# Sex on the Beach

SUSAN LYONS

Heat | New York

**THE BERKLEY PUBLISHING GROUP**
**Published by the Penguin Group**
**Penguin Group (USA) Inc.**
**375 Hudson Street, New York, New York 10014, USA**
Penguin Group (Canada), 90 Eglinton Avenue East, Suite 700, Toronto, Ontario M4P 2Y3, Canada
(a division of Pearson Penguin Canada Inc.)
Penguin Books Ltd., 80 Strand, London WC2R 0RL, England
Penguin Group Ireland, 25 St. Stephen's Green, Dublin 2, Ireland (a division of Penguin Books Ltd.)
Penguin Group (Australia), 250 Camberwell Road, Camberwell, Victoria 3124, Australia
(a division of Pearson Australia Group Pty. Ltd.)
Penguin Books India Pvt. Ltd., 11 Community Centre, Panchsheel Park, New Delhi—110 017, India
Penguin Group (NZ), 67 Apollo Drive, Rosedale, North Shore 0632, New Zealand
(a division of Pearson New Zealand Ltd.)
Penguin Books (South Africa) (Pty.) Ltd., 24 Sturdee Avenue, Rosebank, Johannesburg 2196, South Africa

Penguin Books Ltd., Registered Offices: 80 Strand, London WC2R 0RL, England

This book is an original publication of The Berkley Publishing Group.


Cover design by Diana Kolsky.
Text design by Kristin del Rosario.



PRINTING HISTORY
Heat trade paperback edition / January 2010

Library of Congress Cataloging-in-Publication Data

Lyons, Susan.
Sex on the beach / Susan Lyons.— Heat trade pbk. ed.
p. cm.
ISBN 978-0-425-23216-3
1. Belize—Fiction. I. Title.
PR9199.4.L97S49 2010
813'.6—dc22 2009032049

PRINTED IN THE UNITED STATES OF AMERICA

10 9 8 7 6 5 4 3 2 1

# ACKNOWLEDGMENTS

The idea for *Sex on the Beach* came to me on a cold winter day in Vancouver, British Columbia. I thrive on sunshine and warmth, and I wasn't getting any, so instead I nourished my soul with memories of tropical holidays like the one I took to Belize.

Then I happened upon an article about the popularity of destination weddings, and I remembered how many people I'd seen getting married on tropical beaches. I imagined the sexy fun that might ensue when a group of wedding guests assembled in Belize for the week before an exotic wedding.

The title popped into my head. After that, the synopsis wrote it itself in two days.

Thanks so much to Allison Brandau, the editor who shared my vision for this book and acquired it for the Heat imprint. I'm thrilled to be a Berkley author and look forward to working with the team at Penguin on many future projects.

Thanks also to my own personal team: my agent, Emily Sylvan Kim, and the members of my critique group, Michelle Hancock, Elizabeth Allan, and Nazima Ali. Ladies, I couldn't do it without you.

Special thanks to Tanya Zambrano for research assistance and Doug Arnold for sharing and enriching my own Belize experience.

I love to hear from readers. You can e-mail me at susan@susanlyons.ca or write c/o PO Box 73523, Downtown Postal Outlet, 1014 Robson Street, Vancouver, BC, Canada V6E 4L9. Please drop by my website, www.susanlyons.ca, where I have excerpts, behind-the-scenes information, reviews, contests, a newsletter, recipes, articles, photos, and all sorts of good stuff.

If you drop by my website, you'll find the recipe for Sex on the Beach!

CONTENTS

# War of the Sexes

# Chapter 1

## Ambergris Caye, Belize—Saturday, February 7

"WE'VE decided." Bella's excited voice rang loudly in Sarah's ear despite the poor cell reception on Ambergris Caye. "We want sex on the beach!"

Sarah McCann, swinging in the hammock on her cabana's deck, thought, *Don't we all?* but what she said was, "And you're telling me this why?"

A giggle. "For our *drink*, silly. The theme drink for our wedding."

"Whew. I thought you were asking me to organize your sex life as well as your wedding."

Another giggle. "We can manage our sex life by ourselves, thanks. In fact, right now we're—"

"Stop. TMI." *Way* too much information, especially since Sarah hadn't had sex in *way* too long.

Danny's voice came on the phone. "Hey there, wedding planner."

"Hey yourself, groom." Despite the fact that Danny Trent was, as Bella said, FFR—filthy fucking rich—he was an easygoing guy.

"What my tipsy bride's saying is, we went to the Toucan Bar like you said, and Ric's been making us drinks. We found the perfect one."

"Sex on the beach? What's Ric's recipe?" She'd tasted several variations of the drink using different fruit juices and kinds of alcohol.

"Recipe? I dunno. Fruit juice, booze. Oh, and guess what else?"

Sarah heard Bella saying, "Come on, sweetie, that can wait until tomorrow. I'm horny."

*Really* TMI. She heard a male groan in the background and a muttered, "Jesus, would ya get a room," perhaps from Ric, the resort owner. Danny said a quick good-bye.

How nice if it was that easy. *I'm horny, so come on, you gorgeous hottie, let's fuck like bunnies.* In the loft bedroom of a palm-thatched cabana, with the tropical breeze drifting through the slatted wooden blinds to whisper across your bare skin.

Or maybe on the beach itself, beside an ocean that pulsed to a primal rhythm, under a sky filled with a million stars.

Not to mention with a man you loved madly, who you were marrying in a week. On Valentine's Day.

She felt a twinge of envy—an occupational hazard for a twenty-six-year-old unmarried wedding planner.

Bella and Danny's story was a perfect example of dreams coming true, a concept Sarah had held close to her heart since she was a little girl. She'd been raised by her happily married grandparents after being dropped on their doorstep by her unmarried mom and dad. Her parents had taken off on a journey to find themselves that had ended when their motorbike collided head-on with a semi. And young Starshine—what kind of mom named her daughter Starshine?—had become Sarah.

Dressing her Bride Barbie in a frothy white gown and veil, she'd never tired of sending her down the aisle into Ken's tux-clad arms and into a marriage as loving and secure as that shared by her grandparents.

Now, as a wedding planner, Sarah delighted in giving women a fabulous wedding: the day they'd always dreamed of, a fitting celebration of their love and the perfect launch to a wonderful life as a couple. She wanted all her brides to live as happily ever after as her gran.

Call her old-fashioned, but she believed every woman deserved that special day. And one day, it would happen for her, too.

Tonight she wasn't going to waste time wondering when Mr. Right would come along. She'd count her blessings that she was in warm, sunny Belize in February, rather than back in rainy Vancouver, British Columbia.

Tomorrow the guests would arrive for the pre-wedding week she'd organized after Danny had contacted her three weeks ago. He and Bella had decided to get married and wanted to do it on Valentine's Day—and between Danny and the bride's parents, expense wasn't an issue. The bride and groom could have anything they wanted, which meant a wedding for three dozen people in Belize, where the happy couple had met two years earlier.

It had been a mad scramble to pull everything together. Sarah was tired, and the laze-inducing hammock tempted her to swing to sleep, but she diligently pulled herself out. She wasn't going to enter the theme drink into her spreadsheet until she'd checked it out. Once, she'd made the mistake of assuming a bartender's idea of a mai tai was the weak one she was familiar with, and instead had discovered—at the wedding reception, unfortunately—that his was positively lethal. Never would she repeat that mistake.

Ah well, such a tough assignment, taste-testing a tropical drink.

Clad in white shorts and an orange tie-dyed halter, she pattered down the wooden steps and smiled when her bare feet hit sand that held a warm echo of the day's sunshine.

Oh yeah, she and Andrea, her best friend since kindergarten and now her business partner, had built the perfect career: arranging weddings in exotic locations.

As she walked through the soft sand, golden lights glowed out of the darkness and lilting Caribbean music drifted toward her. The open-air, palm-thatched Toucan Bar was part of the resort she'd booked for the wedding of Bella Moncrieff and Danny Trent.

At the moment, the bar was quiet. Ric Nuñez, an attractive Belizean native in his early thirties, was behind the bar chatting with a customer.

The other man, sitting on a tall stool with his back to her, was a black guy with short, curly hair and a great bod, revealed by a loose black tank top and cargo shorts. Probably a local. The population of Belize was a mixed bag, with ancestors coming from Guatemala, Africa, Europe, India, and a dozen other places.

At a corner table, two middle-aged couples were playing cards and drinking the native Belikin beer. And at their favorite table by the ocean, liqueur glasses in front of them, sat the Everleighs, holding hands, as usual. Married sixty years and still deeply in love, they reminded her of her grandparents.

Sarah greeted the elderly couple with a smile, then walked past them to find an ocean-side table of her own.

Ric came over, his smile a white flash against his brown skin. A man who'd worked his way up from being a waiter to owning a resort, he was resourceful and charming. And he was a large part of the reason she'd chosen the Toucan Resort—named for Belize's exotically colored national bird—as the wedding venue. Thankfully, he'd proved willing to find alternate accommodations for many of the tourists who had booked rooms at his resort.

"I hear you've been playing bartender," she said.

"Bella and Danny were doing the drink tasting, so I figured I'd give Luis the night off. Trust me"—he flashed that smile again—"I'm a great bartender."

"I suspect you're great at pretty much everything you do."

"Try me."

She and Ric got along well, flirting mildly but never pushing the bounds. He was definitely hot, but she didn't feel the zing of chemistry. Which was good, because she and her partner Andi had a rule against mixing business and pleasure. The B&G—bride

and groom—needed to know the wedding planner's focus was on them.

It was likely that Ric, who was professional about his own business, had a similar rule.

She grinned at him. "Seems I need to try sex on the beach."

He grinned back. "I highly recommend it." He headed back to the bar and in a couple minutes returned with a martini glass filled with a peach-colored concoction and decorated with an orange hibiscus blossom.

She tasted it, then couldn't resist another sip. "Oh yeah, that's nice." It was tropical and fruity with a kick—but not, as far as she could tell, a lethal one. And it looked pretty, which was critical. "What's in it?"

"I'll go get you the recipe."

Assuming the recipe checked out, the drink was definitely spreadsheet-worthy. That left only one detail to firm up: the photographer. The guests had been asked to bring their cameras and take photos throughout the week, but the wedding and reception needed something more formal. Danny had said his best friend would do the job as a wedding gift.

Sarah was skeptical. Freeman Lafontaine specialized in travel photography, which was far different than capturing the romance and emotion of a wedding. Plus, for the past few weeks he'd been on a photo expedition in Australia and hadn't returned her e-mails to confirm.

Sarah believed in contingency plans, so she had interviewed local photographers and lined up the best one as backup. Danny's friend was scheduled to arrive tomorrow, and if he didn't show or didn't measure up, she'd go with plan B.

The Everleighs strolled through the bar and exchanged good nights with her, then Ric returned with the recipe.

She studied it. Appropriately tropical, and not too heavy on the booze. "Okay, so you'll make sure you get sufficient quantities of all the ingredients? And serve it in pretty glasses like this with hibiscus blossoms for decoration?"

He chuckled. "D'you ever quit working?"

"I'm stopping now. For the rest of the evening. As of this moment, I'm just a girl on holiday."

"Enjoy." He touched her bare shoulder, but his warm fingers raised no sexy shiver.

Strange, how finicky her pheromones were. Ric was gorgeous and no doubt damned skilled in bed as well. Yet he didn't rouse the slightest hint of lust in her sex-starved body.

Sarah took another sip of the yummy drink. Pheromones were a product of evolution, of centuries of Darwinian fine-tuning, honing the mating instinct. So, if she was correct that there was one right man for her, he must be the one her pheromones were waiting for.

Then it would be her turn for the fabulous wedding. And by then, she'd have scoped out the best locations in the world.

Another martini glass appeared, and she realized she'd finished her first drink. Sex on the beach sure went down easily. "Thanks," she told Ric, "but that's it. I have to be functional tomorrow."

She slid down in her chair, lifted her bare feet to the opposite one, and let the sweet, juicy blend of flavors ease down her throat. Tonight was hers to enjoy the murmur of the ocean, the rustle of palm fronds, the scent of orange blossoms born on the soft breeze.

"Sex on the beach?" a male voice asked. The soft, husky sound seemed like part of a tropical fantasy.

"That would be nice," she said dreamily. Then the world came into focus, and she gaped at the man standing beside her. No, make that the hottie.

Hot enough that every sense zapped into red alert.

It was the guy she'd seen at the bar, and his front view was even better than his back. Tall and nicely muscled, he wore cargo shorts that hung low on lean hips and a black tank top that revealed more than it concealed. His face was great, too, its masculine features set off by an abbreviated mustache and goatee and a tight cap of black curls.

"Sorry." She hoped the dim light concealed her blush. "What did you say?"

He gave a lazy, infinitely sexy grin. “Asked how you felt about sex on the beach.”

Oh my. Here was the zing of pheromones. Her skin pricked into goose bumps, and something hot and juicy surged through her blood and made her pussy throb. Wow, right on target. Her body definitely felt the urge to mate.

“Um, you mean the drink?” she stuttered.

God, his eyes were amazing. Hazel green, startling against his dark skin. Gleaming with humor and definite interest. “Not really, but it’ll do for a start.”

Jesus. The hottest guy she’d ever met was hustling her, and she was acting like a nervous schoolgirl. She pulled herself together. “I think sex on the beach is . . .” *Okay, Sarah, you can do this.* Slowly, she took another deliberate sip, savored it, let it slide down her throat, then ran the tip of her tongue around her lips. “Mmm. Sweet and slow,” she drawled, “with an underlying edge. Delicious and addictive.”

His eyes widened in appreciation. Uninvited, he took the chair beside her, his bare knee brushing seductively against her leg. “A recipe that’s just right for a tropical night.” The gaze he leveled at her held a challenge.

“And it’s definitely a beautiful tropical night.” Even if it was the alcohol talking, it had been a long time since she’d felt so liberated and sexy.

“Nights in the tropics are always special. With the right company.”

How many tourists had this local Lothario used these lines on? But why should she care? This showed every sign of turning into her lucky night, one to gloat about to Andi and to remember when she was back home in rainy, gray, dateless Vancouver.

She extended her hand. “I’m Sarah.”

He held it firmly, warmly in his. “I’m free.”

Free? What an odd thing to say. Did he mean available, or was he clarifying that he wasn’t selling sex to a tourist? Both, she guessed.

He definitely wasn’t her Ken doll, her Mr. Forever, this man who hadn't shared his name. But what the hell, while waiting for Mr. Right, a girl's body could dry out and shrivel up from disuse. At home she had a drawer of sex toys, but this guy would make a far sexier plaything.

Jeez, what was she thinking? He was a complete stranger.

Besides, what if all he had going for him was good looks? She ought to check out the merchandise before she indulged in any more wicked thoughts.

"Want a taste?" She took a swallow of the drink. Then, instead of handing him the glass, she leaned toward him, heart racing. She could do a pretty slick pickup, if she said so herself.

"Definitely." Without hesitation he closed the distance between them and touched his lips to hers. Softly, gently, he flirted with her mouth, dropping teasing kisses, sucking her flesh, and nipping lightly. He smelled of some ocean-tangy shampoo or aftershave, and his breath was scented with rum. As he moved his mouth over hers, the short hairs of his mustache brushed her upper lip, sensuous and arousing.

It was all she could do to hold back a moan. They hadn't even parted their lips, and her body was sparking like it was ready to combust.

She darted her tongue across his lips, and he opened them in an invitation she eagerly accepted. His mouth was hot, sweet, and tropical.

Oh, man, the merchandise definitely lived up to the ads. Tonight she was free from responsibility, so why not enjoy another round of sex on the beach? The literal kind.

No, wait. It wasn't safe to wander off with a stranger, no matter how tempting he was. But he'd been talking to Ric . . . "Excuse me a minute." She stood up.

Sarah gave her hips a sexy sway as she strolled toward the ladies' room. When she reached the bar, she paused and glanced back. The man, sprawled in the rattan chair like a big black cat, made no bones about watching her, and the grin that kinked his full lips was knowing, confident, verging on arrogant.

He thought she was a sure thing.

Was she?

With her back to him, she leaned across the bar and whispered to Ric, "Can you vouch for that man?"

He gave her a wicked grin. "In what sense, Sarah? I haven't personally experienced his talents, if that's what you mean."

"Jesus." The plight of the redhead; she knew her cheeks were pink. "I mean, is it safe to, uh . . . Would you let your sister date him?"

"If she wasn't married. Don't you know? He's—"

"That's okay, thanks." She cut him off, not wanting to hear if the pickup artist was someone she might see around town: a cashier at the grocery store, a waiter, a surfing instructor. All that mattered was, he was hot, it wasn't dangerous to go with him, and he wouldn't be asking for money.

Sarah went into the ladies' room and studied her reflection. Her hair, in its short, deliberately messy wash-and-wear style, looked sexy. Her pale skin, which she always sunscreened liberally, was lit by a flush that made her blue eyes look bright and sparkly.

A flush of arousal at the thought of sex with . . . whatever his name was.

No, she wasn't going to ask. This was a one-night fling. The less information, the better.

# Chapter 2

FREEMAN Lafontaine couldn't believe his luck.

The day had been a crazy one. He'd flown from Australia, where he'd spent the last month going walkabout with a group of Aboriginal Australians, filming the Outback and gradually winning their trust.

After a long, luxurious shower, a burger, and a couple beers, he'd gone to an Internet café to catch up on e-mail.

He'd clicked open Danny's urgent-flagged message, and that's as far as he got. The attached e-ticket had barely allowed him time to grab his gear and catch a cab to the airport. But he did pop off a reply.

> You're fucking insane, man! Call it off. Remember Kimberly!!

Airlines being what they were these days, his flight had been changed. Rather than overnighting in Belize City, he'd capped off the long, cramped flight from Oz by catching a puddle jumper to

Ambergris Caye. It would've been a pretty sunset flight if the kid beside him hadn't kept puking.

The shit Free put up with for his best bud. What the hell had happened to the vow they'd sworn when they were nineteen, to stay footloose and fancy-free? Danny had almost blown it once, hooking up with that fortune-hunting bitch Kimberly and getting his heart stomped to smithereens, and he still hadn't learned his lesson.

Bella was devious. Since Danny had met her, the two of them had been doing fun stuff, and she'd shown no signs of wanting to ball-and-chain him. Then, soon as Free had disappeared into the Outback, she'd shown her true colors. She'd gotten an engagement ring on her finger and a quickie wedding planned, probably hoping Free wouldn't reappear until the marriage certificate was signed.

But she'd mistimed it, and here he was, on a mission to save his bud just like he'd sworn to do after Kimberly's betrayal. He and Danny had been well on the way to getting hammered, but he remembered his tearful friend saying, "Don't ever let me do this again. You know how weak I am when it comes to a pretty girl. I can't go through this again. You gotta promise me you'll save me from myself."

And Free had sworn he would.

Only problem was, since he'd gotten here a couple hours ago, Danny and Bella had been joined at the hip. The only few minutes he'd had alone with Danny were when she'd gone to the ladies' room, at which time Free had said, "What the hell are you doing? This is Kimberly all over again," and Danny had responded with, "No, Bella's different. We're in love."

Yeah, right. What Bella loved was the bling that decorated her ears, wrists, and fingers. Free was about to point that out, but she returned and draped herself around Danny again.

Then she'd used her feminine wiles, and Danny had deserted Free faster than . . . Well, there wasn't much on earth that moved faster than a horny guy who'd been promised sex.

Fine, let Bella think she was winning. There was always tomorrow.

As for tonight, Free had figured he'd finish his drink, then head off to bed.

Then *she'd* come in. Slim but plenty curvy, creamy skin as light as his was dark, fiery red hair tousled like she'd climbed out of bed. Hot. Very hot. His dick had throbbed to life.

Forget about being tired from the long flight. There were better things to do tonight than go to bed alone. He'd waited patiently until she'd finished her first drink, hoping booze and the tropical night would get her mind working along the same lines as his.

And he'd been right.

Gotta love a woman who didn't make small talk, didn't give a damn what you did for a living, or even ask your last name—just wanted to get down to action.

For a moment he'd wondered if she might be a wedding guest, which could make things awkward. But Bella had said the guests wouldn't arrive until tomorrow. The only person who was here now was the wedding planner, who, from what Danny had said, was all about spreadsheets—the kind used for organizing data, not the kind that got rumpled during steamy sex.

The door to the ladies' room opened, and Sarah sauntered toward him, hip-swingy and sexy. "Feel like a stroll on the beach?" she asked.

"Among other things." He shifted his knee so it brushed her smooth leg.

Under that skimpy halter top, her nipples tightened. Yeah, he was looking. And under the cotton of his cargo shorts, his dick did the same.

He handed her the martini glass, making sure their fingers brushed. "Haven't finished your sex, woman. It's no good stopping in the middle."

She took a sip, then held the glass out to him. "Then help me finish."

He let out a surprised chuckle. Damn, she was good.

And so was he. He'd have no problem bringing this babe to a

shuddering climax. Thinking about it made his voice go husky. "Be my pleasure, Sarah."

He drained the glass, the taste of fruit juice sweet and fresh in his mouth. What would the sexy redhead taste like? "Let's go find that beach."

When he stood up and held out his hand, she slipped hers into it.

Outside, bare feet on the sand, Free wrapped an arm around Sarah's shoulders and snugged her body close to his. Her arm came around his waist and she leaned in, soft hair brushing his neck.

She was just the right height, and her skin was warm and smooth. Lots of skin, too, in that brief halter top.

He sure as hell loved warm countries where pretty girls walked around in skimpy clothes. Where the heat melted inhibitions.

As they moved away from the lights of the bar, the night grew darker. Dark enough for privacy, he figured, steering Sarah past a sprinkling of thatched cabanas on stilts.

The night was mellow, all soft breeze, gently rustling palm leaves, the tang of ocean, and the scent of night-blooming flowers. Neither he nor Sarah said a word. All the same, the tension between them was palpable. He felt it in the quick rise and fall of her shoulders, the way his heart raced and his dick hardened.

He sure hoped the woman didn't have second thoughts.

He shouldn't give her time for them. Besides, he wanted to kiss her again.

Free stopped, drawing her to him, putting a hand under her chin and tilting her face up. Her eyes, reflecting starlight, were bright and expectant. Her lips, soft and full, parted.

He bent his head and, just before his lips touched hers, she gave a tiny sigh, the softest sound, a whisper of air on his face.

Then they were kissing, and everything was hot and wet and hungry.

Jesus, he hadn't meant to kiss her like he wanted to devour her, but no way could he hold back. She tasted of tropical fruit; the inside of her mouth was pure, sweet seduction. Even better, she kissed like she was as desperate as he was.

Then she pulled back in the circle of his arms and stared at him, looking dazed. "Wow. That was, uh, intense. I didn't expect . . ." She shook her head.

"Me, either. But it's good?"

The dazed expression faded, her eyes sparkled again, and she gave him a mischievous smile. "Good enough to repeat."

He glanced around. They'd passed the last cabana, and no one else was walking the beach. The shore was lined with palms and leafy shrubs, promising a bit of privacy. He tugged her up the beach and behind the screen of vegetation, searching for and finding a sandy area.

She gazed through the branches at the dim, whispery ocean, then up at the stars, then finally at him. "Beautiful night."

"My lucky night, with a beautiful lady." Again he pulled her close, and she came easily. His dick was hard inside the loose shorts he wore commando style, and he nudged her belly with it.

She gave a soft moan and then rubbed against him, gripping his ass in both hands. Then she went up on her toes, a tantalizing slide of her softness against his hard-on, and captured his mouth.

This time neither of them was in a hurry. The first couple of kisses behind them, both committed now, there was time to explore.

Every guy knew women needed foreplay, and Free was an expert. It wasn't just the girl who benefited. He loved exploring a woman's body, and the happier she was, the happier she'd make him. The hotter they both were, the fierier the explosion when it finally came.

So he pulled off his tank top and settled into stoking the fire for him and Sarah.

Licks and nibbles for her lips, a little slow dancing for her tongue, a hard thrust or two of his own tongue into her mouth to get her pussy imagining what he had in store for it. And, just in case her lower extremities weren't getting the message, a strong press of his pole-hard dick against her belly to remind her he was pure male and purely horny. And damned well hung, too.

She was all soft movement and sound: hips shimmying to tease him, nipples poking through thin cotton and rubbing his bare chest, hands drifting up and down his back, then under the waistband of his shorts. And all the time, she was making a sexy, disjointed stream of whimpers and sighs and moans and *oh, yes*es as her lips joined his, broke away, then came back in their own sultry dance.

Every movement, every sound, fueled the fire inside him. He had to touch more of her, so he untied the bow at her back and then the one at her neck. She shifted so her halter top fell to the sand, then pressed back against him. He groaned when he felt the full impact of those firm breasts with their pebbled buds.

Her fingers rubbed the hollow at the base of his spine, then began to track down his butt crack. Sensation shot through him, making his balls clench and his dick swell even harder.

With a groan he undid his shorts and shoved them over his hips and erection.

She looked down. He knew she would. Gals always had to check out a guy's package.

"Nice," she sighed. "Very nice." Then her fingers wrapped around him. Bold, no hesitation. A woman who took what she wanted.

"Glad you approve."

Deft fingers stroked him, pumped him. Shit, that felt good. Too good. Sarah's fingers were— Oh, man. He had to pull away while he still could.

He took a step back, picked up his shorts, and removed a condom from his wallet.

"Oh God, I'm so glad you have one."

He was glad, too. There were many ways to have sex, but he really wanted to be deep inside this woman.

He spread his shorts and tank on the sand.

"You have a great body," she said. "You look like an athlete."

"Nah. I just like being active." And he'd sure as hell been that, pushing himself to keep up with the tough Aboriginal Australians in the Outback.

God, she was different from the Aboriginal women. Softly curvy, pale skin glowing in the moonlight, nipples dusky and tantalizing. Her torso was so boldly naked, her hips discreetly covered by form-fitting white shorts. "You got a pretty fine body on you, too."

He reached for the button at the waist of her shorts, and in seconds he'd stripped her down to a tiny pair of white panties, only a couple shades lighter than her delicate skin. His dick ached with need as he studied her with hungry eyes.

Her waist was narrow; her hips flared gently. Not only did she arouse him, but the artist in him appreciated her. She was elegant, everything in proportion. Not an ounce too much or too little on any part of her.

Even her short hair was perfect. It focused the eye on a triangular face with even features. Nicely arched brows, big blue eyes that looked silvery in the moonlight, cute turned-up nose, high cheekbones, full lips.

As much as he wanted sex with her, he also wished for his camera. If he photographed her like this . . . Well, if he did, that'd be one photo he'd be keeping for his private collection.

"Hey, are you all right?" she asked, shifting from foot to foot, hugging her arms across her breasts.

He realized he'd gone off into the photographer daze that happened when he saw something he really, really enjoyed looking at and wanted to capture for posterity.

Weird, how his dick could be at rigid, aching attention, and yet he'd almost as soon photograph her as fuck her.

Almost. Besides, his camera and tripod were back in his room, and he had more pressing matters right now than taking Sarah's picture.

"I couldn't be better," he answered her question. "Well, on the other hand, maybe I could." He hooked his index fingers into the sides of her panties and peeled them down her body, revealing a neatly trimmed auburn bush.

Then he took her in his arms and let their bodies slide together, adjust to each other's shapes. Every place they touched felt like a pulse point, throbbing with a sensual heat. And each throb radiated through him until his body was one huge bundle of want and need, with the single goal of getting inside this woman.

She shivered in his arms, raising her lips to his in another wild, hungry kiss that had him thrusting against her belly, pre-come moistening the head of his dick.

He slid a hand between her legs, and yeah, she was wet, too. Both of their bodies were so ready to join.

Her sweet pussy thrust into his hand, and he cupped her, then stroked a finger between her damp folds.

She started up with those moaning, whimpering, murmuring noises again, and he guessed she didn't even know she was doing it. It was so damn sexy, all that stuff happening against his mouth while her body twisted in his arms, telling him how much she wanted him.

He eased a finger inside her, and hot, wet walls gripped him. Man, she was tight. His dick would never fit inside there.

But it had to. Somehow, it would.

He slid his finger in and out, felt her clench, then she softened, eased open. Patiently he stroked, feeling her grow even wetter. Another finger, and now her hips were thrusting. A third finger, and she was grinding against his hand, breath wheezing against his cheek like she was running a marathon.

Between breaths, she kept up with those sexy sounds. "God, yes. Mmm, so good, yes, there. Oh, oh! There, oh, more, harder, right there, like that. Mmm-hmm. Yes, yes."

She was giving him a road map to her pleasure, and all he had to do was follow her directions.

When his thumb, slick with her juices, touched her clit, she rocked harder against him, and her murmurings intensified. He stroked, squeezed gently, and she let out a gasp. He did it some more, and she began to pant, "Yes, yes, yes."

Her whole body clenched.

Then she let out a cry, and orgasm surged through her in pulsing waves that sucked at his fingers.

Waves that made his dick surge in response. In envy.

When Sarah had collapsed against him, he laid her down on his clothes and fumbled with the condom package, eager to sheath himself.

To join with her now, while her body was still quivering with aftershocks.

Her skin gleamed like ivory, her eyes glittered, and he thought there was a hell of a lot to be said for sex on the beach. Then he sank down between her legs, and she smiled up at him and held out her arms.

He went into them eagerly and met that smile with a kiss. Her lips were so hot they seared him, but he went back for more, sweeping his tongue into her mouth. And, as he did, he reached down to grasp his dick and ease it between her slick folds.

She gasped, tightened momentarily, then relaxed as he inched inside. Slowly her body took him in, and she gave an "Mmm" that sounded like pure satisfaction.

Her hips rose, and her legs came up to wrap around his waist so he could plunge even deeper.

When he'd been concentrating on her climax, he'd kind of lost track of just how damned horny he was, but now his body made its needs known. His dick ached, and the moist grip of her channel both soothed and stimulated it. He wanted to slow down, but some primitive drive grabbed ahold of him and wouldn't let go.

He thrust in faster, then faster still. When Sarah started up with that babbly sex talk, it spurred him on, and he pumped so deep and hard he didn't know how either of them could take it without coming apart.

Then she said, "God, yes, now, there, yes, yes! More, there, oh God, I can't—I have to—oh my God!"

And he had to, too. His balls drew up, and he felt his essence surge through him and burst out in hot jets.

Oh my God was right. The top of his head was coming off. Pressure, release, pleasure so intense it bordered on pain. Man, that was one hell of an orgasm.

Laughing exultantly as he came back to earth, he wormed his arms under Sarah, clasping her to him, then he rolled.

She gave a startled squeak but hung on tightly as he tumbled off the rumpled clothing onto his back on the sand, with her cradled atop him. She began to laugh, too, and straightened, sitting up with him still embedded inside her.

He stacked his hands behind his head and admired her sleek curves.

She raised her arms and raked her fingers through her hair, messing it even more. Smiling, starlight shining over her shoulders, she said, "Well, that was very nice."

"Decided you like sex on the beach, woman?" He smiled back. "How was it you described it before?"

Hands pulling her hair back, breasts drawn up high, she tilted her head like she was trying to remember. Then she chuckled. "Something like, sweet and slow with an underlying edge."

"Jesus." He laughed back. "More like hard and fast with some underlying sand."

"Delicious, though."

As he recalled, earlier she'd also said addictive. He noticed she didn't add that word now. Had once been enough for her?

Nah. It might've been a quickie, but it had been damned hot. He rested his hands on her thighs. "Whatcha say, Sarah? Want to try sex in a bed?"

"Mmm, that sounds tempting." A long pause. "But it's late, and I have to work tomorrow. I need a good night's sleep."

The moment she said *sleep*, his body reacted with a wrenching yawn. How many hours had it been since he'd last slept?

Sarah touched his face. "You, too, huh? Hey, it was great. Guess we should leave it at that."

That made sense for tonight, but he'd barely begun to explore her fine body. "You gonna be around tomorrow night? Maybe we could hook up when you get off work." He felt a moment's curiosity about her job. He'd taken her for a tourist, not a local.

She was quiet for a long moment. "I wish, but I have too many other commitments. I need to focus. Not, uh, be distracted."

Hmm. Wasn't often a woman put her job ahead of sex with him. Okay, so she was some kind of workaholic. Definitely not his type, even if she was sexy.

"No problem," he said breezily. He gripped her hips and lifted her free of his body. "I've got stuff to do, too." Mostly, talk his dumb-ass bud Danny out of going through with that stupid wedding.

Sarah began to pull on her clothes. He did, too, then they stood facing each other. "So," he said. "Glad we ran into each other in the bar."

"Me, too." She gave a quick grin. "Gotta say, you deliver great sex on the beach."

He chuckled. "My pleasure, that's for sure."

They studied each other for a moment, then without speaking came together for a kiss that was quick yet intense. After, she turned and walked away.

He watched her disappear into the shadows, and as the soft night breeze brushed his skin, it carried the scent of regret.

# Chapter 3

SARAH woke when morning light filtered through the shuttered windows and slid a gentle ray across her face.

Mmm, the sun felt wonderful. So did her body, all melty and sexually satisfied for the first time in ages.

She marveled over what she'd done last night. That was either one amazingly potent drink or . . . Or what?

She shook her head vigorously and headed for the shower. No point analyzing it to death. She'd met one very hot man, had very hot sex, and that was it. They'd both gotten their rocks off, to put it crudely.

Next time she pulled out a sex toy and wanted a fantasy man, she had the perfect image to call to mind.

Under the pulsing spray of the shower, her fingers toyed with her pussy lips, and she was tempted to indulge right then and there.

No, she needed to review her spreadsheets one more time. Today the guests would arrive. And with them, a new set of challenges.

The biggest would be the MOB and FOB—the bride's mother and father, Giovanna and James Moncrieff. They'd divorced when their daughter was five and, Bella said, mixed as well as Italian olive oil and English tonic water. Left alone in the same room, they might come to blows. All the same, Bella adored both of them, and of course wanted them there when she got married.

Sarah had designed the excursions and seating plans to keep the exes apart as much as possible and could only hope their affection for their daughter would keep them civil.

Then there was Danny's uncle, Zane Slade. He wrote thrillers about a twenty-first-century James Bond who invariably saved the world from some disaster and screwed a half-dozen gorgeous women in the process. The books—and movie franchise—had turned Zane into a celebrity. His date was a Manhattan model, and Sarah only hoped the relatively tame activities she'd planned for the guests would be enough to entertain the glitzy couple.

And, last but not least, was the niggling question about Danny's friend, the photographer. Whenever she asked Danny, he said, "He's always been there for me. I'm sure it'll work out."

Experience told her that when a member of the wedding party said, "I'm sure it'll work out," things were pretty much guaranteed to get screwed up.

Ah well, she was a pro with a plan B. The problem hadn't been invented that she couldn't deal with.

Especially when her sex-starved bones had been so pleasantly jumped last night.

Out of the shower, she fluffed her damp hair, dabbed on a touch of eye makeup, and donned a sleeveless blouse and short skirt in shades of blue.

She checked her e-mail and found a message from her partner, Andi, that read:

> MOB on the Montague/Lee wedding's being a PITA. Remember how she said she'd only pay if it was a formal church ceremony, even though B&G wanted the beach? Well, now MOB says cancel the church and find a beach! LOL. Like I didn't have the beach booked all along.

Sarah chuckled, and e-mailed back:

**Thank God for plan Bs, eh? BTW, on the subject of beaches, remind me to tell you about sex on the beach.**

She'd explain that one when she got home.

Sarah logged off and strolled over to the Toucan's beachside restaurant, where she sipped a glass of orange juice. It tasted bland in comparison to last night's fancy drink. The cocktail had been delicious, and so had the man.

She shook away the thought and turned to the spreadsheet she'd printed off her portable printer, detailing the arrival of the three dozen guests. The planes that flew from Belize City to Ambergris Caye were tiny, and the guests were scheduled for three different arrival times today—the MOB and FOB being on different flights, of course.

Lafontaine, the photographer, was supposed to be with the first group. If he actually showed up, she'd nail him to discuss the wedding photos and see if the guy measured up.

A female voice broke into her thoughts. "Morning, wedding planner."

Looking up, she saw Bella. Her name was Italian for "beautiful," and she lived up to it. Blonde hair with Mediterranean olive-toned skin made a striking combo. She had a natural, casual style, pairing Belizean sundresses with a fortune in sparkly diamond jewelry—gifts from the "filthy fucking rich" Danny—and somehow looking just right.

Sarah hugged her. "Hey there, bride. Where's your groom?"

Bella sat across from her, her sunny expression clouding over. "He went to get—" She broke off. "There they are now."

"They?" Sarah turned, to see Danny walk into the restaurant with another man following behind.

Her last-night lover. Looking as stunned as she felt.

"*She's* the wedding planner?" he asked incredulously.

"Who *are* you?" she demanded, clutching her clipboard to her chest.

"Wedding planner, meet photographer," Danny said. "Sarah McCann, Free Lafontaine."

"Free?" Oh, crap. Freeman Lafontaine. Jeez. Last night, he hadn't been saying he was free, as in available. He'd been giving her his name.

She'd screwed the groom's best friend.

Oh, shit. She'd inadvertently broken the rule against mixing business and pleasure.

This was all the damned photographer's fault. She held out her clipboard and pointed to an entry on the arrivals spreadsheet. "You were supposed to fly in this morning."

"Plans change."

Damn him, he was as handsome in the sunshine as he'd been under the stars. And, double damn him, he still sent her pheromones into overdrive.

Struggling to regain her professionalism, she decided to pretend they'd never met and hope he'd play along. "Sorry. If I'd known, I'd have arranged to have someone meet you at the airport. Anyhow"—she nodded briskly—"it's a pleasure to *meet* you, uh, Free." Would he pick up on her cue?

"Yeah, sure." He didn't look at all happy.

What was with the attitude? Oh God, had he boasted to Danny about last night's hookup? Suspiciously she stared from Free to Danny. The photographer was scowling, but Danny's face wore its usual smile. No smirk. She turned to Bella, who was frowning at Free.

But Bella had greeted her earlier with a warm smile and a hug. She couldn't know about last night.

First opportunity Sarah got, she'd take Free aside. For now, all she could do was shoot him a warning gaze. He met it with a belligerent expression.

Morning-after regrets? Or maybe he was pissed that she'd turned him down when he'd suggested continuing their evening. Yeah, the guy's ego had taken a blow.

She turned to a happier sight, her clients hugging and whispering to each other. If she'd ever seen a perfectly matched couple, it was Bella and Danny. Easygoing and optimistic, they loved the same things, from dancing to deep-sea diving. Both were tall, slim, blond, and beautiful in a natural way. They were going to have the most amazing babies.

"You two are *so* made for each other," she said.

They turned to her with near-identical smiles. "Don't we know it," Bella said. She glanced at Free with a challenge in her eyes.

"Thank God for Ambergris Caye," Danny said. "If we hadn't both come here to dive, we'd never have met."

"Yes, you would," Sarah said. "You were destined to be together."

"Crap." Free, standing beside her, muttered the word under his breath.

"Excuse me?" Maybe she hadn't heard correctly.

"Destiny? Give me a break."

"It seems Free's a cynic." Bella glared at him, tightening her hold on her fiancé's waist. "He doesn't believe in marriage."

Uh-oh.

Sarah squared her shoulders. The wedding issue hadn't been invented that she couldn't deal with. "Let's have breakfast," she said firmly, "and discuss the situation."

"Can't," Bella said. "Danny and I have to go to the airport. Mama phoned, and she's got an earlier flight."

Bella had warned that her mother was dramatic, emotional, and impulsive.

"Giovanna changed flights on a whim?" Sarah frowned. She might as well throw out her spreadsheet if everyone was going to randomly change plans.

"She *said* she's so anxious to see us, she can't wait." Bella rolled her eyes. "Personally, I think she wants to establish her turf before Daddy arrives."

Danny touched her arm. "Come on, sweets. Time to go."

"Hey, Dan the man." Free frowned at him. "Thought we were gonna catch some guy time. Bella can pick up her mom."

"Trust me," Bella said, "that's not the way for him to stay in his future mom-in-law's good books."

Free muttered something under his breath that sounded a lot like "pussy-whipped."

"Should I come, too?" Sarah asked.

Bella shook her head. "No, but could you meet us when we get back? Be the official greeter and help Mama get settled?"

"Of course."

When the B&G had gone, Free said, "Think I'll look for a dive excursion."

As he turned to leave, Sarah grabbed his arm. "Oh, no, you don't. We need to talk. Sit."

He scowled. "You giving me orders?"

Hurriedly she removed her hand, which felt tingly from contact with his warm, bare skin. "Sorry, I didn't mean it that way. Please, can we talk?"

He rubbed his arm where she'd touched it. Reflexively, as if he didn't realize he was doing it. "Talk? What about?" But he sank down in the chair across from her.

Fighting a blush, she said, "Last night, I didn't realize who you were."

"Me, either."

"It was a mistake."

"Yeah, it—" He broke off, and his facial muscles relaxed, his eyes began to sparkle. Under the table a bare knee bumped hers, making her quiver with awareness. "Yeah, but I liked where it took us."

Sex. Amazing sex. She cleared her throat. "I have a policy against, um, having an intimate relationship with anyone who's involved with the wedding."

"That'll be solved when Danny calls off the wedding."

"What? He's not going to do that." She leaned forward. "You may not believe in marriage, but he does. He's head over heels for Bella."

"His brain's in his dick, and she's leading him around by it."

"That's ridiculous. They're in love." What on earth was wrong with this man? "Free, if you think he's making a mistake, why are you here?"

"To stop him."

Her mouth fell open. He had to be joking. "You can't want them to break up?"

"Oh yeah. In the beginning, she was into sex, holidays, fun. I actually liked her. But now it's all about marriage, and Danny sure as hell doesn't need a ball and chain."

Her jaw tightened. "A ball and chain? That's what you think of marriage?"

"Maybe it's okay for old folks or losers who are desperate. But not for a guy like Danny. He's got his whole life ahead of him, and he can get any girl he wants."

"He wants Bella. He loves Bella." She glared at him. "Oh, wait, let me guess. You don't believe in love, either."

"Love? Gimme a break. Bella's a fortune hunter. She may have persuaded Danny he's in love, but it's only hormones. It's temporary."

"Temporary? It's about survival of the species."

"What the hell you talking about?" His eyebrows rose.

"Evolution. Have you heard of it?" she taunted. "Hormones, pheromones, all of those things are highly evolved ways of leading us to our perfect mate."

"What a load of crap."

They glared at each other across the table.

Then, to her surprise, his lips curved and he let out a chuckle. "You saying I'm your perfect mate?"

"You?! Good God, what are you thinking?"

"Gonna deny there's a major hormone thing between us, woman?"

"But that's—" She stopped, her mind spinning. Even now, when she was pissed off with this Neanderthal, she felt that pheromone zing. She'd never felt it as strongly with any other man.

If she believed what she'd said about evolution, then . . .

Under the table, his knee rubbed hers, and arousal danced over her skin, pulsed through her veins. He stroked the back of her hand, and she shivered. Then he turned her hand over and caressed the palm.

How had she never known that knees and palms were erogenous zones, linked directly to her pussy?

Her body was having that totally primitive reaction again. She wanted to grab this guy, drag him off to a cave, and mate with him.

Wide-eyed, she stared at him. She remembered the press of those full, sensual lips, the soft caress of his mustache and goatee, the firmness of his muscles, the impressive size of his cock. The amazing way he'd felt inside her as their bodies merged so perfectly and found climax together.

My God, could this man actually be her Ken doll? The answer to her childhood dreams?

Her Ken had been the opposite of Free: pale-skinned, fair-haired, and genital-free. He'd let her dress him up and boss him around, and he'd definitely believed in happily ever after.

But pheromones had spoken loudly. If Free Lafontaine was her destined mate . . . She owed it to herself, to her future, to find out.

Though how could he be the right mate for her? He was anti-love and anti-marriage.

Okay, so he was immature, or he'd had his heart broken and turned into a cynic. It didn't mean he couldn't come around to believing in happily ever after.

Damn, he had to, or he might try to sabotage Danny and Bella's wedding.

What could she do? There was only one logical answer. It would mean breaking her rule about not mixing business and pleasure, but for the sake of her own romantic future, as well as Bella and Danny's, she needed to fraternize with the enemy and convert Free Lafontaine into a believer. She had her work cut out for her, but she'd never been one to back down from a challenge.

"You have a wicked gleam in your eye, woman," he said in a husky, seductive tone.

So far as she'd seen, there was only one effective way of communicating with the man: sex.

If this was a war of the sexes, then her weapon of choice was sex.

"Wicked?" she murmured, sliding her leg against his. "Mmm, I was just remembering last night. That delicious"—her tongue traced the outline of her lips—"luscious sex on the beach."

His gaze had followed her tongue. "Liked that, did you?"

"It was good enough for seconds."

"Not too early in the morning for you?"

"I can handle it." *And I can handle you, too.*

"Uh-huh. And can you handle this?" Under the table, he lifted her leg, placing her bare foot in his lap. She could feel his burgeoning erection.

Strange how her mouth could be bone dry while her pussy was soaking wet. She wriggled her foot gently, careful not to damage anything, and croaked, "I don't recall having any problems."

"Wanna give it another try?"

She glanced at her spreadsheet. Everything was under control. She tilted her head and teased, "You realize we're sworn enemies? My goal is a happy wedding, and you're trying to subvert my plans."

"I'm gonna win, too," he said confidently.

His attitude was annoying, but he was kind of cute when he got all macho and cocky.

"You don't have a hope in hell." She knew she'd win because, after all, she was *right.*

"Doesn't mean we can't have sex."

"Doesn't mean that at all," she agreed, tickling his cock with her toes.

Wait. If they were going to do this, they needed some rules.

She put her leg down and glanced around, hoping no one had seen. "I don't want anyone to know about this. It might look unprofessional of me." Though, in fact, sexual persuasion was her best strategy for saving the wedding.

He shrugged. "Works for me. Not sure I want to be seen

associating with a *wedding planner*. Could hurt my rep." He raised his fingers to his mustached mouth and pantomimed pulling a zipper.

She needed more. If he told Bella and Danny what was going on, they could lose confidence in her. "You swear you'll keep it a secret?"

"Swear? Yeah, sure, if it's that important to you."

"It is." Okay, but could she trust him? "Sorry, I don't want to insult you, but we barely know each other . . . You are a man who keeps his word, right?"

His jaw tightened. "I take vows very seriously."

She touched his hand. "Thank you."

Then she glanced at her watch. There was no point talking to Free about the wedding photos now, with him so anti-marriage. First she'd have to wage a little sexual warfare. "I've only got an hour before the MOB—Giovanna—gets here. Figure that's enough time?"

His eyes gleamed, and he lowered his voice. "Dunno. How many orgasms d'you want?"

Her sex gave a needy throb. "How many are you up for?"

"Let's find out." He stood, pulling this morning's tank top down over the front of his shorts to conceal his erection.

When she stood, too, he said, "If you don't want people knowing we're screwing, we'd better not leave together."

"Oh, right." She sank down again. Clearly he had more experience with clandestine affairs than she did. No surprise there. "Where shall we meet?"

"I'm in room twenty-two. The second floor at the end."

"I'm in a cabana. It's more exposed to public view. I'll come to your room." Then she raised her voice. "It was nice meeting you, Free." She gave him a sweet smile. "I look forward to working with you to make this wedding a wonderful event."

He chuckled. "We'll see about that." Then he shoved his hands in the pockets of his loose shorts and sauntered away as she admired his rear view.

A few minutes later, she gathered her clipboard and strolled casually toward the lobby. Ric was talking to the receptionist. Damn, she'd forgotten he'd seen her with Free last night.

Her scowl must have caught his attention because he came over. "Something wrong, Sarah?"

She bit her lip. "What you saw last night?" Knowing her cheeks were coloring didn't help her confidence. "I thought he was a local. Didn't know he was Danny's friend. Will you keep it a secret?"

His lips twitched. "I own a resort. Discretion's my middle name."

"Thanks. I appreciate it."

She scooted into the gift shop and pretended to browse until Ric left the lobby. Then she drifted casually toward the stairs at the end of the hall. A minute later she was at Free's door, which stood ajar.

When she pushed it open, she saw a room with two queen-sized beds. One was laden with photography gear. On the other, spread out in the sunlight that streamed through the open window, was Free Lafontaine, naked and fully erect.

# Chapter 4

OH my God. Free looked fabulous, but talk about taking her for granted.

"We're on the clock," he said. "Gonna waste any more time?"

She secured the Do Not Disturb sign, then locked the door.

"Get on over here, woman."

As she walked toward him, he slid over to sit on the edge of the bed. He spread his legs, and she stood between them, staring down at brown thighs and that huge, erect cock. The sight of him made her panties wet.

As he found out, when he reached a bold hand under her skirt and caressed between her legs. "Oh yeah, Sarah. You want this, don't you?"

"Almost as much as you do." Trying not to squirm against his hand, she grasped his cock firmly and stroked up and down. When her thumb circled the head, a few drops oozed out, and she used them to coat him.

He stopped rubbing the crotch of her panties and yanked them down and off.

She let out a startled squeak, then gave a sigh of pleasure when he stroked her damp pussy lips.

"Know what I was thinking about in that restaurant?" he asked.

"Uh, no."

"That short little skirt of yours." He reached for a condom on the bedside table, then gently pried her hand off his cock and sheathed himself.

"My skirt?"

"I was thinking you could sit on my lap, and we could hike up your skirt, and nobody'd know what we were doing." He pulled her skirt up to her waist.

Instinctively she made a move to cover herself. How ridiculous. They'd had sex last night. But that had been in moonlight. Now, in the bright morning sunlight, she felt exposed. Maybe it had to do with how dark he was and how pale she looked in comparison, with her creamy skin and auburn bush.

"So pretty," he crooned, running his fingers through her curls, then dipping down between her legs again. He slid one finger inside, and her vaginal muscles hugged it. Last night, she'd wondered how she could ever open wide enough to take in that impressive cock. Now, she knew it would happen and, as his finger circled inside her, she felt herself widening and moistening, craving more.

Her legs trembled as she pressed herself against his hand, all hunger and need. "Free, that feels so good." When she gripped his shoulders for balance, she found his skin was hot, almost burning, like the sun had baked into him and been trapped there.

"Come up here," he urged. "On my lap."

He helped her climb on the bed so she straddled him, his cock rising between them. She inched forward, nudging it with her pelvis, feeling the tickle of his springy pubic hair against her intimate flesh.

Then she rose up on her knees and watched as he gripped his penis with one hand, and with the other opened her gently. He guided the head of his cock to her entrance, and that first sweet push made her whimper with pleasure.

"Slide down," he said. "Take me in, Sarah."

He was so long, so full, so hot. As she eased slowly down, she could feel every inch of him. Sensation pulsed through her, sweet arousal filling her as completely as he did.

His hands cupped her butt, holding her securely and caressing at the same time. "Yeah, you tell it."

Tell it? She realized she'd been muttering, urging him on, whimpering. Who knew what she'd said, because she hadn't done it consciously. Much better to kiss those firm, curving lips than to babble, so she did just that.

Mmm, he was one hell of a kisser. His soft mustache and goatee brushed her skin sensually. His sexy tongue teased hers, and he set the rhythm of the kiss. Her body picked up that same rhythm, rising and falling on his hard cock, shifting this way and that, swirling and stroking. The caress, the stimulation of flesh on flesh, was a little different each time she moved on and around him.

Every touch, every sensation drove her closer to orgasm. He stroked one hand down the crease between her buttocks at the same time as he reached his other hand between their bodies and fingered her needy clit.

Sensation rocketed through her, and a stunning climax caught her in its grip.

"Yeah, that's it, ride it all the way," Free whispered in her ear.

God, yes. She'd ride this one as far as it took her, her body pulsing and spasming around his rigid length while she moaned her pleasure.

As the final spasms ebbed, he took over, thrusting long and slow, hard and steady, each stroke reaching deep, deep inside her.

"So good." She rocked against him, pelvis to pelvis, as her body caught this new, seductive rhythm.

Giving over control, she clung to him, reveling in the primal beat of their joining. Her body tightened, her clit throbbed, and she could feel another orgasm building.

"I will, yeah. Trust me now. I will," he crooned.

Had she asked him for something? What? Whatever it was, he was hitting all her hot spots.

When she was on the verge of climax, he grabbed her hips, held her steady, then surged deep, deeper, letting out a hoarse cry as his body jerked in orgasm.

She exploded with him, crying out her pleasure.

They rocked together for long moments. She clung to his neck, feeling as if her whole body had melted into a puddle of pure satisfaction. "How on earth do you know how to do that?" she panted.

"Do what?" He was short of breath, too.

"Give me exactly the right thing at the right time."

He chuckled. "Just a talented lover, I guess."

"I'll say."

He stroked down her back. "Come on, don't you know? Really?"

"Know what?"

"You keep telling me. All that stuff you're saying, about yes, there, now, do that. God, woman, you give me the driving directions."

She buried her face in his shoulder. "How embarrassing." Had she always done this? If so, why had no man ever told her—or followed her instructions so well? Or was this a thing she only did with Free?

"Damn, every guy should be so lucky. Takes the guesswork out of it. Not to mention, lets me know you're having a good time."

How sweet of him to put it that way. The man had so much potential. Why was he so set against love and marriage?

She nipped the corner of his mouth. "Danny asked you about taking the wedding photos?"

His lips curved. "Not relevant. There won't be a wedding. You're great in bed, but that's not changing my mind."

"Mine, either. So, let's just say for the sake of argument that I win—"

His low chuckle interrupted her. "Won't happen."

"Mmm-hmm. But *when* it does, I gather you don't want to do the photos, right? And you're a travel photographer, which is quite different than what I'm looking for. Don't worry, there's a competent guy here in San Pedro. His wedding photos are a little conventional, but I guess that's—"

"Crap. I know the stuff you mean."

"He's the best on the island."

"Not now that I'm here."

"But you don't want to do it."

"Keep telling you, there won't be a wedding."

"So you have no objection to me making arrangements with the man in San Pedro? Even though Danny really wants you?"

"Just . . . don't tell him, okay? It'll be another of our secrets."

Sarah reflected, but she couldn't see any reason not to agree. She had plan B in place, and Free could figure out how to explain to Danny when the time came. "Okay. I'll keep your secret, and you'll keep mine."

Then she glanced at the clock on the bedside table. Only ten minutes left. "Oops!" She eased off him and hurried into the bathroom to clean up.

When she came out, he was sprawled on the bed, looking lazy and satisfied. "You want these?" He dangled a scrap of pale blue fabric from his big, dark hand.

Damp panties or a bare crotch? Nope, she'd run back to her cabana and grab fresh underwear.

She smiled teasingly at Free. "You keep them. A souvenir."

A couple days later, Free and Danny were alone on the deck of Danny and Bella's cabana.

Danny flopped into the hammock, and Free tossed his bud one of the Belikin beers he'd bought at the resort bar. "Jeez, man," he complained, "I thought I'd never drag you away from the crowd." And especially Bella, who'd Krazy Glued herself to Danny's side.

It wasn't just Bella, though. Sarah was a compulsive organizer, keeping not only Danny but all of the family and friends busy at all times. Each day's activity spreadsheet had different groups heading out on excursions. Right now, a dozen people were shopping in San Pedro, and another group was exploring the island on the golf carts that were the main form of transportation. Danny's older brother—and best man—and his wife had taken another bunch on a snorkel and dive expedition.

Sarah, Bella, and Bella's mother, Giovanna, weren't on expeditions today; instead they were busy with wedding arrangements.

That Giovanna was damn hot for a mom. Hot-tempered, too, he'd heard. Sarah had said she'd scheduled everything to keep Bella's divorced parents apart, or Giovanna might tear out James's hair.

Free had commented, "You realize, by telling me this, you're giving ammunition to the enemy?"

"As in, you could use it to sabotage the wedding? Free, I think you're a better man than you give yourself credit for," Sarah had replied.

"Cute strategy," he'd retaliated. "It's because I'm a good man and a good friend that I'm going to stop Danny from getting married."

Funny how he and Sarah could be so compatible when it came to sex—which they'd been having whenever they could sneak it in—even though they were at war about the wedding.

So far, damn it, the woman was winning. But only because he hadn't been able to get his dumb-ass bud alone. Right now, Free was supposed to be in San Pedro, and Danny had been scheduled on the golf cart trip, but they'd snuck away for some guy time.

Now Danny swung in the hammock, one hand dangling over the edge by his beer bottle. Free sprawled on a deck chair. A couple of pretty girls in bikinis strolled along the beach. "Nice view," Free said.

"Yup."

"Maybe they'd like to share our beer."

"Don't think Bella'd be impressed."

"Since when does she rule your life?"

Danny put down one leg, got the hammock swinging again, and lifted his leg back up. "It's not about that."

"Sounds like it to me."

"I don't want to be with those girls. I want to be with Bella."

"Jesus, she's got you pussy-whipped. Where's your pride?"

"I'm proud of her. Of being with her. Of who I am when I'm with her."

"You're proud of being pussy-whipped?"

Danny laughed and reached for his beer. "One day you'll figure it out."

"Figure what out?"

"There's more to life than screwing one girl after another. Quality beats quantity."

Quality. Okay, he could kind of relate. What he had with Sarah was primo sex. But that's *because* it was free and easy, no strings attached. "You can have that without getting married."

"Yeah, but I want to marry Bella."

"Jesus, man." Free leaned forward, beer bottle between his hands. "You really figure on only screwing one girl for the rest of your life?"

"Yup. Found the one I want."

"Crap."

"Sure as hell don't want Bella screwing anyone else."

"You're marrying her to stop her from messing around on you?"

Danny laughed again. "You so don't get it."

"Remember that vow we swore when we were nineteen? To never get married?"

"We were kids. A guy can change his mind. It's called maturity."

"It's called a ball and chain." Okay, he'd been playing nice, but Danny wasn't listening. Time to get down and dirty. "Hate to remind you, but you've been engaged before, and you know how that turned out."

Danny's face darkened. "Yeah, I know. You were right about Kimberly. She just wanted my money. But Bella's nothing like her."

"Thought you'd've learned your lesson, man."

"Bella doesn't care about my money."

"Then why does she call you Mr. FFR?"

"It's a joke. Fact is, I'm filthy fucking rich. Besides, her parents aren't exactly poor."

"They're nowhere near rich. Face it, if you were poor, Bella wouldn't marry you. She's hooked on the gifts, the expensive jewelry. The flights on the private jet to go shopping in L.A. and New York, the weeklong dive excursions. It's not you she wants; it's your money." He played his trump card. "Just like Kimberly."

A shadow of doubt crossed Danny's face, then he shook his head. "You're wrong. She'd love me just the same if I was poor. It's like . . ." He thought for a moment. "Okay, she loves sparkly jewelry. I give her diamonds and emeralds and amethysts, but she'd be as happy with junk jewelry."

"Yeah, right."

"What the hell're you doing, anyhow, Free? You're my best bud. You're supposed to be there for me."

Danny's bottle was empty, so Free handed him a fresh beer. "I'm trying to save your fucking life. And remember, you're the one who asked me to do it back when Kimberly ditched you."

"Bella's not like Kimberly," Danny repeated stubbornly.

"Do you remember what a mess you were? I've never seen a grown man cry like that. It wasn't a pretty sight."

Danny winced and took a long slug of beer. "Yeah. I felt like crap. It was hell."

They were both silent for a few moments. Free was making progress. Now, how to drive the point home?

Reflecting, he glanced toward the ocean and noticed a woman slipping out of the cabana with yellow trim. It was the gorgeous Japanese model who was the current squeeze of Danny's celebrity uncle. Willowy in a halter top and short, pink sarong, she had a pink hibiscus blossom tucked into her waterfall of shiny black hair.

"Hey, Tamiko," Danny called.

She froze, then glanced toward them and walked over. "Hello, Danny, Free. I thought everyone had gone off somewhere."

"We skipped out," Danny said. "You and Uncle Zane do the same?"

"You know Zane. He wanted a—mmm, how shall I put this?—afternoon nap. Then that muse of his struck, so he pulled out the computer."

Danny's uncle was a world-renowned writer of techno-thrillers starring a macho secret agent named Lance Connors. Like his protagonist, Zane was a footloose bachelor who dated only the most beautiful women. He'd always been a role model for Free and Danny.

"Want to hang with us?" Danny said. "We have beer."

Damn. Free willed her to say no, so he could get back to making Danny see reason.

Fortunately, Tamiko shook her head. "Thanks, but I think I'll, uh, go for a walk down the beach. Or maybe pop into the gift shop."

"Uncle Zane shouldn't be ignoring you," Danny said sympathetically.

"Oh no," she said quickly. "Zane's wonderful. I adore him, even when his muse takes over. Besides, I don't think he has any control over it; it just happens." She sounded as if she knew him well, and her affection was genuine.

Before Danny could again ask her to join them, Free said, "Why don't you go to the bar? When I picked up our beer, Ric was there, restocking. Get him to make you a fancy drink."

"Ric?" Her eyes widened. "Uh, that's the bartender?"

"Come on, you gotta know Ric Nuñez," Danny said. "The resort owner? He's always around, working with us on the wedding. Great dude."

"Ric," she repeated, her lips giving a brief twitch. Maybe the guy had been flirting with her. Not that he'd stand a chance against Zane, who was not only world-famous and looked like Clive Owen, but was FFR like Danny.

"A drink does sound like a good idea," she said. "Maybe I'll have sex on the beach. I quite enjoyed it when I tried it yesterday."

Free choked back a laugh, thinking about the sex on the beach—and not the liquid kind—that he and Sarah had shared.

He and Danny watched as Tamiko walked away, hips swaying gently, sleek black hair falling almost to her waist.

Any man's wet dream. Except, oddly enough, not Free's. Sarah might not be so knock-you-off-your-feet stunning, but to him, she was prettier, sexier.

Not that he'd toss Tamiko out of bed for eating crackers. He took a swallow of beer and got back to his mission. The model had made him think of his next argument. "Remember how we've always said we wanted a life like your uncle's? There's a guy that'll never get married. He's got world-class babes knocking themselves out to get into his bed."

"Meaningless sex," Danny said dismissively.

"Finest kind. Jeez, I can't believe you're the same guy I've known for more than a decade. That Bella's castrated you."

Danny burst out laughing. "Shit, man, I'm having the best sex I've ever had in my life. And it keeps getting better. There's a lot to be said for love."

"Gag. You sound like a chick flick."

"You just watch. One day you'll be asking me to be your best man."

"Zane Slade will turn gay before that happens."

Danny gave a reluctant laugh. "Or Bella's parents will get back together? Man, you really did take that confirmed bachelor vow seriously, didn't you?"

"Hey, my parents are great role models, just like Zane. Never married, both independent and fulfilled. Still friends, too. If they'd gotten married, they'd be divorced and hating each other like Bella's folks do."

"Her parents are weird, and so are yours. Lots of marriages work."

"More don't. Especially when the girl's a gold digger. Bella'll leave you for a richer guy just like Kimberly did. Besides, you can't believe the great sex will last after marriage. Things'll go stale, she'll have a headache. She'd rather be shopping, spending your money."

Danny wasn't listening. His friend's face had lit up, and he was scrambling out of the hammock. "There are the girls."

Free glanced past him to see Sarah and Bella strolling toward the cabana, arms linked. Both wore skimpy sundresses and had hibiscus blossoms tucked in their hair.

Dimly he was aware of Danny saying, "Be nice to Sarah, okay?" But mainly, Free was feeling that weird, disconcerting physical reaction that always happened around the wedding planner. First, something in his chest jerked, then his stomach did a flip-flop, his dick twitched, and he found himself smiling.

Must have to do with the mind-blowing sex they'd been having. He was always anticipating more.

He wiped the smile off his face. The bride and the wedding planner were his opponents in his campaign to keep Danny from making a huge mistake.

Sarah dipped her sandy feet in the footbath at the bottom of the steps, then climbed the steps, frowning. "Danny, you were supposed to go on the golf cart expedition." She shot an accusing glare at Free. "And you're supposed to be in town."

Danny hugged Bella. "Free and I haven't had much guy time, so we decided to hang out."

"After all, he won't be getting much guy time if he gets married," Free said pointedly.

Bella narrowed her eyes and gave a brittle laugh. "It's *when*, not *if*. And he'd better. I definitely want girl time with my friends. Spas, chick flicks, all the stuff that bores Danny to tears. And I sure don't want to hang out in sports bars watching football."

"You don't?" Danny said with mock surprise.

"That's such a healthy attitude," Sarah said brightly. "Every couple needs some separate friends and interests. It'll make you appreciate your couple time even more." She shot Free a point-to-my-side look.

Damn, but she looked delicious. Her dress was a scrap of cotton with a tropical pattern in oranges and yellows. It wasn't tight, but the fabric was so thin that every whisper of breeze plastered it against her curves. No way was she wearing a bra under that. The question was, what about panties?

It was a pressing question, according to his dick, which was rising to rub against his fly. Not that the answer mattered, because if she was wearing them, he could get them off her in a flash. But the need to know was driving him nuts.

"Something wrong?" she inquired sweetly, lifting a hand to run her fingers through her hair. He knew that she knew perfectly well that the gesture raised her breasts high enough that he could almost see the top of one areola.

"Have to talk to you," he said gruffly. "Now."

"Now?" She raised an eyebrow, trying to be cool. But that redhead skin of hers betrayed her. Her cheeks were pink, and so was her chest and the upper curve of those pretty breasts.

"Now," he said firmly. Searching for an excuse, he added, "About the photos."

"The wedding photos?" Her eyes glinted with humor. "Well, in that case . . ."

"Why don't we go to your cabana?" He added, tongue-in-cheek, "I'm sure you'll want to work on a spreadsheet."

"Spread sheets are good," she said, separating the one word into two, making him envision the huge bed in the loft of her cabana.

Her, stretched out on the bed, skin only a little darker than the white sheet. Sunlight filtering through the slatted wooden blinds to make patterns on her skin. Hmm . . .

"Okay, you go get those spread sheets ready," he said. "There's something I need to pick up, then I'll meet you at your cabana."

"I'm in Orchid, the one with purple trim." Her eyes twinkled, no doubt remembering him sneaking into her cabana in the dark the last two nights.

"Okay." He glanced at Danny and Bella to see if they'd picked up on anything, but they seemed totally absorbed in each other. Damn, he still had to find a way to derail the wedding and save his bud from a reprise of the Kimberly fiasco.

But right now, he had more urgent business.

# Chapter 5

FREE turned the lock on Sarah's cabana door, then took his Nikon from its case and climbed the stairs to the loft.

Oh yeah, she was ready for him, just the way he'd pictured: sprawled on her back, nude body banded with stripes of sunlight, head on a pillow with the peach-colored hibiscus flower still in her hair. She looked lazy and sensual.

He lifted the camera.

She flinched. "What are you doing?"

"We're supposed to be talking photography. Figured I should bring a camera."

"Okay, but put it down."

"I think I should snap off some photos."

"Not of me, like this." She sat up and began to drag the sheet over her.

"Didn't you say you were concerned that I'm a travel photographer? Figure I need to prove I can shoot people."

"Aha! So you agree there's going to be a wedding."

"Nope. Just trying to persuade you to let me take your picture."

She looked pretty cute now, sheet clutched across her body, eyes flashing.

"If you want to shoot people, ask Bella and Danny."

"I'd rather do you."

"Then *do* me, Free, and lose the camera."

"Ever since I saw you, I've wanted to take your picture."

"You have?" She looked startled and flattered. Then she shook her head. "Nice line, camera boy. Bet that works on lots of women. But you're not adding me to your nude photo collection."

"Why not? Self-conscious about your bod? It's really not bad at all," he teased.

He ducked quickly, or the pillow she flung would've hit his Nikon. At least she'd dropped the sheet.

"My body's damned good, as you well know."

"Yeah, I do know. So let me take some pics. Promise I won't use them anywhere without your okay."

"Except for masturbation fantasies," she grumbled, but her eyes were bright and her cheeks had gone pink. The idea turned her on. He'd figured it would.

Turned him on, too. He peeled off his shorts, so she could see how much.

Her gaze fastened on his. "I believe in equality. Do you?"

What was she talking about? "Yeah, of course." That had been one of the fundamental lessons his parents had taught him. And it was one of the reasons they, and he, thought marriage sucked. People lost their identities, they got tied down and confined by old-fashioned roles and expectations.

"So, I get to take photos of you, too?"

His dick grew another inch. She wanted nude photos of him? "Hell, yeah."

"That camera looks fancy. Tell me how it works."

This sure wasn't the time for a lesson on aperture width and shutter speed. He set the camera on automatic and handed it to her, then sat on the bed beside her, his thigh brushing hers. "Lift it up, look through the lens, and focus on something."

She pointed the camera toward a painting of a purple orchid. "How do I focus?"

"Here." He leaned close, smelling the coconut scent of her sunscreen. "Put your hand on this ring and twist out and in. The subject of the photo should be in the middle of the lens. When it's in focus you'll hear a little—" The camera beeped. "Like that. Now click the shutter."

She did; then he showed her how to view the picture she'd taken.

"Well, that's easy. You make a living doing this?"

"Not exactly. The camera's set on automatic. Normally I work on manual and deal with lighting, depth of field, shutter speed, and so on, as well as composition. And then there's the digital manipulation of the image afterward."

He took the camera from her. "You took one. Now it's my turn."

"Hey, wait a minute."

"Equality," he reminded her. "One for you, one for me."

Her arms went around her chest. "I've never done this before."

He could read that on her face: shyness and vulnerability, along with an intrigued curiosity and arousal. Casually he raised the camera and snapped a picture of her head and torso.

"Let me see," she demanded. "If I don't like it, you'll erase it."

It wasn't a question, but he nodded, then held the camera so they could both see the image. "I was right," he said with satisfaction. "Definitely photogenic."

"It's not bad. It's like—" She glanced up. "The best pictures tell a story."

Free nodded.

"The strips of light and shadow are interesting," she said. "And I'm naked, and that's bold like the light. But I'm covering my breasts, which is shy, like the shadow."

Again he nodded. She really got it. "And your expression shows the boldness and the shyness."

"You saw all that? In a couple seconds before you took the shot?"

"It's what I do. And quicker is less intrusive. Like, when I was with the Aborigines the last few weeks. They're shy, and it was incredible they trusted me enough to let me go walkabout and eventually take their pictures. I wanted to respect them and also convey their wisdom, beauty, timelessness, and—" He broke off, embarrassed at how he'd gotten carried away.

"You always seem so laid back. Like you don't take anything seriously. But I'm guessing you've worked hard at this craft. As well as having natural talent. And you love it, don't you?"

Jesus. He'd taken one photo of her, and she'd looked beyond it to paint a portrait of him. Not one he was about to buy into. Hell, he *was* laid back. "Life's about having fun. Right now"—he gestured at her naked body and winked—"photography's a hell of a lot of fun."

Her lips curved in one of those knowing, feminine smiles that drove him nuts. Why did women always want to see stuff in a guy that didn't actually exist? "You'll take excellent wedding photos."

"I have to believe in the story before I can tell it."

"You will."

"Not happening."

Sarah jumped off the bed and took the camera from his hands. "Lie down. Let me find a story to tell for my next shot."

He reclined on her bed, stretching out and spreading his legs. One hand went behind his head, and with the other he adjusted his package and stroked his swollen dick; then he put that hand behind his head, too.

She'd gone to the bottom of the bed and now focused and clicked.

"What's your story?"

"Arrogant male with big cock," she teased, shooting a couple more images.

He chuckled and sat up. "My turn. You lie down."

She handed him the camera and complied, looking nervous again. Rather than taking a picture, he put the Nikon down and leaned over to kiss her. Her lips parted in surprise, then she kissed him back until he could tell she'd forgotten about the camera.

There was one big problem about being with Sarah. He wanted to do everything. Her mouth was so damned seductive, he could kiss her forever. But at the same time, he was thinking about her creamy breasts and the way they responded to his tongue. And how pretty her rosy nipples were. Meantime, his dick was throbbing with the need to bury itself in the sweet heat of her pussy.

Unable to resist the lure of her breasts, he disengaged from her mouth and slid down her body. There was one good thing about not kissing her mouth. She could make all those murmuring, whispery sounds to let him know what she wanted.

He caressed one breast with his hand and laved the other with his tongue, working into the center. Then he sucked her nipple into his mouth, playing with it until it was hard and her hips began to twist.

Slowly he kissed his way down her body, circling her navel with his tongue, breathing warm air on her thatch of red curls. Her body writhed, and her breathy "Yes, oh yes, mmm, lower, go lower, that's so good, keep going" confirmed her enjoyment.

He spread her legs and dipped his tongue to taste her special flavor, musky and spicy and delicious. When her labia were swollen and glistening, he moved quickly up her body again, licking her pebbled nipples, then pressing a demanding kiss on her lips.

Then he sat up and grabbed the camera. Before she realized what he was doing, he'd clicked off a series of shots. Creamy body, red hair, and the gleaming rose of her lips, nipples, and swollen sex.

"Oh my God!" Her eyes flew open. "You photographed me like this?"

"Arousal," he murmured. "The story's arousal."

"That's for sure." She reached for his cock, swollen and glistening from pre-come. "And it's mutual."

"You can take a picture if you want. It's your turn."

She shook her head, face flushed. "Guess I'm not such a devoted photographer. Right now, that arousal story's waiting for a happy ending."

"Let's see what we can do about that." He buried his tongue between her legs again, until she cried out very happily in climax.

Then she said, "So, arrogant male with big cock, how much of you d'you think will fit in my mouth?"

His swollen dick jerked at the thought, and he lay back. "Let's find out."

She leaned over and began to lick his hard-on, from base to crown, each touch of her tongue pulling him closer to orgasm.

Rolling onto his side, he took her with him. She was so engrossed in fondling him that she didn't seem to notice how he was rearranging her limbs.

But maybe she wasn't so oblivious. When he'd matched his face to her crotch, she lifted a leg over him, neatly trapping him between her thighs—which of course was where he'd been headed.

As he began to lick her pussy, she took the head of his dick between her lips and applied gentle suction. Then she opened her mouth wider and took him in deeper, getting him nice and wet and slippery with her saliva, and started to slide her hand up and down his length.

It felt so good, he groaned against her pussy. When he slid his tongue inside, her body quivered and her thighs tightened around him.

She eased back so she was holding just the crown of his penis between her lips, then ran her tongue around it, and all the time her hand was milking his shaft.

The needy ache was building, his balls tightening. He slid a couple of fingers inside Sarah's wet heat and turned his tongue to her clit.

When he knew his climax was close, he paused to gasp, "I'm gonna come," warning her in case she didn't want him in her mouth.

But she only sucked harder as she wriggled her pussy against his face in a wordless demand. He answered it with his tongue, and the deeper, faster thrusts of his fingers. Then, as he let go in delicious release and poured himself into her mouth, she clenched around his fingers and broke in spasms around him.

They lay locked together for a few minutes, both breathing hard. Then she rolled free and sprawled bonelessly on the bed. He collapsed onto his back beside her, eyes closed. "Man, that was good."

"Mmm-hmm," she murmured contentedly.

He realized that, as much as he'd enjoyed having his dick in her mouth, he'd missed her sexy babble. Any lover could give a blow job, but only Sarah could turn him on with her voice. Only Sarah let him know, with all those funny sounds and murmurs, how much he pleased her.

The bed shifted and, eyes still closed, he reached a hand out to touch her. When he found sheets instead of warm, silky flesh, he opened his eyes in time to see her aim his camera at him, and click. "Hey, you caught me off guard."

She grinned. "Aren't candid photos the best? They capture the true personality."

He laughed. "Not sure that one says a whole lot about my personality."

"A portrait of satisfaction."

"You got that right."

She clicked off a couple more, then came back to the bed, bending to pick up the hibiscus blossom that had fallen to the floor.

When she lay down, he took it and arranged it on one breast. "Looks so nice against your skin. You've got such subtle coloring."

She caught his hand, interlaced her fingers through his, and held their clasped hands away from their bodies. "I love how your skin looks against mine. Wish we could take a photo of us together, but I'm sure not inviting someone in to do it."

"The camera has a timer. Got a tripod in my room, but I'm not going back for it now. We could set the camera on the windowsill."

He studied her face. "It doesn't bother you, me being black?"

She lowered their clasped hands, shaking her head. "Any reason it should?"

"There's places in the world where it'd matter."

"Not Belize. Not Vancouver, where I come from." She curled on her side facing him and shot him a quizzical glance. "Where do you live, anyhow?"

"Vancouver's home base. But I go wherever the job takes me."

"Me, too. I share a town house in Vancouver with my partner, Andrea. That's our business office, too. But mostly we meet clients at their homes, and we're away a lot at weddings."

"Strange life, running other people's weddings."

"Every woman, every couple, deserves their special day. The right start to their life together."

"Jeez, Sarah, half of marriages end in divorce, and a lot of the rest are miserable."

"People give up too easily. They expect everything to be perfect, and when they run into trouble, they bail. Most marriages could work if the spouses put some effort into them."

"The reason marriage doesn't work is because it's an old-fashioned institution. It's based on traditional roles—the woman needing a breadwinner, the man needing a homemaker and mother for his kids. Now that men and women are *equal*, they have better options."

"There's no better option than a loving marriage."

He groaned. "Come on. It's lust that gets people to marry each other, and it burns out."

She shook her head, red hair brushing the white pillow. "Sure, it's often lust—pheromones—that first attracts people. But pheromones are the product of evolution, so don't sell them short. They get the right prospective mates together, spending time, finding common interests and values. Like Bella and Danny."

He groaned louder, but she went on. "They met here on the beach, two beautiful people lusting after each other, sexually compatible. They discovered common interests, like diving. So they went on dive trips and shared that underwater world. They had drinks, talked, found more and more in common, more to like and respect in each other."

Listening, Free had to admit that what she said matched up with what Danny had told him. But that was before Bella had set her sights on his bud's money and a marriage certificate.

"So, lust turned into love," Sarah went on. "And they're getting married. Their love will deepen the more years they spend together. They'll be motivated to stick with the relationship, work on it, build it. They'll move into their new house, have babies, maybe come back to Belize each year on their anniversary. Go diving, drink a couple glasses of sex on the beach."

He'd been shaking his head as she spoke. "Lose their freedom. Their independence." And the only sex they'd be having was from a martini glass.

"Find different priorities in life. More mature ones."

"Ouch," he said mildly, thinking the woman was nuts. "Whatcha doing with me, if you figure I'm so immature?"

She sat up, propping pillows behind her and gathering the sheet across her breasts. "That's a good question. Tell me, Free, why are you so dead set against marriage? Did some girl break your heart?"

He snorted, sitting up, too. "No way. I'd never put my heart out there to get broken. I'm footloose and fancy-free. I value my independence. And"—he shot her a warning look—"I like women who value theirs."

"Independence," she echoed. "By which you mean the ability to take off whenever you want on a photo trip? To screw whatever woman comes along? Without taking anyone else into consideration or having anyone care what you do?"

"Yeah, that'd be it."

"That sounds . . ." She paused.

"Perfect." He finished her sentence just as she said, "Lonely."

He gave another snort. "Why're we even discussing this? You trying to win the war by talking me to death? Let's stick to the stuff we agree on. Like sex. Now, why don't I set the timer on the camera?"

She stared at him for long seconds, and he guessed she was deciding between being pissed off versus letting it go and having some more sexy fun. Finally she shrugged and said, "Sure. Why not?"

* * *

WHEN he left Sarah's cabana, Free's legs felt as weak as if he'd downed a half-dozen potent tropical drinks. Man, that woman packed a punch.

He showered and then downloaded the afternoon's images to his computer. Oh yeah, he'd been right about Sarah being photogenic as well as sexy.

The pics she'd taken of him gave him a laugh—she sure did seem fascinated by his dick. He e-mailed all the photos to her, figuring they'd both have something to keep them warm at night once they were back home.

Home. Her home base was Vancouver, too. Maybe they could hook up from time to time—if he could convince her of the merits of no-strings sex.

He'd made a good argument this afternoon, and she'd had no problem getting down and dirty with him—with a guy who'd made it crystal clear he wasn't into commitment.

Oh yeah, he was winning her over.

Whistling, he checked the latest spreadsheet. Damned if Sarah didn't slip them under each guest's door every day, accounting for every minute of their time. Tonight the group was scheduled for a seafood dinner at the Toucan. Not much chance of getting Danny alone until tomorrow, when he'd again do his best to pry his bud away from Bella and knock some sense into his head. It was one hell of a job, trying to save a guy who seemed determined not to be saved.

He headed for the bar. It was empty but for the bartender and Ric, who were discussing something on a computer screen. Everyone must be getting ready for dinner.

Drinking alone was okay, but company was better, so he said to Ric, "Buy you a drink?"

To the bartender, Ric said, "Yeah, let's try this one." Then, to Free, "Sounds good. Everything's under control for dinner, and the chef knows where to find me if he needs me."

As they seated themselves on high stools, the elderly English couple came through, saying hello as they headed for the adjoining restaurant.

"How come you let those two stay?" Free asked the resort owner. "You cleared out pretty much everyone else who isn't with Danny and Bella."

Ric grinned. "Couldn't ditch the Everleighs. They're my good luck charm. They stayed here the first year I opened the Toucan Resort, and they've come every year since for their anniversary. Been married sixty years." He chuckled. "Hey, maybe Bella and Danny will do the same thing."

"Not gonna happen," Free muttered under his breath.

"What's that?"

"Nothing. So, what're you drinking?"

When they were both sipping tall icy rum drinks, Free said, "Thanks for being cool about the thing with Sarah and me."

"No problem. Everyone's entitled to their secrets."

Yeah, Ric was a good guy, just like he'd told Zane's girlfriend. "Did Tamiko find you?"

Ric's drink must've gone down wrong, because he started to cough. "Tamiko?" he choked out. "Who's that?"

Like any man within a hundred miles could have missed her. Free raised his eyebrows. "The gorgeous Japanese babe who's warming Zane Slade's bed?"

The other man's eyes heated, but his tone was noncommittal when he said, "Oh, right, her. Did she say she was looking for me?"

"Zane was writing, and she was at loose ends. I told her to find you, and you'd make her a fancy drink." He snorted. "Beats me how a guy could ignore a girl like her."

Ric shrugged. "He's a writer. Don't you ever get caught up in something? So deep you're kind of obsessed?"

Free thought about taking pictures and how hours could pass without him noticing. He gave a rueful grin. "Been known to happen. So, did she find you?"

"Tamiko? She dropped by, but I had to go into San Pedro for something." His lips curved. Free expected some comment about how hot the model was, but instead Ric said, "She's a nice person."

Maybe. And when she'd been talking to him and Danny, she'd sounded as if she really cared for Zane. "Then I hope she knows what she's gotten herself into."

Ric choked and coughed again. "How d'you mean?"

"Since I met Danny, his uncle's always had some eye-candy babe hanging around, but he never gets serious with them. If Tamiko's nice like you say and has actually fallen for the guy, she'll end up getting hurt."

Ric sighed. "What can you do when you're falling for someone? Tell your heart it's not a good idea?"

"Hell, yeah." Take Sarah, for example. She was pretty, fun, smart, and incredible in bed. But he wasn't going to do anything stupid like fall in love.

"Had much luck with that approach?" Ric asked.

"Sure." He took another sip of the potent drink. "Well, truth is, I've never been seriously tempted. I love women, lots of women. We have some fun, great sex, until one of us gets bored. I'm not the kind to settle down."

"Lots of guys think that. Until they meet that special one."

"And have you met yours, Ric?" Sarah's teasing voice asked.

Free turned to see that she, along with Danny and Bella, had come up behind him. He thought he heard Ric murmur, "You never know," but Danny's voice overrode him as he said, "I've definitely found mine."

*Yeah, sure,* Free thought cynically. His bud had said the same thing when he was engaged to Kimberly, before she'd fucked him over. Why wouldn't Danny see reason?

Free usually avoided confrontation. There wasn't much in life that was worth fighting over. But he couldn't walk away from this. He had to find some way of saving Danny from making the same mistake twice.

He studied Bella, who was smiling as she polished her huge engagement ring against the fabric of her purple sundress. More diamonds, along with amethysts, sparkled at her neck and dangled from her ears.

"Aren't you going overboard with the bling?" he taunted. "It's the beach, for God's sake."

Defiantly her gaze met his. "I like sparkly jewelry."

"And it looks so pretty on her," Danny chimed in.

Damn, couldn't the idiot see that the carefree girl he'd met a couple years ago had turned into another money-grubbing Kimberly? Bella was out to hook him—at least until a richer sucker came along. At least Kimberly had found the richer guy *before* the wedding ceremony.

Holy shit! He had a lightbulb moment. Desperate measures were called for, and he knew what he had to do to make Bella reveal her true colors.

Abruptly he stood. "Just remembered some business I have to take care of."

"Aw, come on," Danny said. "Can't be so important it won't wait 'til tomorrow."

"This is."

"There you go again." Sarah winked. "Blowing that laid-back rep of yours."

If she only knew what he had in mind.

"I'll be back for dinner." As he hurried to his room, he felt a moment's guilt over what he was planning. But then, he and Sarah had declared war from the outset, and he'd bet she believed all was fair in love and war.

Bella had brainwashed Danny, and he wasn't listening to reason. And Sarah was seeing their relationship through those completely unrealistic rose-colored romantic glasses of hers.

But actions spoke louder than words.

The scheme was forming in his mind. He even knew the perfect guy to pull it off: Jeff Tomaso, the actor. A mutual friend had introduced them when Free had been doing some work in Manhattan. They'd hit it off, kept casually in touch.

Free crossed his fingers that Jeff didn't currently have an acting gig.

# Chapter 6

THE next day, plans made, Free bided his time and played nice.

He was scheduled on a golf cart expedition heading north to view scenery, then have lunch. Cars were rare on Ambergris Caye, and so were good roads. Golf carts were ubiquitous. Damned slow, but they had an island charm.

In bed last night, Sarah had told him she'd paired her name with his to share a cart, and he'd teased her about whether she'd ever made out in a golf cart. She hadn't taken him seriously, but he was definitely going to be on the lookout for an opportunity.

Mid morning, the group assembled in the resort parking lot. Free had brought his camera along and snapped a few shots.

Tamiko and Zane were there, and Danny's brother and his wife. Danny's cousin Jennie said, "Who am I paired with?"

Sarah, slim and lovely in shorts and a sleeveless top, consulted her spreadsheet. "Brad, one of Danny's friends. Do you know him?"

"Uh-huh." The young woman didn't look thrilled. Brad was an overweight guy who spent most of his time talking about sports. Spectator sports.

Bella's gorgeous mother, Giovanna, leaned against a cart chatting to Danny's widowed dad, Al, her partner for the outing.

"You matchmaking the parents?" Free muttered to Sarah.

"No. Giving future in-laws a chance to get acquainted." She glanced past him, and her eyes widened. "Shit!"

He turned to see James Moncrieff striding toward them. Despite the lovely weather, Bella's father wore long pants and a long-sleeved shirt and tie. He wasn't bad-looking for a guy his age, but he dressed like he was lecturing at a university.

The man stopped and stared at his ex. "What are you doing here?"

"I'm *supposed* to be here," she snapped. "You're not."

Free smothered a grin as Sarah hurriedly stepped between them. "She's right, James. Didn't you do the golf cart trip yesterday?"

"No. Brad wanted to switch. Sorry, we should have told you."

Giovanna shot James a dagger glance as Sarah said, "Yes." She held up her ever-present clipboard with its bundle of spreadsheets. "I make these spreadsheets for a reason."

Free had to wonder what the guy had been thinking. Hadn't he realized his ex might be taking this trip?

Jennie gave James a bright smile. "Well, I'm Jennie, in case you don't remember my name, and I'm happy to have you as my partner, Mr. Moncrieff. Or would you rather go with, uh—" She broke off, glancing between James and Giovanna.

"Of course not," he said quickly. "I'm delighted to be with you. And please, call me James."

"Well, I'm *delighted* to accompany Al," Giovanna said, taking Danny's dad's arm. Today she wore a skimpy hot pink top with a flowery skirt, showing off her killer figure. When she leaned toward her companion, her impressive cleavage was on full display. Any red-blooded guy had to look—and appreciate the view.

"I can't believe you'd appear in public like that," James huffed.

"Why don't you—?" Sarah started.

But Giovanna, who'd dropped Al's arm and stepped past the

wedding planner, interrupted. Brown eyes flashing, she said, "This is the beach, not your office."

One red-tipped hand touched the knot of James's tie. "A tie. *Madonna mia!* Still the stuffy professor." She flipped the knot open, and with one swift movement yanked the tie from around his neck. Then she began to undo the top button of his shirt.

He raised a hand and trapped hers.

She gave a soft gasp, and for a moment their gazes locked. Dramatic brown eyes met sky blue ones, exchanging some message that made the warm air sizzle.

Free snapped a shot. Man, what a great photo. That picture told a story, but it was a complex one each viewer would interpret differently. To Free, it said sex. But then, to him, most things did.

"Can't keep your hands off me, Giovanna?" James asked, a dangerous note in his voice.

She jerked her hand free. "Don't flatter yourself. I'm simply trying to save you from looking *inappropriate*."

The way she ground out the last word, Free guessed it had special significance to the two of them. And that the sizzle was about anger, not sex.

Then Giovanna tossed her head, which sent waves of rich, dark brown hair rippling, and went back to Al Trent's side.

James turned to Jennie. "Which golf cart is ours?"

Free lowered his camera, and Sarah let out a long breath and rejoined him. "Crisis averted," she murmured.

"Guess it's true they can't be near each other without fighting."

"It's so sad that love can turn into anger, bitterness."

"So much for marriages with happy endings." Score one for his side.

"They weren't right for each other," she said with certainty. "Look at them; they're complete opposites. The passionate Italian and the ivory-tower academic."

She glanced toward the closest cart, where Giovanna was saying, "Please drive, Al. I'm sure you'll be so much better than I."

Sarah's lips curved. "Hmm. She's gorgeous and charming. Not to mention, a woman who really appreciates men. He's been widowed quite a while, right?"

Free thought back. "Six or seven years."

"And never remarried." She tapped a finger against her clipboard. "This just might work." With a wicked grin, she added, "And you were the one who first suggested it. Thanks, Free. We'll have you turned into a real romantic before the week is over."

When he gave an exaggerated groan and made an I'm-gonna-puke gesture, she laughed. "All right, time to get going. Shall I drive?"

"Guess you're not an old-fashioned woman who appreciates men?"

She chuckled again. "If that means you want to drive, just say so. I thought it might be beneath your dignity to drive a golf cart."

"Gotta admit I'd prefer a sports car." But he slipped behind the wheel as she climbed in the passenger side.

"Want to lead the caravan?" The plan was that they'd see some scenery for an hour or so and end up at a beach restaurant for lunch. "If you could survive in the Outback, I'm guessing you can get us to the Crazy Monkey."

"Gee, thanks."

"Besides, there's only one path. It's impossible to get lost."

"You're so good for a guy's ego." He made it sound like a grumble, but he enjoyed sparring with Sarah. At least when she wasn't going on about the joys of marriage.

He revved the engine and steered the cart past the others.

Sarah put on her sunglasses, thinking she'd gotten the best of that little exchange. Then she craned around to call, "Follow us, single file."

After she'd seen the carts fall into line, she settled back in her seat and watched as Free navigated a few unpaved streets lined with houses and stores, then got on the narrow road that led north. She had to admit, the guy was more than competent at pretty much anything he chose to do: photography, sex, golf cart driving.

Her pheromones had chosen well. Free was smart, fun, considerate.

Well, maybe he wasn't so smart, if he couldn't grasp the concepts of love and marriage.

Why was he so opposed? It wasn't normal for a human being to choose a lonely, independent life with no one to care for or to care about him.

At least he'd laid off trying to get Danny alone and talk him out of getting married. Free must be mellowing. She was having an influence, even if he wasn't ready to acknowledge it.

"Hey, what's this?" His voice broke into her thoughts.

She glanced ahead and saw a stretch of green water with a primitive open-air ferry boat on the other side. "There's a channel dividing the Caye. We cross on a hand-drawn ferry."

When he stopped, she said, "We'll break into two groups. I'll tell the others."

She hopped out of the cart and made her way back, filling the others in on what was happening and giving them a photo-op advisory. To the women, she said, "Check out the muscles on the ferry pullers."

She climbed in beside Free again, and they waited while the boat unloaded a couple golf carts and half a dozen passengers. Then Free drove on and turned off the cart's motor. They sat back as the ferry loaded and began its slow journey. On the far side, a few cyclists in shorts awaited the boat.

Free took some photos, and Sarah enjoyed watching the half-naked dark-skinned Belizeans pulling on the ferry cable.

She glanced at her companion. His muscular body, revealed by his faded sage green tank top and cargo shorts, was even better than those of the ferrymen. The guy was so damned attractive.

Wondering if he really was mellowing, she said casually, "Tell me more about your views on marriage."

"Nothing to say. It sucks." He turned to her.

God, the man's face was so purely beautiful she'd never get tired of looking at it. Phenomenal bone structure, skin as rich and sinful as the best dark chocolate in the world, and those amazing greenish eyes, almost the exact color of the water that surrounded the ferry.

He wasn't sounding so mellow, though. "Why are you so opposed?" she asked. "Have you ever been married?"

A snort. "Gimme a break. I have more sense."

"Sense? Why is it sensible to stay single all your life?"

Leaning back in the seat, he crossed his arms over his chest. "People're built that way."

Men. Honestly. They should be required to take a communication skills course in elementary school. But, as a wedding planner, she had lots of experience translating. So she said, "You think human beings are designed to remain single? Sorry, but survival of the species depends on procreation and on children being protected and nurtured."

He was staring straight ahead. but she was studying his face, so she saw his frown and look of concentration.

"We've extended the human life span," he said. "Maybe monogamy can work short-term, when people's lives are all about survival. But not in the long run. Not nowadays. That was a Dark Ages concept."

"Dark Ages? What's that mean? When people died before they were thirty?"

"Uh . . . I guess. It's just what my parents always said."

Ooh, this was getting interesting. "Tell me about your parents."

"They're cool."

"Married? Divorced?"

"Married? Shit, no. I said they're cool."

She bit her lip to hold back a laugh. "Marriage isn't cool?"

"God, no. It's a patriarchal, chauvinistic, religion-based, oppressive institution."

The laughter died on Sarah's lips. That was probably how her own parents had felt. Gran and Gramps said they were hippie kids who'd never had the chance to grow up. Clearly, they hadn't cared enough to marry each other or stick by their kid. It was her grandparents who had taught her about love and commitment. Cautiously, she said, "That's what your parents think?"

"Yeah. And me."

"Tell me about them." Out of the corner of her eye, she saw the ferry had almost reached the other side of the channel.

"Mireille—she's the Lafontaine part of my name—does international aid work."

"Impressive. She's French?"

"Québécoise. My dad's American."

"Do you speak French?"

"*Mais, oui.* Two or three other languages, too, that I picked up when I was a kid. Comes in handy now when I travel."

He'd learned English, French, and another *two or three* languages? Wow. She lived in a country that was supposedly bilingual and had barely survived high school French.

"And Jamal," he was going on, "is a painter. Jamal Freeman. They met when they were in university in Montréal. Hooked up, had me."

And didn't get married. The same as her parents. This was just plain wrong. "You have a child, you should take responsibility."

"They did. But as separate and *equal* individuals."

"*Equal* doesn't have to mean separate. A wife and husband can be equal."

He started the engine and drove off the ferry, then parked. "Gotta wait for the others, yeah?"

"Yes. But Free, are you saying a man and a woman can only be equal if they aren't married? That's a pile of crap."

He chuckled. "You got a mouth on you, woman."

She stared at him, and his gaze drifted down to her lips. The air between them sizzled, and she knew they were both thinking about all the ways she'd used her mouth on him. But this conversation was important. "You honestly don't see marriage as a partnership of equals?"

He snorted. "Not likely."

"Okay, I know there are some marriages where the man is the

boss and others that are the reverse. But there are also lots where the spouses are equal," she argued. "Each couple should create the union that works for them."

"My parents have done that. But as friends. If they'd married, they'd have ended up divorced and hating each other, like James and Giovanna. This way, they've had the freedom to pursue their careers, have other lovers."

"Spouses can pursue careers, and rather than do it alone, they have someone else's support. As for other lovers . . . I'd rather build a loving relationship than leap from partner to partner. That's too superficial for me."

"Well, you're different than me and my folks."

A depressing thought. She probed deeper. "What was it like, growing up? Did your mom and dad live together?"

"Not usually. They were always doing different stuff career-wise. They lived in different countries, had different partners. They like variety, excitement. Don't like it when things get stale."

Sarah tried to imagine it. Not so much for his parents, but for him. What would it have been like to have been the child of parents who got bored easily and flitted from place to place, job to job, lover to lover? "Where did you fit in?"

"Sometimes I was with one, sometimes the other. For a week, a year, whatever." He gave a warm, reminiscent smile. "I grew up in three provinces, six states, four European countries, Singapore, Vietnam, Africa."

"It sounds . . ." She thought it sounded horrible. Yes, she loved visiting different countries, but roots, a home, security—that's what counted. And he'd had none of them. No wonder the poor guy was so screwed up.

But he was grinning, a big flash of white teeth in his chocolate face. "It was fantastic."

Her heart plummeted. Despite the message that pheromones—and evolution—kept sending her, maybe the two of them were a horrible match. "Really?"

"So many great experiences. I learned so much."

She tried to imagine the places he'd seen, the people he'd met. At least his parents had loved him and not abandoned him. How much better it would have been, though, if they'd had a happy marriage.

A horn sounded, and she saw the ferry had reached the other side and was letting people off.

Sinking back, she thought about how Free had grown up compared to how she had. "My upbringing was different," she mused softly. "My parents weren't like yours."

"Let me guess," he said dryly. "They were married."

She met his piercing gaze. "Wrong. They grew up in the sixties and seventies. Believed in sex, drugs, rock and roll," she said bitterly. "And freedom. So they dumped me on mom's parents and took off."

Those hazel green eyes of his softened. "Your parents ditched you? That sucks."

"Yeah. But if they'd taken me along, I'd probably be dead. They went off on some journey to find themselves. Drugged out, they smashed their motorbike head-on into a semitrailer. Me, I was safe with Gran and Gramps. Even though they'd already raised a kid and I shouldn't have been their responsibility, they were wonderful." Thinking of them made her smile. "They loved me, gave me everything."

"And they were married."

"Oh yeah." She beamed happily. "Their golden wedding anniversary is in August."

"Golden? Which one's that?"

Of course he wouldn't know. "Fifty."

"Jesus."

His heartfelt tone made her raise her eyebrows. "The right marriages work, Free. They last. Their foundation is love and attraction; the building blocks are hard work. In the long run, the glue that sustains them is the complete and utter knowledge that this is the person you're destined to be with. What could be better than that?"

Their gazes locked for a long moment.

Was there any hope he'd change his mind? Become a man her heart and her brain, as well as her pheromones, could choose?

A horn beeped, then another. She peered over her shoulder and realized all the golf carts had driven off the ferry. Pulling herself together, she said, "Okay, just follow the track."

As he drove off, he said, "My parents would tell you their way is better."

"Do they each live alone now, or are they with partners?"

"I dropped them an e-mail when I got to Belize, but haven't heard back. When I headed into the Outback a few weeks ago, Mireille was in Afghanistan doing relief work. Don't think she was involved with anyone."

"Afghanistan. Wow."

"Yeah, I hope she's okay. But she always is. That's one tough woman. And Jamal, he was in Paris, living with a dancer half his age."

"I e-mail with my grandparents every day or two," she said pointedly. "I know exactly what's going on with them." Although their lives revolved around bowling, bridge club, the garden, and new recipes for lemon cake, not war zones and younger lovers.

"And they know what's happening with me," she added. Though not that she'd met a man who might be her perfect mate. Or might break her heart. They loved her so much—wanted for her the same beautiful thing they had—that she wasn't about to get their hopes up unless she was sure.

"Each to their own," he muttered.

That must be why he'd laid off harassing Danny. He was reconciled to letting his friend and Bella follow their own path.

As to Sarah's path, and Free's, was there any hope they'd converge? Any hope she could convert this beautiful, frustrating man into marriage material, and with him build a wonderful future? Damn, she liked Free and, despite their differences, she felt a growing sense of connection, of caring.

Dangerous thoughts. So instead she concentrated on the scenery and kept the conversation casual. The landscape ranged from sandy stretches to lush vegetation to lagoons with tangles of mangrove, broken by patches of development. They saw everything from picturesque homes with lovely landscaping to abandoned shacks and areas of raw new construction.

Sarah gestured toward a particularly charming house with hibiscus, bougainvillea, and an orange tree flourishing in the yard. "Living in Vancouver, I can see the allure. One day, if I stop traveling all over planning weddings, I could see having a winter home here."

"Belize has a lot to offer," he agreed. "Ocean, beach, all the conveniences. And I doubt they'll ever get strings of high-rise hotels like on the beach at Cancun, just a couple hours north."

Their golf cart wound its way through a thicket of small trees and emerged onto a long, thin stretch of pale sand beach. A salty breeze ruffled her hair, the view was perfect, and Sarah stretched back in her seat and sighed with contentment. "I love the tropics. They make me feel so mellow."

"Mellow?" He chuckled. "Seems to me you're always in high gear, running around organizing stuff."

"Who, me?" She slapped his thigh gently below his cargo shorts, then let her hand rest there. Her fingers trailed under the edge of his shorts, feeling the warmth of his skin, the firmness of his muscles.

"Seems to me I haven't been running all the time," she said. "In fact, I recall a fair bit of lying down. At least when we've been together."

He glanced over and winked. "I do recall some lying down, now you mention it. And lots of other positions as well."

"Mmm-hmm." She caressed his warm, bare skin. "Some great positions. Do you have a favorite?"

"Nope. Depends on the mood. Speaking of which, you're getting me in the mood right now. What you trying to do to me, woman?" His gaze held humor and also heat.

Glancing down, she saw his cock was growing under the fly of his loose shorts.

"Turn you on, it seems." And herself. Her nipples had tightened, her blood was warm from more than the sunshine, and a sexy pulse beat in her pussy.

Unable to resist, she abandoned his thigh for a more rewarding playground. But caressing him through a layer of cotton wasn't enough, so she undid his fly and freed him. He filled her hand with throbbing heat and, under her own shorts and bikini panties, her crotch grew damp.

"Do you ever wear underwear?" she asked.

"When it's cold. In the tropics, I like loose clothes, and as few as possible." He adjusted position, thrusting into her hand. "And, oh yeah, I like your hand on me. Next best thing to—"

"My mouth?" she broke in, circling him and stroking from base to tip.

He sucked in a breath. "I was gonna say, being inside you. But yeah, your mouth's damned fine, too." He slanted her a teasing glance. "It'd feel really good, right about now."

"Free! We can't." And yet her mouth watered at the thought of sucking on that gorgeous brown cock. Tasting him, teasing him, testing his self-control. And then . . .

The idea of making him come in circumstances like this was unbearably erotic.

# Chapter 7

SARAH glanced over her shoulder. The next golf cart, the one carrying Tamiko and Zane, was quite a ways back.

This was crazy. And yet, irresistible.

In one swift move, she bent so her head was in Free's lap. In the next breath, she'd taken him between her lips.

He jerked with surprise, then gave a moan of pleasure. "Shit, Sarah, I didn't think you'd really do it."

She lifted her head. "Complaining?"

"God, no." His hand came down to ruffle her hair. "Don't stop."

She licked the head of his cock, the salty drops and the musky scent of arousal telling her how much he wanted this. Then she swirled her tongue around him and down the sides of his shaft, flicked the thick, pulsing vein, sucked one of his balls into her mouth, and heard his gasp.

His hand gripped her head, then released it. "Need two hands on the wheel," he said, voice rough.

Cautiously, because the cart was jouncing on the uneven track, she took him into her mouth as deep as she could, bathing his length with wet heat. She lifted her head, let him slide out a ways, then sucked him back in, lips tight around his shaft. Her vaginal muscles clenched with the ache of need.

She closed her eyes so all she saw was an orange red haze behind her lids and gave herself up to the experience. Free was sunshine, vitality, pure masculinity. Greedily she sucked and tongued him, wanting all of him, everything he had to give.

Her hands cupped his balls and felt them tighten as he gasped, "Jesus, Sarah. That's so good I can't take it."

His cock jerked, thrust, and he groaned as his essence jetted into her mouth. Once, twice, and a third time, as she swallowed and smiled against his pulsing flesh. Now this was the true taste of sex on the beach.

After a few moments, she tucked him back inside his shorts and did up the zipper. "Is the coast clear? Can I come up now?"

"Yeah. No one can see."

She swung up, head reeling a little, and settled back in her seat, squirming against the need he'd ignited between her thighs.

He must have noticed because he said, "It's your turn."

*God, yes!*

But wait a minute. Up ahead she saw the sign for the Crazy Monkey. "Oh jeez, we can't, we're almost at the restaurant."

"Then I guess you'll have to take a rain check." He wriggled his eyebrows suggestively. "You know I'm good for it."

"Yeah, but we're not waiting until it rains."

"Okay, a sunshine check. Or starshine check."

"Starshine? That was my birth name." The words were out before she'd thought. Rarely did she tell anyone about the silly hippie name her mom had given her. When she was a baby, her grandparents had renamed her Sarah, which fit her much better.

"Really?" He pulled the cart to a stop in the restaurant parking lot. "Cool. It suits you."

Hmm. Maybe it did. At least it suited the woman who was Free's secret lover.

He climbed out of the cart, and she did the same, wishing her crotch didn't feel so sticky.

Zane pulled his golf cart up beside her, and she tried to forget about arousal and put on her professional hat as Tamiko got out. "Have a nice drive?" Sarah asked.

"Delightful. What a lovely place this is," the model said.

"You're enjoying your holiday?"

As Zane came up beside her, Tamiko slipped an arm around his waist. "So long as I'm with Zane, I'm happy, and it's a bonus to escape to the sunshine when there's snow on the ground back home."

Her lover—a ruggedly handsome older man whose photo appeared regularly in the tabloids—hugged her tightly, and she gazed up at him adoringly as he steered her toward the restaurant.

Sarah didn't realize she was shaking her head until Free said, "What's wrong?"

"They act all lovey-dovey, but it seems to me there's something off."

"Off?"

"Like, it's not real. They're both nice, but I don't sense any chemistry between them."

"Yeah?" He glanced after the departing couple. "I got the sense they like each other. But who knows, maybe it's an arrangement of convenience. He gets arm candy and a hot lay, and she gets to be with a celebrity."

"Maybe so. Guess there's nothing wrong with it, as long as they're honest with each other." Just like herself and Free, she thought. He'd never deceived her. If she risked her heart and got hurt, she had only herself to blame.

He glanced past her. "Uh-oh."

"What?" She swung around to see the MOB and FOG, Giovanna and Al, approaching arm in arm. Behind them, James was rooted in one spot, staring at them.

She hurried over to him, noting that he'd undone a few shirt buttons and rolled up his sleeves. The man had quite the physique for an academic. Lean and classy, his looks were the kind that improved with age. She could see why he wouldn't be the dramatic Giovanna's type, but it was amazing some other woman hadn't snapped him up.

Giovanna's laugh drifted back to them, and his jaw tightened.

Sarah squeezed his arm gently. "James, I didn't plan for you both to be on this trip. Please—" She shrugged.

"Behave myself? For Bella's sake? Yes, Sarah, I hear you."

"Thanks."

"I do love her," he said, sounding almost sad.

"Of course you do. Bella knows you and her mom both love her."

"Bella? Yes, I know. So I'll try to behave." He patted her hand, then said he was going to find his golf cart partner, Jennie.

On the restaurant patio, Sarah made sure he and Giovanna were seated out of each other's line of vision. And, thank heavens, the meal went smoothly.

Everyone drank nonalcoholic tropical drinks, ate coconut shrimp, scallops, and squid, took pictures, and chatted easily. The patio was open-air, with huge umbrellas shading the tables and planters of hibiscus adding bright splashes of color. The gentle rhythm of the waves breaking on the beach was a soothing backdrop, and just past the railing the ocean was a constantly changing pattern of Caribbean blues and greens of every tone from subtle to vivid. The scent of seafood mingled with the fresh tang of salt air, and a gentle breeze cooled their cheeks.

Unfortunately for Sarah, that breeze failed to cool the heat Free had aroused in her. Playing it safe, she'd chosen to sit on the opposite side of the patio from him, but even so, she was super-aware of his presence. Her body throbbed and hummed, anticipating the orgasm he owed her.

When dessert—a selection of homemade tropical ice creams—was served, Danny's brother and his wife excused themselves to go for a walk. Sarah guessed, from the blush on the woman's cheeks, they weren't going to remain vertical any longer than it took to get out of sight.

Zane said, "Tamiko, do you feel like a *walk*, too?"

"Mmm," she purred. "I always enjoy a little exercise after a meal."

Then they, too, were gone, heading hand in hand down the beach in the opposite direction.

Free caught Sarah's eye and raised an eyebrow suggestively.

Regretfully she shook her head and tucked into her coconut-ginger ice cream. Her body was abuzz with unfulfilled lust, and she'd like nothing better than a good orgasm, but she didn't dare sneak off with Free. Nor could she trust Giovanna and James to behave if she wasn't there to keep an eye on them.

After lunch, when the two "walking" couples returned from the beach tousled and glowing, everyone headed back to the golf carts.

James Moncrieff volunteered that he and Jennie would take the lead, commenting diffidently, "It's not likely we can get lost."

"You never get lost," Giovanna put in, and for once the abrasive tone was missing. "James, you have the sense of direction of a"—she flung her arm up dramatically and gazed at the blue sky—"an eagle."

"Thanks," he said quietly, and their eyes met in a long gaze that looked almost fond.

Hmm.

But then Giovanna gave a snort. "It can be very frustrating. Sometimes we mere mortals like to think we know where we're going, without always being corrected."

His lips quirked. "Getting lost is a waste of time."

"Getting lost can lead to interesting adventures," she snapped.

Hurriedly Sarah clapped her hands to shut them up and get everyone's attention. "We'd best get under way so you'll have time for a rest or swim before dinner."

Free ushered her into their own cart. "Want to bring up the rear? More privacy. You can claim that sunshine check."

"God, yes," she said fervently. "I'm crawling out of my skin."

"I can fix that."

"I'm counting on it."

He steered their cart into the last spot in the line, behind Al and Giovanna. Once they reached the beach, he slowed so they slipped farther back.

He leaned over to give her a quick kiss that seared her lips. "You missed the view last time, so sit back and enjoy it." Steering with one hand, he reached over to touch her shoulder, then slid his fingers down her bare arm, skimming the surface.

The sensual touch made her shiver and brought her body to full awareness. She sighed, a sound that blended contentment and need. Gazing at the multihued water, the sunny sky, the pale sand, she felt his fingers caress up her arm and then back again. Amazing how he could arouse her with such a simple touch.

Glancing down, she thought that her skin was barely darker than the sand, while his was the color of the sinfully rich dark chocolate wafer that had accompanied her ice cream dessert.

Making a humming sound of pleasure that matched up with the hum in her blood, and especially between her legs, she turned her gaze back to the ocean and gave herself up to the sensations Free was creating.

His hand moved from her arm to her thigh, stroking back and forth with that same light caress that brought every nerve to attention. Then he spread his fingers over the front of her shorts, warming her belly underneath. From there, he moved between her legs, cupping her needy pussy. "Would have been easier if you'd worn a skirt."

She wriggled against his hand. "I hadn't planned on this when I got dressed." Last night he'd made some comment about fooling around in a golf cart and, silly her, she hadn't taken him seriously. "Do you need some help?"

"There's lots I can do with one hand." Without turning his gaze from the track that followed the upper edge of the beach, he deftly undid the button of her shorts and worked the zipper down.

She lifted herself off the seat and slid the shorts down her legs, then—damn it, she'd been waiting for this orgasm a long time—slid her panties down, too.

"Take them off and spread your legs."

She took a towel from her tote bag, covered the seat, then kicked off the garments and settled back. No one else was around, but she felt so exposed, her bottom half completely naked in the open-sided golf cart.

Free gazed over. "Now, that's a pretty sight." The cart lurched over some obstacle, and he quickly gripped the wheel with both hands and straightened their course. "Damn, how can I concentrate on driving when you're sitting there like that? Let's stop the cart."

"No! Someone will notice and come back." She'd instructed everyone to keep an eye on the cart ahead and the one behind.

The track was smoother now, and he reached out again, resting his palm on her stomach and threading his fingers through the short auburn hairs of her neatly trimmed bush. His hand was so big, it almost covered her whole pelvis, making her look so feminine and delicate in comparison.

She pressed herself against him, urging him to move lower, and he obliged. When his hand was lodged between her legs, it felt so good that she moaned and instinctively tightened her thighs around him, squeezing him closer.

"I can't until you spread your legs," he said.

"Can't what?"

He gave a soft laugh. "You really don't know what you're saying, do you? You asked me to stroke you, open you."

Embarrassment flooded her. "I can't help it, it comes out without me knowing."

"Don't apologize, Sarah. It's fucking sexy. Now, spread your legs."

She did, and then he did stroke her, somehow knowing how firm to make his touch as he slid his finger back and forth across her damp flesh. And now—oh, yes—that's what she wanted, to have that finger slide inside and tease her just—yes, there. How did he know how to—oh, because she was telling him. With words, and with her body's response to his touch.

Thank God he found it sexy.

His palm cupped her, stimulating her tender flesh, pressing against her clit while his finger swirled inside her. She whimpered with pleasure, trembling as the tension built. The need, the pounding need for release.

The cart ahead of them turned right abruptly, and she realized they'd almost neared the end of the beach track. From there, they'd cut up through the scrubby trees, then be in a construction zone. "No," she gasped. "I can't wait. Make me come, Free. I need to come." She ground down against his hand.

One finger still inside her, he rubbed his thumb over her clit.

"Yes!" Pleasure so intense it was almost pain zinged through her. "Yes, more, now."

He stroked that sensitive bud of flesh, and she felt another zing, and then his touch triggered a wave of hot, rushing pleasure that surged through her lower body and made her buck against his hand.

When it was over, she laughed in exultation and flopped loose-jointed back in the seat. "That was wonderful."

She looked over at his crotch, to see an erection under his shorts. "But how about you?"

"You've given me something to look forward to—when I sneak into your cabana tonight, Starshine."

Laughing softly, she bent to pull on her clothes.

She and Free were quiet as he steered the cart through the bushes and past a construction zone where a half-dozen new houses were going up. Visiting Belize—and the other exotic places where she'd organized weddings—was fun, but what would it be like to live in a foreign country? The way Free had done numerous times when he was growing up.

"Where did you go to school?" she asked.

"Here and there. Sometimes my folks did home schooling. What can I say? I'm bright and adaptable."

"Humble, too," she joked, though she believed him.

"Besides, I got real-life learning, which beats dry facts in textbooks."

"Mmm," she said noncommittally.

"Don't be so down on it," he said easily. "Your work takes you lots of places. You telling me that's not a great learning experience, as well as being fun?"

"Good point," she admitted.

And yet, despite all she'd learned about other cultures, religions, traditions, she clung to the basic values her grandparents had taught her, the values that had given her a home, love, and security, when her parents had abandoned her.

"In some ways my parents were like yours," she said. "Free spirits who believed in independence, discovery." It always made her so sad to think about them. Maybe they'd have grown up, married each other, and come back for her if they'd had the chance.

"They didn't believe in marriage either," she murmured. "And it killed them." She almost hoped he didn't hear her, because the words sounded kind of silly, spoken aloud.

He drove in silence for a couple of minutes, then touched her thigh. "It was drugs and a semi that killed them, Sarah." His words, like his touch, were compassionate.

That compassion touched a chord in her heart. "If they were married, they wouldn't have left me." Damn it, her eyes were filling with tears. She was always more emotional after orgasm.

Free squeezed her thigh. "They were rotten parents. They didn't deserve a kid. And you deserved better than them."

True. Not that it made things any better. Still, Free was trying to help, so she swallowed hard and blinked back the tears. "Thanks."

A few minutes later he said, "But it didn't have anything to do with whether they were married. My parents went their own ways, lived their own lives, but they never dumped me. They always let me know I was loved."

As Gran and Gramps had with her.

Her belief in the institution of marriage owed a lot to her grandparents, just as Free's view had been influenced by his parents. "I hear what you're saying. That they're happy in the lives they've chosen. But they're unusual. Most people do better with a committed relationship."

"You gonna make me quote divorce statistics again, woman?"

She shook her head. "I know lots of people fail at marriage. But many try again. People want to be loved, to love, to share the highs and lows of life with a partner." Did he really not want that? "Can you honestly say you never feel lonely?"

The golf cart lurched over a bump. "I like my own company. And when I don't, there's always a pretty girl around."

Like her. Was that all she was to him?

No, she didn't believe that. The problem was, he seemed determined to.

Did she have any hope of making him see the light? She'd come to care for him—let's face it, she was halfway in love with him—but could he ever allow himself to open his heart and return that emotion?

Time was running out. The wedding—which at least he'd stopped trying to sabotage—was on Saturday, three days from now. On Sunday she'd head home and Free would . . . do whatever he damn well wanted.

THE next day, after again playing nice—though it grated on his nerves every time Bella flashed her diamonds or cuddled up to Danny—Free got the call he'd been hoping for.

Jeff Tomaso rang his cell to say he'd arrived at the Crown Jewel, the ritzy beachside resort where the wedding group was scheduled to have dinner.

The last-minute flight and the classy accommodation would do serious damage to Free's MasterCard, but rescuing Danny was priceless.

"Everything go okay?" Free asked. "You're playing the role?"

"Flinging your money around like it's water," Jeff said cheerfully. "A guy could get used to this lifestyle."

"You have the right clothes?"

"*You* are asking *me* about clothes? Like you'd know good taste if it bit you in the ass?"

"Yeah, yeah."

"So, how far do you want me to take this thing with the girl?"

"How d'you mean?"

"Into bed?"

"Crap, Jeff." He hadn't envisioned that.

"Well, you said this Bella's pretty hot."

Man, if Bella slept with Jeff, Danny'd be shattered. Free felt a twinge of guilt. Yeah, for his poor deluded friend's sake, he had to get Bella to show her true colors. Danny had to learn the truth now, rather than after he was married, more emotionally invested, and Bella had a claim on his assets.

He thought about Jeff's question. "I don't think it's gonna happen." Bella was a conniving money grubber, but she wouldn't go straight from Danny's bed to Jeff's. Would she?

"Whatever. So, what's the plan? Set the scene for me, and tell me about the other players."

# Chapter 8

WHEN Sarah checked e-mail Thursday afternoon, she found a panicked message from Andrea.

> #$%^&*&^%$#!!!! Can you believe, Justine Carmody and Brian Bender have split? It's 2 freaking weeks before the wedding!!! The wedding in freaking BIMINI!! So what the hell do I do? Try to cancel and get refunds, or hope they'll make up?

Well, crap. Sarah rubbed her fingers over her temples. Scrap their losses or be optimistic? Pre-wedding jitters could happen to anyone. Justine and Brian had dealt mostly with Andi, so Sarah didn't know them well. Were they a meant-for-each-other couple who would make up this spat, get married, and live happily ever after?

She e-mailed back.

> What does your gut say, Andi? Do these 2 belong together? If so, put the suppliers on notice but don't can-

**cel. Play counselor and super-matchmaker for a couple days and I bet B&G will get back together. Hugs! And don't stress out over this.**

As she logged off, she thought about Bella and Danny's upcoming nuptials. Free might spout that anti-marriage crap, but when it came to stopping the wedding, he'd thrown in the towel pretty easily.

Yes, she was absolutely confident the wedding would happen. The only question was, would he agree to do the photos? Danny'd be so hurt if he didn't.

Yet it would be horrible if Free took the photos and botched them. He told a story with his images and, if he persisted in seeing the wedding as exploitation rather than romance, how would the pictures come out? Surely he wouldn't be so petty as to ruin the wedding photos.

Free might have his blind spots, but he didn't strike her as petty. For example, he'd honored his vow to keep their relationship secret, when he easily could have spilled the beans to Danny and Bella and damaged her professional reputation.

She did have to resolve the photo issue soon, though. It wasn't fair to keep the San Pedro photographer on standby any longer. Tonight, when Free made his late-night visit to her cabana, they'd have to have a serious talk.

But now she needed to dress and get over to the Crown Jewel to make sure everything was set up the way she'd discussed with the manager.

Half an hour later, her taxi drove through the village of San Pedro and down the coast a mile or so, then turned into a beautifully landscaped drive. Although the Crown Jewel was only a few years old, it was designed to resemble a British officers' hotel and club in an outpost of the old British Empire—as indeed Belize had once been.

Sarah stepped into the spacious lobby where the heaviness of gleaming mahogany antiques was offset by wooden ceiling fans and flowered fabrics. Brass shone, flowers overflowed giant Chinese vases, and windows and doors were flung wide, letting sunshine stream in.

She wandered through the bar and glanced out to the patio, where people sat under striped umbrellas, nursing sunburns and cold drinks.

Her gaze snagged on a man who was alone, his tall body sprawled in a padded chair in the sun. He looked very *GQ* in khaki shorts and a crisp white shirt, sleeves rolled up and open down the front to reveal an impressive physique. His strong bone structure, wavy black hair, and Mediterranean complexion could easily have belonged to a cover model. And so could the perfect white teeth that flashed as, catching her watching, he sent her a dazzling smile.

Wow.

He raised his highball glass in a toast. Sun glinted off a heavy gold chain bracelet and a diamond ring.

If she hadn't met Free and hadn't been working, she'd have been tempted to join him. Tall, dark, handsome, apparently wealthy, and seemingly charming. What more could a girl want?

How about that inexplicable, primitive zing of attraction she felt every time she saw Free?

She smiled back at the handsome stranger who didn't tickle her pheromones, then turned to hunt for the manager.

Fifteen minutes later, with all the items on her spreadsheet ticked off, she went to meet the Toucan van with the first load of wedding guests.

"Hey there, bride," she greeted Bella, as the other woman emerged, looking put out.

"Hey, wedding planner." Bella sounded subdued.

Giovanna and more guests climbed out, but no Danny.

"Where's your groom? He's supposed to be with you."

"I *know* that," Bella snapped. "He and Free got to drinking beer and lost track of time. Honestly, when those two get together, they can be such *boys*."

Sarah bit her lip. Was Free making a last-ditch effort to talk

Danny out of marrying Bella? The bride's disgruntled expression suggested she was thinking the same thing.

Not that Free could win. Danny and Bella definitely weren't like Andi's cold-footed couple.

"I know I'm supposed to be playing hostess," Bella said, "but my cohost is missing, and I need a drink."

This wasn't how Sarah had planned things, but a little flexibility wouldn't hurt.

"Okay, everyone." She raised her voice to reach the others. "Come on in and explore this lovely hotel, or head straight to the bar for a nice cold drink."

Giovanna linked her arm through her daughter's. "Sarah, I'm sure there's a sunny patio somewhere, and drinks for Bella and me."

As Sarah guided the pair through the bar, Giovanna went on, "Warm sun and a cold drink. What more could a woman want? Except, of course, for an utterly charming and devastatingly handsome man."

Sarah smothered a giggle as they went through the open door to the patio.

Giovanna stopped dead. "*Che bello!* From my lips to God's ears."

Yes, the *GQ* guy was still lounging negligently in his chair. A smile widened on his face, then he came to his feet and walked toward them. "Ladies, this lovely day has grown even brighter."

Giovanna gave a delighted laugh as Bella and Sarah exchanged eye rolls. Bella leaned close to Sarah's ear. "Over the top," she whispered, "but God, he's cute."

Sarah poked her in the ribs and whispered back, "You're engaged."

"Tell that to my missing fiancé." Her voice rose slightly.

"Fiancé?" the man said. "No, don't tell me you're engaged. I'm desolate." He glanced at Giovanna. "Tell me you're not engaged or married."

She threw back her head, hair rippling over her tanned shoulders, and let out a husky, sexy laugh. The MOB was looking especially lovely today, skin glowing and eyes sparkling. "Let me guess, you're Italian, yes?"

His teeth flashed. "My father was from Assisi. How did you know?"

"No one but an Italian could be so outrageous and get away with it."

Watching them, Sarah thought that Giovanna had a quality—a confident, almost earthy sensuality—that she and Bella could never achieve. The two of them might have youth on their side, but male eyes gravitated to Giovanna.

"Shall we leave you two to your flirtation?" Bella asked dryly.

"Oh, Bella, don't be silly," her mother said.

"Bella? Now, there's a perfect name for such a beautiful woman." He held out his hand. "I'm Jeff Tomaso."

She reached out her hand, clearly expecting to shake, but he raised it, touching his lips to it in a European gesture that seemed totally natural. And appreciative.

Pink stained Bella's cheeks.

"I just arrived, and I'm lonely," Jeff said. "Will the three of you do me the honor of letting me buy you a drink?"

"That's the best offer I've had all day," Bella said.

"How kind of you." Her mother held out a graceful hand. "I'm Giovanna."

"Giovanna." He repeated the name, drawing it out with an Italian flourish. Then he kissed her hand as well, lingering over the gesture.

Giovanna, unlike her daughter, accepted it as her due.

He turned to Sarah.

"I'm the wedding planner," she said briskly, "and *I* have guests to look after."

His eyes twinkled. "My loss. But I shall console myself with these two lovely women."

Sarah turned and headed back to the hotel lobby, wondering about this Jeff Tomaso. Was he for real, oozing all that charm? Or a gigolo, taking advantage of wealthy women tourists?

Oh well, Bella was getting married in two days, and the worldly

Giovanna would be more than a match for Jeff. Let him give it his best shot.

The Toucan van arrived again. More guests got out, including the FOB, looking pretty damned fine. For some reason, Tamiko had offered him a makeover, and he'd agreed. She'd transformed him from pleasantly attractive to strikingly handsome and stylish.

Oh yes, James was loosening up this week. Sarah thought back to the morning, when a Belizean couple had come to the Toucan to give lessons in a sexy dance called punta, followed by salsa. Sarah hadn't been the least bit surprised that Giovanna had looked as skilled and sultry as the female instructor. She hadn't expected James to be equally as good.

Nor would she ever have predicted that the exes would have danced together. Or that the floor would have come close to bursting into flames, the way the two of them smoked. For a moment, she'd imagined them young and in love, and wondered if they might possibly reunite. But when the dance had ended, they'd stalked off in opposite directions.

Now, she trailed James into the bar, knowing he was bound to glance out to the patio and see his ex and daughter chatting with Jeff Tomaso.

When he did, he stared for a long moment, face expressionless. Then he said, "She was not an easy woman to be married to." For once he sounded reflective rather than angry.

All the same, not willing to risk an incident, Sarah touched his arm. "James, there's a library I think might interest you."

He tore his gaze away from the threesome. "I can always be tempted by a library."

Gratefully, she steered him in that direction and hovered in the doorway until he'd pulled down a volume and immersed himself.

She greeted more guests, guided people in the direction of rooms and activities that would interest them, and kept an eye out for Danny and Free.

They came in the last group of arrivals, together with a couple of Danny's friends.

Sarah took Danny aside, and Free came with him. "You're late," she told the groom.

"Sorry." The scent of beer wafted across her face.

"Does he have to play host at every social function?" Free asked.

She raised her brows. "May I remind you, it's *his* wedding? Hosting is something he and Bella specified when we did the planning."

"Is Bella pissed?" Danny asked sheepishly.

"She was, but I think she got over it. She's on the patio with someone she and Giovanna met."

"You mean she's not playing hostess?" Free asked.

Sarah scowled at him. Despite the fact that Bella, too, had violated the sacred spreadsheet, she'd at least had justification. "Why should she, when her fiancé was missing?"

"Let's go find her." Free sounded eager, which was unusual.

Wishing the two of them had stuck to the spreadsheet and skipped the beer, Sarah went with them to the patio.

Bella waved but remained seated as they walked over. "You decided to show up," she said coolly to Danny.

Jeff inclined his head. "You must be the fiancé. I congratulate you. You're a very lucky man."

"I know," Danny muttered uncomfortably.

Under his breath, but loudly enough that Danny and Sarah could hear, Free said, "So the *someone* is a man."

Jeff rose, every movement full of masculine grace. "I must go and dress for dinner." He leaned toward Bella's mother. "Giovanna, such a pleasure." They did a lingering European kiss-both-cheeks thing.

Then he turned to Bella. "A delight, *bellissima* Bella." He caught her hand and again raised it to his lips, brushing it with a kiss and holding it a moment too long. "An utter delight."

She flushed. "Thanks for the drink, Jeff."

"I will hope to see you both later." As he passed Sarah, he said, "And you, the unnamed wedding planner. And of course the groom and his friend."

As he walked away, Free said, "Gotta hate guys like that. All smarm."

"*Charm* and *smarm* are two very different things," Giovanna said pointedly. "A man should let a woman know she's appreciated."

Danny held out his hand to Bella. "Come on, sweets." He tossed her a wink. "Let's find a private spot, and I'll show you how much I appreciate you."

Sarah winced and held her breath. He was no Jeff Tomaso.

His fiancée stared at him like she was making up her mind whether to still be mad. Then she rose with a smile and gave him a hug. "You're incorrigible."

Sarah let her breath out in a sigh of relief. "Don't sneak off too far. It's almost time for dinner."

It took a while to round everyone up, but eventually they were all seated in the dining room at three long tables. Waiters deftly poured Chardonnay and presented salad plates with shrimp atop sliced avocado and mushrooms. Sarah noticed when Jeff Tomaso, looking casually elegant, took a table by himself.

Five minutes later, a waiter appeared with a bottle of Dom Perignon and presented it to Bella. "From the gentleman in the corner."

"What?" Bella glanced over, and Jeff gave her a smile and a nod. "How kind. I guess it's to celebrate our engagement?" She looked questioningly at the waiter.

He shrugged and began to take off the foil. "He said it was for you, miss."

"Not for her and her fiancé?" Free asked.

The waiter didn't reply as he busied himself with the cork. Bella flushed and murmured, "Please give him my thanks," while Danny scowled.

"That's damned expensive champagne," Free grumbled.

Jeez, this wasn't good. What was Jeff doing? And what was going on with Free?

The e-mail from Andrea had been a reminder that pre-wedding jitters could hit even the most loving of brides and grooms. The last thing Sarah needed was Free fanning the flames.

For the last couple days, he'd been sweet, and she'd thought she was making progress on her mission to convert him into a romantic. But now he was acting like a jerk. She was disappointed and hurt.

But this wasn't the time to worry about her personal emotions. She had to concentrate on her job. There'd be time later to sort through her feelings for Free.

She glanced around, making sure everyone was enjoying the food and finding someone to talk to. Danny was drinking too much, thanks to Free constantly refilling his wineglass. Why did guys think it was fun to get the groom plastered?

When the main course was served, piano music started up. An attractive woman sat at the bench of a grand piano at one end of the room, playing a classical piece Sarah recognized but couldn't identify.

"Debussy," Bella said. "I love it."

"It's got no beat," Danny complained.

"And you have no culture," she said tolerantly. Then, to the others at the table, "We have absolutely opposite tastes in music. He's into stuff with a pounding bass."

"And you like that tinkly classical stuff?" Free asked.

"Mmm. I got that one from Daddy. And Mama taught me to enjoy opera." She laughed softly. "But I confess, my guilty pleasure is romantic show tunes and movie sound tracks."

"Really?" murmured Free. A few minutes later he excused himself and headed toward the lobby, presumably to find the men's room.

When he came back, Sarah glanced up and noticed that Jeff Tomaso was no longer at his table. He must have finished his meal and headed off in search of night life, thank heavens. One potential source of trouble was gone. Now, if she could only get Danny to stop drinking and Free to stop sniping.

The dinner plates had just been cleared when Bella said, "Oh, this is one of my favorite songs."

The piece was "Moon River" from the old Audrey Hepburn movie, *Breakfast at Tiffany's*. Poignant and romantic, Sarah liked it, too.

Bella pointed, eyes wide with excitement. "It's Jeff."

Sure enough, the handsome Italian was caressing the keys and flashing his charming smile. So he wasn't a rich guest, only a hired entertainer. One who'd had the audacity to send champagne to a hotel guest. "Did he tell you he's one of the pianists here?" Sarah asked.

"No, he said—" Bella broke off as the hotel manager walked over to the table.

"Is everything to your satisfaction?" he asked Sarah.

"It's excellent." She gestured toward the piano. "We were just commenting on how good your pianist is."

"Matter of opinion," Free muttered, and Danny laughed too loudly.

The man ignored them and nodded. "He doesn't work here; he's a guest. When Ramona went on her break, he asked if he could play. He assured me he knows what he's doing, and he's a hard man to say no to."

Bella tilted her head. "I met him earlier and found him quite charming."

"Oh, yes, very much so."

"And generous," she said.

"Indeed." The manager, who Sarah had learned lacked Ric's discretion, added, "He's in our best room and has been *most* generous with the staff."

Sarah happened to be gazing at Free and saw him frown. Then he asked, "What does he do? I mean, for a living."

It was Bella who answered. "He invented some gizmo used in diamond mining and made a fortune."

"A rich playboy," Danny said.

"Takes one to know one," Free joked. "But it sounds like he's richer than you. And he doesn't even have to go into an office."

"I *choose* to work," Danny said defensively. His family owned a huge chain of clothing stores, and he worked in the public relations division. He'd told Sarah he enjoyed the job, so long as he got time off to travel with Bella.

"Shh," Bella said. "He's playing 'All I Ask of You' from *Phantom.*"

"God," Free groaned. "We're going to have to listen to hokey love songs all night?" He poked Danny. "Wanna go to the bar?"

"That's a—" Danny started eagerly, then Bella clamped a hand on his arm, and both Giovanna and Sarah glared at him. He finished lamely, "Not such a good idea, I guess."

But later, after they'd eaten a delicious Key lime pie and the woman player had completed her second set and surrendered the piano to Jeff again, Free said, "Okay, really. This is enough."

Sarah could see that some of the others—particularly the men—were restless. Most of the women, though, were watching Jeff with dreamy expressions, swaying gently to the music.

This called for a spreadsheet adjustment. Given the way Danny was drinking, she should probably drag everyone back to the resort early. But if she did, some guests would complain.

Quickly she debated the wisest course of action. Separating Bella and Danny for half an hour wasn't such a bad idea, and so what if the groom wanted to hang out with his guy friends and get mildly hammered? Tomorrow he'd have a hangover, which would serve him right. He'd be fine by the next day, in time for the wedding.

"All right," Sarah said. "Why don't the people who want to listen to music move up to the empty tables near the piano, and the others head into the bar?"

"Now you're talking," Danny said as he and Free jumped to their feet. "I'll go tell the others."

Sarah and Bella collected a group of more than a dozen women, plus both the FOB and the FOG, and settled into chairs with a better view. Jeff acknowledged them with his dazzling smile and launched into "It Had to Be You." So far, he'd been doing instrumentals, but this time he sang—softly, in an appealing voice.

He was playing without sheet music, and his gaze lit on Bella, so it seemed as if he was singing directly to her. It was a long minute before he, seemingly with difficulty, looked away.

The next song was "Younger Than Springtime" from *South*

*Pacific*. And this time, as he sang, he didn't even try to look away from Bella.

Damn the man, he knew she was engaged. What was he trying to do?

Sarah glanced at the bride. Her eyes were sparkling, and she mouthed the words to the song.

Jeff broke off. "Bella, you can sing this, yes?"

She shrugged, looking embarrassed. "I know the whole soundtrack. It's old-fashioned, but . . ."

"Romance is never old-fashioned." He patted the bench beside him. "Come, *bellissima* Bella, and sing with me."

"Oh *tesora*, do it," Giovanna urged. "You have a lovely voice, and when will you ever again have an opportunity like this?"

Sarah bit her lip. She wasn't comfortable with Jeff's behavior. Yet she knew Bella truly loved her fiancé, and as her mother had said, why turn down a once-in-a-lifetime experience?

"Well . . ." Bella rose, lovely in a sky blue linen dress complemented by sapphire and diamond jewelry, and went to perch on the piano bench. "I've done karaoke, but this is different."

"Relax and enjoy." Jeff smiled into her eyes. "Think about the music, the romance."

A smile lit her face. "Okay, that helps."

He played the opening notes and sang the first line, then she joined in, voice tense and wavery. But soon she loosened up and seemed to be thoroughly enjoying herself. Their voices blended well, and when they finished, their audience applauded. Not only the wedding guests, but other diners as well.

Giovanna and James exchanged glances, and for once there was no animosity, only shared pride in their daughter.

Sarah noticed Free and Danny had slipped into the room to stand near the door, highball glasses in hand. Oh great, they'd gone from beer to Chardonnay to hard liquor.

On the piano bench, Jeff and Bella had a whispered consultation, then launched into "Up Where We Belong" from *An Officer and a*

*Gentleman*, then followed it with "I Had the Time of My Life" from *Dirty Dancing*.

When they finished, Jeff kissed Bella's cheek. "You are a delight, *carissima*."

"You gonna let him do that?" a male voice asked.

Sarah turned to see Free staring at Danny.

"They're just singing." Danny sounded doubtful.

"Get a grip. That rich dude is hustling your girl." Free said something else that Sarah, stunned, didn't quite catch. It sounded like, "You gonna let that happen again?"

"Hell, no!" Danny's voice was loud. He lurched over to the piano and grabbed Bella's shoulder. "We're going. Now."

She gaped up at him with a shocked expression.

Sarah gaped, too. Should she intervene?

"Hey," Jeff said. "Take it easy with the lady."

"Back off. She's *my* fiancée, and she's going with me."

# Chapter 9

GIOVANNA started to rise, but James was on his feet first, and she sank back to perch on the edge of her seat. Sarah did the same, vibrating with tension.

Bella, crimson-faced, was trying to shake off Danny's hand. "Stop it," she hissed. "You're making a scene."

"Danny, you've had too much—" James started.

"And you're acting like a slut," Danny said to Bella, "throwing yourself at this rich guy."

"Oh!" Bella jerked to her feet, and Danny's hand fell away.

James quickly stepped between the two of them, facing the groom. "Calm down."

Jeff rose and put an arm around Bella. "Yeah. Stop insulting her and go sleep it off."

"Who the fuck do you think—?" Danny tried to lunge at him, but James blocked him.

"You've had too much to drink, and you're overreacting," he told the younger man. "Bella was just singing."

Free came to stand shoulder to shoulder with Danny. "Singing love songs like she meant them," he said coolly, sounding far less drunk than his friend.

Of course he'd take this opportunity to drive a wedge between the bride and groom. In fact . . .

Sarah leaped up. She glared at Free, anger bubbling and spilling over. "This is your fault. You got him drunk."

"I'm not drunk," Danny protested, his slurred speech belying his words. "I'm mad. Bella, what the fuck are you—?"

Again he tried to get past James, and again James blocked him.

Sarah looked at Bella, who was staring wide-eyed at her father and fiancé. "Maybe it's best if you just take Danny home," she told the bride.

Bella straightened in the curve of Jeff's arm and folded her arms across her chest. "I have no intention of going home with a drunk. It's Free's fault. He can take him home."

"I'm not going without you," Danny said.

"Yes, you are." Bella and her father spoke together.

Sarah raised her hands. "Let's everyone just—"

Jeff broke in. "Bella, you don't have to put up with this. Come, I'll buy you a drink. I bet you could use one."

Didn't he care that he was making things worse? "I don't think that's a good idea," Sarah said. "Bella, I'll take you back to the resort."

The usually easygoing young woman stuck out her jaw. "No, thanks. I'd rather have a drink with Jeff." She gave him a glittery smile. "It's so nice to be with a man who knows how to treat a woman."

Sarah groaned as the two walked away, arm in arm. When Danny made a move to go after them, she jumped in front of him. "Stop. You'll only make things worse. Go home and cool off, then apologize in the morning."

"Crap, I—" he started.

"Apologize?" Free broke in. "What's he got to apologize for? He's the one who got dumped for a richer guy."

What the hell was he talking about? Bella hadn't dumped Danny;

she was just pissed off. As Sarah herself was. What a disaster the evening had turned into.

Was this day jinxed? First, Andi's B&G had split, and now Sarah's were fighting. Of course, she was positive Bella and Danny belonged together, and in the morning she'd ensure they made up.

As for her and Free . . .

Damn him, he actually looked triumphant. "Shut up! You've done enough harm."

He looked surprised, as if he didn't understand why she was so vehement. Nausea surged through her, temporarily replacing anger as she realized how wrong she'd been. Free wasn't her life mate. She'd spent the last few days drifting in a romantic dream, believing they might belong together. But it was never going to happen. What a fool she'd been.

While she'd believed she was turning Free into a romantic, he'd just been biding his time, waiting for the right opportunity to strike.

She took a deep breath, forcing down the nausea. Then she turned to the group of gape-mouthed spectators. "A pre-wedding spat," she said with forced lightness. "Happens to the best of couples. They'll sort everything out in the morning. Time to get back to the Toucan."

All she wanted was to sink into the bed she'd shared so many times with Free and cry for her lost dreams.

But hey, she'd only met the guy a few days ago, and it was her own stupidity that had gotten her into this state. The person who truly deserved sympathy was Bella.

Squaring her shoulders, Sarah said, "Go!" to Free and Danny. Then she waited until they both—Danny looking hangdog and Free edgily triumphant—headed out of the room.

Some of the other guests, expressions suggesting they wished they were anywhere else, started to leave, too.

James had moved over to speak to Giovanna, and Al was sitting by himself, shaking his head.

Sarah said, "James, Al? Could you get everyone back to the resort? I'm going to stay and talk to Bella."

"As will I," the MOB said quietly.

Giovanna had a drink in front of her, and sipped from the tall, slim glass as the two dads went into organizational mode. When the guests had all left the room, she rose. "Let's find her, Sarah. Knowing Bella, she's about to crash."

Together they headed for the bar, where Bella sat with Jeff. As they approached, she gave a bright, utterly artificial smile. "Hey there."

Giovanna sank into the seat beside Bella and gave her daughter a hug. "I see you've inherited my flair for the dramatic."

"Danny's a whole different person tonight. I don't know what got into him." She sagged, like the spirit had gone out of her. "He doesn't trust me."

"He was jealous," Sarah said. "And drunk. And Free Lafontaine's an asshole." Damn, she and Free had acknowledged they were at war. She shouldn't have let her guard slip just because he'd been nice for the last couple days. He'd only been biding his time, waiting for the perfect opportunity to sabotage the wedding.

"Free doesn't want us to get married," Bella said. "I thought he liked me, so I don't get it."

"He hates marriage in general," Sarah said bitterly. "He thinks he's saving Danny from a fate worse than death."

"What?" Giovanna said. Then, to Bella, "You didn't tell me this."

"Mama, I'm an adult. I can handle my own problems."

The MOB opened her mouth, likely to point out that she wasn't doing a great job of it, then closed it again.

Sarah glared at Jeff. "Then there's you. You sure didn't help matters."

Free must have been ecstatic when Jeff had started flirting with Bella. Even in his wildest dreams, he couldn't have imagined such a scenario.

"Hey." The Italian raised both hands in disavowal. "If the lady prefers my company, I'm not going to complain."

"But I don't," Bella said. She colored. "I'm sorry, that came out wrong. You're great company. I've enjoyed talking to you, and singing together was amazing. But I'd never . . . I mean, I love Danny."

"You do?" Jeff sounded surprised. He took a long sip from a brandy snifter. "But does he really love you? He's insecure and possessive, and a bully. Better you find out now, before he's your husband."

"I don't know." Bella shook her head, eyes growing damp. "Everything's gone wrong."

"He'll apologize in the morning," Sarah said. "Yes, he acted stupid, but this is all Free's fault. And Jeff's."

Slowly Giovanna said, "I hate to say this, but perhaps an apology isn't enough. I've never seen this side of Danny before. And ultimately, he's responsible for his own behavior. Bella, you can't be with a man who doesn't respect and trust you. Believe me, I learned that lesson a long time ago."

"N-no. I can't." Tears slid down her daughter's cheeks.

Oh God, were they saying the wedding was off? That even if Danny apologized, Bella wouldn't take him back?

That Free Lafontaine had won?

He'd not only broken Sarah's heart, he'd broken Bella's as well.

THE next morning, Free woke to the sound of snoring coming from the other bed. Last night Bella's father had told Danny not to go near the cabana he shared with Bella, and Free had been happy to take him in.

Well, not exactly happy, because Danny had been in a foul mood, interspersing curses with maudlin ramblings, just like after Kimberly betrayed him. Fortunately, it hadn't been long before he went to sleep. Or passed out.

Free had wandered over to Sarah's cabana, only to find the door locked. She'd refused to talk to him. He wondered how long she'd hold the grudge. Hell, they'd declared war in the beginning, and he'd won. Maybe his tactics had been a little shabby, but he'd proved Bella was just after the richest guy.

Surely when Sarah calmed down and realized the truth—that Bella had never loved Danny—she'd let the victor reap his rewards.

And Danny, when he got over being hurt and pissed off at Bella, would thank him for honoring the vow he'd sworn in the post-Kimberly days.

It had cost Free several thousand dollars to pay Jeff's bills and the loss of a night of hot sex with Sarah, but saving Danny was worth it.

He opened the slatted wooden shutters and glanced over to see Danny sprawled in a mess of tangled sheets. Deciding to give him a few more minutes' sleep, he booted up his laptop and checked e-mail.

Still nothing from Mireille. But e-mail must be virtually nonexistent where she was in Afghanistan, so he wasn't going to worry.

Jamal had e-mailed him, though.

> Hey, kid. Glad you had fun in Oz. Bet you got some awesome pix.
>
> How's Ambergris Caye? I went there once with some girl who was into diving. Cool place. Say hi to Danny for me. Can't believe he's actually getting married. Thought he had more sense.
>
> BTW, I split with Thérèse, she got some job in Rome, so I'm on my own. Want to come to Paris and we can hang together for a while?
>
> No, haven't heard from Mireille, but she'll be OK. Always is.
>
> Lemme know about Paris. The women here are sweet.

Hmm. He hadn't seen Jamal in over a year. Could be fun to spend some time with him.

On the other hand, if he went back to Vancouver, maybe he could hang out some more with Sarah, and that'd be even more fun. He figured she wasn't the type to hold a grudge.

He showered, then shook Danny awake. "Want to go diving?" Activity would distract his friend from his woes, and help him get over Bella. Maybe he'd even find a hot babe to soothe his wounded pride.

The response was a groan and a muttered, "Leave me alone. Wanna die."

"You're hungover." Free knew Danny well and had used that knowledge last night. Danny rarely drank to excess, but when he did, he got insecure and obnoxious—and Kimberly's betrayal was a very, very sore point for him.

"Have a shower," Free said. "You'll feel better." He hustled his bud out of bed and into the shower, then turned on the cold water.

This time he got a yelp and a string of curses. He put a bottle of aspirin on the counter beside a bottle of water and left Danny alone in the bathroom.

Ten minutes later, his friend emerged with a towel around his waist. His face was not only unshaven but red and blotchy, like he'd been crying. "I feel like shit."

"Food will help."

"It's not the hangover. It's Bella."

"Look, man, I know it's tough she turned out to be like Kimberly. But it's better you found out before you married her."

Danny sank down on the spare bed and buried his face in his hands. "I can't believe this." His shoulders heaved, and he let out a sob. "We're supposed to get married tomorrow. How could she do this to me?"

"Hell, man, she showed her true colors. Women always do, eventually."

"I didn't think Bella was like that." He raised wet, bloodshot eyes. "Damn, I really love her."

Love, lust, call it whatever you wanted. It was crazy to love someone who'd dump you for a richer guy. "Hey, Dan the man, there's always another girl," he said encouragingly.

Danny shook his head, then winced and turned green. "Not like her. Never." He squeezed his eyes shut and said in a tortured voice, "You think she slept with him?"

"Dunno," he said uneasily.

"Crap. I fucking blew it. If I hadn't acted like such a shit . . ." He scrubbed his eyes with both hands. "Maybe if I apologized."

"Apologize? You gotta be kidding. She's the one who went chasing some other guy."

"Yeah, I guess. Crap." He buried his head in his hands, then groaned and dashed to the bathroom.

No big surprise, Free thought as he listened to his friend hurling, it was going to be a rerun of Danny's reaction after Kimberly dumped him.

A few minutes later Danny, looking ashen, slunk out of the bathroom, eased into bed, and pulled the covers over his head.

Free decided to get some breakfast and then try again later.

When he walked into the Toucan restaurant, several people turned their backs on him, mostly girlfriends of Bella's. Apparently female loyalty extended to supporting your friend even when she betrayed her fiancé.

A small group of Danny's relatives and friends beckoned him, and over eggs, bacon, pancakes, and fruit, they discussed the previous evening.

Most people saw fault on both Danny's and Bella's sides, and there was great speculation as to whether they'd make up.

Danny's brother said, "Of course they will. They're like Nance and me." He put his arm around his wife's shoulders. "The real thing."

Free snorted. "There's no such thing."

"Confirmed bachelor." The other man winked to the rest of the group. "One day he'll learn."

*And one day you'll be divorced, Nance will have cleaned out all your money, and the two of you will be fighting the way James and Giovanna do.*

Sarah didn't make an appearance, so Free headed to her cabana to see if she'd gotten over being mad. As he neared the cabana Bella and Danny had shared, he saw Sarah and Giovanna standing on the deck.

"You!" Giovanna tossed her hair back, dark eyes spitting fire. "*Faccia di merda!* Stay away from my daughter."

Italian was one of the languages he spoke. She'd called him an asshole, a bastard, a scumbag.

Should he tell the women he'd been looking for Sarah, not Bella? She was scowling at him, too. "I wasn't going to—" he started.

Giovanna cut him off. "Get lost. If you make Bella cry again, you'll have James and me to answer to."

Her and her ex? Weren't they sworn enemies? And what was this about Bella crying? Free had figured she'd be happily moving on to her new boyfriend.

Giovanna went inside, and Sarah turned to Free, stony-faced. She started down the steps. "You heard her. Stay away from Bella."

"It's you I was looking for."

"Stay away from me, too." She stalked off.

Crap. She was overreacting, too.

He caught up and walked beside her. "Don't be pissed. We both knew where we stood. For a while you were winning, and we were still, uh, friends. What's changed?"

She swung to face him, hands on her hips, eyes blazing. "Jesus, Free. This isn't about us. You went too far. You sabotaged a forever-after love."

"But it isn't, for God's sake!" Why was he the only one who grasped that simple point? "Bella chose Jeff over Danny. The guy with the deeper pockets."

"What?" Her brows drew together. "You total idiot! Bella was heartbroken. She came back here in tears last night."

Heartbroken? He frowned. "But she and Jeff were getting along so well. I thought they—"

"They what?" She didn't let him finish or answer her question. "You thought she was going to leave Danny for him? Get a grip. She loves Danny, you idiot."

That was two *idiots* in less than a minute. "But she—"

Again she cut him off. "She was annoyed at Danny—and that was your fault—and she was flattered by Jeff's attention. You kept pouring booze down Danny's throat and trying to make him jealous, and finally he snapped. I am so *furious* with you."

Tense with anger, cheeks blazing, blue eyes glittering, Sarah looked truly gorgeous and utterly sincere in her anger. And that was even without knowing he'd brought Jeff to Belize, with instructions to try to seduce Bella.

"You're going to let this come between us," he guessed, even as a niggle of guilt made him wonder if he'd been wrong. Was Bella really heartbroken?

Sarah snorted. He guessed that, if she'd known that Italian expression of Giovanna's, she'd have used it. Instead she said, "Get off Ambergris Caye and leave us all alone."

As she strode away, back rigid, he thought he'd do exactly as she suggested. Things here were a mess, and Sarah'd made it clear playtime was over.

Well, shit. He'd enjoyed spending time with her. Matching wits, discussing photography and travel, screwing each other's brains out. Damn it, the thought of not seeing her again really pissed him off.

He stalked back to his room. Danny was a lump under the covers.

Should he tell his friend what Sarah had said about Bella? But hell, then the wedding might be back on. Even if Bella wasn't another Kimberly, he'd still promised to stop his bud from ever getting married. Marriage, misery, divorce. He couldn't let Danny walk that road.

"You awake?" Free asked.

His answer was a groan.

"I'm gonna pack up and leave. You should come, too." When women turned into problems, you left them behind and moved on.

"Yeah." But he didn't stir.

"Your stuff over at Bella's cabana?" Free started to toss clothes into his duffel.

Another groan.

"Leave it. You can buy more."

"Don't care."

Free pulled down the sheet that covered his friend's face. Damn, Danny had been crying again. His face was puffy and red. "You okay?" Free asked tentatively. He hated to see him in this kind of pain. Why the hell hadn't Danny learned from Kimberly's betrayal and not let Bella worm her way into his heart?

"Shit, no. I wanna die."

"Things'll get back to normal," he promised. "You and me, both footloose and fancy-free. Hey, come to Paris with me and visit Jamal. He says the women are sweet. You'll find another girl. Or two or three."

Even as he said the words, he felt an achy kind of emptiness. It'd take a pretty fine woman to make him forget Sarah.

"Don't want another one. Bella's the one. The only one. And I fucking blew it. I'm such an asshole. My life is over."

Shit. Women could really mess a guy up.

Free stared down at his half-packed duffel. Yeah, he wanted to blow this joint, but Danny was in no shape to travel, and he couldn't leave him alone.

He sat down on the bed. "I get it that you feel like shit, but your life's not over."

Danny glared at him. "What's the point to life if I can't share it with Bella?"

Bella had really done a number on this guy. What had happened to the old carefree Danny? "You can share stuff with me and your other buds," he pointed out. "With dozens of pretty girls who are just waiting to meet you."

"You so don't get it. Sharing *stuff* is different than sharing life. Knowing the two of you are a team. I thought Bella and I were. But I act like a jerk just once, and what happens? She dumps me for some rich guy in fancy clothes who can fucking sing!"

Again guilt poked Free between the shoulder blades as he thought about Bella, crying in her room rather than hooking up with Jeff.

He tried again. "Look at my parents. They're both independent, and they're perfectly happy."

"They didn't love each other. Probably neither of them's ever loved anyone except you." Danny propped himself on the pillows. "Mireille cares more about causes than individuals, and Jamal's the same way with art."

"They're free to live their own lives rather than being tied down." And they'd taught him that was the best way to live.

"Look, I like your parents. Though I've never had a chance to really get to know them." Danny leaned forward, blotchy face earnest. "Think about that. We've been best friends since we started college, and I've met Mireille twice and Jamal not much more. You're their kid, and they love you, but they're always off doing their own shit."

"They did okay by me."

"Sure. But they taught you to keep emotional distance."

"Now you're talking pop-psych shit."

"Whatever. But it's true."

"What's wrong with a little distance? At least I won't get hurt the way Bella's hurt you." As for Sarah and that empty, achy spot inside his chest, he just needed to find another hot woman.

Danny sagged back. "Yeah, you got me there. I'd never been so happy. Never imagined I could be so happy. And now, shit, I'm miserable. I'll never be happy again." He pulled the sheet over his head. "Fuck, yeah, be independent. Look after yourself. And leave me alone."

Full of a restless energy that needed direction, Free headed out for a run on the beach. As he drove his body to its limit, his mind puzzled over what was going on with Danny and why the fight with Sarah had left Free feeling so crappy himself.

He'd always believed his parents were right, that monogamy was an archaic institution and that familiarity killed passion. That self-fulfillment was the highest possible goal.

And yet, when he was old and gray, did he want to be alone with his independence, or did he want the kind of relationship Sarah said her grandparents had?

Sweat poured off him as he ran, and he wished he'd brought a bottle of water. That stupid pain in his heart didn't go away, either, and he had a kind of sick feeling in his stomach. Couldn't be a hangover—he'd been careful about his own alcohol intake. Maybe he'd caught some tropical bug.

Danny had accused Free's family of emotional distance. What the hell did that mean?

So, okay, his mother was in Afghanistan, and neither he nor his dad had a clue whether she was all right. It wasn't that they didn't care, just that they never kept tabs on each other. Independence, right?

He could bet Sarah's grandparents always knew where she was. He told himself it'd stink, being tied to apron strings like that. But maybe there was something to be said for having someone give a damn where you were and what you were doing.

Now that he thought about it, there'd even been a pathetic undertone to Jamal's e-mail. He'd once been on Ambergris Caye with *some girl.* His lover had left to take *some job.* He was on his own, had nothing better to do than hang out with his kid. It was so impersonal, so distant.

Yeah, so maybe there was something to be said for closeness. The kind Danny said he'd had with Bella. The kind Sarah talked about—and maybe even the way he felt when he was with her. There was definitely something special about her, and it wasn't just the sex.

Pelting along the beach lost in thought, he caught up with the Everleighs. He remembered what Ric had said about how long the two of them had been married.

And yet they were always holding hands, and it looked like more than a habit. There was a glow in their eyes when they gazed at each other.

Maybe Sarah's grandparents had that same glow. Had his parents, even back when they were lovers, ever looked so happy? So much like they belonged together?

"Good morning," Mr. Everleigh called as he passed them. "Could we ask a favor?"

"Uh, sure." He stopped and went back.

The man handed him a small digital camera. "Would you mind taking a picture of us?"

"No problem."

He studied the light, the scenery, then gestured. "How about you stand there? With the beach and those palm trees for background."

As they moved into position, he asked, "How long have you been married?"

"Sixty years." Mr. Everleigh wrapped his arm around his wife's shoulders.

She smiled up at him, and the two of them exchanged a glance that was so sweet, Free clicked the shutter and captured it.

He checked the image on the display screen. Well, damn. A picture told a story, and the story this one illustrated was love.

The same kind of love he'd seen on Danny's and Bella's faces.

Why had it taken him until now to realize it?

But even if Danny and Bella did make up, could they beat the statistics and have one of the marriages that survived?

"That's a long time," Free said, lifting the camera again and studying them through the viewfinder. "What's your secret?"

Mrs. Everleigh gazed at her husband, her own expression serious. "Many things. Patience, communication, compromise."

Her husband nodded as she spoke, and Free clicked a couple more shots.

Then, eyes twinkling, Mrs. Everleigh added, "But I'd have to say, the biggest one is sex."

"S-sex?" Free almost dropped the camera. Weren't they too old for all that? Besides, sex was about lust, and lust burned out. Didn't it?

But Mrs. Everleigh was nodding firmly, and a rakish grin split her husband's face. "Oh yes," she said, in her sweet little-old-lady voice. "It's the best motivation for all that patience and compromise."

"And the best way of making up after a spat, isn't it, love?" Mr. Everleigh chimed in.

"Well, actually, any excuse will do," she said, laughing.

Shaking his head in wonder, Free returned their camera and hurried back to the Toucan. He needed to talk to Jeff, but he didn't want to do it in front of Danny, so he found a pay phone.

Jeff answered his cell. "Hey, Free. I'm lazing by the pool. How'd it go at your end?"

"Weird. What happened with Bella after we left?"

"Either she's a good actress, or you were wrong about her. She said she loves the guy. But now she's pissed that he doesn't respect and trust her. Her mother—God, I can't believe Giovanna's her mom, that woman's truly hot—basically told her that was a deal-breaker. So my guess is, the marriage is off. That's what you wanted, right?"

"That's what I wanted," Free echoed glumly. Maybe he really had been an idiot. "Okay, you've done your bit. Go home and stop depleting my bank account."

Jeff chuckled. "I'm enjoying the sun. Maybe the hotel will give me a gig as pianist."

"Whatever."

When Free returned to the room, Danny was still curled up in bed.

In the shower again, washing off the sweat from his run, Free thought about Danny and Bella, the Everleighs, his own parents, and Sarah. "Attitude readjustment," he muttered. Crap, if he'd been wrong all along, and he'd broken up a good relationship and cost Danny and Bella their chance for a future as happy as the Everleighs' . . .

By the time he'd put on fresh shorts, Danny was sitting on the side of the bed.

"I gotta talk to her," his friend said grimly. "I have to apologize. Maybe she doesn't really want that piano guy; maybe she just went with him 'cause she was mad at me."

Well, okay. Maybe Danny and Bella would patch things up. And he could stop feeling guilty.

Except . . . Oh fuck, he had to confess and do his bit to help. Man, Sarah would laugh her head off at the thought of him playing matchmaker. Grimly he said, "Before you go, I have to tell you something. I think I screwed up."

"You?" A flicker of interest lit Danny's swollen eyes. "Don't think I've ever heard you say that before."

"Yeah, well, I've probably never screwed up before. But this one's big. That guy Jeff? I brought him here."

"Huh?"

"I thought Bella was after your money, and she'd ditch you the way Kimberly did if something better came along."

Danny's eyes narrowed. "Who the hell is Jeff?"

"An actor friend from New York. I paid his way, told him what role to play. Got him to hustle Bella."

"Shit! What the hell?" Danny jumped to his feet, fists clenched.

"I thought I was doing it for your own good. I didn't understand. And you made me swear that oath, back when Kimberly—"

Before Free saw it coming, a fist connected with his nose. "Shit! Ow!" Followed by another that popped him in the eye.

He ducked, raising both arms to protect his face. Warm blood gushed down and dripped off his chin. A couple of punches landed on his arms.

"Bella's miserable, too," he said, tasting blood. "She didn't go with Jeff."

Danny stopped swinging. "Really?"

Warily, Free lowered his arms. "That's what Sarah says."

"Wow." Danny's face lit. "She still loves me. I can apologize for acting like a jerk, and everything will be okay."

"Well, uh, it might not be that easy. Jeff says she's pissed off that you didn't trust her."

"Shit." Danny glared at him, and Free raised his arms again, in case another blow was coming.

But then his friend crumpled and sank down on the bed. "I didn't. She's right. And I should have."

Free used the back of his hand to swipe blood from his chin. "Yeah, but you were drunk, and I pushed your hot buttons so you overreacted."

"Asshole." Danny glanced at the blood and shuddered. "Did I break your nose?"

Free touched it gingerly, wincing. "Don't think so."

"Too bad," he said halfheartedly.

It was still bleeding though, so Free pinched his nostrils closed. His voice came out nasally when he said, "I'll explain to Bella. Tell her it's my fault."

"Yeah. Yeah, that'd be good." Danny sprang to his feet and began to pace. "Persuade her to see me. Let me apologize. Damn, I'll do anything to make it up to her. We're supposed to be getting *married.*"

"I know." And for the first time, Free found himself wanting that marriage to happen. Really wanting it. He clapped his friend on the shoulder. "I'll fix it. I promise I'll fix it."

He headed for the door but caught a glimpse of himself in the mirror over the dresser. "Better wash first, or I'll scare her."

"Just goddamn hurry!"

Five minutes later, Free knocked on Bella's door. Her father, James, answered.

When he saw Free, he shook his head. "Haven't you made enough trouble?"

"Yeah. I've come to fix things."

James's eyebrows rose. "Are you sure?"

"Positive."

He leaned closer, inspecting Free's face. "What happened to you?"

"Danny."

"Ah." He gave a knowing smile, then called, "Bella, Free's here to see you. I'm sending him up."

"No!" she screeched.

James gestured toward the staircase to the loft. "Give it your best shot. And if you hurt her again, you'll be feeling my fist, too."

Wondering if Bella was going to punch him as well, Free took the stairs.

She was standing by the bed, wearing a robe. The shutters were closed, but even in the dim light, he could see her face was as swollen and miserable as Danny's. Her eyes narrowed and she spat, "Asshole!"

"That's me."

"Ever since you got here, you've been trying to stop the wedding."

"Yes."

"Why?" She sank onto the bed. "I thought you liked me."

"I did. I do. But when you got engaged, I thought you were trying to tie Danny down. To own him. To get his money, take away his freedom."

"That's stupid."

"Is it?" He leaned forward and touched her arm. "Bella, he's my best bud. Tell me the truth."

Her eyes went misty. "Danny's my soul mate. We belong together. I love—" She broke off. "No, that's how I used to feel. But last night he ruined it all."

Seeing the hurt and hope and love on her face, he knew she was no Kimberly. He'd been such a shit. "It was me who ruined it."

Slowly, sadly, Bella shook her head. "You didn't help the situation, but it's Danny who ruined it. He didn't trust me. He didn't trust in our love."

"He was jealous."

"I refuse to be in a relationship where I can't have fun with another man. I didn't think Danny was like that. I have other guy friends, and Danny has female friends. It's never been an issue before. I don't understand where he was coming from."

"Did he ever tell you about Kimberly?"

"Who?"

"The girl he was engaged to a few years ago."

"He told me he was engaged once before, but it was a big mistake and he didn't want to talk about it. I figured it was the past, so I didn't push."

"She dumped him for a richer guy. She'd just been after his money. It shattered him."

"Bitch!" She reflected. "Oh no, you don't mean he thought I was like her? That the thing with Jeff was . . . Damn! Jeff was just . . . an interesting guy who was nice to me when I was annoyed with Danny. It was all just coincidence. Him playing the kind of songs I loved, then— Why are you shaking your head?"

"It wasn't coincidence he played those romantic songs. I told him you liked them. I set it all up, Bella."

"Set what up?" she asked, looking puzzled.

Again he made his confession. This time he didn't get a punch, but the pillow she heaved did send a trickle of blood running from his battered nose.

When she saw it, she put a hand to her mouth. "Oh my God, did I do that?"

"Danny punched me."

"He did?" She sounded pleased and leaned closer, squinting in the dim light at his swollen, aching nose.

"Yeah. When I told him the same thing I just told you. He really loves you, and he feels like crap that the two of you fought."

"He shouldn't have acted the way he did."

"He knows that. But he's human, Bella. I played on his weaknesses."

Grudgingly she said, "He can act stupid when he drinks too much."

"I know. And Kimberly's betrayal really hurt him."

She nodded slowly. "I played into your hands, too, didn't I? You got Danny drinking and made him late for dinner, so I was pissed off and all ready to let Jeff sweet-talk me. To even flirt back a little."

"You and Danny have some things to work out." He remembered something Sarah had said. "The foundation of a good marriage is love, but the building blocks are hard work." Then he threw in a bit of advice from the Everleighs. "It takes patience, communication, compromise." He left out the sex part, guessing she and Danny could figure that out for themselves.

She eyed him warily. "You sound like a marriage counselor."

Free managed not to wince. "He wants to apologize. He says life isn't worth living if he can't share it with you."

Tears leaked from her swollen eyes. "I feel the same way. Maybe we can work things out."

Relieved, he said, "Can I tell him to come see you?"

"Yes. No! Wait, I look awful."

"So does he." He shuddered. "Believe me."

She leaped off the bed. "Give me fifteen minutes, then send him over."

"Okay. And Bella?"

"What?"

"Thanks."

Her eyes narrowed. "I haven't forgiven you."

"Nor has Danny." Nor would Sarah. But even if confessing had cost him the best friendship of his life, and one very special woman, it was worth it if he brought Danny and Bella back together.

From downstairs, they heard a hard knock on the door and Danny's voice calling, "Bella, I'm such a jerk. I don't deserve you. Let me in."

"Forgive him, Bella," Free said urgently.

Her lips twitched. "Maybe."

# Chapter 10

SARAH was so distraught, she couldn't do anything but pace the beach. James had told her Danny was with Bella, apologizing. Would the two of them make up?

At noon, the couple emerged, arms around each other, faces swollen and blotchy yet glowing with love.

"It's on," Bella said. "The wedding's back on."

Relieved and brimming with curiosity, Sarah trailed them to the restaurant, where they made the same announcement to the assembled guests.

Giovanna, who'd been sitting with the elderly English couple, the Everleighs, stood up and walked over. She hugged her daughter, then gave Danny a stern look. "I want to talk to you two."

The young couple's friends moved away, but Sarah hovered as Giovanna went on. "I'm concerned, Bella. I want to know you've really resolved things. I'm sure both your father and Danny's father do, too."

James added, "We love you, sweetheart. We saw how upset you were, and we need to be sure you know what you're doing."

"You're right," Bella said. "Let's find some privacy and talk. And Sarah, too. She's put so much into this wedding." She gave the wedding planner a hug.

They all settled at a table in the bar and, taking turns, Bella and Danny explained what had happened, including Free's role.

When Sarah realized the lengths to which he'd gone to sabotage the wedding, her blood pressure climbed so high, she was sure she'd have a heart attack.

How could she have ever thought he might be the right man for her? How could she have believed she was falling in love with him?

The thing that made no sense was his confession and apparent attempt to play matchmaker. Did he actually possess a shred of human decency?

To her chagrin, she felt tears welling and had to blink hard to fight them back. It was agony to force a smile and say to the B&G, "I'm so happy you worked things out. True love triumphs in the end. Now, if you'll excuse me, I have some details to arrange before the rehearsal."

She fled back to her cabana and had a good cry. If Free had been there, she'd have torn his head off, but surely he was already on his way home to Vancouver.

After her sob fest, she washed her face and applied more makeup than she normally wore, then grabbed her rehearsal spreadsheet and went to meet with Ric.

There were so many details to attend to that she was kept frantically busy, which was a very good thing. She did stop to watch as Bella and Danny, standing under the thatched canopy by the ocean, rehearsed the wedding ceremony, beaming brighter than the sun.

Clipboard at the ready to note any details that needed tweaking, Sarah glanced at the assembled guests seated in folding beach chairs. The MOB and FOB were side by side, so close their shoulders might even be touching, and she was relieved they were managing to be civil. Their daughter's trauma seemed to have brought them together, at least temporarily.

Tamiko and Zane whispered as they watched the rehearsal, and Sarah wondered if she'd been wrong about them. Maybe they'd be the next couple to announce their engagement.

The Everleighs, who'd also been invited, sat holding hands, beaming.

Ric, standing at the back, had his PDA out, ready for note-taking.

Sarah's eyes widened as she glanced past Ric. It was Free!

His camera was up to his face as he moved unobtrusively around. What was he doing here, taking pictures? He had to know he wasn't welcome.

Her heart raced. She wanted to steam over and tell him off, but that would interrupt the ceremony.

Perhaps he felt her glaring, because he lowered the camera and glanced her way.

She gasped at the sight of his swollen nose and black eye but then narrowed her eyes and tried to project a "Get fucking lost!" message.

The sound of applause drew her attention, and she realized the B&G had kissed, concluding the mock ceremony.

As Bella and Danny walked happily down the aisle, Sarah strode over to Free. "What the hell are you doing here? Is this some new plan to stop the wedding?"

"God, no." He bit his lip. "Sorry. This has been hard on you."

*"Hard?"* The word came out with the same edge as a fingernail scraping a blackboard. "Oh, you figure? Look, just get lost. Leave the Caye, go home, let Bella and Danny get married in peace." *And leave me in peace*, she added silently, *so my heart can start healing.*

"What?" It was Bella. She and Danny had come up to them, overhearing Sarah's last comment.

"Man, you can't go," Danny said.

Sarah stared at him. "He tried to sabotage your wedding, you punched him in the nose, but still you want him here?"

Danny shrugged. "He fucked up. He fixed it."

Was it really that easy for him?

Then Danny added, "He's my best bud. He thought he was looking after me."

"And we need him to do our photos," Bella said.

"No," Sarah said. "I've booked a photographer from San Pedro. He'll do a fine job."

Bella shook her head. "But he doesn't know us. He wouldn't understand."

"Understand what?" she asked, frustrated.

"The story." The bride hugged her groom's waist and smiled up at him. "Our story." Then she gave Free a mischievous grin. "Free's thickheaded and it took him a while, but now he's got it. That's why he helped us make up. He understands how much we love each other. That's what his photos will show. Right, Free?"

Stunned, Sarah watched as he smiled at the bride and groom. "Yeah, that'll be the story." He shot a sheepish glance at Sarah. "Sorry I messed up."

Although he'd apologized to *her*, it was Bella who said, "Actually, it helped. It got some stuff into the open. Danny and I met and fell for each other, and our love grew, and everything went smoothly. Our love was never tested until now."

"Could've lived without the freaking test," Danny muttered, and the two of them chuckled.

Bella squeezed his butt. "Come on, groom, let's find some privacy. And leave Free to grovel to Sarah some more."

When they'd gone, Free said, "Not sure what else I can say. I was wrong. Can you forgive me?"

She shook her head, baffled. "Do you—?" She broke off as a couple guests paused to compliment her on how well the rehearsal had gone.

After responding, she said to Free, "We need to talk. Let's go for a walk."

In silence they walked, not touching, to the edge of the water and turned north. Sarah remembered strolling this way the night they'd met, under a starlit sky. She'd thought of him as a one-night sexy encounter.

So much had happened since then, and now she didn't have a clue what to think or how to feel. She'd been on the verge of falling seriously for Free, and her heart felt as bruised and achy as his nose looked.

"Why?" she asked. "You'd got what you wanted and broken them up, so why the about-face? I have trouble believing it's for real."

He gave a long sigh. "I saw how shitty Danny felt. He told me what Bella meant to him."

"He's told you that before."

"Yeah, but . . . Guess I didn't have a context."

"Context?" Honestly, talking to a man could be like pulling teeth.

He turned to look at her. "I've done a lot of talking this week."

"I haven't a clue what you're *talking* about," she said in frustration.

His lips twitched. "To you, to Danny. Ric. The Everleighs." A pause. "They're like your grandparents."

Surprised, she said, "Yes, they are. So, are you saying . . . you've come to believe that happily ever afters are possible?"

"I guess." He walked away from the water, and automatically she followed. "And that people like Danny and Bella deserve their chance at one," he added.

"Well, hallelujah," she said softly. So the wedding was definitely on.

But what about her and Free? He'd screwed up, admitted it, done his best to fix things, and the B&G had both forgiven him.

Had she been right about him all along? Might he truly be the man for her?

Hope gave a tentative flutter inside her battered heart. "And how about Free Lafontaine? Does he want—or deserve—a chance at romance?"

He gave a wry laugh. "I probably don't deserve it. Not after acting like such a shit." Then he stopped and touched her arm, halting her, too. "I told you about me and my parents. That's the only way I know how to live. But, yeah, it can be lonely and . . . kind of meaningless."

She put her hand over his. "You don't have to be like your parents."

"Guess not. When I look at the Everleighs, it's hard to be cynical. Hard not to think it'd be pretty cool to have something like that."

The flutter in her heart became a flood of warmth that soothed the aches. "It would."

He raised an eyebrow. "No 'I told you so'?"

"I'm not so petty." She couldn't help grinning, though, because she felt as if a whole future of possibilities had opened up. If Free could believe in true love and happy endings, then maybe he was her destined mate.

But did he see their relationship that way?

"Sarah?" He gripped her shoulders gently. "Do you forgive me?"

She searched her heart, which now felt all soft and mushy. "Yes." Then she rose to touch her lips to his.

She'd meant it to be a quick kiss, but it sparked a fire, and suddenly they were wrapped in each other's arms, kissing deeply, hungrily, like they couldn't get enough of each other. Her body zapped into instant arousal.

But wait, she still had an important question. Breathlessly, she broke away. "Wow. But I have to ask. Free, what about us? Is this just a holiday fling for you? Or are you ready to think about something more?"

He touched her cheek in a soft, lingering caress. "If I hadn't met you, I wouldn't have understood what Bella and Danny have. I feel like we're doing what they did. Instant attraction, great sex, having fun together, but more. You know?"

More? Was his "more" the same as hers? She blew out a puff of air, half thrilled and half exasperated. "If we do keep seeing each other, we've got to work on your communication skills. You're saying we have feelings for each other that go beyond lust? Feelings that could deepen into something—"

She was going to say "serious and long-term" but stopped herself. Free had already taken a giant step. She wasn't going to scare him off now.

"Yeah." His grin suggested he had a pretty good idea where she'd been heading. "Definitely into *something*." Then he laughed exultantly. "And it feels damned good."

She laughed, too, blinking back a rush of happy tears. "It does." She touched his bare forearm. "So, what are we going to do about it?"

His smile turned teasing. "I asked the Everleighs the secret of how they've stayed married so long."

"You did? What did they say?"

"Well, she said it, but he agreed." His eyes twinkled.

"Okay. And what was it?"

"Sex."

A laugh burst out of her. "No! Seriously?"

"Yup. So I figure, in the interest of moving toward that *something* between us, maybe we ought to try out their secret." His finger traced the V neckline of her sleeveless dress, pricking every cell to alertness and making her nipples bead.

"That sounds like a very good idea. We could go back to my cabana. People would think we're discussing the wedding photos."

As she spoke, he'd started to shake his head. "Nope."

"No?"

"We have a tradition to maintain."

Tradition? Free believed in tradition? "We do?"

"Look around you, Starshine."

For the first time since they'd stopped walking, she took in their surroundings. He'd steered her up the beach to a sandy area shaded by tall palms and fringed by pretty shrubs with green and red leaves. "This is where we came the first night," she said.

"It's private. Or at least semiprivate. What do you say?"

"To sex on the beach?" She laughed and flung her arms around him. "I say yes."

Sex with the
Proper Stranger

# Chapter 1

Ambergris Caye, Belize—Sunday, February 8

THE Toucan Resort van pulled into a gravel parking lot bordered by a white trellised fence laden with bougainvillea. Tamiko Sato, a Manhattanite, smiled at the extravagance of the blossoms—fuchsia, red, white, pink, orange.

"Here we are, folks," Danny Trent said. "The Toucan Resort. Your home for the next week." He jumped out, opened the van door, and extended a hand to Tamiko.

She took it and slid out into sunshine and balmy air. "This is heaven. Back home the temperature's hovering at freezing and there's snow on the ground."

As her wedding date stepped out to join them, she said, "I'm in paradise, and I'm here with the sexiest man in the world." Though he was old enough to be her father, Zane Slade had an appealing combination of rugged masculinity and suaveness. He was a celebrity, the author of testosterone-driven thrillers that had spawned a movie franchise.

"And I'm here with the most beautiful woman." He put his arm around her.

She beamed at him. This was the first real holiday in all her twenty-five years, and he'd given it to her. A week in Belize, all expenses paid, leading up to the Valentine's Day wedding of Zane's nephew Danny and Danny's fiancée, Bella Moncrieff.

The rest of the dozen wedding guests climbed out of the van, and Bella, who'd been sitting up front with Danny, hugged her fiancé. "Well, groom, now everyone's here, and we're ready to party."

The young couple looked perfect together, both tall, slim, and blond, him in shorts and a tee, her in a flowered sundress and stunning jewelry. So obviously in love, the two sparkled as brightly as Bella's gemstones. Though they were her own age, beside them Tamiko felt old and jaded. Her experience with men—with life—had been so different than the carefree Bella's.

Sarah, the wedding planner, clapped her hands. A vivacious and super-efficient redhead, she'd been at the airport to greet the arrivals. "Let's get everyone checked in."

Holding a clipboard, she led them into a tropical garden with hibiscus, bougainvillea, shiny green fan-shaped leaves, and spikes of vivid red flowers. Two yellow butterflies flirted on a cluster of orange hibiscus blossoms, and Tamiko smiled with delight.

She and Zane followed the others toward a thatched-roof octagonal building that adjoined a three-story block of rooms. Everything was painted in pastel shades of turquoise and green, accented by bright pink and fuchsia bougainvillea and white patio furniture.

What bliss to live in a place like this. Of course, with her job in Manhattan and her family to take care of, that would never be an option. Still, she had a week to enjoy paradise.

She and Zane entered the octagonal building, where Sarah was organizing the guests into two lines in front of the reception desk. Tamiko's attention was drawn by a store with tropical clothes on display. She needed some casual clothing, the kind of things she, an image-conscious model, never normally wore.

She tugged Zane in the direction of the store, and he dropped a kiss on the top of her head. "That's my girl."

A tall, middle-aged man wearing khakis, a long-sleeved white shirt, and a tie, of all things, came out of the store, a bag in his hands. "Hello. Newly arrived wedding guests?"

Zane held out his hand. "Hi there. I'm Zane, the groom's uncle, and my lovely lady is Tamiko."

The other man shook his hand, then Tamiko's. "Welcome. I'm the bride's father, James." He spoke with a hint of an English accent. His features and coloring reminded her of Pierce Brosnan, though Pierce wouldn't have been caught dead with such a terrible haircut.

She was busy thinking how she'd make James over—a hobby of hers—when she saw his gaze drift past them. His body tensed, and Tamiko got the sense he'd stopped breathing.

She turned to see what he was looking at.

Near the registration desk, a gorgeous woman was staring back at James. Tamiko almost sensed a sizzle, like a current of electricity or bolt of lightning, sparking between the two.

The woman reminded her of someone, with her lush figure, Mediterranean beauty, and dramatic style, but before Tamiko could place her, she'd tossed a mane of wavy dark hair and turned her back. The movement revealed the man she was talking to.

That was one totally hot guy.

He was dark-skinned, and his tan shorts and short-sleeved white shirt with a Toucan Resort logo accented a lean, muscular physique. The clothes were smartly tailored, an interesting contrast to his casual rope sandals and the rather wild black hair that curled over the collar of his shirt. Leaning against the counter, face expressive, a hand gesturing as he talked to the woman, there was a relaxed grace, an easy elegance about him. He'd look as great in a tux as in those shorts. Though it'd be a pity to cover those legs.

This was a man who definitely didn't need a makeover.

He glanced over and caught her staring. For a long moment, their gazes held, and she felt a zing of . . . Was that attraction? It wasn't a familiar feeling.

Perhaps Zane noticed, because he pulled her tighter into the curve of his arm. "A striking couple," he murmured.

The man by the reception desk turned back to the woman he'd been talking to, and Tamiko took a shaky breath. What had just happened?

"She's a decade older than him," James said disapprovingly.

"She's timeless," Zane said. "Any red-blooded male would find her attractive." Despite his words, she knew he, too, was watching the man.

Because Zane was gay. And though he had a longtime companion, a closeted one, he did appreciate a hot guy.

Tamiko was one of less than a handful of people who knew the truth. Zane figured his career depended on projecting a macho image, just like his superspy protagonist Lance Connors, who was known as the James Bond of the twenty-first century. So Zane always appeared at events with a "hot babe" on his arm and had the reputation of being a playboy who'd never settle down.

He was a sweet guy and Tamiko's dearest friend. They often posed as each other's date at events, and she'd been delighted to play his lover—his "beard," as he termed it—in exchange for this vacation in Belize.

Playing her role, she flicked her waterfall of glossy black hair in an eye-catching gesture she'd learned when she was all of fourteen, and pouted teasingly. "Hey, lover, are you making eyes at another woman?"

James gave a snort, then turned it into a cough. "Sorry, that's my ex-wife. We're, er, not on the best of terms."

Ooh, that should be interesting. But she didn't care so much about the woman. "Who's the man?"

"Ric Nuñez. He owns the resort." Though he spoke to Tamiko, his gaze rested on the couple, and he was scowling.

Perhaps the wedding planner noticed the tension, because she hurried over to their group.

James's scowl turned into a rueful smile. "Here's Sarah, to make sure the dog and cat don't get close enough to fight."

Sarah gazed evenly at James out of big blue eyes. "This is your daughter's week. We don't want anything to spoil it, do we?"

He raised his hands, the bag dangling from one. "I'm behaving myself. I came in to buy swim trunks and got to talking." He turned to them. "See you at dinner."

Tamiko and Zane made their way toward the registration desk. It was hard to peel her gaze off the resort owner, but she forced herself to glance away, at James's ex-wife.

And now, up close, she recognized her. Tamiko gasped. "Oh my gosh, you're Giovanna!" This woman was a goddess, a legend.

Excitedly she said to Zane, "She's the head of Venezia Cosmetics." The woman had founded the company, shunning subtlety and muted tones and going for something dramatic and sexy. The style wasn't Tamiko's, but on the right woman it was gorgeous, and the relatively new business was really taking off.

The other woman smiled. "How flattering to be recognized. Yes, I'm Giovanna Moncrieff."

"And I'm Ric Nuñez," the hot guy said. "Welcome to the Toucan." He gave her and Zane a warm smile, and she wondered if it gave Zane the same tingles she experienced.

"Zane Slade," her companion said, "and Tamiko Sato." He shook the man's hand, then turned to Giovanna. "I'm delighted to meet you, Giovanna."

"My pleasure." Her dark eyes gleamed flirtatiously as she presented her hand in a manner that indicated she expected a kiss not a shake. As Zane obliged with a sexy flourish, she went on, "I've seen your picture in the papers. Such a thrill to meet the man who created Lance Connors."

Then she studied Tamiko from head to toe and back again. "And you, Tamiko, are even lovelier than your photos. And that's saying a lot."

"My pictures?" Yes, she was a model, but her work hadn't been high enough profile that she'd be recognizable. Yet.

"The face of Sakura. You're perfect."

So the industry was already buzzing about the contract

Tamiko had recently been offered, to launch a new line of beauty products.

"We must talk," Giovanna said.

"I'll look forward to that."

Giovanna rose on her toes and pressed a light kiss to Ric's cheek. "Ciao for now, darling."

Were they lovers or just two beautiful people who had an easy, sensual confidence and enjoyed each other's company?

"The line at reception has cleared," Zane said. "I'll get us registered." He stepped away from her, so she stood alone with Ric.

The man gave her another of those charming smiles. "Is this your first time in Belize, Tamiko?"

"Yes." Her first time anywhere other than the States, or up to Canada for an occasional modeling assignment. She'd never enjoyed Manhattan, but her work required her to live there, and she'd cultivated the image of a sophisticated city girl. Now, though, excitement spilled out. "I love the weather, the flowers, the butterflies. And I can't wait to see the beach."

"It's a seductive place, all right," he said teasingly. His eyes, a brown so dark they were almost black, danced the way they had when he was talking to Giovanna. Was he flirting?

No, of course not, because he believed she was with Zane.

All the same, the sparkle in his eyes made her feel alive, aware. Normally, when men looked at her, she felt like an object, as if they were appraising her beauty, calculating what they could get from her. But she didn't get that feeling from Ric, only a sense of appreciation.

Again, sheer joy filled her. "And I think I'm in a mood to be seduced," she confessed. Then she clapped a hand to her mouth. "Oops. I mean by Belize."

His lips twitched, but the sparkle in his eyes had dimmed. "I know. You're with—"

Zane's arm came around her waist. "Okay, babe, we're all set. We're in a cabana called Hibiscus."

Ric nodded at both of them. "Enjoy your stay, folks."

She felt a twinge of regret. For once in her life she actually felt an attraction, wanted to flirt. It wasn't a situation she'd ever contemplated when she'd agreed to play the role of Zane's lover. But, loyal to her friend, she linked her arm through his. "Let's find the beach."

They went outside to find sand, palms, and cute signs with toucans pointing the way to the restaurant, the beach bar, and the cabanas.

Zane slipped off his loafers, and she followed his example and scrunched sand between her toes. "I can't believe this. It's the first honest-to-God holiday I've ever had in my life."

He pulled her into a hug. Not the fake, flirty kind they shared in public but a warm, affectionate one. "You're such a contradiction, Tami. You look the epitome of exotic sophistication, and at heart you're a little girl who's had a bum rap."

She hugged him back. "On the subject of contradictions, look who's talking."

"We're two big fakers, aren't we?" He gave her a rueful smile. "Guess that's why we get along so well. It's nice to have one person in the world who knows your secrets."

"It is." Though even Zane didn't know all her secrets—like how her dad had died. No one ever would.

He grabbed her hand and tugged her down the beach, and she shoved the past away.

The pale sand was hot enough to make her step quickly, and the abrasiveness was like a gentle scrub with a loofah. They passed a palm-thatched beach bar, then there was the ocean.

"Oh, my!" The color was so incredible, she couldn't believe it was real. Every imaginable shade of turquoise and blue and green blended and rippled, shifting continually under a cloudless blue sky. "I have to put my feet in it."

She stepped in until both feet with their pink-painted nails were planted right where gentle waves breathed in and out against the beach, and smiled rapturously. White gulls soared overhead, water caressed her feet like cool silk, and the sun kissed her head and shoulders, melting every ounce of tension. "I could stand here forever."

He laughed. "Yeah, it's great, but you'd soon get bored. You'd miss Manhattan. High heels and high-rises."

She doubted that but said, "Okay, maybe I'll only stand here for a week."

Glancing down the beach, she saw sunbathers on towels, an elderly couple strolling hand in hand, a good-looking black guy in shorts running on the wet sand, and half a dozen people her age splashing in the ocean. "When I was a kid, there was a community pool. I sort of learned to swim. Wonder if I still remember how?"

"You can find out tomorrow."

He steered her down the beach where, set back from the ocean's edge, she saw half a dozen thatched cabanas. Each stood on stilts and had a porch with a woven hammock. Every door was painted a different color, with shutters to match. "They're adorable."

"And only for the most prestigious guests." Zane winked. "So be glad you're with me, babe."

The first cabana they passed had trim almost the color of the ocean, and on the door was a plaque with a painting of waves. The next, with purple trim, had an orchid.

As they strolled, Zane said, "That Ric guy's hot."

"Very. You don't really think he's with Giovanna, do you?"

"No, I think they were just appreciating each other." He grinned. "Nothing wrong with appreciating." Then he pointed to a cabana with yellow trim and a painted hibiscus blossom. "That's us."

She hugged his arm. "Just remember who you're with, you macho dude, you. Me, here, and Graham, back home." Graham was his personal assistant and his live-in lover of many years.

"Yeah, yeah. I'll try to refrain from pinching Ric's butt. Provided you do the same, girl."

"You know me. I have no interest in men." But even as she said the words, she thought of the warm pulse of awareness Ric had aroused in her.

Zane pulled her closer and waved at a couple who'd been on the same flight as them, who were going into a green-trimmed cabana.

"I know you've had a shitty history with men," he said softly, "but there are some nice guys out there."

The memory of her father's hands on her adolescent body made her shiver. Though sessions with a counselor had gotten her to the point that she could tolerate a man's touch, she rarely enjoyed it.

She dipped her sandy feet in the cute ceramic footbath at the base of the wooden steps. "It's not like I have time to mess around with a relationship anyway. You know where my priorities lie." Providing financial security for her mother and sister was all she cared about.

"I've never seen anyone as focused," he admitted as they went up the steps. "But the Sakura deal will really set you up. You're going to take it, right? Sounds like word's already out on the street."

"Giovanna's very business savvy. She'd have her ear to the ground. And yes, of course I'll sign with Sakura." This was her big break, and she was damned lucky. She'd done all right with modeling—her height and build made her ideal as a fashion model, her hair had netted her shampoo commercials, and she had graceful, elegant hands—but she'd never hit the big time.

Thanks to Sakura, she'd be able to pay off the medical bills that had been hanging over her family's heads for more than a decade and pay down the mortgage on the little house she'd bought for her brain-injured mom.

Stepping inside the cabana, her gaze skimmed over rattan furniture with cushions in shades of blue and green, white walls with watercolors of tropical flowers, and an orchid plant with dozens of tiny yellow blossoms. The windows had no glass but instead were open air with slatted wooden shutters. A staircase led up to what she guessed was a sleeping loft, and a wooden ceiling fan churned the air lazily. This was so not Manhattan.

The concept of being on holiday was sinking in more and more each moment.

Zane took her chin in his hand. "This lovely face will be plastered all over billboards. Every magazine will have Sakura ads. You're going to become more recognizable than me."

A shudder went through her. She couldn't hate her beauty, because it was the only tool she had for achieving her goals. Yet, all her life, guys had come on to her and women sniped at her just because of how she looked. When she signed with Sakura, it would only get worse.

But this was a wonderful opportunity, and—at the ripe old age of twenty-five—it might well be her last significant modeling gig. She'd invest wisely, because after this, she'd probably be back to waitressing, and she had her mom to support for the rest of her life.

"It's a clever bargaining ploy," he said, "telling Sakura you need a week to decide. They'll ante up with a bigger offer."

"That's what my agent says." Yes, she needed the money, but she also wanted this week of R & R.

"You're worth it." He released her chin. "You're worth a lot more than just a fancy modeling contract, if only you realized it."

"I keep telling you, work and my family are all I have time for. I'll leave the romance to you and Graham."

# Chapter 2

SEVERAL hours later, the beach dark and quiet now, Tamiko and Zane headed back to their cabana. The wedding guests had enjoyed a delicious dinner at the Toucan restaurant, where Tamiko had played her arm-candy role.

Her head was filled with a blur of faces and names. Thank heavens the guests had been pretty laid back. Many of them already knew Zane, so there hadn't been much of that gawking-at-the-celebrity thing. She'd seen a few eye rolls over his dating habits, but people seemed willing to accept her.

Her gaze had been continually drawn to Ric Nuñez. He'd attended to every detail, unflappable and charming, conferring occasionally with Sarah. In black pants and a white shirt with the sleeves rolled up, he'd again had a casual, natural elegance that intrigued her.

A natural charm, too.

When he'd handed Tamiko a drink and said teasingly, "Feel like a little sex on the beach?" and their hands had brushed and he'd gazed into her eyes like he couldn't look away, she'd known it was just his manner.

And yet she'd felt a tingly awareness. She, who so rarely enjoyed a man's touch, had wished his hand would linger.

Very strange.

As she and Zane took the steps to their cabana, he yawned. "It's been a long day. Think I'll hit the sack."

She paused in the doorway. Yes, she was exhausted, too, and stressed from meeting a bunch of strangers. And yet she was reluctant to go in.

The night air felt balmy on her skin, stars glittered against a dark canopy, and the ocean was a quiet, breathing presence.

"Do you mind if I take a short walk? I want to unwind. Listen to the quiet." Something that didn't exist in Manhattan.

He nodded understandingly. "Want me to come?"

"No. Sarah said it's safe here."

"All the same, if you're worried . . ."

"I've survived Manhattan for eight years. Think I'll be okay on Ambergris Caye."

He kissed her forehead. "Enjoy. I'll leave the door unlocked."

She set out with nothing but the black cocktail dress she'd worn to dinner. The designer dress, which she'd been given at a photo shoot, was classy and worth a small fortune. It was a staple of her wardrobe.

When she'd dressed for dinner, she'd coiled her hair in a fancy style to look like a Japanese version of Audrey Hepburn in *Breakfast at Tiffany's*, seeking a sophisticated image to match her role as Zane's lover. Now she wished for a sundress or sarong, like many of the other women had been wearing.

At least she could let her hair down literally as well as figuratively. She pulled out the hair clips, stuck them onto the neckline of her dress, then ran her hands through her hair and shook it, loving the sense of release.

When she reached the edge of the water, she turned and walked away from the lights of the resort into a night lit only by the moon and stars. Maybe she should have been scared or lonely, but at the moment all she felt was an amazing sense of peace.

It was as if real life was suspended. As if the worries and responsibilities had been lifted from her shoulders. Tonight, she was just a woman on a beach.

The moon's beam cast a swath of light across the dark, shifting ocean. Like a beacon, drawing her.

As a girl, she hadn't swum enough to become good, but she'd enjoyed slipping through the water. She'd had that same sense of release, of freedom, as tonight. Of being away from a life that was anything but carefree.

Tomorrow she'd put on a bathing suit and take a dip.

The beach was deserted, silent but for the quiet, seductive breath of the ocean. Tomorrow it would be crowded. People would be watching her.

Right now, not a soul was watching but the moon.

Tamiko reached for the zipper at the back of her dress. Moments later she'd peeled off the garment, folded it, and placed it on the dry sand. Clad only in a black bra and thong, she deliberated.

What the hell. She was alone, and she'd want dry underwear when she got out of the water. Besides, just the thought of the ocean's caress on her naked skin was unbearably tantalizing. Belize was bringing out a side of her she'd never known existed. A sensual one.

Decisively she stripped off her underwear, then rushed into the water. It was cooler than she'd expected, but her body adjusted to the temperature.

She held her breath and ducked, then straightened and shook her head, hair fanning out and scattering drops. Delighted, she laughed aloud, knowing there was no one to hear.

Thinking back to those long-ago swim lessons, she tried out the breaststroke, sidestroke, and crawl. Her technique was terrible, and she kept rolling onto her back to rest, kicking gently with her feet and sculling with her hands to stay afloat.

She made progress, though, and loved feeling the water sliding past her naked skin. But then, as she was swimming a slow breast stroke, she felt a pain in her calf.

Trying to breathe through it and relax the muscles, she used her arms and other leg to stay afloat.

Damn, it was a real cramp, like the ones she sometimes got when she was modeling, strutting around in high heels under bright lights, getting dehydrated.

Now that she thought of it, she'd had very little to drink today, with all the travel.

Struggling against the pain, Tamiko gazed toward shore. It seemed an impossible distance. How stupid to swim out to sea, rather than parallel to shore where she could have dropped her legs, touched bottom, and hobbled in.

The pain was even stronger, and she was cold now, so cold, teeth chattering as she gasped for breath and flailed her arms through the water.

She couldn't drown. Her mom and sister were relying on her.

Staring at the beach, she thought she saw a figure, movement.

She summoned all her strength and cried, "Help! Help me."

Yes, there was someone there. The figure had stopped moving.

"Help!" she cried again, flinging up one arm in a quick signal. She swallowed a mouthful of salt water and coughed.

"Coming!" a male voice shouted. He tossed something aside and ran toward the water.

Coughing and shivering, she focused all her energy on staying afloat. Would her rescuer make it in time? She stared toward that distant figure, her only hope of survival.

Ric Nuñez plunged into the ocean.

Who was that stupid woman? What was she thinking, swimming alone at night? And what had happened to her?

He sliced through the waves in an easy crawl. Thank the Lord he'd decided to go for a walk on the beach before turning in.

The sea was calm, and each stroke brought him closer to the swimmer. She'd stopped screaming once she saw him coming. At least she had the sense to save her breath, conserve her strength.

But she was flailing her arms, coughing, obviously in serious trouble.

Stroking fast, he pushed himself harder. He had to make it in time. There was no other option.

"It's okay," he called as he narrowed the gap. "Hang on. I'll be there in a minute."

The woman's face was a white mask in the moonlight. Black hair gleamed, dark brows arched, wide eyes fixed on him with desperation and hope.

Well, damn, it was Tamiko Sato.

Treading water, he put an arm around her to steady her. "I've got you. What happened?"

"C-cramp," she choked out, teeth chattering. "Calf. I c-can't—"

"It'll be okay." Thank the Lord it wasn't a heart attack. "Float on your back and try to relax, and I'll do the rest."

Those huge eyes stared at him, and he had the feeling trust didn't come easily for her. But then she tilted her head back and let her body rise until she was floating.

He hooked an arm around her—she was tall, but so slim she weighed next to nothing—and with his other arm began to sidestroke as fast as he could.

What the hell was Tamiko doing, swimming on her own?

When he'd walked past the Hibiscus cabana twenty minutes earlier, he'd assumed she and Zane were having sex in that king-sized bed in the loft. And that had pissed him off no end.

Now, here he was, rescuing another man's woman. A woman he was strongly attracted to. Life was unfair.

His arm was tiring, so he switched sides and stroked out with the other one.

He was short of breath by the time he could finally put his feet down and touch bottom. "Stay on your back," he told her, towing her into shallower water. Then, with one arm around her shoulders and one under her thighs, he scooped Tamiko up in his arms.

She quaked with deep shivers that wrenched her whole body as he strode toward shore.

That's when he realized she was naked.

Before, her body had been mostly underwater, and he'd been focused on saving her. Now he saw the soft curves of small breasts, the vulnerable triangle of a completely waxed mound.

He forced his gaze away as he stumbled out of the water onto the sand, his unerring sense of direction leading him straight to the shirt and water bottle he'd discarded.

She stirred weakly, trying to free herself. Averting his eyes, he set her down gently, and she crumpled to a sitting position, hugging her knees tightly and coughing.

"Here, put this on." He tossed her his shirt and forced himself to look away as she struggled into it.

Then he glanced back, to see her rubbing her calf. "How's the cramp?"

"It's"—shivers racked her body—"a bit better. But I'm f-freezing."

From shock and pain, as much as the water temperature. He sat on the sand and pulled her awkwardly into his lap, cradling her in his arms. When she struggled, he said, "Body heat. We need to get you warm."

Despite the cool water and the fact that he wore only soaking-wet shorts, he was overheated from exertion. He rubbed her back, her arm, whatever parts of her body he could reach.

As his warmth began to transfer to her, she slowly relaxed against him.

At dinner she'd looked like a princess, and now she was a pitiful, shivering bundle of damp shirt, cold skin, and dripping hair.

Damn it, the woman could have died tonight.

"Where the hell is Zane?" he demanded. "What was he thinking, letting you go swimming alone?"

"He d-didn't know. I went for a w-walk." Gradually the shivers were easing. "It was an impulse to go swimming."

She ducked her head, wet hair trailing across his bare chest. "A stupid one. I'm out of practice, and I got out too far. And I think I'm dehydrated."

He picked up the water bottle, unscrewed the top, and handed it to her. "Sip it."

"Thanks." She sipped, coughed, sipped again. Then a shudder wrenched her. "Thank you," she whispered. "You saved my life. I could have—"

"Don't think about it," he said roughly. "You're fine. Just, for God's sake, don't do it again."

"Believe me, I won't." She sipped again, prodded her calf gingerly. "The cramp's gone, and I'm starting to warm up." A shiver rippled through her, and her body tensed, fighting it. "I can probably walk back now."

Maybe. But now that her skin wasn't so deathly cold, she felt wonderful. He'd rescued the woman, so didn't he deserve a few minutes of holding her? "Don't rush things. The cramp might come back."

"Okay. Whatever you think, Ric."

She knew his name. With all the people she'd met today, she'd remembered his name. Perhaps he hadn't imagined that odd sense of connection, one that shouldn't exist, considering she'd come here with another man.

Slowly her body softened against him until she was snuggled close, arms around her knees, head resting on his shoulder. His arms encircled her.

They were both soaking wet, her hair was dripping cold water on his chest, and a bony elbow poked him in the ribs. And yet he'd have been happy to sit this way for hours.

Except her warm, naked bottom pressing against his lap was too damned arousing.

Zane Slade's woman. Not only that, but a resort guest. He never messed around with guests or staff. He'd built this business from the ground up and struggled every day to keep it in the black. He wasn't going to screw things up over some woman.

Not when he had Mara, his sweet four-year-old daughter, depending on him.

Sex . . . It was easily found, if he wanted it. Mostly, he was too busy to care.

He'd gone without for too long. That, combined with the warm curves of a lovely woman on his lap, must be why he was feeling so horny.

Of course, he'd felt horny from the moment he laid eyes on Tamiko.

She was so different from his ex-wife—blonde, curvy Jane, who'd deserted both him and Mara. So different from the Belizean women and tourists he'd occasionally dated.

Tamiko was elegant, like a bamboo orchid: simple, clean-lined, utterly perfect. A touch mysterious; sexy, yet with a hint of purity and innocence.

No, that was crazy. There was no innocence. She was another man's lover and a successful model.

He'd bet few men had seen her like this: scared and vulnerable. His arms tightened protectively around her.

Quietly, warm breath brushing his neck and making his blood surge, she said, "I'm sorry for being so stupid. But when I was walking on the beach, I felt so alive, so free. The ocean, the moon's path, it drew me in."

"I know. The ocean's seductive." As seductive as she was. "But you have to be careful. It can be dangerous."

"I thought I was going to drown."

"It's over, Tamiko. Don't hang onto the fear. Don't let one bad experience scare you off."

She was quiet for a long moment, then looked up at him. "I'm not a coward." But her expression was uncertain.

"Things will look different tomorrow, when you've had a good night's sleep and the sun is out."

She nodded, then shifted position, and her hip brushed the front of his shorts where his boner tented the wet fabric. She froze.

Should he apologize? Hell, a woman like her must be used to men getting turned on, right, left, and center.

"I should go back," she murmured, shifting again awkwardly, trying to get her feet under her. Her hip rubbed provocatively against his erection as she rose.

He jumped to his feet just in time to catch her as she stumbled in the soft sand.

Off balance, she fell against him, and he gripped her shoulders to steady her. Her body, with his shirt plastered against her damp skin, pressed against his from chest to thigh. Small, firm breasts with nipples as hard as pearls. Gently flaring hip bones and softly curving thighs.

He was totally aware of every inch of her and of the way his rigid shaft prodded her stomach.

He should have stepped back, but he didn't.

He expected her to move away, but she didn't.

She stared up at him, those huge, dark eyes starry as they reflected the moonlight. Her lips parted, and she drew in a shuddery breath that made her breasts shift against his chest.

Caught in her spell, he lowered his mouth to hers until their lips touched. Still she didn't move away. Her warm breath puffed in and out rapidly, and he captured it in a kiss.

Her arms came up, not to push him away, but to twine around his shoulders. Long fingers threaded into his thick mass of unmanageable hair. Her lips answered his tentatively, almost as if she was as out of practice with kissing as with swimming.

He responded in kind, cherishing her mouth with soft brushes and gentle licks, sucking and nibbling her flesh tenderly.

"Oh," she sighed. Her tongue ventured out to flirt with his, and when it retreated, he followed it back into her mouth. She was sweet, tasting like a fruity cocktail. Sweet, too, in the ingenuous way she met his kiss.

How could a drop-dead gorgeous woman like this, with so much sexual experience, kiss like a virgin?

# Chapter 3

THE thought brought Ric to his senses. He jerked backward abruptly.

What the fuck was she doing? She'd come here with Zane, and now she was kissing him?

Disgusted with her and himself, he swiped a hand across his mouth. No, her kisses weren't sweet and innocent; that was the taste of betrayal.

"Sorry," he said roughly. "I should never have kissed you."

"I . . ." She ducked her head. "Me, too. I . . . I don't know what came over me. I shouldn't have—" Wet black hair gleamed in the moonlight as she shook her head. "I'm with Zane. I'd never . . . It must have been the fear and shock. The relief of being rescued."

She did sound truly apologetic, totally flustered.

And, after all, he'd behaved as badly. "Let's forget it happened." Though how he'd forget the feel of her firm little breasts, the delicate touch of her tongue, was beyond him.

"Yes, please," she said strongly.

"Time to go."

She glanced around. "I left my dress and, um, underwear on the beach."

"By a palm tree or some other marker?"

She shook her head. "I wasn't thinking."

He gave an exasperated sigh. "We'll never find them."

"But I need that dress."

"Buy another tomorrow," he said impatiently.

"You don't underst—" She took a breath. "Yes, fine." She began to limp along the beach toward the distant lights of the resort.

His damp shirt clung to her body. Her hair hung in a black waterfall down the white back, and her bare legs reminded him of all the other naked skin he'd glimpsed earlier.

Naked skin that only Zane Slade would be caressing.

Ric swore and caught up with her.

When they reached the cabana, the lights were off. The woman had almost drowned, and she'd kissed another man, and Zane had slept through the whole thing.

If she was Ric's woman . . .

But she wasn't. Would never be.

"Have a shower." He kept his voice low less out of concern for Zane than for the guests in the neighboring cabanas. "Make sure you're warm all the way through. And drink lots more water, in slow sips."

She nodded, head down, not meeting his eyes. "I will."

Feeling bitter, jealous, and downright mean, he said, "Don't have sex tonight. You might cramp up again." It probably wasn't true, but he couldn't stand the thought of her in another man's arms, not when his own body ached from holding her.

"Thanks again. And . . . I'm sorry." Then she'd slipped inside, and the door closed.

He stomped away. It was going to be one hell of a long week with that woman around.

Inside the cabana, Tamiko went into the bathroom and stared at herself in the mirror.

She was pale, her wet hair a straggly mess, and the oversized shirt didn't do much to conceal her body. With makeup and the right photographer, the image could be turned into a sexy one. And, in fact, under the shelter of that cotton shirt, her body hummed in an unfamiliar way.

Arousal.

She'd felt whispers and murmurs of it before, but whenever a man had kissed her, she'd gone cold.

Remembering.

Her mom's muffled cries in the night, the tearstains on her face, and the bruises she tried to hide.

Her dad's hot breath on Tamiko's face in the darkness. His threats.

The memories were ice water, banishing arousal and turning her back into the frozen woman she knew herself to be.

Yet when Ric had kissed her, his mouth so gentle and caressing, she'd felt herself thawing. The rigid thrust of his erection hadn't scared her but had made her want to press against it.

She stepped into the shower and, as the pulsing spray beat against her body, she imagined Ric's hands stroking her. Those fantasies, more than the heat of the water, warmed her through and through.

WHEN Tamiko woke, Zane was downstairs by an open window, laptop on his knees.

As she paused on the stairs, clad in a short, kimono-style robe, he glanced up with a smile. "Morning, Tami. I didn't hear you come in last night. Have a nice walk?"

"I did have a nice walk. Then I tried to swim and almost drowned, and then I . . . I kissed Ric, and I liked it."

"What did you say?" He stood, dumping his computer on the coffee table. "My God."

The sunshine out the window was irresistible. "Can we sit on the deck and talk?"

"Sure." His brow was furrowed with concern.

He opened the door, then picked something up: a white bag with the Toucan logo. He glanced inside, then, frowning, handed the bag to her.

She reached inside and pulled out her dress from last night. How sweet. Ric had found it for her. As it unfolded, her lace bra and thong fell out. She snatched them off the floor.

"You came home *naked*?"

"No, I had his shirt." She moved past Zane, out into the sunshine.

He followed. "Tell me what happened." He sat in a lounge chair and pulled her down to sit beside him.

"Stupidly, I went for a swim, then I got a leg cramp. Ric was on the beach, and when I called for help, he rescued me."

"Jesus!" He gripped her shoulder. "Are you all right, girl?"

She nodded. "Yes, though I was scared. And freezing. He held me, warmed me, and . . ."

"One thing led to another." He studied her face. "As is wont to happen. But not in your life. You never let a man get close, because of . . ."

The abuse. She swallowed hard. "People have gotten over much worse things. But, despite counseling, I haven't. I'm frigid, Zane. Besides, I don't have time for a relationship."

"But you said with Ric, you felt . . ."

"Aroused," she whispered. "The way he kissed me, held me, it was so tender. He didn't push. It was like he let me come to him. And I wanted to. I actually felt as if I might want . . ."

"Sex."

She nodded. "Of course, if he'd gone any further, I'd probably have frozen the way I always do." She'd only had two lovers, and she had barely been able to endure having sex.

"Maybe not. Tami, I don't think you're frigid. You're . . ." He paused. "Sensitive. You've been hurt, and you're afraid."

She bowed her head. Label her frigid or label her sensitive, the truth was, she was flawed.

And yet she was strong and had her priorities straight. She didn't need a man.

"You're also sensual, and capable of joy," Zane said. "The gentle, wondering way you touch a flower petal, the subtle way your body moves to music. The light in your eyes when you see a child playing in the park or reach down to stroke a dog."

Zane's words struck a chord. "Maybe." The delight she'd felt, seeing the butterflies in the garden. The silky caress of ocean air on her bare skin. She tipped her face up to look at him. "Yes, maybe."

He took her hand and held it gently. "If this was any other place and time, I'd encourage you to get to know this man. But this week . . ."

"I'm Zane Slade's date. I know. It's all right." She told herself it was better this way. Chances were the thing with Ric had been a fluke, brought on by dehydration, danger, relief. The moon. If she put it to the test, she'd freeze, like always.

Better to have the memory of, for one time in her life, feeling like a real woman.

THE morning after he'd rescued—and kissed—Tamiko, Ric was working in his office, avoiding her and Zane, when a knock sounded on his door. Tamiko herself stepped into his office, looking wary.

When she closed the door, he drank in the sight of her. Gone was yesterday's sleek sophisticate. Today she looked like an island girl in a pink sundress and flip-flops.

Damn, he couldn't resist. The window was open, and he reached out to pluck a hot pink hibiscus blossom. Then he got up and walked toward her. "How are you feeling?" As he approached, her draw was magnetic. His dick stirred.

Last night, she'd been naked in his arms. She'd kissed him as if she was a virgin awakening to sensuality.

"I'm fine. I slept well. Thank you." The words came out choppily, and her chest rose and fell quickly. In public she was poised, but being alone with him made her nervous? Was she afraid he'd come on to her? "And thanks for finding my dress and my, uh . . ."

Underwear. Those black lacy bits that had so tantalized him.

Was she wearing a thong under that sundress? The thin straps suggested she was braless.

On the Caye, people walked around half-naked all the time. Crazy that the sight of this woman in a simple sundress made his body stir with need. "You're welcome."

She jiggled a gift shop bag she held. "I brought back, uh, your . . ." She ducked her head. "Shirt." The word came out as little more than a breath of air.

It conjured the image of her clad only in his shirt, its fabric clinging to her damp skin.

He was hard now, aching for her, for another man's woman. Trying to keep his voice steady, he said, "Thanks."

She nodded. "I should go." But she didn't move. Her gaze was fixed on his face as if she was mesmerized.

Mesmerized himself, he lifted his hand to tuck the pink blossom in her shiny hair. His fingers brushed her cheek, the shell of her ear. Her skin was so smooth, and she smelled like gardenias. A creamy, delicate blossom with an aroma that was lushly sensual. Yes, the scent was perfect for her.

Her eyes gleamed; her lips parted as if she wanted to kiss him.

She was tall, only an inch or two shorter than him. He wouldn't have to bend down to touch his lips to her soft, trembling ones. Words tumbled out of his mouth. "God, Tamiko, I want you."

She jerked backward, the bag falling. "I can't. I'm sorry. I . . . I'm with Zane. I just came to return your shirt. I have to—"

"Shit, yeah, I know." He scrubbed his hands across his face. "I don't know what—"

A knock interrupted him, and the door opened. Zane Slade, clad in shorts and a linen shirt, stepped into the room.

As he turned to close the door behind him, Ric grabbed the bag from the floor and straightened, holding it to conceal his boner.

Zane's sharp-eyed gaze raked him, then focused on Tamiko. Expression softening, he walked over to her. "I like the flower. It suits you, Tami." He stroked her cheek, a gesture that struck Ric as almost more a father's than a lover's.

The man turned back to Ric. "You saved her life."

"I happened to be on the beach."

"Thank God you were." The other man paused, then said, "You're attracted to her."

Shit. He tried to shrug it off. "What man wouldn't be? You're a lucky guy."

Zane nodded slowly. "Yes, I am. Tamiko is special."

She gave a start, then slipped her arm through his and hugged herself up against him. "Oh, lover, you always say the sweetest things. I'm the one who's lucky to be with a sexy man like you." The words tripped off her tongue, but her expression was strained.

Zane smiled at her, then said, "Ric, I need a moment alone with the lady. Could we use your office?"

Evicted from his own office? The guy sure had cojones.

Ric stepped outside and pointedly closed the door. He wouldn't stoop to putting his ear against it, but he was sure as hell tempted.

He ran his hands through his hair and paced.

Finally the door opened and Zane said, "Come in."

Tamiko was seated in one of the guest chairs, lips pressed together in a thin line. Had the two of them quarreled?

Zane pointed to the other guest chair. "Sit down, Ric."

"I'd rather stand." The better to defend himself, and Tamiko, if that's what this was about.

"Fine. Okay, I've asked around about you."

"What the hell?"

"A writer can get away with anything in the name of research. Anyhow, I hear you're a decent, hardworking guy. You and your mom are raising your daughter after your wife ran out."

"Shit! You have no right—"

"You have a daughter?" Tamiko asked.

"Yes, Mara, she's four. But what does that—?"

"You treat women with respect," Zane went on. "You don't fool around with staff or guests. You've hardly dated since your divorce."

Tamiko rose. "Zane, I've changed my mind. This is insane."

"What's insane?" Ric demanded.

She went to the window, her back to them.

"You're attracted to her," Zane went on, "and she's attracted to you."

*Damn.* "I know she's with you. She's made that clear. I'd never do anything." His protest sounded hollow. He'd never before been tempted to mess with another man's woman, but when Tamiko was around, it was so damned hard to keep from touching her. And he sensed she felt the same.

Zane studied him for a very long moment, his whisky-colored eyes seeming to peer into Ric's soul. Then he said, "No, she's not."

"She's not what?" Ric spoke at the same time as Tamiko swung around from the window saying, "Zane, don't do this. You don't have to."

"Hush, girl," Zane said. Then, to Ric, "She's not with me."

Ric frowned in puzzlement as Zane went on. "People say you can be trusted, so I'm going to trust you. Because I care about Tamiko."

"Uh, all right," he said warily.

"Tamiko is my dear friend, but not my girlfriend. I have a significant other who couldn't come on this trip. It's a long story, but I didn't want to come alone. I'm tired of getting hit on by people who are attracted to fame. I wanted a relaxing holiday. So did Tami, and she agreed to come along and pretend to be my lover."

That was just plain weird. But then, Zane was a celebrity. They could be eccentric.

Wait a minute. Tamiko was unattached? He glanced at her, standing by the window. She didn't meet his eyes, yet he felt that magnetic pull. "Why are you telling me this?" He addressed his question to Zane but couldn't look away from Tamiko.

"I'm matchmaking the two of you," Zane said. "For this week, if you're discreet and no one finds out."

A secret affair? Oh, Lord, did that sound good. To hold Tamiko again, feel her naked body against his. But . . . "I never get involved with guests," he said regretfully.

"A wise policy," Zane said. "Things could get messy. And an added incentive for you to be discreet."

"I . . ."

Tamiko raised her head and gazed steadily at him, and he couldn't read her feelings. Did she want this? She must, or why would Zane have proposed it?

"This won't get messy," Zane said. "Tamiko's a New York model with a big new contract. You're a Belizean, building this business and looking after your little girl. You both work hard, so why not have some fun for a week?"

"Why are you doing this?" Ric demanded. "You want us to have a holiday fling?"

"Exactly," Zane said.

"It's probably not a good idea," Tamiko said softly, uncertainty in her voice. Again, he had that sense of innocence.

"That's for the two of you to decide," Zane said. "I'll leave you alone." He went over to her, rested his hands on her shoulders, and kissed her forehead. Then he whispered something in her ear.

She nodded slowly but didn't look convinced. Her expression reminded Ric of last night, when she'd said she wasn't a coward.

Why would it take courage to have a sexy secret fling with him?

Zane left the office, closing the door behind him.

"Well, that was strange," Ric said. "I don't get it."

"He's a good friend," she said softly. "I told him we . . . kissed, and he felt guilty."

"For having you pretend to be his date, so you weren't free to . . ." To what? Have sex with Ric?

Her shoulders lifted in something that was as much a shiver as a shrug. "It's probably a crazy idea. We might not even be compatible."

She was selective, that's what she was saying. A classy model who regularly dated celebrities like Zane Slade. Yeah, why the hell would she be interested in a man like Ric?

Yet he had felt the chemistry between them.

He'd rarely been tempted to break his rule against getting involved with a guest. But now, for this woman, he was willing to toss it out the window. So long as it was their secret, and, as Zane had said, there'd be no complications afterward.

"I think we'll be compatible." He took her slim, graceful hands, and they trembled in his. He felt the strangest mix of sensations: lust, because Tamiko was the sexiest woman he'd ever seen; awe, because she was the most strikingly beautiful; and tenderness, because something about her made him want to treat her gently.

She gazed at him, biting her lip. He hadn't a clue what she was thinking.

"Last night," he said, "when we kissed, that was special."

Her dark eyes went luminous, and her lips parted. "Yes. But that was . . . You'd just saved my life and we were . . . There was moonlight and . . ."

Was that all it had been for her? For him, he'd never wanted a woman so badly, and it had nothing to do with moonlight. "Before we decide what we want to do, let's find out if we're compatible."

Her slim throat rippled. "H-how do you suggest we do that?"

He moved past her to lock his office door. "Another kiss. Here and now. No moonlight, no lifesaving." His heart raced as he waited for her answer.

# Chapter 4

TAMIKO'S entire body quivered with nerves. Ric was so masculine and vital with his lean, muscular body, that beautiful dark skin showcased by his simple shirt and shorts, the black hair that sprang off his head with a will of its own. She felt pale and insignificant in comparison.

Yet the heat in his eyes told her she was very significant.

Many men had looked at her with lust, but she'd felt as if they never truly saw her. They admired an image: the model with her exotic beauty.

With Ric, the desire felt personal.

Her desire for him certainly was. She'd never before looked at a man and felt like . . . she wanted to lick him all over. Like she wanted to feel his fingers touch every inch of her body.

A shiver ran through her—of arousal, and fear.

What if they kissed, and she froze? What if they had sex, and she was so clumsy and inexperienced she didn't satisfy him? Her last lover had left her in disgust, calling her frigid. She couldn't stand it if that happened with this beautiful man.

But if they didn't kiss, she'd never find out if she could be the sensual woman Zane believed her to be.

She took a breath. Her mind was racing too far ahead. "A kiss." That's all he'd asked for.

She touched his bare forearm, brown and sprinkled with black hair. It was firm, warm, and felt wonderful under her hand. She stroked his skin gently from wrist to elbow, feeling a sense of connection. The warmth from his skin sank into her, calming her nerves even as it made her blood sing.

She tilted her face toward his in invitation.

He let out a sigh, as if he'd been holding his breath. "Tamiko."

"What?"

"I just had to say your name. Your lovely name. Now, you say mine. Ricardo."

"Ricardo," she murmured, feeling as if they'd made some kind of vow.

He put his hands on her waist, then his lips whispered across her forehead, stringing a daisy chain of soft kisses that drifted past her temple and down to her ear. His hair brushed her cheek, and she smelled coconut.

Each kiss sensitized her skin, made her body more aware of him, teased her toward arousal.

Those butterfly-light kisses trailed across her cheek toward her mouth, and she sucked in her breath in anticipation. Then he was drifting kisses across her lips, following the outer line of her top lip, then the bottom one.

He was so male yet so gentle. In his dark eyes she saw a heated gleam that was as much appreciation as lust.

It gave her confidence to stop passively accepting his attention, to firm her lips and catch his. He had such full lips, such a sensual mouth. A mouth that had been designed to kiss.

And he knew how to use it.

He didn't push his way into her mouth but played with her lips. Each lick and teasing nibble made her body tingle with pleasure and awareness.

Her hand crept from his shoulder to the back of his neck, under the thick curls of hair, and she went up on her toes, easing closer.

His hands left her hips and began to stroke her back, over the fabric of the sundress and then up to her shoulders, shifting her hair out of the way so he could caress her bare skin.

His tongue teased the seam between her lips, and she opened to let him in, hoping he'd continue the slow, sensual dance of mouths rather than thrust forcefully. As if he'd read her desire, he sent the tip of his tongue to flirt with hers and explore the ultrasensitive secret places in her mouth.

She closed her eyes and sighed with pleasure, with mounting need. The need for . . .

Until last night, she'd never longed to feel a man's erect penis against her body.

Yes, she'd had sex several times, with two different men. She'd forced herself to tolerate the touch, but never had she craved it. Until now. Her pussy throbbed with a pleasant ache.

Cautiously she shifted closer so the front of her dress brushed his shirt. His shorts. Where, yes, he was rigid with arousal.

His hands drifted down to cup her butt cheeks, but he didn't pull her tightly against him. He left it up to her to decide how much she wanted, and how soon.

Emboldened, she tilted her hips to press her pelvis against that hard jut of cock, and a moan rippled through her. This feeling was amazing. Pleasure, and need.

It was like taking one bite of ice cream, perfect in itself and yet not enough. A teaser that left you greedy to devour an entire bowl of delight. When it came to ice cream, she, always conscious of her weight, never allowed herself more than a bite. But Ric . . . He was calorie free, and she craved him.

She wanted to see him naked. To feel him naked. Last night, even though she'd been traumatized by the near drowning, she'd noticed the musculature of his torso and the way the wet shorts had draped his assets.

Last night, when she'd gone for her walk on the beach, she'd had a sense of freedom and release. She'd felt alive. And now, with Ric, she felt that same way. As if he was liberating her from her chilly slumber and awakening the passionate woman inside.

She moaned and freed her mouth from his. "You feel so good."

"So do you, Tamiko. God, I want you."

He slipped one of the spaghetti straps down her shoulder and kissed the skin he'd revealed. And then her collarbone. And then he . . .

Began to whistle cheerfully?

"Damn!" He pulled away from her, and she realized the whistle was coming from outside the window. "It's Ramon, the gardener." Ric yanked down his shirt to cover the bulging front of his shorts.

Hurriedly Tamiko pulled up the strap of her dress and took a few steps backward. "Will he—?"

Before she could finish the question, a sturdy black man carrying a rake came from behind the pink hibiscus bush and peered in the open window with a broad smile. "Hey, boss. How ya doin' today?"

"Good," Ric's voice sounded strained. "I'm good, Ramon. How about you?"

"Can't complain." The gardener touched his broad hand to the brim of a battered straw hat. "Mornin' miss. You have a good day."

"I will. Thank you. Uh, you, too."

When Ramon had moved off, Ric blew out a long breath. "Sorry, I got carried away."

"So did I." She eyed him, not daring to step closer. Her damp sex throbbed, and her skin felt twitchy, craving his touch. So this was what it felt like to be horny.

His gaze seared her, even from several feet away. "I don't think we have a compatibility problem."

At the moment, she felt more like combusting than freezing. And yet . . .

Anxiety skittered across her skin. Would things really be different with Ric? Could one man, a man she'd barely met, banish the fear, the memories?

Zane had suggested she consider telling Ric about her past, but she couldn't. If this had any hope of working, she had to hang on to some degree of confidence and poise. She couldn't tell him she was damaged, maybe frigid. She didn't want to *feel* that way, much less acknowledge it.

Besides, what man would take on a woman like that? Ric was looking for a discreet, sexy fling.

And so was she, damn it.

"Tamiko?" he asked, the heat in his dark eyes now replaced with concern.

Trying to sound flirtatious, she said, "What do you propose we do next, Ricardo?"

"Find a time and place when we can be alone together." He glanced toward the window. "Where no one's going to interrupt. And then I want to kiss you, and kiss you some more, and we'll take it from there."

She liked the way he'd phrased it. Not specifying sex, leaving it open. For some reason she, who trusted no man but Zane, believed Ric wouldn't pressure her to go any further than she was comfortable.

"That sounds good," she said softly. "But it's our secret. Agreed?" She'd never betray Zane.

"Yes. So, let me think." He moved to his desk and consulted a piece of paper. "Sarah has you and Zane down for the snorkeling trip, and I guess you need to go, right?"

"That's the whole point of me being here. To act like Zane's lover so he doesn't have to worry about other women coming on to him." She had to be careful to stick to the story Zane had told Ric, and not out her friend.

"You'll be gone for several hours on a catamaran. There's a picnic lunch, and sunbathing, swimming, snorkeling, diving for those who are certified. Go in the water, Tamiko, or you may always be afraid of it. And don't forget the sunscreen. Your skin's so beautiful, you sure don't want to burn."

"I'll be careful." How sweet that Ric wanted to take care of her.

"After you get back, there'll be an hour or two before dinner, but people will be wandering around. It'd be hard to find any privacy."

An embarrassed expression crossed his face. "I live across the street from the resort. I wish I could invite you to my place, but my mom and daughter live there, too."

"I understand." Briefly she wondered about his daughter and the ex-wife who apparently had abandoned them. What was wrong with the woman?

"I know it's a little primitive, but what about the beach? Tonight, late."

Last night, she'd felt so sensual and alive by the ocean. Excitement rippled through her. Yes, she'd be less inhibited on the beach. "Good idea."

"Half an hour after the group gets back from dinner in San Pedro, you walk away from the resort in the same direction as last night. I'll find you."

He gestured toward the locked door. "Now, you should go."

"No kiss good-bye?" She wanted to touch him again, to let that contact reassure her she was doing the right thing.

He took a deep breath, then let it out. "If I kiss you, Tamiko, I won't be able to stop." His gaze seared her across the room.

She quivered with that aware, alive, sexy feeling only Ric had ever given her. Yes, this was right. "Tonight, then." On legs that trembled, she left his office.

Out in the sunshine, crossing the sand toward the cabanas, she felt young, excited. A feeling she'd rarely experienced since she was a child. The day was bright with promise and the night even more so.

Before she'd gone to Ric's office, she had packed her new beach bag and was all set for the boat trip, but first she needed to talk to Zane.

As she approached their Hibiscus cabana, she saw him lazing in the hammock on the deck. "You're not writing."

"I am. In my head. Working out a plot point." He maneuvered himself out of the hammock. "How did it go?"

They went inside, and she said, "Good." Her face, her whole body, felt like they were glowing. "But Zane, why did you do this?"

"Told you in his office. It's what you need."

"Need? I've gone years without sex, so obviously I don't really need it."

"Not just sex. Good sex. You're—" He broke off and grinned. "What's that Madonna song? 'Like a Virgin'? Well, that's what you're like. Remote, afraid."

"I've done sexy photo shoots," she protested.

He waved a hand dismissively. "Sure, you know the moves, but you don't feel it. Now you've found a man who turns you on. Awakens that slumbering sensuality. So, go for it."

She hoped it would be that easy.

"You're always saying you don't have time in your life for a man, so Ric's perfect. Once you get back to Manhattan, you'll be your normal, driven self, and working with Sakura. Ric'll be here in Belize. But you'll have great memories to remind you you're a woman."

"I hope so."

"And maybe one day, you'll have time in your life for romance, and you'll be open to loving a man."

Maybe. Once she was too old to model, and was back in Oregon living with her mom. Was it possible she could have a real life? Love? A husband, maybe even kids?

Zane, who knew her better than anyone else in the world, seemed to think so.

"It'll help your career, too," he went on. "When you're flirting with the camera, you'll remember Ric. Sakura wants you because you're exotic, and there's a pureness to your beauty. Combine that with a gleam in your eye that says you've had amazing sex, and every female consumer will want to be you."

Sakura again. It was an incredible honor being chosen over dozens, maybe hundreds, of other models. This could mean financial security for her small family.

And the world would know her face. Every moment she was out in public, she'd have to *be* Sakura.

Oh well, it wasn't like she wasn't used to being stared at.

Or like she had other options. She'd barely scraped through high school, and all she had going for her was striking beauty and street smarts.

"Tami, are you okay?"

She focused on how lucky she was, both with Sakura, and to be here. And tonight she had a secret date with a beautiful man who knew how to be gentle and take things slow. It would be good. Maybe even great.

Maybe she'd have the first orgasm of her life.

# Chapter 5

IT was around eleven when Tamiko tiptoed down the steps of the cabana.

*I'm going for a walk on the beach. That's all anyone would see.*

Laughter sounded from Bella and Danny's cabana, and Tamiko imagined them romping in the king-sized bed. For them, life seemed so happy, so easy. Of course, Danny had tons of money, which made things a lot smoother.

Yes, she was envious.

Then she remembered Zane's parting advice. *Try for once to live in the moment.*

He was right. She was always worrying about her mom, her sister, the fact that her face and body were commodities with a short shelf life, and that modeling was all she knew how to do except waitressing.

Becoming responsible for her family at the age of thirteen had wreaked havoc on her ability to be spontaneous and carefree.

But tonight, the warm air whispered across her face, reinforcing Zane's advice to live in the moment. As did the dozens of stars, dazzling in the clear night sky. And the murmur of the ocean, an ocean she'd made peace with this afternoon.

Despite the mellow night, her body was taut with tension. Was this a wise idea? What if things didn't work out, and she couldn't relax?

Ric's voice, a soft murmur not much louder than the sea, spoke her name.

She gasped in surprise. Then, when he materialized from behind a screen of palm trees and shrubs that lined the beach, she went to meet him.

His dark hair and skin seemed like part of the beautiful night. In shorts and a T-shirt, more casual than the ones he wore for work, he could have been a sexy beach bum, not the owner of a successful resort.

In one hand he held a rolled-up towel. With the other, he reached toward her, and she put her trembling hand into his. "Hi, Ricardo."

His warm grip was reassuring, but she felt her inexperience. What was she supposed to do now?

He answered that question by drawing her gently toward him. "I've never seen a prettier sight than you in the moonlight, Tamiko." He pressed soft kisses to her forehead, her nose, her lips, then drew back and simply gazed at her.

His hair was damp, and he smelled of coconut. He'd showered and shaved before coming, and already she knew his scent.

A sense of belonging filled her, a subtle mix of arousal, trust, and anticipation. It wasn't the least bit logical, given her history and the fact she barely knew Ric, yet it helped her relax.

"Let's walk," he said. "Up here, rather than along the shoreline. There's less chance of being seen."

They strolled along in the soft sand, clasped hands swinging between them.

"Was it a problem for you to get away?" she asked quietly. "What about your daughter?"

"We had dinner, she had a bath and a story, and she's sound asleep. Mom's there. She knows I get called out on work things all the time."

She was glad Ric hadn't initiated a sexy embrace. Walking and chatting like boyfriend and girlfriend helped her relax.

"You've got your life well organized," she said approvingly. "A house across the street from your business, and your mom there to help raise your daughter."

"Things are working out. But it's a struggle. The tourist industry isn't the most reliable way to make a living these days."

"Nor is modeling. But we do the things we're suited to."

"Did you always want to be a model?"

Never. But that was a truth she kept to herself. So she did the hair toss that always distracted men. "My looks are my biggest asset, so modeling was the logical choice."

"Your biggest asset? I doubt that."

She tilted her head to stare at him. "Sorry, I don't understand what you mean."

He shrugged. "I've just met you, Tamiko, but already I know you're a loyal friend. That counts for more than physical beauty. Don't you think?"

"It does," she said slowly, appreciating that he saw her as more than a pretty face. "But I was talking about marketable assets."

"Let's stop here. This is a nice spot."

It was a sandy space with a view of the ocean framed by palms and shrubs. He set the towel down, and she saw there'd been a plastic bottle wrapped in it.

He touched her cheek. "You look classy, like you were born rich. But I get the feeling that's not true."

If he knew the truth, he'd be shocked. Appalled. She'd buried it long ago. Back when she was thirteen, and she and her badly injured mom and sister moved from California to stay with her mom's cousin in Oregon. There, they'd used her mom's maiden name long before they'd had the money to change their names legally.

Now, all she said was, "I grew up without much money. But I've done pretty well."

"We have more in common than I'd thought."

"What did you think?"

"That I was drawn to you from the moment I saw you. You're not just beautiful, but arresting. You make a man stop, look again, look longer. It's hard to stop looking."

The execs at Sakura had said the same thing.

"But there's something more," he said, studying her face. "A quality that makes me feel . . . young. Almost like I'm a boy with my first girlfriend. Like I want to go slow and—" He shook his head. "I don't know how to say it."

"Slow is good," she said, relieved. "I'd like that."

He spread the towel. "Have a seat."

She sank down, sitting with her legs curled to one side.

Ric sprawled beside her, a man at ease with his body. He held up the bottle. "I'd have brought a picnic basket, proper glasses, but if anyone had seen me, it would have looked suspicious."

"What's in the bottle?"

White teeth flashed. "Sex on the beach."

"Seriously?"

"Is it too cliché?" He unscrewed the lid and handed her the bottle.

Not cliché, but it didn't help her nerves. Of course he was expecting sex, even though he'd said he would go slow.

She took a sip, hoping the alcohol would loosen her up.

When she handed him the bottle, he drank, too. She liked the intimacy of his lips covering the place where hers had been, liked the way he threw his head back, and his throat rippled as he swallowed. He was so physical compared to the men she knew in Manhattan, so outdoorsy and natural, yet just as intelligent and successful.

"I like your style, Ricardo," she said shyly.

"I like yours." He touched the flower she'd tucked behind her ear. "You're wearing a hibiscus again. It suits you." His fingers plucked it from her hair and brushed its petals across her cheek.

She'd worn it because it made her think of him. And in hopes it would make her feel new and fresh, sensual and free.

He drifted the blossom across her lips, then down her neck, and she arched, shivering with pleasure at the gentle, sensuous touch.

The hibiscus traced the neckline of her sundress, lingered in the cleft between her small breasts. He tucked it there, like a decoration, and the tight top of her dress held it in place.

His touch made her body hum, her nipples tighten, but she tensed. Would he reach under her dress, fondle her breasts? Did she want him to?

Instead, he used both hands to smooth her long hair behind her ears, running his fingers through it again and again. "Like silk," he said. "A waterfall of black silk."

She'd wanted to touch his hair since she'd first seen him, and now she did. It might be the same color as hers, but the texture was the opposite. It was so thick and almost wiry, she couldn't weave her fingers through it. She chuckled. "How do you comb it?"

"Fro pick," he said. "My dad was African American. When I was in my teens, I had dreads."

"I like it like this." The conventional choice for a businessman would have been to cut it short, but she was glad he hadn't. "It's sexy." Wasn't there supposed to be a tie between a man's hair and his virility?

"You're sexy." He leaned toward her and touched his lips to hers, light as a butterfly wing or hibiscus petal.

Nice. Not the least bit threatening, just tantalizing.

"More," she whispered against his mouth.

He began to kiss her the way he had in his office, teasing her flesh until she opened her lips and begged him to come inside.

The times she'd had sex, nothing had felt natural to her, not even the kissing and foreplay. She'd felt pressured and anxious. Inhibited, scared.

But with Ric, kissing was wonderful. He took things so slowly, she could savor it, enjoy the heady pulse of growing arousal.

And she did the same things back to him, not because she had to but because she wanted to.

He clasped her shoulders and tipped her backward until she was lying on the towel with him leaning over her, and for a moment she felt the familiar, instinctive panic. But he didn't quicken the pace, just nibbled her lips and explored her mouth with his tongue, and soon her tongue was slow dancing with his again.

Her arms circled his back, and his soft T-shirt brushed her chest. Last night his torso had been bare, and she wanted that again. She wanted to see him, to feel his firm, warm brownness. She tugged on the shirt, pulling it upward.

He broke the kiss, peeled the shirt over his head, tossed it aside, then waited for her to decide what to do next.

What she did was stare. Ric could have been a model. Put him in an ad for expensive cars, watches, or cologne, and buyers would flock to the stores.

But that would never be his world. Taking him to New York and sticking him in front of cameras and lights would be like caging one of those soaring black frigate birds.

She stroked his skin wonderingly. Her fingers weren't used to touching people in anything but the most superficial way, and now they lingered.

His skin quivered under her touch, but other than that, he didn't move, as if he sensed she needed to be in control.

Muscles, strength. And yet he didn't scare her. Power and gentleness were a potent combination, one that made a hungry pulse beat between her legs, a throb of arousal that was so rare, so welcome.

His skin was smooth, rich chocolate. She raised her head and licked his shoulder, almost surprised to find the taste of salt on her tongue rather than chocolate. "You taste good," she whispered. "You feel good."

Leaning on one arm, he lifted the hair that fell over her shoulder and kissed the skin he'd revealed: the cap of her shoulder, her neck, the vulnerable hollow at the base of her throat where her pulse fluttered.

He reached behind her and touched the top of the zipper that ran down the back of her sundress. "Yes?"

She wanted those kisses to move lower, wanted his tongue to lave her aching nipples. "Yes."

He drew the zipper down slowly, fingers brushing the knobs of her spine with soft deliberation.

As the dress loosened, the blossom it had held in place tumbled free, drifting down between her breasts.

When he'd lowered the zipper fully, he circled the base of her spine with his thumb, brushing the upper curves of her buttocks, the cleft between.

As he slowly drew her dress straps over her shoulders and began to ease the top of her dress over her breasts, she had a nervous impulse to cross her arms over her chest and stop him. Last night she'd been naked, but he'd barely glanced at her body before tossing her his shirt.

Yes, she wanted his touch, but she had a fashion model's body: skinny, with barely there hips, butt, and breasts. The camera loved her, but was she woman enough to please a vital man like Ric?

Time to find out.

As he stared at the body he was revealing inch by inch, she watched his face. She saw the glitter of his eyes, the flare of his nostrils, the way his lips parted.

The dress cleared her breasts, the cotton whispered across her ribs, her flat stomach. The hibiscus flower tumbled to the towel beside her.

She lifted up so he could keep going. Now her lower body, clad only in a tiny flesh-colored thong, was exposed, and then he was pulling her dress off.

"You lying there in the moonlight . . ." His voice was husky. "Someone should paint that picture. You're so lovely. A moon goddess."

"Not a goddess. Just a woman." A woman who, before coming to Belize, had never felt the breath of a tropical night on her naked skin or yearned for a man's touch the way she craved Ric's.

The corner of his mouth curved. "Lucky for me."

He caressed her breast, her taut nipple, his touch featherlight.

She gasped with surprise, pleasure, anxiety.

"Are you cold?"

"A little. And . . . aroused. And," she confessed in a rush, "a bit nervous."

"I make you nervous? Damn, Tamiko, I don't want to do that."

"It's not you, it's . . ." She swallowed and came up with a half-truth. "It's been a while, and my last relationship ended badly." She didn't tell him that had been three or four years ago, and her lover had called her a snotty, frigid bitch.

"We'll take it as slow as you want. We won't do anything you don't want to."

But she did want to have sex. She wanted to have good sex for once in her life, and something told her this was the man who could give it to her. If only she could get over her nerves.

She had an idea what would help, but she felt so foolish, she couldn't look him in the eyes. "Could you take off your clothes and just hold me? So I can, uh, get comfortable with you."

He didn't respond for a moment. "Your last guy. Did he . . . push you? Before you were ready?"

She ducked her head, letting her hair slip from behind her ears so it hung in two wings, hiding her face. Ready? She'd never had a clue what *ready* meant until her body had hungered for Ric's. "We just weren't very compatible."

"I meant what I said. We won't go any further than you want to."

"I want you to take your clothes off. I want to see you." If she was going to freak out, it would happen when she saw his erect penis, when she felt it press against her.

Still hiding behind the curtain of her hair, she listened to the *zzzz* of his zipper, the rustle of clothing.

He stroked her upper arm. "Let's lie down together. How about you lie on top of me?"

That sounded good. If she was on top, she wouldn't feel overpowered by his size and strength. "Okay," she whispered.

Beside her, he moved, stretching out. His knee bumped hers, then, as he settled, his thigh brushed her hip.

Trembling with anticipation, she lifted her head and looked at him. His face first, framed in springy dark curls, a tender smile on his lips. Then his torso, beautifully muscled. Finally she let her gaze shift lower.

She sucked in a breath. His hips were lean, his belly flat, but those weren't the attributes that held her attention. His erect cock, rising out of a nest of curly black hair, was firm and beautifully shaped, not too thick but definitely not skinny. His penis looked so much more appealing than any others she'd seen.

It made her mouth water and her hand itch with the desire to touch it.

It made her pussy throb with need.

And yet, competing with those feelings was the surge of fear she always felt.

In her experience, sex was at best a mildly painful encounter that made her feel dirty and inadequate. At worst, it was a violation.

A shiver rippled through her. Damn, even with Ric, the past was rising to haunt her.

"Come lie down." His voice was gentle. "Let me hug you."

Trying to quell her nerves, Tamiko eased down so she was lying half across his body, breasts against his chest, one leg across his thighs, low enough so it didn't touch his package. She buried her face against his shoulder.

Slowly he put his arms around her and stroked her upper back. "Hey, it's okay. Nothing bad's going to happen." She felt his breath, his kiss, against her hair. "You're so tense, I'm thinking some guy really did a number on you."

"I'm sorry. I didn't realize how much it still affected me." She was such a loser, letting herself be trapped by scars from her past. Damn it, she'd had counseling. She should be past this.

Ric would get impatient, he'd realize her sexy image was false advertising.

"Don't apologize. It's okay. Just relax. Everything's okay." His tone was low and soothing. "It's going to be all right, Tamiko. Or can I call you Tami, the way Zane does?"

Her friend was the only person who called her Tami, and she liked having a nickname. "Yes, please."

She relaxed slowly, her body adjusting to the contours of Ric's. He was so firm and warm, he felt wonderful. His hands caressed her back lightly but didn't roam below her waist, and now she was beginning to wish they would.

She was also growing increasingly curious about his package. She raised the leg she'd curved across his thighs and felt the fullness of his scrotum, the slight tickle of hair, the firm root of his cock.

He stirred and gave a sigh but didn't thrust against her. His hands, though, did dip below her waist, circling the upper curves of her buttocks. He paused, giving her a chance to say no.

Cautiously she raised her leg an inch higher along his shaft, and his hands began to move again, exploring an inch lower down her backside.

Her nipples were hard and sensitive, pressing into his chest. She felt moisture on her inner thighs as her pussy hungered for contact with the organ she'd now trapped under her leg.

Slowly she shifted position, sliding her lower body over his until she was sprawled across him, his erection hard against her stomach. She'd never been on top of a man before, and his cock felt good. A deep pulsing need overrode her nervousness.

"Come and kiss me, Tami." His voice whispered across her hair.

She raised up a little, which made their lower bodies press even closer together.

But he didn't take advantage, didn't seek to probe between her legs. Instead, when she'd lifted her face to his, he gazed into her eyes. "Are you okay?"

"This is nice. Thanks for being so patient. I feel so stupid for—"

Ric cut off the apology with a kiss. It started out soft and tender, then, as passion rose in her, she demanded more from him, and he gave it to her.

His hand slipped between their bodies to tease her nipple, and delicious sensations radiated outward, making her moan and press harder against his cock.

He was rigid against her belly, but that wasn't where she craved the pressure. Without conscious thought, she shifted her pelvis, lifted higher, until the base of his penis rubbed the ache between her legs.

He groaned against her mouth, and she froze, but he didn't thrust against her or try to enter her. "So hot and sexy," he murmured. "You feel so good, Tami."

"You, too." Unbelievably good.

Suddenly, she felt the need to take him now, before something changed. Before she lost that delicious sparky burn of arousal. Before she got scared.

"Did you bring protection?" she whispered.

"Yes, but . . . Now? You want this now?"

"N-now." Her voice quavered, but she wasn't going to back out. She wanted this so badly. Quickly she pulled off her thong and straddled his hips, so his shaft rose between her legs.

*I'm in control. This is Ric, he won't hurt me. I can do this.*

He reached for the shorts he'd tossed aside, then held up a condom package. "You want to put this on?"

"I . . . Yes, please." She wanted to touch him, liked the idea of staying in control.

With shaking fingers, she ripped open the package and removed the condom. When she started to sheathe him, his shaft felt amazing under her fingers. Such soft skin, yet underneath she felt his pulsing strength.

He was so strong, so hard. Her fingers fumbled as she rolled the condom into place.

# Chapter 6

"HEY," Ric said softly, "what if I'm not ready yet?"

He was fully erect, his cock beautiful in the moonlight. "Looks to me like you're ready."

"Mmm. Not quite." He raised himself slightly, bracing his weight on one arm, and reached up to tease her nipple again. "I need to do this for a while longer."

It felt so good, she pressed forward into his hand. A whimper escaped her lips, and she felt moisture between her legs.

"And then, there's another breast I need to touch," he said, and his hand drifted over to play with the other one.

Restlessly, she shifted, pressing her crotch against his shaft. But that wasn't good enough; she needed more.

His fingers stroked across her rib cage, her belly, her waxed mound.

"So smooth and soft, Tami." His hand slid lower, between her legs, his touch so erotic it made her quiver with pleasure. "And here, so hot and lush, so slick and moist."

He stroked her folds, and she pressed against his hand, feeling needy, shameless, wanton.

The tip of one finger slid between her labia, entered her, then stopped.

She knew he was asking if it was okay, and it was. Very much so. "Yes, oh yes," she breathed, and he slid farther.

He parted her, explored, made her moan and tremble as her body gripped his finger, and more moisture gushed.

Gently she gripped his shaft, imagining how it would fill her. How it would stimulate all those needy spots his finger was toying with.

She was beginning to understand the conversations she'd heard while getting her hair and makeup done. The women who'd boasted about how well hung their men were. And how well they used their equipment.

She had no doubt Ric knew exactly what to do with his. His kisses, his hands, his words were those of a lover who knew how to please a woman, even one as wary as her.

"That feels good, Tami," he murmured.

"So does that." His finger was still inside her, and now his thumb rubbed gently against her clitoris, collecting all the arousal, the sexual tension, making it coil tight inside her.

He looked so amazing, sprawled naked beneath her, and her body was alive with sensation. For the first time, with a man, she felt sexy and empowered.

She let go of his shaft and leaned forward, even though it meant he had to slide his finger out of her body. Then she flicked her long hair across his belly, his cock, the way a sexy woman might do.

He shuddered, and his cock jerked. "God, Tami. You could drive a man crazy with that hair."

"Could we settle for crazy with desire?" She tried out her newfound sense of power.

"Oh yeah, that's definitely the kind of crazy I meant. Do that again."

This time she rested her hands on the towel by his shoulders and let her hair tumble around their faces as she bent to drift a kiss across his lips.

When he tried to capture her mouth, she shifted away with a breathless laugh, moving down his body. With a quick shake she sent her hair rippling across his chest, then captured a nipple in her mouth and sucked it hard, feeling a tug of need in her sex.

He groaned and reached up to capture a handful of hair, but she'd already moved.

She let a waterfall of hair flick over his erect cock. His balls. She shouldn't have been so quick to sheath him. He'd have felt the sensations even more strongly.

Next time.

Or the time after.

There'd be lots of time this week to do everything she wanted to do with him, to touch him with her fingers, her tongue. Her pussy throbbed at the thought.

"Ricardo?"

"Yeah?"

She took his shaft in one hand. "I want you. Now."

Holding him, she rose on her knees, guiding him to the drenched folds between her legs.

Usually, at this point, her body closed up, rejecting the idea of being invaded. But tonight, she felt another pulsing gush of juicy need, and the tip of his penis slid into her. "Oh," she cried softly, amazed at how good his hardness felt against her sensitive flesh.

But then she felt pressure, a hint of pain, because she was so tight after years without sex. She lifted up, eased down again, felt her body soften with pleasure, loosen, and take him in. Up and down she moved, her moisture coating his shaft, and each time he sank deeper into her.

His hands held her hips, steadying and reassuring her. Other than that, he didn't move, though the quick rise and fall of his sculpted chest and the tension on his moonlit face spoke of the effort it cost him.

He touched her breast gently, then took the nipple between his thumb and index finger and rolled it. "You're so sexy, Tami. So lovely. Damn, I'm a lucky man."

No, she was the lucky one. Her body had come alive under his praise, the provocative tweaking of her nipple, the pulsing heat of his cock. Foreign sensations, womanly and erotic, rippled through her vagina and gathered in that delicious ache between her legs.

The ache was like an itch that demanded to be scratched, and instinct told her to twist her hips and grind against him where their bodies touched. And then to rise slowly, until his shaft was almost free of her, then glide down quickly, ending with another twist—hard—against him.

"God, Ric, this feels . . . You're so . . ." No, there were no words. She was gasping for air; her brain wasn't functioning, she was all about sensation.

About chasing something she knew was there but just out of reach, something unbearably tantalizing yet elusive.

Inside her, it was like a spring was tightening, a delicious, achy pressure building and coiling. Eyes closed, whimpering with pleasure and need, she concentrated, focused.

She was on a journey she'd never taken before, and she knew something wonderful awaited her at the end, but she didn't know how to get there. She wanted it so badly, but maybe she couldn't achieve it.

Then she gasped. Ric had reached between her legs, found her clit, and was softly rubbing his thumb across it.

"Oh, God!" Yes, that was the magic button.

That blissful ache built, she focused, she reached, and then . . .

The world stopped. All thought, striving, worry ended, and her body took over. Pleasure peaked, burst, surged through her in waves that made her cry out with wonder and joy.

This was it: orgasm.

She wasn't frigid, not damaged beyond repair.

She was a woman, whole and sexy.

Shivers and ripples of pleasure still trembled through her body as she leaned forward to kiss Ric, lips eager and grateful.

"Tami." He broke the kiss, touched her cheek, and she realized she was crying. "Did I hurt you? Are you all right?"

She sat up and brushed the tears off her cheeks. "I'm wonderful. So happy. That was amazing." He must think she was nuts to be so excited about an orgasm. "Your turn now," she said, feeling his rigid erection deep inside her.

"Want to stay on top?"

She felt safer there, in control, not pinned down by a man's weight. But this was Ric. With him, maybe she could conquer another level of fear.

Besides, if she asked him to let her go on top again, he would.

Somehow, this man she barely knew had done what no man other than Zane had achieved. He'd won her trust.

"No, I want you on top." She eased down until she was sprawled atop Ric's body, feeling all those hot, firm muscles press into her soft flesh.

He put his arms around her and rolled them until she was on her back and he was above her, taking his weight on his knees and forearms. She bent her legs, cradling his hips between her thighs.

His face blocked the moon, and for a moment she felt overwhelmed by the big, dark body that loomed over her. Then his lips touched hers, sensual and enticing, and she fell into the kiss and forgot to worry.

Slowly he pumped his hips, his cock filling her in long, smooth glides.

Her body, so recently satisfied, was sensitive, responsive. She caught his motion and lifted to meet him.

"Okay?" he murmured.

"Oh, yes." She stroked his muscled shoulders, and the sense of controlled strength aroused rather than frightened her. Her hands traveled down his back, reached his waist, and went on to explore the firm curves of his butt. He probably swam every day and ran on the beach.

An outdoor man, yet he ran a successful business.

A powerful man, yet he was gentle, sensitive to her needs.

A man of contrasts.

The sexiest man she'd ever met.

That sweet achy feeling of building arousal filled her again. Might she actually have a second orgasm?

His strokes quickened, his breath came fast and shallow. The controlled man was losing control, getting carried away by need, by passion.

That excited her, as did the harder, faster thrusts of his cock.

She whimpered with pleasure and spread her legs wider, pushed up against him, and felt her body reaching for what only he could give her.

Not only was she aware of Ric moving against her and inside her and of her body welcoming him, but all her senses seemed sharper. The towel beneath her was pleasantly rough against her skin. The humid night air was a caress. Stars glittered like tiny diamonds, accenting the serene, glowing moon. And the ocean murmured, a steady backdrop to the harsh sound of Ric's breathing.

She felt as if she and this man had always been here and would always be here, making love with only the ocean and sky as witnesses.

It felt primal, right, inevitable.

His pace quickened, his strokes became jerky, and she forgot about everything but their two joined bodies and the incredible way he made her feel, the response he pulled from every cell of her sensitized pussy.

She arched, grinding against him, and he gave her exactly what she needed. Just the right pressure in just the right place, and now she was coming apart again.

And so was he, his climax plunging deep into her core as she shattered around him.

She clung, body racked by deep, shuddering waves of pleasure, sobbing his name over and over.

He plunged hard again, then again.

And then, panting as if he'd run a marathon, he gradually slowed.

Braced on his arms, his body heaved as he sucked in air, and then slowly he collapsed on top of her. “My God, Tami.”

Before she could react to his weight pinning her, he rolled them so they were both on their sides, still joined.

He smiled. “That was incredible. You’re really something.”

“No,” she said honestly. “That was you. You helped me get over . . . a bad experience.”

“I’m glad. Though I’m sorry some guy . . .” He paused, giving her an opportunity to fill in the blank.

“It’s in the past. Way in the past now.”

He didn’t press her, and gradually their breathing returned to normal. He pulled out of her and dealt with the condom, then handed her the bottle containing the sex on the beach cocktail.

She took a long, slow swallow, enjoying the tangy sweetness of the juice with the bite of alcohol behind.

When she gave back the bottle, he drank, too. “Are you warm enough?”

“A little cool without you to keep me warm.”

“Roll over.”

Obediently she rolled away, then he spooned her from behind, curling one arm around her. She felt cozy, protected. What would it be like to fall asleep this way, and wake with a man’s warm body wrapped around you?

If a man like this loved you, how could you ever walk away?

Zane had said Ric’s wife had abandoned him and her own child.

To Tamiko, who put family above everything else, that was inconceivable.

Somehow, she knew Ric was a good father, responsible, protective, and loving. She rested her hand on his. “Tell me about your daughter.”

He gave a soft laugh. “What can I say? I’m a proud daddy. Mara’s perfect. Smart, pretty, a sunny personality. She’s loaded with natural charm, and the toughest thing for Mom and me is to make sure she gets enough discipline in her life.”

“My sister’s like that.” With the wisdom of adulthood, Tamiko knew she'd spoiled Midori. But she'd wanted to shelter her and make up for the shit their family had gone through. "She's in college now, and having to learn self-discipline."

Tamiko had been so proud that her sister, unlike her, had done well in school. She was happy to pay for her college education.

"Is she your only sibling?"

"Yes. Midori's six years younger."

"And you're . . . ?"

"Twenty-five. How about you?"

"Thirty-two. Are your parents both alive?"

She'd been asked so many times, her answer came automatically. "My father died when I was thirteen, in an accident. Mom's healthy and active." Except for the brain injury she'd suffered in that final beating.

An injury that fortunately had stolen her memory of what her husband had done to her and how she'd saved her own life. How she'd grabbed the knife she'd been using to chop onions and plunged it into her husband's heart.

Tamiko hadn't been there, but she'd imagined the scene so many times. Now, with Ric's arm around her, she could push away those images and concentrate on here and now.

"What about you?" she asked. "Your mom lives with you. Does that mean your dad passed on?"

"More like moved on," Ric said easily. "It was hippie days, Vietnam War days, and some of the kids drifted down here. Mom hooked up with a draft dodger. They lived together for several years. Didn't plan on her getting pregnant, but it happened.

"Then President Carter declared amnesty for draft dodgers," he went on. "My dad missed the States, and his parents wanted him to come back. He asked Mom to go, but she didn't. When I got older, she told me they didn't love each other enough for her to follow him to a new world."

"Did you grow up knowing him?"

"No. I was born after he left. They stayed friends, kept in touch. He sent money. When I finished high school, I went to Chicago to meet him. He's a good guy, married with a couple daughters. We don't have much in common."

"How about you and your ex?"

He sighed, then lifted her hair and kissed her nape. "Jane's a Bostonian. An investment banker. She was involved with a colleague, it broke up badly, and she left the place she'd been working. Came here for a break. We fell in love, got married. Jane loved the romance of it. Loved sending snaps of herself on the beach in a bikini to friends back home."

Tamiko smiled. "I can see the appeal." Not only with Belize but Ric as well.

"Then reality set in. She'd gone from being a big city investment banker to changing diapers on an island with a population of fifteen thousand. A backwater, she called it."

"But—" A person didn't bail on their responsibilities.

"She missed the city, her high-powered job, life in the fast lane. We argued all the time, didn't even like each other anymore. She went back to the States."

"I can see a marriage breaking up. Sometimes that's for the best." Tamiko's mom should have divorced her dad, but she'd been so traditional. The husband was boss, the wife subservient. No matter what the man did. "But to leave her little girl . . ."

"Yeah. Well, it worked out for me. Rather than trying to share custody with a woman in the States, I got Mara to myself."

"Are you in touch with Jane?"

"No. She wanted to put the Belize part of her life behind her."

"That's rough." And inconceivable to Tamiko. "For you, but especially Mara. She's bound to wonder about her mother."

"I know. I hope Mom and I can give her enough love that she won't be too upset."

"She's a lucky child to have you."

Lying under the stars, her body fitting so comfortably in the curve of Ric's, she could think about her own father without as much of the usual pain and anger. Yes, he'd ruined their family, but Tamiko—with help for the first few years from her mom's cousin—

had looked after the three of them. They were so much better off without him.

And, though he'd abused her, it hadn't been permanent. Thanks to Ric, she now truly believed she would heal. She squeezed his arm affectionately.

"I guess you can relate to the city and career thing, can't you?" he asked.

"Oh, yes. I grew up in small towns and hated them." Anonymity was impossible in a small town, and she had so craved it, what with her brain-injured mom, the family's poverty, and Tamiko's failures in school. "And in my line of work, Manhattan is an ideal place to live."

Ric nuzzled into silky black hair, kissed the nape of Tamiko's neck, smelled her gardenia scent, and thought how perfect she felt in his arms.

But her words were a reminder that this was temporary. He couldn't let himself fall for another big city woman. "What kind of modeling do you do? Fashion?"

"Yes, and shampoo, nail polish, cosmetics."

"Giovanna said you were the new face of, uh, was it Sakura? A cosmetics line?"

"Beauty products, skin care, cosmetics. A new line. Very expensive. Sakura is Japanese for cherry blossom."

"Sounds like a big career step."

"It is. Many lines choose movie stars, but Sakura decided to go with a relative unknown. They don't want people looking at me and remembering a certain character in a movie; they want a, uh, blank slate. That they can create on."

"I wouldn't call you a blank slate, but I don't know anything about your industry. Will you have fun with this job? I guess all the makeup and hair and photo shoots are exciting."

She drew in a breath and let it out slowly. "Kind of, in the beginning, though scary, too. Now, it's hard work, like any job. It's not easy being on display, standing under hot lights, turning this way and that, and doing what people tell you. And then there's the weight thing. My agent's always on my case about that."

"Sounds tough."

Her shoulders moved in a shrug. "With Sakura, the money will be good. Job security doesn't exist for models."

"Nor for resort owners," he said ruefully. "But I do love this business. I get to live in a beautiful place, and my hours are flexible enough I can spend time with Mara. I enjoy meeting people, and I love organizing things and solving problems."

Tentatively he said, "I get the sense you don't love being a model."

She tensed, then shrugged. "It's fine, as jobs go. The money's good."

"Is money so important to you?" he asked quietly.

Again she stiffened, and he was afraid he'd offended her. "It has to be," she said flatly. "You can run this resort for the rest of your life, but in a few years I could be too old to get jobs. There aren't many for women in their thirties or older."

She'd said her beauty was her biggest asset, yet she had so much more going for her. Oh well, it wasn't his place to question or criticize. Besides, the hour was late.

He nuzzled into her hair one last time. "We should head back."

She sat up and turned to face him, folding her arms across her naked breasts. "I've disappointed you. You think I'm shallow."

"God, no." He sat, too, then lifted both hands and used his fingertips to trace her features. High, unlined forehead, perfectly arched black brows over almond-shaped eyes with dark fans of lashes, delicate nose, cheeks as soft as a bougainvillea blossom.

"Not shallow," he said. "Complex. Career-driven, yet a caring friend, a passionate lover, a woman who'll go swimming all alone in the moonlight."

"That's not complex, it's stupid." Her expression had lightened, though, and she let her arms drop so they no longer hid her lovely little breasts.

"Impulsive. A quality I bet doesn't show up much in your work life."

She shook her head, hair rippling around her face and down past her shoulders. "No. And I probably should avoid it. Last night proves I don't have very good judgment."

"And tonight?"

She smiled. "That's a different story. This, with you, is definitely good judgment." She picked the hibiscus blossom off the towel and stuck it in her hair. Miraculously, it hadn't been crushed.

"So we'll do it again?" His heart raced, and he willed her to say yes.

"I want to. As long as no one finds out."

"Tomorrow night? Same time, same place? Though I don't know how I'll wait that long."

Her eyes danced. "We'll see each other during the day."

He groaned. "With my staff and the other guests around. It'll be torture."

"When you see me . . ." She rose and stood in front of him, naked, as graceful and lovely as an exotic blossom in the moonlight. "Remember me like this."

He threw back his head and laughed softly. "Like I said. Sheer torture."

THE next afternoon, Tamiko put on a halter top and a short, flowered sarong—she loved the casual clothes Zane had insisted on buying her here in Belize—and headed for the cabana door.

Zane, at his computer, raised a hand. "Have fun, but be discreet."

"I will. Ric may not be able to sneak away anyhow."

Sarah had organized various excursions, but as everyone was leaving, Zane had excused himself and Tamiko. He'd hinted about preferring a little afternoon delight. Then, when he and Tamiko were alone, he'd suggested she might find some private time with Ric.

The idea made her blood hum with anticipation as she ran barefoot down the cabana's steps and headed across the sand.

"Hey, Tamiko," a male voice called.

She stopped dead, then turned. It was Danny. He and his best friend, Free Lafontaine, lazed in shorts on the deck of Danny and Bella's cabana.

Reluctantly she went over. "Hello, Danny, Free. I thought everyone had gone off somewhere."

"We skipped out," Danny said.

They chatted for a few minutes, and Danny invited her to join them, but she said no thanks. They joked about Zane ignoring her for his writing.

"Why don't you go to the bar?" Free suggested. "When I picked up our beer, Ric was there, restocking. Get him to make you a fancy drink."

"Ric?" Oh no, did Free suspect something? "Uh, that's the bartender?"

Danny said, "Come on, you gotta know Ric Nuñez. The resort owner? He's always around, working with us on the wedding. Great dude."

Oh yes, he certainly was a great dude. "Ric," she repeated, trying to keep her lips straight. "A drink does sound like a good idea. Maybe I'll have sex on the beach. I quite enjoyed it when I tried it yesterday."

# Chapter 7

RIC was in the bar, restocking and whistling cheerfully as he remembered last night and looked forward to spending more time with Tamiko.

A voice called, "Daddy, Daddy!" and he turned to see Mara, clad in blue shorts and a T-shirt with turtles on it, skipping toward him. "Hey, baby girl." He swung her up in his arms. and they exchanged a smacking kiss. "What're you doing here?"

Glancing past her, he saw his mom enter the bar. She looked striking in a purple dress, her black hair with its streak of silver pulled back from her face with a band of flowered silk. "Hi, Mom. What's up?"

She gave him a quizzical look. "I'm taking Otty Martinez to the lawyer to talk about her husband's estate. Remember, I told you at breakfast? She says she never understands his legalese."

His mind had been too full of Tamiko to pay attention. "Sorry. Sure, you go ahead. Me and my best girl will hang together."

"I'll be back in an hour and a half." She turned to go.

Behind her, Ric saw Tamiko climbing the steps to the bar. Alone.

Casual and stunning in a halter top and sarong. This was *not* the time to remember her naked in the moonlight.

His lover's wide eyes took in the picture. "I, uh, thought I'd get a drink, but I see you're busy." She turned to go.

"No, wait."

Mara tugged on his shirt. "Daddy, put me down." When he did, she skipped over to Tamiko and announced, "You're pretty."

Tamiko, a New York model who'd won a prestigious contract, beamed like a kid herself and kneeled down. "Why, thank you. So are you."

God, they looked cute together, and he loved the easy way she related to his kid. Grinning, Ric walked over. "Mara, the pretty lady is Tamiko, one of the guests for the big wedding that's happening on Saturday. And Tamiko, the pretty girl is my precocious daughter, Mara."

The sound of throat-clearing made him turn to see his mom's raised-eyebrow glance.

"And this lovely woman is my mother," he said quickly. "Perlita Nuñez."

Tamiko rose lithely and held out her hand. "I'm pleased to meet you."

His mom shook her hand firmly. "Me, too. And now, I must go." She ruffled Mara's hair and hurried away.

Ric turned to Tamiko, wishing he could touch her. "So, what would you like to drink?"

She waved a hand. "Don't worry about me. You and Mara go and—"

Charlie, the chef, took the steps in a flying leap and burst into the bar, cutting her off. "The seafood supplier's fucked up—" He stopped dead when he saw Mara and Tamiko. "Hi, kiddo. Good afternoon, miss. Can I interrupt for just one moment? I need a word with Ric."

"Of course," Tamiko said.

Charlie took Ric's arm, pulled him over to a corner of the bar, and spoke urgently. "The supplier's delivery guy didn't bring the barracuda. We could switch to snapper, but it's not the same."

"Damn." Sarah had requested a meal of seafood specialties, and he didn't want to swap snapper for the more exotic barracuda. "You called the supplier?"

"Yeah. He says he doesn't have any, but I think he's lying. Can you go see him?"

"Okay. And assume for now that we'll get the barracuda."

As the other man left, Ric went over to Mara and Tamiko. Things with the supplier could get heated. Did he really want to take his daughter along? He could ask the receptionist to keep an eye on her, but if she got busy on the phone or computer . . .

"Ric, I couldn't help but overhear," Tamiko said. "Do you need someone to stay with Mara?"

"I can't ask you to do that." Besides, what did a Manhattan model know about looking after children?

Tamiko gazed steadily at him, a hint of humor in her eyes. "I grew up looking after my sister. I'll take good care of Mara."

Tami might look like an exotic flower, but she was caring and responsible. Yes, he did trust this woman with his precious child.

He turned to Mara. "Is that okay with you, baby?"

She glanced between the two adults, frowning slightly.

Tamiko bent down to Mara. "Do you like butterflies? I've seen some in the garden."

"The big blue ones?"

"No, these were little yellow ones. Why don't we look?" She held out her hand.

Mara took it. "Okay. See you later, Daddy."

He gave her a kiss, then said to Tamiko, "Thanks. If there's any problem, ask the receptionist to help. And she has my cell number."

"We'll be fine."

Hand in hand, the pair headed for the exit. With their straight, slim backs and long black hair, they could have been mother and daughter.

Tamiko glanced over her shoulder and gave him a warm smile.

The sight of the two of them together did funny things to his heart.

* * *

RIC loaded a cooler full of fish into the back of the Toucan Resort van, then opened his cell and dialed Charlie. "I have the barracuda. After delivering a rant about the meaning of contracts and penalties."

"So he did have it all along. I thought so."

"Yeah. But he'd got a rush order from the Sea Witch, and they offered to pay a premium price, so he was going to give it to them. Anyhow, they'll be getting snapper, and we've got our barracuda."

"Thanks, boss."

Rick snapped the phone shut and jumped into the driver's seat.

As he drove back to the Toucan, he wondered how Tamiko and Mara were getting along.

He parked by the kitchen delivery entrance, off-loaded the cooler into the waiting hands of one of the kitchen staff, then headed for the garden.

It was deserted.

He stuck his head into the lobby, which was empty except for the receptionist. "Sandy, did you see Mara?"

"Ms. Sato said they were going over to your house."

"Okay. That's where I'll be if you need me."

As he hurried out, he wondered how Tamiko would view his two-story bungalow. It was just big enough for the three of them, and it was homey rather than impressive.

The garden, though, was something special, thanks to his mom's green thumb. She'd done the landscaping for the resort and for numerous clients on the Caye. In their own yard, she'd created a beautiful and sweetly scented paradise, specializing in plants that attracted butterflies. No doubt Mara had wanted to show Tamiko the butterfly garden.

When he crossed the street from the Toucan to his home, he saw the family car in the driveway. His mom was home already?

He went around back, to see a cluster of females sitting around the umbrella-topped patio table. His mom, Tamiko, Mara, and Otty Martinez, a gray-haired neighbor who'd recently lost her husband.

Tami glanced up, and her face lit. "Ric."

He grinned back, thinking how surprisingly natural she looked sitting there. He wished he could kiss her, claim her as his girlfriend. But of course she wasn't, and their affair had to be kept a secret.

Besides, she'd be gone in a few days. Tamiko was a model, a city girl who didn't like small towns, and the Caye was, as Jane had said, a backwater.

Mara ran over to throw herself into his arms. "Daddy, want a cupcake?"

"Sounds good." With her clinging to him like a monkey, he went over to the table, noting the teacups and a half-empty plate of the miniature chocolate cupcakes Mara loved. "Hi, ladies. Otty, how did it go with the lawyer?"

The woman huffed. "We got there, and he'd just left. Seems like the oldest Teague boy got hisself arrested again."

"So we drove home." His mom shot him a questioning look. "And found Mara and Tamiko hunting butterflies."

"I had a work crisis."

"So Tamiko explained." It was clear she wondered about his relationship with Tamiko, but what could he say?

He went into the kitchen for a glass of milk, and when he returned, the women were chatting again. He helped himself to three cupcakes, and Mara hopped onto his lap. As he munched, his mom and Otty talked about gardens and the tropical climate. Tamiko listened and asked questions.

She was so pretty, face animated and eyes sparkling. And she fit in easily. Strange, considering she must be used to wearing fancy clothes and sipping martinis with other Manhattanites.

He wished he could touch her, even to rest his hand on hers. It sucked pretending they were near strangers.

His mom was talking about her part-time landscaping job, and how lucky she was to be able to take Mara along. "And the work is pure joy. I love everything about gardens, from the planning to the execution, from the tending to the sitting back and enjoying. Seems to me, we all have one thing we're born to do, and that's mine."

"Mine's cooking," Otty said. "Especially the sitting back and enjoying part." She patted her round belly, then sighed. "Sure miss having Joey to cook for." Then she forced a smile and turned to Ric. "Your thing's the resort, right?"

"Yeah. And this little monkey." He hugged Mara. "How about you, sweetheart? What's your favorite thing in the whole wide world?"

"Chocolate cupcakes," she said promptly, reaching for the last one on his plate.

They all laughed, then his mother said, "What about you, Tamiko? Have you found your special thing?"

"Still looking." She grinned at Mara. "But I agree, chocolate cupcakes are pretty nice."

"You only had one," Mara said.

Tamiko reached out to tweak her nose. "One cupcake is a lot for someone in my line of work."

"Seriously, Tamiko," his mom said. "What's your favorite thing in the world?"

"I'm not sure I've ever thought about that." She reflected. "I have an eye for color and design. Like you with your gardens, except for me it's with people. I'm good at makeovers. Helping people find the right clothes, hairstyles, makeup—not the expensive ones necessarily, but the ones that fit their personality and lifestyle."

"That sounds fun and creative," his mom said.

She nodded. "I like helping people feel good about themselves, whatever their budget."

"What would you tell Otty and me?" his mother asked.

Tamiko didn't even pause. "Perlita, I'd tell you purple is an excellent color for you, but you already know that. It's your favorite color, isn't it?"

After his mom laughingly agreed, Tamiko turned to the older woman. "Otty, your long hair is lovely, but you'd look ten years younger if you got a shorter, more modern cut."

The woman touched the thick hair coiled at the back of her head. "My Joey, he did like long hair. But it's so hot, and a danged nuisance. I'll think on what you said, Tamiko."

"How about Ric?" his mom asked, a gleam in her eye. "What would you suggest?"

Tamiko flashed her a smile. "He's your son. You know he's perfect just as he is."

The other two women laughed, but his mom again glanced curiously between him and Tamiko.

Thinking about what Tamiko had said, Ric asked her, "This company you're going to model for? The cosmetics are expensive?"

"Yes." Some of the animation had faded from her face.

"Wouldn't you be happier working for a company that's more, like, for the average woman?"

Her brows rose. "Happier? Ric, I don't pick and choose my work. I'm amazingly lucky to get the offer from Sakura."

Lucky. Meaning she'd make a lot of money. Even though Sakura didn't make her eyes sparkle the way her makeovers did.

She narrowed her eyes. "Yes, I care how much I make. My dad's dead, and I have my mom to support. And my younger sister, until she finishes her education."

"Your mother doesn't work?" his mom asked.

"She was in an accident and has a brain injury."

Her words created a shocked hush, and she hurried on. "Mom's a sweet person and quite happy. She's capable of living alone. A home care worker helps organize housework, shopping, laundry. Mom goes to a sheltered workshop on weekdays, enjoys socializing and being productive, but she doesn't make a real income."

He heard what Tamiko didn't say. That she'd be supporting her mom for the rest of her life.

This wasn't a woman like Jane, who'd walk away from her family responsibilities.

"I admire you for taking care of your family," he said, and his mom and Otty murmured agreement.

"Thanks. Sakura will be a huge help." She shoved back her hair and stood. "I should get back. Perlita, thanks for the lovely tea. Otty, it's been a pleasure talking to you. And Mara, thanks for sharing your butterflies."

Otty heaved herself to her feet. "I should head home, too, though the house sure does seem empty these days. Tamiko, I'll walk with you to the road. I want to know what hairstyle you think would suit me."

Ric stood, gave Otty a kiss on the cheek, then couldn't resist touching Tamiko's hand, though he tried to make it look casual. "Thanks for helping out with Mara. Guess I'll see you around." *Later tonight, on the beach.*

Humor sparkled in her eyes. "I imagine we'll bump into each other."

When Tamiko and Otty had gone, Mara went to give her favorite doll a cupcake, and Ric and his mom began to clear the table.

"Imagine my surprise," she said, "to come home and find Mara in the garden with a stranger."

He glanced up from stacking plates. "Tamiko's a responsible person. Don't you like her?"

"Question is, do you?"

"She's a guest at the Toucan."

"You're seeing her."

"You know I have a policy against getting involved with guests." He didn't mention that Tamiko was in Belize as Zane's date, since it seemed she hadn't done so herself.

"I know you do. And I know that mostly you have a brain. But I think maybe you're losing it, when it comes to her."

Damn. His mom had a sixth sense about this kind of thing.

She put a hand on his arm. "Yes, I like her. But son, you've gone down this path before. With an American. Same way I did with your dad. They belong there; we belong here."

"I know. And I didn't even say I was seeing her." He grabbed a handful of dishes and headed for the kitchen.

"No. You didn't." He felt her disapproving gaze on his back.

SEEING Ric Tuesday afternoon, so efficient at work and so loving with his family, made Tamiko eager to be alone with him that night.

But, after dinner, a bunch of guests had a party on the beach, and she didn't think it wise to try to sneak past them. When they showed no signs of stopping by midnight, she went to bed, frustrated.

The next morning, she and Ric managed to exchange a few words, promising to try again that night. But night seemed a very long way off.

Fortunately, the day would be busy. Tamiko and Zane were scheduled on a golf cart expedition, with lunch at an oceanside restaurant.

As the guests gathered in the parking lot by the fleet of shiny red carts, she saw Giovanna, looking stunning as always. She was paired with Al, Danny's widowed father, who'd been married to Zane's sister.

Sarah was always careful to keep Giovanna and her ex, James, separated, so Tamiko was surprised when James appeared. Again her fingers itched to make him over.

He stalked over to Giovanna, and the two exchanged words, though Tamiko was too far away to hear what they said. But perhaps Giovanna, too, had issues about James's wardrobe. She reached for his tie, released the knot, and yanked the tie off. Then she undid his top button.

He lifted his hand and caught hers.

And for a long moment neither of them moved.

"Unfinished business," Zane murmured in Tamiko's ear. "And sexual tension."

"But don't they hate each other? I thought they fell out of love long ago."

"The opposite of love is indifference, and those two sure aren't indifferent."

James broke the spell, saying something to Giovanna. She jerked away from him and went back to Al.

A few minutes later, everyone was settled in their assigned golf carts, and heading off.

The trip proved interesting. Tamiko enjoyed the pull ferry, the quaintness of traveling on a cart track, the intriguing construction sites. As they passed houses with lovely gardens, she wondered if any were Perlita Nuñez's work.

Her thoughts kept turning to Ric. If she didn't see him tonight, she'd go crazy. Now that he'd helped her discover her sensuality, she yearned for more.

Their cart came out onto a lovely strip of pale beach. Beach, like the one where she and Ric had hoped to meet last night. "I'm still annoyed about that party last night."

"Poor Tami." He patted her leg. "You're sexually frustrated. You and Ric need a contingency plan."

"What?"

"You aren't used to subterfuge the way I am. You should always have another plan in case you need it. Graham and I do."

What a terrible way to live. "Would it really be so bad if you came out of the closet? Lots of people in the entertainment industry are gay."

"Yeah, but not the ones with the supermacho images. Could you imagine if the world found out that Daniel Craig was gay?"

Her eyes widened. "Is he?"

He snorted. "No, of course not. But look how shocked you were at the idea."

"Zane, you're an author. You being gay doesn't make your hero gay."

"It makes him suspect to some of my readership."

"Who's more important? Your homophobic readership, or Graham, the man you love?"

"Graham is." He scowled at her. "He knows that."

"How do you think he feels when you flaunt a beautiful woman on your arm?"

"He understands." Her friend's tone was grim.

"Sorry." She touched his arm. "Guess I'm being bitchy. I just think, if two people love each other, they ought to be able to make it public without anyone dumping on them."

"Would that it were so." He glanced at her. "At least I have someone to love. You keep saying you're not looking for that, but you're missing something."

Last week, she'd have argued. But now . . . She'd discovered she could be sensual and sexual with the right man. And she could care. With Ric, her heart was awakening.

Not only that, but she'd felt a deep yearning when she'd played with Mara.

# Chapter 8

THEY arrived at the Crazy Monkey, a picturesque beach restaurant, and took the seats Sarah assigned them, sharing their table with Free Lafontaine, Giovanna, and Al.

The meal was al fresco again, a habit Tamiko could easily get used to. She stole a yellow blossom from a planter of hibiscuses and thought of Ric as she tucked it into her hair.

She chose the lowest-carb lunch, seafood ceviche, but she didn't refuse when Zane offered her one of his delicious coconut shrimp. In the back of her head, she heard her agent's voice nagging about her weight, but she let the ocean's murmur drown it out.

Giovanna, seated with her back to her ex, entertained Tamiko with her witty comments about colleagues in the cosmetics industry. Zane and Al, his brother-in-law, chatted easily. Free joined in sporadically but seemed distracted and kept glancing over to another table. At Sarah, if she wasn't mistaken.

And the wedding planner was glancing back, color high. Something was going on with those two. A quarrel? Or was it possible they, too, were secret lovers?

During the dessert course, Danny's brother and his wife, looking flushed, too, announced they were going for a walk on the beach.

She could guess what they had in mind and envied them.

Zane put his arm around her shoulders. "Tamiko, do you feel like a *walk*, too?"

Amused, she leaned into him and purred, "Mmm, I always enjoy a little exercise after a meal." Besides, it would get her away from the coconut ice cream, which smelled like Ric and was too darned tempting.

Hand in hand, she and Zane left the restaurant and headed down the beach, going in the opposite direction to the other couple. After checking that they were out of sight and no one had followed them, they waded in the ocean and beachcombed.

Then they strolled back, arms tight around each other's waists, and joined the group for the trip back to the Toucan.

When they arrived at the resort, Zane said he wanted to write, so Tamiko drifted into the gift shop to browse.

She found James Moncrieff studying a shelf of books. "Hi, Tamiko."

"If you're looking for a good book, I can recommend Zane's," she said with a grin.

"I'm afraid I'm not much of a fiction reader. I bought a history of Belize, and I've finished it, so I guess I'll move on to the flora and fauna."

The book he selected reminded her of a textbook—the kind she'd never had time to read when she was at school. She must have made a face, because he said, "Yeah, I know. Boring. I'm sure your life is far too exciting for you to want to sit down with a book, much less something like this."

"My life's not that exciting." She wasn't a party girl. Most of her earnings went to her family, and while there were always men happy to buy her drinks and dinner or take her dancing, they expected something in return that she wasn't prepared to give. "Most evenings, I'm home watching TV and knitting."

"You knit?" The expression on his face was comical.

"My mom taught me when I was little. It's relaxing. And creative."

"You're full of surprises." He reached up as if to adjust the knot of his tie. "Damn, that crazy woman took my tie."

"Dare I ask why you were wearing one?"

"It's habit. Every morning I put on pants and socks, a shirt and a tie. Sandals in summer, when classes are out."

She pursed her lips, deliberating. Normally an academic like him would have intimidated her, but he seemed genuinely nice—and a little clueless.

"James, I don't want to insult you, but you dress like a stodgy old professor."

"Well, I guess I am." He gave a dry laugh. "I started dressing this way when I was the youngest assistant professor. They called me the Baby Brit. I wanted to look older, more impressive."

Poor guy. She could relate to that kind of pressure. "Well, now you have silver threads in your hair, and didn't I hear you tell Zane you're head of the department? That sounds pretty impressive. Besides, you're in Belize."

She touched the blossom in her hair. "Believe me, this isn't how I dress in Manhattan. Look, you're a handsome man, but you hide it behind a bad haircut and boring clothes, so why not—?"

Realizing he was staring at her, she said, "What?" Had she offended him?

"You think I'm handsome?"

"Hello? Haven't you noticed some of the women checking you out? You look like Pierce Brosnan."

"Who?"

She shook her head in amusement. "You need to get out more."

A rush of excitement swept through her. "You, my friend, need a makeover, and I'm just the woman to help."

"A makeover?"

"Give me two hours, and you'll be turning female heads."

Tamiko expected him to dismiss the idea as frivolous. But instead, his lips—very sexy lips, now that she noticed—curved. "You can do that?"

She studied him. Classic bone structure, amazingly blue eyes with long dark lashes, those great lips. A dreadful haircut, but thick, glossy hair. Ho-hum clothes, but she'd seen him in swim trunks on the boat cruise. He might be a desk sitter, but he either worked out or had amazing genes, because his tall body was lean and lightly muscled, not chubby or saggy.

Her lips curved, too. "James, it'll be a snap." She took his hand. "Put yourself in my hands."

RIC was due home for dinner, but he hung out in the lobby as the wedding guests congregated before going to an Italian restaurant in San Pedro. He wanted a glimpse of Tamiko to tide him over for the next few hours.

Free came into the room, and Ric noted that his gaze went straight to Sarah, who was talking to the groom's father. Free didn't join them, though, instead choosing a group of Danny's friends.

Since Free and Sarah had hooked up that first night, not knowing each other's identity, Ric had kept a curious eye on them. He sensed he and Tamiko might not be the only ones sneaking around in the dark.

Giovanna swept into the lobby, and Ric gaped, blinked, refocused. No, she wasn't naked, but her form-fitting dress was close to her own skin color. Man, that was one hot woman. She had that same sexy, olive-skinned lushness as Salma Hayek and Jennifer Lopez. He'd overheard a couple of the young male guests calling her a MILF.

She caught his eye and blew him a kiss, and he made a gesture of catching it from the air and pressing it to his heart.

She smiled, then glanced around. Her expression sharpened, and he turned to see what had caught her attention.

Well, how about that. He'd heard from the receptionist that Tamiko and James had gone off in a golf cart, and now he understood what they'd been doing.

Tamiko, the makeover artist, had found a project.

And damn, she was good.

James looked fit and casually elegant in linen pants; a slim-fitting, short-sleeved blue shirt; and glossy leather sandals. A new haircut made him look younger and more vital.

"You're staring." It was Tamiko's voice, full of humor. She and Zane had come over to him while he was gaping at James.

Ric turned to her with a smile. "You're very good." And lovely, in a simple yellow dress with a yellow hibiscus blossom in her hair.

She gave a pleased laugh. "How did you know it was me?"

He tucked the flower more securely in place, an excuse to let his fingers caress her ear, her cheek. "James would never have put together that look on his own." He remembered her joking comment yesterday about Ric being perfect, and now he felt self-conscious about his own tousled hair and simple Toucan shirt over shorts. "I should get you to make me over, too."

Her eyes sparkled as she assessed him from head to toe. "I wouldn't change a thing."

The warmth in her voice, as well as the way her gaze lingered and her body shifted closer, made his blood heat.

Zane cleared his throat. "Hate to tell you, Tami, but Giovanna's shooting eye daggers at you. I don't know what you've done to piss her off, but methinks you don't want that woman as an enemy."

"I wonder if she's mad that I took James in hand?" she mused, attention still focused on Ric. "But why would she care?"

"Maybe because he's being flocked by a bevy of young beauties?" Zane said.

Ric chuckled at his phrasing, and he and Tamiko tore their gazes away from each other and glanced over at James. Sure enough, three of the female wedding guests were competing for his attention. And Giovanna, watching, didn't look the least bit pleased.

"You'd better go," Ric said, "and smooth things over with her." Quietly he added, "See you later."

SEVERAL hours later, aching with need, Ric waited in his and Tamiko's special place.

At last, she came into sight.

"Tami," he called softly.

She flew into his arms. "Ricardo."

He caught her, lifted her off her feet—light as a butterfly—and swung her around exultantly. "Finally!"

Then he lowered her and kissed her.

Their mouths knew each other now, and there was confidence in this kiss and a passion that took them from zero to a hundred in seconds flat.

He wore a short-sleeved shirt, unbuttoned and loose, and she wore a tank top. Braless. He could feel her budded nipples against his chest. Just as she would be feeling his rigid shaft through his shorts and her thin sarong.

He wanted her, ached for her, needed desperately to be inside her. The fire in her kiss, the bite of her nails on his shoulders, told him she felt the same.

And yet he remembered how she'd acted the first time they'd made love: shy and tentative, almost afraid. Some man had hurt her. The last thing he wanted was to reawaken that memory.

So he forced himself to break the kiss. To touch her gently, stroking her hair back from her face. "I missed you."

"Me, too."

He kissed her forehead, the delicate arch of her brows. Her eyes drifted shut, and he kissed the closed lids, felt the soft whisper of her lashes against his lips.

"It's been so hard," she whispered. "Seeing you, talking to you in public, and having to pretend we barely know each other."

He kissed his way down her slender nose, then licked her soft lips. "I know."

"There are downsides to having a secret affair."

A lot of them. But that was all they could have, so he focused on the positive. "This part's fun."

"Yes, it is." She nibbled the corners of his mouth, then darted her tongue inside.

Passion flared again, and a couple minutes later he had to pull away, gasping for breath. Hands on her shoulders, he said, "Tami, slow down. I'm so hot for you I'm going to explode."

She rested her hands at his waist. "And slowing down will help that?" He couldn't tell if she was teasing or if it was a genuine question.

He gave her an honest answer. "At this point, nothing's going to help."

She glanced down, then up at him through her lashes. "I'm hot for you, too. You don't need to . . . hold back. Last time was . . ." She gave an impatient toss of her head. "Look, I had a couple bad experiences, but you were wonderful. I trust you, and I want you."

Her words made his heart, as well as his dick, swell. "If you ever need to slow down or stop, tell me. Promise?"

She nodded solemnly. Then her eyes began to sparkle. "Right now, I'd rather speed up, if that's okay."

"Lord, yes."

With one quick gesture, she flicked his shirt off his shoulders. "I love your body."

"I love yours." He pulled her tank top over her head, gave a shuddering sigh at the sight of her pale, perfect breasts in the moonlight, then pulled her against him so he could feel her, flesh to flesh.

Her hands grappled with the fastenings of his shorts, and then they were dropping. He hadn't bothered with underwear, so now he stood naked in front of her, fully erect.

She ran her tongue around her lips, and he didn't think she was aware of doing it. The fact that it was natural, not deliberate, made it even more sexy.

Then she untied the bow that held her sarong in place, pulled the fabric away, and—oh shit, she was naked. Not even a tiny thong, just her own flat tummy, waxed mound, and slender thighs.

He had trouble tearing his eyes away. But when he did, he noted the curved palm tree behind her. It was shaped almost like a chair with a sloping back.

Grabbing the towel from the sand, he draped it along the trunk of the palm. Then he urged her toward the tree until she was half sitting, half leaning against it, her body as slim and pale in the moonlight as the curving tree trunk behind her.

"Ric?" she breathed.

"So beautiful." He ran a hand down her body, feeling the hard nub of her nipple, the smooth skin of her belly, of her mound.

Then he knelt on the sand and gently parted her thighs.

She let out a squeak, tensed, then slowly opened her legs.

He trailed his fingers between them, stroking her swollen folds, feeling hot dampness. He urged her to lie back a little more, to spread her legs farther. She smelled delicious, all musk and flowers and woman: delicate yet earthy.

The sand grated against his knees, but he didn't care as, holding her by the waist, he leaned in to lick her center.

Just the lightest touch at first, but when she moaned and pressed against him, he licked harder. He ran the flat of his tongue along her slit, then dipped the point of his tongue inside to taste her tangy essence.

She whimpered, grabbed his head, and held him there as he continued to lick. Gently, he inserted a finger, felt her grip it. Then she relaxed, so he could slide it in and out, and she grew even wetter, slicker, sweeter.

Her fingers bit into his scalp, her hips rocked, and she panted a breathy string of yeses.

Each rock of her hips, each thrust of his finger, resonated in his own body. His dick wanted warm heat, pressure, friction. It wanted to thrust and thrust and explode inside her.

He took her clit between his lips, sucked it gently, flicked his tongue across and around it.

She ground against him in a wordless plea, and he added a second finger inside her, sucked her clit a little harder.

Her muscles tightened, then she let out a soft cry and climaxed, pulsing against his mouth, around his fingers, in waves as relentless as the tides.

Waves that called to him and urged him to plunge in and follow her in climax.

Desperately he reached for his shorts with his free hand, found a condom in the pocket, and ripped the package open with his teeth. Only then did he ease his fingers out of her to sheathe himself.

Then he rose to stand between her thighs. Her head was thrown back against the tree trunk, her eyes closed. "So beautiful. Tami, do you want this?"

She opened her eyes, her expression glazed, then her focus sharpened and dropped to his dick. Staring at it, she said, "Yes. I want you, Ric."

He stepped closer, parted her moist folds, and eased the tip of his penis between them.

Her head went back again. "Oh, yes."

He wanted to lodge himself deep inside her in one urgent thrust, but instead he forced himself to go slowly, though it was sweet torture to hold back.

She took him in, embracing him with the heat of her narrow channel. Her arms came around his neck, and she leaned back against the trunk, pulling him with her. Her legs lifted to wrap around his hips, and the bulk of her weight rested on the palm trunk seat.

Slowly Ric began to pump in and out of her, fighting to stay in control.

Fortunately, her soft moans told him she wasn't far behind.

Lord, he just couldn't hold back any longer. He changed the angle slightly so his dick rubbed her clit, and she responded by pressing against him and whimpering needily.

"Now," she breathed.

He groaned with relief and let go, plunging hard once, twice, letting all the power of pent-up need gather and tighten his body. Then he thrust again, the climax roaring through him and surging into her as she cried out.

She clenched around him, then milked him with internal spasms that drained him dry.

Stars spun in the sky. Except his eyes were shut, so they must be spinning beneath his closed lids.

Tamiko still clung to him, but he could feel her arms and legs loosening, so he eased out of her then gathered her up. Cradling her with one arm, he managed to pull the towel from the palm trunk and throw it down on the sand, then he lowered her.

He lay beside her, an arm around her shoulders, and she curled her body into his, one leg under his and the other across his thighs, her head resting on his shoulder.

Gently she stroked his chest. "That was wonderful."

"It was."

"I'll remember this back in New York. It'll seem unbelievable."

Damn, yes, she'd be leaving soon. "I'll remember it, too." He'd miss her like crazy. Though he'd had to deny their relationship to everyone, for him it was special.

Tamiko was special. He barely knew her, yet already he felt closer to her than he'd ever felt to Jane or any other woman in his life. He could fall in love with her so easily.

It was crazy to think this way. Next week she'd be gone.

But she'd remember. This was special for her, too. The way she looked at him, responded to him, told him that.

Tonight he'd brought a very light blanket, just enough to keep her delicate skin from getting chilled by the night air. He tossed it over them, and it seemed almost as if they were snuggling cozily in bed together.

Stroking her hair as it lay over her shoulder, he said, "How was dinner tonight? I know Sarah figured people would be ready for a change from seafood and native dishes."

"They were, and the food was good. I had a tomato, bocconcini, and basil salad."

He waited, and when she didn't go on, said, "That's it?"

"I have to watch my weight."

"Don't you get hungry?"

"I've learned to ignore it. If I gain weight, my career's over." She lifted her head to gaze at him. "I know some people think models are too skinny, but we have to be to get fashion work. Do you think . . . ? I know I don't have very big breasts . . ."

Was she asking if he thought she was too thin? "Tami, you're beautiful. But you'd also be beautiful with another ten or twenty pounds on you. It seems so unfair, not being able to enjoy a good meal. Especially when you're not all that keen on modeling."

She shrugged and again rested her head on his shoulder. "A person has to work with what they've got. If I'd been smart and plain, I'd be an engineer or something."

"You're smart."

She shook her head. "No, Ric, I'm not." There was such certainty in her voice.

"Why do you say that?"

"I barely scraped through high school."

"Then the teachers were doing something wrong. You're smart. And you're responsible, looking after your mom and sister."

"We're family."

"How long have you been looking after them?"

"Since I was thirteen, when my father died and Mom was injured."

"Wow. How did you manage, if your mom couldn't work?"

"We lived with her cousin, but she didn't have much money either. I had part-time jobs. Being pretty helped. I was always tall, and with the right clothes and makeup, I looked older." She gave a soft snort. "Then, my family's survival depended on me looking older. Now, I have to look younger."

A quick hair toss, then she went on. "After school I cleaned houses for neighbors, which didn't pay much. Evenings, I worked in a bar. The owner knew I was underage and paid me off the books. I drew business and got great tips."

Exploitation of a minor. Yet how else would she and her family have been able to stay together? What a brave, amazing woman Tamiko was. "No wonder you had trouble with school if you were working so much."

"I had to stay home a lot, too, to look after Mom when she had a bad day or get her to the doctor. She was in pretty bad shape for a while."

"She was injured in the same car accident that took your dad?"

"She was injured the same night he died." She seemed to have chosen her words carefully.

He kissed the top of her head. "There's more to the story. I can hear it in your voice."

"It was a long time ago."

"Tami, I know we won't have much time together, but . . ." He shouldn't let himself care for her, yet he was powerless to resist. "I feel close to you. I want to know you. Don't shut me out."

"Oh, Ricardo." She pressed a soft kiss to his chest. "My mom has amnesia, and my sister was too young to know what was going on. It's . . . buried, and that's how it has to stay."

Buried? "You mean Zane, your friends, no one knows?"

"Zane knows part of it."

He thought that he'd never known a lonelier person. She'd been carrying such a burden since she was thirteen, and doing it all alone. He wished he could help.

"You don't always have to be so strong. Sometimes it's good to share. I'd like it if you trusted me that much."

# Chapter 9

UNDER her cheek, Tamiko heard the thump-thump of Ric's heartbeat, slow and steady. She felt so connected to him, and yes, she did trust him. "If anyone found out, it would ruin my career."

"I'd never tell a soul."

She believed him. But all the same . . . "You'd think less of me," she whispered. "It's pretty bad."

"I'd never think less of you."

Ric had given her an intimacy she'd never experienced before nor believed herself capable of. One that was both physical and emotional. He'd made her see that she might be able to love and perhaps even be loved.

She took a breath. "You gave me my first orgasm."

His hand, which had been stroking her shoulder, stilled. "Go on."

"I told you I'd had a bad experience or two. Well, back when I was a kid, it was worse than bad."

He gripped her tightly, too tightly. "Damn, Tami. You were abused?"

"Yes. Let go; you're hurting me."

"Jesus." He released her, and his fingers trembled against her skin. "I'm sorry. Who was it?" He started to roll onto his side to face her.

"No, don't. I can't look at you when I say this." She paused, waited for him to lie back.

He clasped her hand where it rested on his chest.

She took a breath. "It was my f-father." She had told Zane her dad had abused her, and left it at that. Not even her counselor had heard the rest, because it wasn't relevant to her frigidity. Now, the urge to share was compelling.

"He raped and beat my mom, too. She'd been brought up to obey her husband. He kept her almost imprisoned. They were immigrants."

Now that she'd broken the long, painful silence, words poured out. "He wouldn't let her learn English or have friends; she had to account for every moment of time, every penny of money. If she tried to stand up to him, he beat her up."

His body was tense. "Oh, Tami. I want to say she should have left, taken you kids away, but I know abused women get trapped. They don't see alternatives. And particularly if she didn't speak English, didn't know the services that might help."

She nodded, grateful he hadn't judged her mom. Over the years, she'd tried so hard herself not to judge.

"She killed him." The words slid out on a whisper of air. Tamiko didn't know if she'd intended to say them or if a force stronger than her own will had taken over.

"Shit." Ric's hand squeezed hers, hard. "The poor woman."

"She found out he was . . . coming to my room at night. She told him it had to stop. He beat her up, but she still didn't leave him."

Tamiko took a breath. "I don't know exactly what happened that afternoon, just what a neighbor and the police figured out. My parents had another fight, he smashed her around, and her head hit the kitchen counter. Before she passed out, she grabbed the knife she'd been using to chop onions, and swung at him." She swallowed. "It went into his heart."

Ric's strong arm tightened around her, and she curled gratefully against his solid warmth. Perhaps he expected tears, but she'd cried herself out years ago, and it hadn't solved a damned thing.

"A neighbor heard them screaming, called nine-one-one. When the police arrived, he was dead, and Mom was unconscious. She had an aneurysm, and it caused injury to her brain. She's never remembered what happened. The police didn't charge her."

"Tami, I'm so sorry." His voice sounded ragged. "That's horrible. I don't know what to say."

"Yeah. Well, it happened, and we moved on. The neighbor took Midori and me until Mom could leave the hospital, so we didn't have to go to Social Services. Then the three of us moved from California to Oregon to live with Mom's cousin. We changed our last name, started a new life. I told Mom and Midori that there was a car accident. That's what everyone believes."

She sighed. "There was some money in the bank, but no medical or life insurance. Mom's medical bills were horrendous. I still haven't paid them all off."

"You could have declared bankruptcy. That would have wiped out all the debts. Didn't anyone tell you that?"

"A social worker. But . . ." She shook her head. "It was a point of pride. We owed that money, and we were going to pay it. We *are* going to pay it. Once I sign with Sakura, I can finally be free of it, and that's going to feel so good. And I can pay out, or at least pay down, the mortgage on the cottage Mom's living in." What a relief that would be.

He rolled onto his side, and this time she let him gaze into her eyes. "You're the strongest person I know, Tami."

His words warmed her. She should say no, she'd only been doing what any good daughter would. But sometimes it had been hell, and she wanted to accept the pat on her back. "Thank you, Ricardo."

"Thanks for trusting me."

For a few minutes they just held each other under the light blanket he'd brought.

She felt exhausted yet at peace. Not so alone. Ric was right that sharing helped.

But she could only have done it with him. How, in such a short period of time, could she have come to feel this sense of connection, belonging, intimacy?

Gratefully, she kissed his lips. He responded, soft and tender.

They exchanged little kisses, ones that were almost innocent.

Against her belly, she felt his cock grow, but he made no move to thrust against her or deepen the kisses. He knew she was fragile.

Except she didn't feel so fragile anymore. Being with Ric empowered her.

Boldly she took the lead, sliding her tongue between his lips. Passion rose in her body, and she let him know with her kisses, with the wriggle of her hips, with the stroke of her fingers down his firm backside.

She tore her mouth from his and began to kiss every part of him she could reach. His cheek, his neck, his shoulder. She planted soft butterfly kisses and big, sloppy wet ones; she licked delicately and sucked so hard she might leave marks.

She cherished him and ate him up greedily, all at the same time.

And he did the same to her. Their bodies shifted under the blanket, twisting this way and that, always reaching for a new spot to kiss. And while they kissed, they caressed each other hungrily, legs twining together and then coming apart. They laughed breathlessly and sighed with pleasure.

The blanket was getting in their way. Tamiko, not the least bit cold now, threw it off. How beautiful Ric looked in the moonlight: his sleek, dark body; his wild, black hair; the flash of his white smile.

She sat up so she could stare at him and marvel, but he tugged her down again. His thigh was between hers, and she rubbed against him, her pussy damp and throbbing, hungry for contact.

He didn't let her stay there long. He was shifting position again, twisting his body to stay on the towel. They ended up both on their sides but reversed, so her head was near his bent knees. His face eased between her thighs.

She parted to give him access, and soon he was giving her big, wet licks that made her moan.

Arousal came so easily with Ric. Sex seemed so natural, so wonderful.

His tongue rubbed over her clit, and she gasped.

He knew just how to tease, to build that needy ache of pleasure. Long, firm tongue strokes, little lapping ones, the soft sucking pressure of his lips on her clit.

She writhed against him as tension mounted, then gave a shuddery gasp and came apart under his tongue.

As she drifted back to earth, she realized he was still licking her, but very slowly and gently now. She realized, too, that his erect cock was only inches from her face.

He made no demand, didn't thrust it closer.

She'd never imagined wanting to put a male organ in her mouth. But Ric's cock was so beautiful. With it, he'd given her so much pleasure.

She reached out to grasp it in one hand and ran her fingers up and down his shaft.

He pulsed, let out a soft groan. "Feels so good. But Tami, you don't have to."

His skin was silky over that hard, pulsing strength. She circled the crown with her finger. It was like warm velvet, with a drop of moisture in its tiny eye.

What did he taste like?

The thought was tantalizing.

She leaned forward and touched the tip of her tongue to that drop.

It was a little salty and made her think of the ocean.

"I want to, Ric."

Bolder now, she ran her tongue delicately over the crown, then circled under it. She licked down his shaft, tracing a big, throbbing vein.

Tasting him, feeling him, wasn't a turnoff; it was arousing, enhancing the sweet tension he was again creating in her pussy.

She licked her way back up, then, shivering with desire and a little fear, opened her mouth and closed her lips around his crown. She waited, hoping he wouldn't thrust, hoping she wouldn't panic. Neither thing happened, and gradually she relaxed.

Slowly she slid her lips down his shaft, taking more and more of him into her mouth.

"Mmm, I like that," he murmured, but still he didn't thrust.

Braver now, she swirled her tongue around the head of his penis, then began to slide her mouth up and down, her lips rubbing damply against his shaft.

She didn't feel choky or panicked; she felt like she was in control. Again, in their lovemaking, Ric had given her control.

And she knew from his moans that she was giving him pleasure.

Each time he moaned, his breath trembled across her intimate flesh, making her quiver in response.

She felt so sexy, so whole.

Arousal was building inside her, mounting toward orgasm.

The tension in Ric's body told her he felt the same way. She stroked his balls, caressing the furry sac, feeling them tighten.

Was she ready for him to come in her mouth? Again, anxiety shivered through her.

Ric kissed her between the legs, then pulled away from her, easing his cock from her mouth. "I need to be inside you, Tami."

Did he, or was he sensing her uncertainty? Either way, she was relieved and grateful. Taking things slow worked for her.

He sheathed himself and shifted position so they were side by side, then pulled her into his arms and kissed her.

Losing herself in that kiss, she almost didn't notice when he slid his knee between her thighs, but when his cock probed her sensitive folds, she sighed happily against his mouth.

He slipped inside her easily, and she gripped him, savoring the sensation.

He fit perfectly, and he made her feel so incredible. It was all so natural and right.

He pumped his hips slowly, his cock sliding almost all the way out, then pressing in, that velvety crown teasing her labia, brushing her clit. The fact that she'd explored him with her mouth, tasted him, made this even more intimate and intense.

And he'd tasted her. That was the flavor on his lips as he kissed her.

Physical intimacy, to match the emotional intimacy of sharing her deepest secrets.

Intimacy was a new word for her, a new experience.

Their bodies moved slowly, smoothly together, each motion erotic and arousing, each one building the sweet ache inside her. It felt as if their bodies had been designed for each other.

"Ric," she whispered. "Ricardo, you're amazing." And she meant much more than just sexually. What a special man he was.

He gave a soft laugh. "No, Tami, that's you."

His eyes were melting pools of reflected moonlight, and she stared into them, unable to look away.

"Come with me, sweet lover," he murmured.

The motion of his hips, the slide of his cock, were as smooth and even as the pulse of waves on the beach, as mesmerizing and enticing.

He had gripped her hand, woven his fingers through hers. Such a simple thing. A boyfriend-girlfriend kind of thing.

But she'd never really had a boyfriend, not one who respected and cherished her as Ric did. If she'd met someone like this years ago, how different her life might have been. It might have held love.

"Now, Tami." His breath brushed her lips. "Come and fly with me."

He filled her, hard and deep, and she shattered around him in pulsing waves of orgasm that went on and on as he jerked and cried out.

And then she shattered again, in a flood of tears that took her completely by surprise.

"Tami! God, are you okay?"

"I'm . . . good," she managed to choke out. "So good. Th-thank you." She wanted to thank him for healing her and bringing her to life. For urging her to share and for his understanding.

She wanted to thank him for the first true intimacy she'd ever experienced, for making her believe love might be possible.

There was so much to thank him for, but she was crying too hard to get the words out.

He didn't fuss, just gathered her close, stroking soothing circles on her back, brushing kisses against her hair.

Eventually, when Tamiko was all cried out, she sat up and reached for her beach bag. Inside was a small pack of tissues, and she used several, blowing her nose and drying her face.

Ric sat, too, arms looped around his knees, watching the ocean through the screen of bushes, giving her privacy.

When she tossed her bag aside again, he turned to her. "Feel better?"

"Yes." Her voice sounded choky from tears. "I've cried more with you than I have in the last ten years. But it's good. It's all good."

Except for one thing: the fact that their relationship was only temporary. This man was so special. She cared for him deeply, and the way he treated her told her he cared, too.

He was making her want things that weren't possible.

Love and family. With him.

# Chapter 10

TAMIKO woke to see morning sun through the slatted wooden blinds. She felt light, as if a burden had been lifted. But she was sad at the thought that soon she'd have to leave Ric.

Realizing she'd overslept, she hurried downstairs to find Zane tapping away on his computer. "You should have woken me. We've missed breakfast with the group."

"Don't worry about it."

Half an hour later, when they walked into the Toucan restaurant, only a handful of wedding guests lingered over coffee. A white-haired couple sat at a table on the ocean side.

"Who are they?" Tamiko whispered to Zane. "I've seen them around, but they're not part of the wedding group."

"I heard they come every year for their anniversary, and Ric let them stay despite the wedding."

Wasn't that just like him?

When she and Zane walked by their table, the older man said, "Good morning."

"Isn't it a fine one?" Zane said. "We're Zane and Tamiko, and we're here for the wedding."

"Pleased to meet you. We're Bill and Ellie Everleigh." His accent said they were from England.

"I understand it's your anniversary," Tamiko said. "Congratulations."

"Sixty wonderful years," Mrs. Everleigh said.

Her husband sent her a twinkling glance. "Glad you made the right decision, aren't you, love?"

"The decision to say yes?" Tamiko asked.

"Yes to Bill," the woman said. "I had another young man propose to me, too. My dad thought I should marry him because he was a solicitor, whereas Bill was just a gardener."

"Obviously you disagreed," Zane said.

"My granny had a word with me." Ellie Everleigh gazed at him, then Tamiko. "She said, 'You need to follow your heart. It won't steer you wrong.' "

"I agree," Tamiko said. And she was, in looking after her mom and Midori. It was a pity that her heart also yearned for Ric. The more she saw of him, the deeper her feelings. It would be so easy to love him. Or maybe she already did.

She sighed, then told the other woman, "I'm so glad things worked out for you."

"Oh, yes, my heart steered me well." Ellie reached over to squeeze her husband's arm. "Years of happy marriage, children, ten grandchildren, and four great-grands so far. Not to mention, my gardener here ended up owning the biggest nursery and landscaping business in the county, and we have the prettiest yard you ever did see."

The two of them went off to stroll the beach, and Tamiko and Zane settled at a table and ordered breakfast. "So," Zane said, "let's hear about last night."

She couldn't tell him she was falling for Ric. Zane had wanted her to find her sensual side, and she had. He'd be devastated to know she'd been foolish enough to fall for her holiday lover and would be going home with a bruised heart. "I'm having a ball with Ric. He's the sweetest, sexiest man."

"Next to Graham."

"Ah, but Graham's taken."

FROM breakfast, they went to the resort lobby, where Sarah had scheduled dance lessons for the guests.

She and Zane danced a bit, a lively Belizean dance called the punta, then he said he needed a break, and they moved off the floor. He pointed toward James Moncrieff, who was dancing with the female instructor. "That man's in damned good shape for a middle-aged desk jockey like me."

"He told me yesterday he plays basketball. And he sure knows his way around a dance floor." The man looked pretty darned sexy, too.

So did Giovanna, who was dancing with one of Danny's friends. The young man was awkward but enthusiastic, and Giovanna looked the epitome of fiery sexuality with her swirling hips and tossing hair. Her gaze was fixed not on her partner but on James.

She was an emotional woman, Tamiko knew. Last night she'd kind of lost it, accusing Tamiko of making a play for James. Once she'd heard the makeover story, though, she'd apologized profusely.

As Zane had said earlier, the opposite of love was indifference, and Bella's parents were anything but indifferent to each other.

RIC was in his office meeting with the accountant, but it was hard to concentrate on numbers when the sexy pulse of punta music penetrated the closed door. Was Tamiko out in the lobby, dancing?

Just as he and the accountant finished up, the music ended. Ric headed for the lobby to see how things were going. To see if Tamiko was there.

This week was going sideways. Tami was so much more than a sexy secret fling. He'd never met a stronger, sweeter, more fascinating woman. What he'd felt for Jane was shallow compared to the emotions Tamiko aroused in him. And he knew she cared for him, too. Not only had she trusted him with her lovely, fragile body but with her deepest, darkest secrets.

When he saw her talking to Zane and Giovanna, he couldn't stay away. They all greeted him with smiles, and Tamiko's was particularly warm.

Their eyes exchanged a secret message before she gave a tiny, rueful shrug and refocused on the conversation.

The three Manhattanites were comparing notes on their favorite restaurants. Zane raved about the sauces at a place with a fancy French name, Giovanna praised the white truffle risotto at an Italian bistro, and Tamiko weighed in with her favorite place for sashimi.

Ric had nothing to offer to the conversation.

Nor to Tamiko, after this week.

Listening to them was a harsh reminder that, much as he might care for her, she belonged with people like this, not with him.

The instructors called for attention and asked the dancers to reassemble to learn the salsa.

He wished he could dance with Tamiko, but since he couldn't, he was glad she and Zane decided not to hang around. It would drive him nuts to see her in another man's arms, dancing as if they were lovers.

As they left, Tamiko's gaze met his with a special message. *Tonight.*

Giovanna did a sexy shimmy in front of him. "Come be my partner, darling?"

He raised his hands, smiling. "You're too hot for me, Giovanna."

She gave a mock pout.

As he watched the guests, clad in shorts and tropical shirts, sarongs, even bathing suits, Ric thought Sarah had been clever to plan the dance lesson for Thursday. Earlier, some of the guests might have been inhibited. But now they'd mixed and mingled for days, they'd swum in the ocean and burned their noses, they'd downed tropical cocktails and Belikin beer.

He realized Giovanna was staring at James. The man clearly knew the dance, and his partner was picking it up quickly, putting extra oomph in her hip wriggles.

With seductive grace, Giovanna walked over to the couple. "Let me show you how it's done," she said to James. And, to the girl, "You'll excuse us, won't you?"

The girl looked stunned, and Ric quickly strode toward her. "Want to dance?"

"You bet, Ric."

He'd danced salsa most of his life, and his partner had a good sense of rhythm, but her sexy hip action didn't arouse him one bit.

He glanced over to make sure the exes weren't fighting and sucked in a breath. Now, that was salsa. So hot you could almost see the air around them smoking.

These were the two who hated each other? Looked more to him like they wanted to fuck each other's brains out.

Of course, maybe they were both just excellent dancers.

The instructors had that fiery look, too, and they weren't a couple. It was all about the performance.

The tune ended, and James dipped her. Slowly down, slowly up, their gazes locked together.

He murmured something that made her gasp.

She muttered something in reply, and they stalked off in opposite directions.

Ric let out a whistle under his breath. At least this time the sparks hadn't combusted into a quarrel.

FRIDAY morning, Ric's mom was scrambling eggs and toasting banana bread while he sliced papaya. Mara, at the table, enthusiastically crayoned in a coloring book.

"You have a good time last night?" his mom asked softly.

"Yes." He'd given up trying to hide what was going on, though he'd sworn her to secrecy.

"You're getting yourself in deep."

Oh yeah.

But that was his problem, not his mom's. He shrugged, trying to act nonchalant. "That'd be silly, with her going back to New York on Sunday."

"Uh-huh." She popped the toast. "You thought of asking her to stay?"

If only that was a possibility. "And repeat the J-A-N-E mistake?" He spelled it out so, if Mara overheard, she wouldn't recognize the name of her absent mother.

"I like Tamiko. Maybe she's different."

"She is, in a lot of ways." Family-oriented, responsible. Yet there was one big similarity. "But she's a city girl, too, and hates small towns."

She sighed. "I'm sorry, Ricardo."

The warm sympathy in her eyes got to him, and he said, "Yeah. Me, too."

When they were all seated, eating breakfast, she said, "You're going to have a busy weekend, what with that wedding."

"Sure will." Last night Tamiko had told him the bride and groom had had a major spat, but they'd agreed Bella and Danny were so much in love they'd surely make up.

"Seems like a good time for Mara and me to go on a sleepover at Vicky's house." Rick's cousin, her husband, and their little girl lived a few miles away.

Mara looked up from her eggs. "Yay! Sleepover."

If they left, he'd have the house to himself. He and Tamiko could make love in a real bed. They could be as noisy as they wanted, without fear of anyone walking by on the beach and hearing. Maybe she could even stay the night.

He studied his mom's face, and she gave him a sweet, sad smile. "Take the moments you can, son, and store up the memories."

ON Friday night, after the wedding rehearsal and dinner, Zane and Tamiko walked back to their cabana.

"That was quiet compared to last night at the Crown Jewel," he said. "No fireworks."

"I'm so glad Bella and Danny worked things out. They're so in love, and it's obvious they belong together."

Perhaps she sounded wistful, because he shot her a sharp glance. "It's your second to last night with Ric."

"I know." There was a bittersweet poignancy to every remaining moment with him.

Inside the cabana, Zane said, "It's become more than a fling, hasn't it?" He touched her shoulder gently. "I see how you look at him, girl. You've gone and fallen for him."

She ducked her head and didn't answer. Admitting out loud that she loved Ric would make it even more real, more painful, and it would make Zane feel guilty.

Sure enough, he said, "It's my fault. I thought it would help you, and I didn't realize . . ."

She raised her head. "It did help. I'm a different person." She'd discovered so much about herself. If a bruised heart was the price she had to pay, so be it.

"Guess there's a reason I write thrillers, not romances," he said ruefully. "A love story's supposed to have a happy ending."

She hugged him. "Mine can't, but what about you and Graham?"

He sighed.

She stared him in the eyes. "You have a huge audience, Zane. If you come out of the closet, yes, maybe you'll lose a few fans and a few friends, but you'll gain some, too, and find out who your true friends are."

"But, it's—"

She cut him off. "How can you compare sales figures to being able to be yourself? To living openly with the man you love?"

He gazed at her in wonder. "Damn, Tamiko, you've never talked to me this way."

"That happy ending is within your reach, Zane, if you have the guts to go for it."

"Are you sure it's not within yours? I see how he looks at you, too."

She bit her lip. Ric was gentle, considerate, passionate. Her heart told her he genuinely cared for her.

Since she'd been thirteen, practicality had ruled her life. Except for this past week, when she'd let sensuality, romance, even a dream or two slip in.

She shook her head. "Ric belongs here," she said sadly, "and my whole life is in New York. I need my career, Sakura, the income to look after my family."

# Chapter 11

IT was around eleven when Tamiko strolled from the cabana, trying to look casual in case someone saw her.

She loved the idea of going to Ric's home, yet it scared her, too. All week, their affair had kept moving to deeper levels of intimacy.

For the first time in her life she was in love. And in a couple of days she'd be gone. She and Ric could keep in touch by e-mail, but that would only prolong her misery. It would keep a dream alive, when she had no business dreaming.

When she reached the main building of the resort, she didn't walk through the lobby. Instead, as Ric had instructed her, she took a path that led toward the garden and parking lot. The route was unfamiliar, so she picked her way slowly, with only the light of the moon and the stars to show her the way.

Suddenly a tall body barreled out of the darkness and nearly ran her down. They both gasped, and she saw it was James.

"Oh!" She put a hand to her chest where her heart thudded quickly. "You startled me."

"I'm, er, going for a walk."

More like a run, she thought, though he was lugging a bulging tote bag. "Me, too."

"On the beach," he clarified.

Where else would a tourist be walking on a balmy evening on Ambergris Caye? Though of course she was going in the opposite direction. "The garden," she said. "It's, uh, so peaceful."

"Oh. Yes. Well, have a good walk."

"You, too."

Relieved he hadn't questioned her story, she carried on. She'd only gone a few steps when something rustled ahead of her. Human or animal? Nervously, she said, "Hello?"

Another man stepped toward her. "Hello?" It was Free, clad only in shorts. "Tamiko?"

This time she had her story ready. "I'm going for a walk in the garden. It's so peaceful."

"Garden? Yeah, I guess. I'm, uh, going to the beach. For a run."

"You may see James. He just headed out for a walk."

"Oh, uh, okay. Bye now." And he hurried off.

Was anyone else wandering around on this fine Friday night?

It seemed not. She hurried through the garden and parking lot, then across the road. After making sure there was no car in Ric's driveway, she went around to the back of the house. The door was unlocked, as he had said it would be.

A muted light burned in the kitchen. "Ricardo?"

He rushed into the room. "Tami, you're here." He caught her tight and kissed her warmly, and she thought how totally right it felt.

Before she could settle into the embrace, he took her hand and tugged her down a hallway. Instrumental music with a seductive tropical beat beckoned.

When she stepped through the open door, she gasped.

The queen-sized bed was strewn with hibiscus blossoms of every color imaginable. Shutters slanted open, and a whisper of tropical night air made half a dozen candles flicker. She glanced around, noting framed underwater photographs of colorful fish on the wall, together with Mara's artwork. On the bedside table was an ice bucket with a draped bottle in it, and two flute glasses.

She was touched that he'd done all of this for her. "Ric, this is wonderful. Thank you."

"The best Belize has to offer." He made a rueful face. "I'm sure it's a long stretch from what you're used to in Manhattan."

Gently she shifted some of the blossoms on the bed and sat down. The scent of flowers drifted in from Perlita's garden, and she thought about the traffic exhaust smell of New York's streets. She smoothed down the sundress she was wearing, so comfortable compared to her New York wardrobe. "Yes, Belize is definitely different."

And Belize had Ric. Returning to New York was going to be so hard.

The first day she'd arrived here, she'd thought it would be bliss to live in Belize, and that was before she'd even met Ric Nuñez.

Forcing a smile, she took the glass he handed her. "Here's to Belize and the most amazing week I've ever experienced. And to you, Ricardo, for being so wonderful."

"Ah, Tami." He sat down beside her and clinked his glass with hers. "Here's to you. And to Zane, for bringing you into my life."

They both took a drink, then gazed at each other.

"Will you think of me?" she asked softly. "And miss me?"

"More than you can imagine." He gripped her arm.

The sincerity in his voice, the way his fingers trembled, warmed her heart. Not having the nerve to say she loved him, she put her hand over his and settled for, "Me, too. I wish this didn't have to end so soon."

"I feel the same."

For one crazy moment, she let herself dream. "I guess there's no way you'd move to New York?"

"Oh, Tami." He bit his lip. "The resort, Mara, my mom . . . I just don't see how."

"And besides," she said sadly, "it wouldn't suit you. You belong here."

"Yeah. And you'd never come here. You belong in Manhattan."

Would he want her to come if she could? She stared down at their joined hands, letting her hair fall in wings around her face. Dreams were nice, but she had to face reality. Her family's future depended on Sakura. No way could she make that kind of money in Belize. "Sad, but true."

"Sad?" He tilted her face toward him, hooking the hair behind her ears. Expression puzzled, he said, "But you love Manhattan."

"No. I make my living there."

"You once said you hated small towns, so I thought . . ."

Had she? "I hated the towns where I grew up, because everyone gossiped, and it was so tough for my family. At least New York has let me be anonymous. Though that'll end with Sakura." She sighed, then shrugged off that thought. Loss of anonymity was a small price to pay. "But the city is intimidating, and so fast-paced."

Ric stared at Tamiko as she said, "Belize is so much nicer. You're lucky to live here."

He put his arm around her, having trouble understanding. "But what about all the restaurants and theaters and shops?"

She snuggled into him. "I'm on a tight budget, and it's not really me, anyhow. Well, food would be, but my agent yells if I gain a pound."

He'd imagined Tamiko perched on a stool in a ritzy martini bar, wearing a sophisticated cocktail dress and mile-high heels, gossiping with beautiful women and handsome, successful men. Now he had no image to replace that one with. "How do you spend your free time?"

"Yoga, walking, reading, knitting in front of the TV. Calling my mom or sister." Softly, almost under her breath, she said, "Sometimes, hearing their voices is the only thing that keeps me going."

Then she squared her shoulders. Tone artificially bright, she said, "Thank heavens for my long-distance calling plan."

"You really miss your family."

"Of course."

She supported a family she couldn't even be with. He raised his glass. "I do admire you."

"I admire you, too. You're building a wonderful business, you're doing a great job raising Mara, you and your mom have a terrific relationship, and you're just . . . a really nice man, Ric."

Her words were ones to remember and treasure. "When I first saw you, this gorgeous model from New York, I was attracted to you but thought we had nothing in common. And yet we do."

She nodded. "It's going to be so strange—so awful—not having you in my life."

His breathing hitched. "In less than a week, you've somehow become a part of me." When she left, she'd tear a chunk out of his life. His heart.

Misty-eyed, Tami said, "Me, too."

And he realized he really was in love with her. He'd been fighting the idea because he knew she'd have to leave.

If he loved her, he had to think about moving to New York, much as he hated that idea. He needed to be near Tamiko, to find out if she might come to love him, too.

But what would he do for a living? How would Mara adjust? And what about his mom? She hadn't loved his dad enough to leave her beloved home. She'd do it for him and Mara, but was it fair to ask her to move to a place that grew skyscrapers rather than the lush plants she so loved?

Tamiko lifted her chin. "Damn, this is feeling like good-bye, and we still have tonight and tomorrow night."

"We do." He spoke absently, his mind racing. At breakfast, his mom had asked whether he might ask Tamiko to stay in Belize. And he'd said her life was in New York.

But she didn't like her work or the city. She missed her mom but had to live apart from her in order to support her. And she didn't see any alternative.

He needed to lay his heart on the line.

"Tami." He grasped her hands and held them tight. "I've fallen for you in a big way." Her eyes widened, but before she could speak, he went on. "Fallen in love with you."

"Oh!" Her face lit with wonder. "You have? I can't believe . . . I mean, no one's ever . . ." She took a big breath, then beaming, laughing a little, she said, "I'm in love with you, too. I just can't believe this."

"You are?" Exultation filled him. "Lord, I can't believe it. Tami, that's—" What the hell was he doing talking when he could be kissing her?

He pulled her into his arms and touched his lips to hers. Gazing into her eyes, seeing the truth of her love in them, he kissed her gently. A loving kiss that made the world stand still.

Until Tamiko eased away. "Oh, Ricardo, this is wonderful, but it's awful, too. What can we do?"

"We should be together. We need a chance to see where our relationship's going to go."

"But you can't move to New York, and I can't make enough money here to support my mom."

"I can help."

Her lips parted, quivered. "You'd do that? You are so sweet. But you've told me how tough it is to make a go of the Toucan. And you've got Mara and your own mom to think of."

He thought back to the day he'd come home to find Tamiko with his mom, daughter, and Otty.

An idea hit him, maybe a brilliant one that would work for everyone. "Otty Martinez is lonely since her husband died."

Tamiko looked at him as if he'd lost his mind. "Poor Otty."

"She was used to looking after someone, having company."

"I'm sure it's tough."

The confusion on her face and his own nervous energy brought him to his feet. Staring down into her lovely eyes, he scrubbed a hand across his jaw. "I bet she'd like it if your mom moved in."

Tamiko's hand flew to her throat. "Mom?"

"It could be good for both of them." He strode to the door and back again to stand in front of her. "Options. Let's think about options. There's more than one way the future could go."

"I guess, but—"

"You could sell the house in Oregon. No more mortgage, and

the proceeds would help pay the medical bills. I can help, too. I was saving money to add a spa to the resort, but it can wait."

"Ric! I can't let you—"

"Tami, stop." He grabbed her hands. "We've come so far this week, it doesn't feel right to go back to being two separate people with careers in different places. Damn, I wish we had more time."

He shook his head vigorously. "That's what I want to do. Buy us more time, to see where our love takes us."

Her wide eyes searched his face. "I'd like that, too, but if . . . if I did move here, what would I do for work? I doubt there's much modeling in Belize." She swallowed. "Actually, I'm a pretty good waitress."

"No. You did that when you were a desperate teenager." There'd be bad memories. Besides, what a waste of her talents. An idea struck him. "You transformed James. And Otty's thrilled with that new hairstyle you talked her into. You have a real talent for makeovers."

"Thanks. I love helping people. But, are you thinking . . .?"

"I'm thinking you could make money doing what you love, like I do. And Mom, with her landscaping. We could offer makeovers as a special feature at the Toucan, and you'd get resort guests as well as locals. The stores and hair salons would give you commissions on sales, I bet, and—"

Shaking her head, she broke in. "Ric, this is too much to take in. I—"

"I know. It's a lot to think about." He knelt in front of her and rested his forehead against hers. "It's too soon to decide all these things. I'm only raising ideas."

He gave a soft laugh. "If we'd known each other a couple months, I'd probably be proposing."

"Proposing?" she echoed breathlessly. "Wow. Oh Ric, I've never felt this way before. And what you're suggesting . . . It's so big."

"I know. We need time. But if you sign with Sakura, we won't get it. You've always been so responsible; I know how hard it must be to think of turning down the contract."

She nodded solemnly.

"Of gambling on our love and a future together."

"Together," she breathed. "It's always been just me."

"Remember what I said about sharing? Well, how about sharing your present and future?" He took a deep breath, trying to calm down.

Framing her delicate face with his hands, he said, "Think about it. We'll talk some more. But right now, you lovely, sexy lady—Tami Sato, the woman I love—I want to hold you and make slow, sweet love with you."

As he'd spoken, the tension had eased from her face. Now she gave him a tender, glowing, misty-eyed smile. "That sounds perfect to me, Ricardo Nuñez, the man that I love."

How he loved to hear those words.

She rose, pulling him up with her, and they stepped into each other's arms. He loved how she fit there. He didn't have to lean down; she didn't have to stretch up. Their bodies had been made for each other.

Their lips met, and when they kissed, he knew it was love they shared, and tenderness, passion, and hope.

She stepped away, pulled her sundress over her head, and skimmed a tiny thong down her hips. Naked in the flickering candlelight, she was slim and elegant with her pale skin and long, black hair, soft and sexy with her pink-tipped nipples and gentle curves.

No way would he let this woman go.

Ric hurried to strip off his shirt and shorts.

He lifted her and gently placed her on the bed, an Asian orchid amid the bright hibiscus blossoms.

One day this beautiful, brave, incredible woman might be his wife, his partner in life.

He sat beside her and bent to kiss her reverently.

Her fingers buried themselves in his thick hair and held him as she took charge and deepened the kiss.

When they broke for air, she pulled him down onto the flowery bed and rose over him, long hair drifting across his body as she kissed and licked her way down his chest and rib cage.

She showed no hesitation. In the last few nights, she'd turned into a confident lover, secure and unafraid.

Her deft hands explored his dick, then she wrapped a handful of black hair around it and slid it up and down in a thousand silky caresses. And then she let her hair go, cascading across his belly. Behind the black curtain she took him into her mouth.

The press of her lips, the glide of her tongue, made his blood pound, and after a few exquisite minutes he had to catch her shoulders and stop her.

He pressed her down among the crushed blossoms and took his turn kissing her.

One by one, he cherished all her secret places.

The inside of her elbow, the hollow of her armpit.

The sandy-tasting Vs between her toes, the back of her knee.

The curve of her hip bone, the sweet dimple of her navel.

She giggled, whimpered, and moaned as he left his mark.

By the time he reached the sweetest place of all, the slick, swollen petals between her legs, the delicate pearly bud of her clit, it took only a few firm strokes of his tongue to bring her to a shuddering climax.

She cried out, "Ric, oh yes, my love!"

He sheathed himself and slid inside her. "I love you, Tami." His dick was surrounded by the gentle waves of aftershock that rippled through her vagina.

He rolled so she was on top, her thighs hugging his hips. Together they began to move, her rising and falling on him as he thrust gently, gazing into her beautiful face.

Smiling, she gazed back, dark eyes passionate and loving. "This feels so good, Ricardo. So right, you and me."

Lithe and flexible, she bent to kiss him. Her soft breasts pressed against his chest, and he hugged her close as their tongues mirrored the motions of their lower bodies.

Slow and gentle soon gave way to hard and driving.

As they both reached the breaking point, they stopped kissing, too busy gasping for air. Gazing into each other's eyes, they made wordless sounds of need and pleasure and breathed each other's names.

Then their bodies surged into climax, and they cried out together, "I love you."

They stayed locked together until the last ripples of orgasm had faded. And long after.

Ric sighed. Drained, satisfied, joyful.

Finally, they separated, and Tamiko rolled onto her back. He sat up, shoving pillows behind his back. "Sit up, pretty lady, and I'll give you some more champagne."

She shifted position, each motion of her slender limbs graceful among the hibiscus blooms. When she was sitting, she took the glass he handed her and had a small sip. "Pity this yummy stuff has calories."

"Move to Belize, and you can forget about counting calories." He grinned. "Not that I'm trying to bribe you or anything."

She took a larger sip. "I was talking to Mr. and Mrs. Everleigh this morning. Those two are so happy together. She told me it's all because she followed her heart."

"Wise woman. So, Tami, what does your heart tell you?"

She studied his face, eyes bright with hope. "That my story can have a happy ending after all."

Sexy Exes

# Chapter 1

Ambergris Caye, Belize—Sunday, February 8

GIOVANNA, walking arm in arm with her daughter Bella, followed the wedding planner toward a cute thatched cottage on stilts, with a bright red door and shutters.

"This is your cabana," Sarah said. "Wild Ginger."

"It's adorable," Giovanna told her. How lovely to be in this sunny spot with her beautiful daughter and see the way she glowed with happiness. Her fiancé, Danny, was a nice man, a good match for her.

The only cloud on Giovanna's horizon was having to see her ex again after all these years.

She shoved that thought away and focused on the charming details: the ceramic footbath and the hammock, a gecko sunning itself, the stylized painting of wild ginger on the door.

Inside, she glanced around the room. Rattan furniture, ocean-colored fabrics, white walls, dramatic paintings of flowers, orchid plants here and there. "This is delightful."

Bella gave an impatient bounce, like the little girl she'd been not so long ago. "Mama, I want to see the dress!"

"Of course, *tesora*." Getting a designer wedding gown on such short notice, and without the bride available for fittings, would have been impossible for most women. But Giovanna Moncrieff was not most women. She was friends with Fabiana, one of New York's hottest designers, and could afford the gigantic price tag. Only the best would do for her daughter's wedding. She couldn't wait to see Bella's face when she saw the gown.

Giovanna turned to the wedding planner. Touching her shoulders with red-tipped fingers, she gave her a light kiss on each cheek. "Sarah, you've done an amazing job. Thank you so much."

"You're very welcome. I'll leave you two alone."

Bella was already hurrying up the steps to the sleeping loft where Sarah had said Giovanna's luggage—the two big cases she'd brought for herself plus the wardrobe bag with the wedding gown—would be waiting.

Her mother followed, crossing her fingers. She was confident her daughter would love the dress, but would it fit? "I brought matching thread and lace. You're sure there's someone here who's competent to do alterations, if they're needed?"

"Ric says there's a woman across the street, Otty something, who's a great seamstress." Bella unzipped the garment bag and eased out the dress, then squealed and hugged Giovanna. "Oh Mama, it's even more beautiful than the pictures."

She hugged her back. "And you're going to look so lovely in it." She shoved her daughter away. "Go on, I can't wait. Try it on."

While Bella pulled off her shorts and tank top, Giovanna unbuttoned the back of the dress, then she helped her daughter into it and buttoned her up.

Bella turned around, her expression anxious. "Do I look okay?"

Oh, yes. Giovanna's eyes filled with tears as she stared at the vision in front of her. "*Bellissima*. Go and look."

She blinked hard as her daughter walked toward the full-length mirror.

Fabiana had worked magic. She'd combined classic lines, feminine touches, and a casual feel to create a dress that absolutely matched Bella's joyful personality and the beach setting of the wedding.

"It's beautiful," Bella breathed.

"It's utterly gorgeous, and so are you." She remembered the day she and James had decided to name their newborn Bella. Italian for beautiful. Already the two of them had been having problems, but Giovanna, hormonal and even more emotional than usual, had hoped that their tiny, lovely girl would meld them into a loving family.

And now, there was no "she and James," and her little girl was grown up and getting married.

"Mama, are you crying?"

"Just a little. I'm entitled."

Bella flung her arms around her. "Thank you so much. This is the best dress in the world. I love you."

"I love you, too." If Giovanna could have one wish, it would be that her daughter's marriage to Danny was a happy one.

Her mind flashed back to the day seven months before Bella was born, when she and James had climbed on the plane in Rome, bound for a new life in the United States. After a wildly passionate summer, she was leaving Italy, engaged to the young Englishman she'd fallen madly in love with.

She had been as full of hopes and dreams as Bella was now.

What a fool she'd been.

A waitress, engaged to a university professor who lusted after her but was only marrying her because she'd gotten pregnant. His true love wasn't her but his brand-new appointment at Tufts University.

The thought of James made her jaw tighten. "Your father gets in this afternoon?" Giovanna had switched her own flight to make sure she arrived first and had private time with Bella.

"Yeah." Bella bit her lip. "You know how much I appreciate you coming. I couldn't get married without both of you here."

Giovanna managed a smile and teased, "If you ever had any doubts, now you know how much I love you, *tesora*."

"It'll be okay. Sarah's scheduled events to minimize contact between you."

But he'd be *there*, which he hadn't in ages. They'd barely even conversed since they split up when Bella was five. If they tried to talk, they fought. Or, more often, she screeched like a banshee and he slashed her with icy disdain.

Their wisest decision—after the one to divorce—was hiring a mediator to handle communication and help sort out matters relating to Bella.

"Why did your father have to come for this pre-wedding week?" Giovanna demanded. "He should have had the decency to just fly in for the actual ceremony."

"He had the *kindness* to come and be with me, the same way you did."

Ha! A pointed reminder that she, too, could have waited until the last minute to arrive.

And now she almost wished she had.

It was all very well, in the safety of her elegant apartment on Park Avenue, to be curious about how James had aged. In her mind, she'd thinned his thick, dark hair and given him a huge bald spot. A potbelly, too, which was likely, given how out of shape he'd been when she last saw him.

The crucial thing was that he'd look much, much older than she.

Which of course he would, because she looked fabulous. Everyone said so, and the admiring looks she received from men of all ages didn't lie.

But James would likely still think she looked flashy and cheap. The man wouldn't recognize a designer dress if it bit him on his no doubt saggy ass.

Back then, her clothes had been inexpensive, but in Italy he'd thought she looked hot. It was only when they reached Medford, and bloody Tufts University, that he'd changed his opinion. There, everything she'd done was wrong. "He wanted me to dress like his pompous friends." Too late, she realized she'd said the words aloud.

Bella held up her hands. "Mama, you know I don't want—"

"I know. Sorry. I didn't mean to say it." The one thing she and James had actually agreed on when they split up was to not bad-mouth each other to Bella. Which meant they never spoke about each other, because neither had kind words to say.

Giovanna resisted asking whether he still had his hair. Still, she couldn't stop herself from saying, "You're sure he's not bringing a date?"

"Positive. Things are going to be awkward enough."

But was he dating anyone seriously? She knew Bella would have let her know if he had married, but in general she'd told her daughter she didn't want to hear about James. That way, she could avoid thinking about him. But now . . .

Damn. It would be beneath her dignity to ask. "It's going to be a very long week," she grumbled.

"Don't frown, Mama. You'll get wrinkles."

"Pah!" It was a standing joke. Giovanna, now the head of Venezia Cosmetics, had been giving Bella similar beauty tips since she was ten.

Her little girl. A woman now, and in a week she'd be Danny's wife. Sniffing back fresh tears, she flung her arms around Bella. "I want this to be a beautiful, unforgettable week for you. I'll be good, *tesora*. I promise."

JAMES walked into the shop in the Toucan Resort lobby. His daughter Bella had laughed her head off when he'd admitted he'd come to Belize without a bathing suit.

He'd retorted that she and Danny had decided to get married on such short notice, he'd barely had time to pack at all.

As chair of the Department of History at Tufts, he had many responsibilities. He'd had to persuade his teaching assistant she was capable of covering his lectures and go over his notes with her. Then there'd been meetings with the grad students he supervised, and administrative tasks to either handle, delegate, or postpone.

In his few spare moments, he'd found himself wondering about Giovanna.

They'd divorced when Bella was five, believing a broken family would be healthier for their beloved daughter than listening to their constant battles. Giovanna, who exaggerated everything, probably told her friends the divorce had saved her from killing him or vice versa.

Since then, they'd rarely spoken to each other. And Bella, hating tension and refusing to take sides, didn't talk to him about Giovanna. Pretty much all he'd learned over the years—mostly by catching his daughter off guard or stooping to eavesdrop on her phone conversations—was that Giovanna had taken some college courses, now worked in cosmetics, and had dated lots of men but never settled down with one.

The cosmetics and the men were no surprise. College was. His ex had never shown the slightest interest in academia.

"Sir, would you like to try those on?" A polite female voice interrupted his thoughts.

He realized he had his hand on a pair of board shorts in vivid orange and yellow. "Do you have something more conservative?"

Even as he said the last word, he imagined Giovanna's snort. The first year they'd been married, he had been the youngest assistant professor on faculty—the Baby Brit, they'd called him—and desperate to look dignified. He'd chosen a wardrobe that was conservative. She'd told him he looked stuffy and pompous.

Well, at least *he* had looked respectable. Those revealing clothes she'd worn in Italy had been completely inappropriate for a professor's wife. Giovanna had been so voluptuous, so sensual, she should have dressed to tone down those qualities rather than flaunt them. He'd hated the way the male profs and students had looked at her.

"How about these, sir?" The salesclerk handed him a pair of navy trunks.

"Great, thanks."

"Want to try them on?"

"No, they look fine."

"Anything else for you?"

"Do you have books on the history of Belize?"

They had one, so he took it.

As the clerk rang up his purchases, James glanced at his watch. When he'd arrived, he and Bella had spent an hour catching up. She'd rattled on about the wedding, and he'd smiled to see her so happy. He approved of Danny and hoped the young man truly appreciated what a treasure he was getting.

The only rough spot had been when Bella had raved about the fabulous wedding dress her mama had bought for her.

Remembering Giovanna's wardrobe, he'd said, "You're sure it's, uh, tasteful?"

Her blue eyes had widened. "Dad, it's incredible. It's a Fabiana."

Fabiana? That sounded Italian and flashy, just like Giovanna. All the same, he bit his lip and shut up. If his daughter liked it, that was what mattered.

Besides, his ex was middle-aged now, with a grown-up daughter. Surely her taste had matured.

The salesclerk handed him a Toucan bag. Now he had an hour or two before the group was dining. Perhaps he'd take his new book to the bar and have a beer.

Giovanna might be there.

Perhaps he should read on his balcony instead.

Damn, he refused to let the woman rule his life. Besides, he had to confess, he was curious to see her.

He remembered the first time he'd laid eyes on her in Rome, on a fine May morning. She'd stepped out of a dark coffee shop—or bar, as they called them in Italy—onto the sunny *terrazza*, and dazzled him with her curvy body, her amazing hair, her sparkling smile. She'd asked him something in Italian, then English, then English again, before the words sank in. Her question had been whether he wanted to sit inside or out for his morning coffee.

He'd wished she was asking if he wanted to make mad, passionate love, explore Italy, and fall head over heels in love with her.

Create a wonderful child together, take her home with him, and marry her.

Because his answer would have been yes.

And in fact, that's exactly what he'd done.

Proving that twenty-five-year-old men had no judgment when hormones were involved.

As he stepped out of the store, a couple were walking toward it, holding hands. The woman was young, stunning, Asian, and the man looked older than James. Not that he was about to judge anyone else's relationship.

Smiling, he said, "Hello. Newly arrived wedding guests?"

The man held out his hand. "Hi there. I'm Zane, the groom's uncle, and my lovely lady is Tamiko."

"Welcome. I'm the bride's father, James." After shaking their hands, he glanced toward the reception desk, where more new arrivals were lined up.

And . . . there she was: Giovanna, staring back at him.

He sucked in his breath. Was he in a time warp? She hadn't changed a bit.

Damn her, she was still the most beautiful woman he'd ever seen. He hated that he felt a surge of lust, just as he had on that first day. How unfair that he'd never felt that attraction to any of the highly compatible academics he'd dated.

He could almost feel the air between them crackle for the long moments their gazes held.

Then she tossed her hair, that same mass of glossy dark brown hair, and turned her back.

James raised a hand and ran it through his own hair, conscious of the couple dozen silver strands. Damned if his fingers weren't shaking.

He saw that his ex was talking to Ric Nuñez, the resort owner, and now the man looked in their direction. And focused on Tamiko. What man wouldn't, unless of course he was talking to the even more lovely Giovanna?

Zane pulled his date closer, maybe warning the other man off. "A striking couple," he murmured.

Ric turned back to Giovanna. She said something, flicked her hair, laughed.

"She's a decade older than him," James said, disapproving eyes fixed on her.

"She's timeless," Zane said. "Any red-blooded male would find her attractive."

Timeless? Giovanna should damned well dress, and act, her age.

Tamiko flipped her own hair. "Hey, lover, are you making eyes at another woman?"

Without intending to, James let out a snort, then tried to turn it into a cough. "Sorry, that's my ex-wife. We're, er, not on the best of terms." Talk about an understatement.

"Who's the man?" Tamiko asked softly.

"Ric Nuñez. He owns the resort." Giovanna never missed the opportunity to flirt. Nor to wear some bright, figure-hugging item of clothing like the blue dress that accented her curvy ass. And, when he'd seen her front view, showcased her splendid bosom.

A young woman scurried into his line of sight, heading straight toward him. The wedding planner, with a determined expression on her face. "Here's Sarah," he said ruefully, "to make sure the cat and dog don't get close enough to fight."

Bella had warned him to be on his best behavior, and Sarah had told him she'd scheduled events to keep him and Giovanna apart. They were treating him and his ex like children who couldn't play nicely together.

Which, unfortunately, was the truth.

Sarah raised an eyebrow. "This is your daughter's week. We don't want anything to spoil it, do we?"

He raised his hands in protest. "I'm behaving myself. I came in to buy swim trunks and got to talking." He turned to Zane and Tamiko. "See you at dinner."

Now he really needed a drink, and at least he knew Giovanna wasn't in the bar. He strode out of the lobby, refusing to glance in her direction.

All the same, her image was etched in his mind, taunting him.

She was still so damned seductive, so glamorous and out of his league.

Not that he wanted to be in the same league with her. From what he could see, they were no more compatible now than when they were married.

It was going to be a very long week.

GIOVANNA tried to concentrate on Ric, but her first sight of James had shaken her.

There was no good reason for it. He was the same stuffy professor, even down to his tie. Ooh, it had always irked her when he looked that way, so pompous and unapproachable.

A tie at a beach resort. Pah!

He hadn't gained weight—in fact, he'd slimmed down—though his clothes did nothing to flatter his tall, lean build. His hair hadn't thinned, but he was in desperate need of a stylist. If he had a woman in his life, she either had no taste, or she'd had no more luck than Giovanna at polishing his appearance.

He was still kind of hot, though. Even from a distance.

But nowhere near as hot as when she'd first seen him. She'd been waiting tables at a bar in Rome when he had approached the door. Standing in the fresh morning sun, he'd been irresistible: lanky and nicely muscled in khaki shorts and a T-shirt, black hair glossy and blue eyes bright with interest.

She'd stepped toward him, asking whether he wanted to take his breakfast outside in the sun. What her heart had been saying was, "Take me. Please, take me in your arms and kiss me. Make mad, passionate love to me."

What had it been about him? She'd been popular in Rome, even if she was only a simple girl from the country, waitressing in the restaurant where her cousin worked. She'd come to the city to have fun, go a little wild, and men were always asking her out. But never had she felt the same chemistry as with James.

And sadly, though she'd dated everyone from actors to oil tycoons, she never had since.

Now, a hum in her blood told her that chemistry might still exist.

Oh yes, it was better to avoid the man.

Giovanna tuned back into what Ric—a handsome, charming man, even if he didn't make her blood sing—was saying about the wedding preparations.

In a few minutes, the couple James had been talking to came over. What a small world it proved to be. She recognized Zane Slade from photos in entertainment magazines, and Tamiko Sato was all the buzz in the cosmetics industry.

Giovanna, who'd launched Venezia Cosmetics, a line with a bold yet sophisticated European sexiness, had wondered at Sakura choosing a relatively unknown Japanese American model. But Tamiko was exquisite. She'd give the new line a delicate, exotic look, quite different from Venezia's more sultry style.

She would enjoy talking to Tamiko, but right now Giovanna wanted a cool drink and a relaxing bath. Seeing James had unsettled her.

Resting a hand on Ric's shoulder, she went up on her toes and kissed his cheek. "Ciao for now, darling."

She strolled toward the bar to ask for a fresh lime to add to the sparkling water in her fridge. And there, sitting at a table, was James. His head was buried in a book. How often had she seen him like that? Oblivious to the world around him.

Oblivious to her.

Breath coming quickly, she stared at him. She could walk away, but she wanted that lime. Probably, she could get it, and he still wouldn't notice her. Damn him.

They had to speak sooner or later, so why not make it now, when it was her choice?

She sauntered toward him, shoulders back, wishing she was in heels rather than barefoot.

Normally, when he was concentrating on a book, nothing could rouse him short of fire or flood. But today, he looked up as she crossed the floor.

His eyes widened—damn, he had beautiful eyes—and tension tightened his shoulders.

# Chapter 2

GIOVANNA reached her ex-husband's table and stood with one hip cocked. "James," she said flatly.

"Giovanna." He looked wary, as if he thought she might yell or slap him. Both things she'd done more than once in the past.

She snorted. "Don't worry. Annoyed as I am that you're here, I—"

"I'm here because my daughter wants me here." His voice held that familiar note of disdain.

"*Your* daughter? *Madonna mia!* Seems to me it took two." The moment she said the words, she regretted them because they made her remember all the times, all the places, all the ways she and James had made love.

His blue eyes had gone dark, intense. In the early days, that would have meant he was thinking about sex, but that wasn't likely now.

Though seeing his eyes like that, and the clean, masculine bone structure of that familiar face, a face she'd once loved to caress—

No. She refused to get aroused by her ex. She tossed her hair and glared at him.

His eyes narrowed. "Yes, it took two, together with some carelessness about birth control."

"Ooh!" She'd been on the pill that summer, but she and James had lived a happy-go-lucky life, traveling, staying up all night, sleeping in hostels and even on the beach. She'd always worried he thought she'd gotten pregnant deliberately, to trap him into marriage, though, surprisingly, he'd had the decency to never say so. Was that what he was implying now? "I did *not* intend to get pregnant."

"I know that," he snapped. "No more than I intended to knock you up. I only meant we both should have been more careful."

She planted her hands on her hips. "Oh yes, I know perfectly well that having a wife and baby was the last thing you wanted when you were just starting your precious career."

"And I know your plans were more along the lines of party, party, party than changing diapers."

So that's why he'd never accused her of getting pregnant deliberately.

There was truth to what he'd said. She'd enjoyed traveling, going dancing, having fun. Staying up all night—and not with a crying baby. "Bet on it."

He raked his hands through his hair. "Shit. If Bella heard us talking this way, she'd think—"

"I love her." She glared at him. "I've never regretted having her."

He glared right back. "Nor have I. She's the best thing in my life."

Pah! Where had he been when it was time to change diapers? In his damned office. She'd never doubted that he loved Bella, but his career always came first.

"So, James, did you ever get that damned tenure you were so desperate for?" She knew he had. In fact, a few years ago she'd eavesdropped on one of Bella's phone calls to a friend and heard he'd been appointed chair of his department.

"It didn't take long, once you were out of my life," he said sardonically.

She was so steamed, she couldn't think of a good comeback. How could she still feel the spark of arousal when the man pissed her off so damned much?

Pouring that bottle of beer all over him would feel so good—and that's what she'd have done in the old days—but now she had more dignity.

"Well," she drawled, "*delightful* as it's been to chat, I have more important things to do."

She turned and sauntered away. Her back tingled as if he was watching, though that was probably her imagination. The dratted man had likely gone right back to his book. Just in case, she put a little extra oomph in the swing of her hips to annoy him. In Medford, he'd told her to keep her hips under control.

But in Italy, he'd loved the way she walked. In Italy, they'd had such passion.

In truth, even though she'd had her share of lovers over the years, the sex had never been as good as in those early days with James.

Before they'd begun to tear each other to pieces.

A couple days later, James was breakfasting with cousins of Danny's, trying to ignore Giovanna at a table across the room. Not only did she still royally piss him off, but she also—damn her—aroused him in an irrational and very primitive way.

The woman was hard to ignore, though. Animated and outgoing, touching people and calling everyone darling, always ready to throw back her head and laugh, she still had to be the life of the party.

When they'd lived in Medford, she'd nagged him to go out and party like they had in Italy. The woman hadn't given a damn that he was working his ass off developing lesson plans, doing research, and writing journal articles, trying to establish credibility with his older colleagues and set his feet firmly on the tenure track.

And not only for his own professional glory but for financial security for her and Bella. A fact she'd never appreciated.

"Hey, man," a voice broke into his thoughts. He looked up to see a somewhat overweight young man. "I'm Brad, a friend of Danny's. You're James Moncrieff, right?"

"I am."

"Wondered if I could swap trips with you today? You're on the golf cart trip, and so's Heather." He gestured across the room toward a blonde with a ponytail, and gave her a wave and toothy smile. "I'd really like to ride with her."

Sarah had the guests going on excursions each day. Yesterday, he'd been on a boat trip and gone snorkeling, and it had been both educational and fun. "What excursion were you scheduled for, Brad?"

"The trip into town."

"Fine." He'd be just as happy to explore San Pedro today, history book in hand.

THE next morning he went to the parking lot to join the golf cart expedition.

And damned if the first thing he saw wasn't his ex, clad in a figure-hugging top in an eye-grabbing shade of pink and a flowered skirt that showed off her curvy hips. She was leaning against a red golf cart in one of her seductive poses, flirting with Danny's widowed father, Al.

James stalked over to her. "What are you doing here?" Was she deliberately tormenting him? Sarah had scheduled them on separate outings.

"I'm *supposed* to be here," she snapped. "You're not."

Oh, damn. She was right.

The wedding planner stepped between him and Giovanna. "She's right, James. Didn't you do the golf cart trip yesterday?"

"No. Brad wanted to switch." And he'd never thought to mention it to Sarah or worked out the possible consequences. "Sorry, we should have told you."

"Yes. I make these spreadsheets for a reason."

Giovanna was scowling at him, eyes blazing. He knew what she was thinking, because she'd said it often enough. He was the typical absentminded professor.

That had to be the reason he'd forgotten. It certainly wasn't some subconscious desire to see her.

Not when just standing near her made him feel so damned uncomfortable. Pissed off and, yes, turned on. His skin heated, and he pulled at the knot of his suddenly too-tight tie, aware of Giovanna's gaze following his hand.

A young woman who'd been standing nearby—a cousin of Danny's, he thought—gave him a smile. "Well, I'm Jennie, in case you don't remember my name, and I'm happy to have you as my partner, Mr. Moncrieff. Or would you rather go with, uh—?" She glanced at Giovanna.

*God, no!* "Of course not. I'm delighted to be with you. And please, call me James."

"Well, I'm *delighted* to accompany Al," Giovanna said. She grabbed Al's arm and leaned toward him, flaunting her cleavage.

How many times had she done that kind of thing with his fellow professors? She'd embarrassed him, and his colleagues had teased him about how a ho-hum guy like him had managed to win a gorgeous sexpot like her.

Those old insecurities rushed back. "I can't believe you'd appear in public like that."

"Why don't you—?" Sarah started.

Giovanna dropped Al's arm and stepped toward James. Eyes spitting fire, she said, "This is the beach, not your office."

He could smell her scent. She'd changed perfumes, and this one was even more seductive than her old one. Spicy, earthy, sensual, exactly like her. His cock pulsed.

She reached out one hand. Slim, expressive fingers, red-painted nails.

He watched, not breathing. Mesmerized.

She touched the knot of his tie. "A tie. *Madonna mia!* Still the stuffy professor."

What was wrong with a tie? The group was going for lunch, weren't they?

Deftly she flipped open the knot of his tie and yanked it off.

Memories flooded back, of passion overcoming them, of their desperate rush to strip off each other's clothes. His cock surged, and he was glad his trousers were baggy.

She started to undo the top button of his shirt, and her fingers brushed his neck. The soft pads of her fingers. So many memories. Gentle touches, passionate ones.

He had to stop the memories. Had to stop her.

Had to touch her.

He lifted his hand and caught hers.

Giovanna gasped, and her gaze lifted to meet his.

She had beautiful eyes: warm, sultry, dramatic. Her expression was intense, almost like when they'd first met, when she'd said she was crazy about him.

The air between them heated and sparked, ready to burst into flame.

Damn, but he wanted to kiss her. And that was insane. What was she up to? Was this a game, pretending she wanted to seduce him so he'd make a fool of himself?

Which he would, if he didn't stop this now. Any longer, and he'd have a raging hard-on no baggy pants could conceal.

With an edge to his voice, he said, "Can't keep your hands off me, Giovanna?"

Her eyes widened, and she yanked her hand free of his. "Don't flatter yourself. I'm simply trying to save you from looking *inappropriate*."

Inappropriate. The word he'd so often used for her own wardrobe. And her behavior.

She tossed her hair, that same glossy mass of rich hair. Nearly black, with chestnut highlights gleaming in the sun.

Then, head high and hips swinging, she sauntered back to Al.

James sucked in a breath, held it, and forced his cock to subside.

He willed his gaze to turn from Giovanna to Jennie, willed his voice to sound calm when he asked, "Which golf cart is ours?"

She linked her arm through his. "Over here. Who gets to drive this cute little thing?"

Who gave a damn? All he could think about was that charged exchange with his ex. "Go for it, if you want."

He climbed into the passenger side, placing his Toucan tote bag on the floor. In it, he had his book on Belize, a water bottle, towel, sunglasses, sunscreen, and a bathing suit. He'd thought of everything he might possibly need for the day.

The only thing he'd forgotten was that Giovanna might be there.

Jennie pulled their little vehicle into the single-file line leaving the parking lot, and he forced his ex to the back of his mind.

The trip proved to be interesting. He read bits from the Belize book to Jennie, and she talked about her life in Vancouver.

She'd recently broken up with her boyfriend, which was why she'd come to the wedding alone. "He was too young. Honestly, young guys are so, you know . . ."

Teaching university students and coaching a basketball team for disadvantaged kids, he had a fair idea. "Yes. But eventually they grow up."

She shot him a twinkling glance. "It's so nice to be with a man who's mature."

Was she flirting? No. What would a pretty girl like her see in a middle-aged guy like him? After all, if Giovanna was to be believed, he'd been a pompous bore long before he turned thirty.

Damn, he wished she hadn't touched him. He wished he hadn't touched her. His hand still burned from the contact, and every time he thought about her, his cock throbbed.

He blew out air and rolled up his sleeves, undid a couple of buttons at his neck. What game had Giovanna been playing?

Didn't she realize how foolish she looked, flirting with every man in sight?

Then he remembered Zane's words. He'd said Giovanna was timeless, and any red-blooded male would be attracted.

"Isn't this the most beautiful beach you've ever seen?" Jennie asked.

He realized they were now driving on the beach itself, a lovely strip of pale golden sand. "It is." And he should relax and enjoy the scenery.

But when their cart pulled into the parking lot for the Crazy Monkey, he tensed again. His ex was walking toward the restaurant, arm in arm with Al Trent, so close that no doubt her full breast pressed against his forearm.

Jennie said something about wanting to dip her toes in the ocean, but he barely heard.

Sarah came up to him, but he barely noticed her, either. Giovanna's head leaned toward Al's, and her infectious, sultry chuckle drifted back. What the hell were the two of them talking about?

He ground his teeth. Then he felt insistent pressure on his arm. Sarah was squeezing him gently. "James, I didn't plan for you both to be on this trip. Please—" She broke off.

He took a deep breath. What the hell was he doing? Was he jealous of Al Trent?

Yeah. Because, despite all the hurt, bitterness, and anger, Giovanna was still the girl he'd fallen in love with in Rome, the one he'd wanted to spend his life with.

He glanced at the wedding planner and gave a rueful smile. "Behave myself? For Bella's sake? Yes, Sarah, I hear you."

"Thanks."

But his gaze snuck back to Giovanna, and he admitted something to himself. "I do love her." It seemed as if you never truly stopped loving your first love, even if mostly you hated her.

"Of course you do. Bella knows you and her mom both love her."

"Bella?" Good God, he'd spoken that last thought aloud. Thank heavens Sarah had misinterpreted it. "Yes, I know. So I'll try to behave." He patted her hand. "Now, I need to drag Jennie out of the ocean and bring her in for lunch."

A couple hours later, the group had finished dessert and was preparing to leave. James had been seated with his back to Giovanna and

Al, which had calmed his nerves. Though, when two couples had gone to—wink-wink—walk the beach, he'd felt a twinge.

Impossible not to think about that summer in Italy when he and Giovanna had been so hot for each other, they'd made love every place imaginable: the beach, an olive grove, an ancient ruin, even in a gondola in Venezia while the gondolier pointedly looked the other way.

"James," Jennie said, "I'm going to make a trip to the restroom."

Yes, he and Giovanna had made love there, too. The single bathroom in a tiny restaurant in Milano. It had been a quickie, and an impatient patron had kept banging on the door.

"I'll see you at the cart," he said.

"This time you can drive."

As people straggled out to the parking lot, James said to Sarah, "Would you like Jennie and me to take the lead? It's not likely we can get lost."

"You never get lost." It was Giovanna's voice.

Surprised, he turned to see her and Al standing behind him. For once, there was humor rather than rancor in his ex's voice.

"James," she said, "you have the sense of direction of a"—she flung her arm up toward the sky—"an eagle."

No snipe about him being absentminded.

And another reminder of traveling in Italy, his sense of direction keeping them on track. "Thanks," he said quietly, gazing into her eyes and wondering if she, too, was remembering.

Once, they'd shared something incredible, something he'd believed would last forever.

In fact, it had lasted less than a year.

# Chapter 3

PERHAPS the same bittersweet thought occurred to Giovanna, because she jerked her head and gave that familiar snort. "It can be very frustrating. Sometimes we mere mortals like to think we know where we're going, without always being corrected."

"Getting lost is a waste of time," he pointed out with some amusement.

"Getting lost can lead to interesting adventures," she snapped back.

Sarah clapped her hands, the sharp sound as effective as if she'd told them to shut up. "We'd best get under way so you'll have time for a rest or swim before dinner."

Jennie joined James at their cart. As he started the engine, she said, "You do look better without the tie and with your sleeves rolled up. You have strong arms."

"I play some basketball."

"Mmm, I bet you have good legs, too. I like a man who keeps in shape."

Giovanna used to nag him about that, but he'd never had time.

Now, he knew he was healthier and more productive for getting a workout two or three times a week.

"James?"

"Yes?"

"You aren't interested in me, are you?"

"Of course I am. I've enjoyed hearing about your job, your friends, and so on."

She rolled her eyes. "No, I mean *interested*."

Oh damn, she had been flirting. "Er, I . . . There's a significant age difference."

She gave an amused huff. "It's okay, I get it."

They were quiet a few minutes, then she said, "I'm going to ask you something. I want you to answer without looking at me."

Women could be very peculiar. "All right. But why?"

"What am I wearing?"

Instinctively he began to turn his head but she said, "No! Don't look."

He focused on the beach again, and tried to picture her. "I'm not good at noticing that kind of thing. But I did think you looked nice."

"Thanks. Okay, now look."

He gazed at her. She wore a skimpy yellow and white striped top and white shorts that barely covered the tops of her thighs. She was slim, lightly tanned, attractive. "Yes, very nice."

"Do you think I look okay to appear in public?"

"Of course."

She made an amused sound. "You realize I'm wearing less clothing than Giovanna."

She was? "But she's so . . ." Jennie looked cute and healthy in her shorts and top. Giovanna, in her skirt and slightly less skimpy top looked like . . . sex.

"Sexy?" Jennie echoed his thought. "Voluptuous? She's got that whole sensual, worldly European woman thing going on. All the guys, whether they're twenty or eighty, think she's hot. I wish I had what she has."

"You do?"

"But each of us has to develop our own style, make the most of what we've got, to be attractive."

She was no older than his students, yet she was teaching him a lesson. Seemed as if his insecurity had made him too judgmental about Giovanna. Well, damn.

Uncomfortable with his thoughts, he asked Jennie about her job as a paralegal, and that topic occupied them until they arrived back at the Toucan.

He thanked her for her company, then went into the store to see if they had any other nonfiction books on Belize, since he'd finished the first one.

Tamiko came in, and they chatted about books and what they did for entertainment. He got the surprise of his life when the lovely Manhattan model said she spent most evenings at home knitting.

That was his second lesson about judging by appearances.

Flustered, he went to adjust the knot of his tie. Except he wasn't wearing one. "Damn, that crazy woman took my tie."

"Dare I ask why you were wearing one?"

"It's habit. Every morning I put on pants and socks, a shirt and a tie. Sandals in summer, when classes are out."

She studied him, lips pursed. "James, I don't want to insult you, but you dress like a stodgy old professor."

Like he hadn't heard that before from Giovanna? "Well, I guess I am." Then, because she wasn't Giovanna, just a nice girl who liked to knit, he told the truth. "I started dressing this way when I was the youngest assistant professor. They called me the Baby Brit. I wanted to look older, more impressive."

"Well, now you have silver threads in your hair, and didn't I hear you tell Zane you're head of the department? That sounds pretty impressive. Besides, you're in Belize."

Touching the hibiscus flower in her shiny black hair, she said, "Believe me, this isn't how I dress in Manhattan. Look, you're a handsome man, but you hide it behind a bad haircut and boring clothes, so why not—?"

He was gaping at her, which was probably why she stopped talking.

"What?" she asked.

"You think I'm handsome?" No, he wasn't fishing for a compliment, he was genuinely surprised.

She cocked her head. "Hello? Haven't you noticed some of the women checking you out? You look like Pierce Brosnan."

"Who?"

"You need to get out more." Her face lit up. "You, my friend, need a makeover, and I'm just the woman to help."

"A makeover?"

"Give me two hours, and you'll be turning female heads."

What a ridiculous idea. And yet . . . He'd never had a clue about clothes. Giovanna had criticized, but he hadn't trusted her clothing advice. Tamiko was a model. She'd know about these things.

Could she actually make him over into an attractive man? "You can do that?" What would Giovanna think?

Tamiko gazed at him appraisingly, then grinned. "James, it'll be a snap." She took his hand. "Put yourself in my hands."

GIOVANNA returned from the golf cart expedition wondering what on earth had possessed her to touch James. To let her fingers brush the soft, firm skin at the base of his throat. That hollow where she'd so often pressed a kiss and felt his heart race.

She'd felt that quick pulse this morning, too, despite the way her fingers had trembled.

And she'd seen the heat in his eyes as they darkened. Indigo eyes, the beginning of a tan, the way the breeze had ruffled his hair—he could have been the old James.

Bad enough the chemistry between them was still amazing, but now she kept remembering those magical days in Italy. Each day, she'd fallen more deeply in love with him.

Damn him. He was the only man she'd ever loved.

And yet they were completely incompatible and still drove each other crazy. Why did matters of the heart so rarely make sense?

When she reached her cabana and saw the hammock, she let out a snort of annoyance. She'd meant to pick up a book to read.

She stalked back to the lobby. As she entered, James and Tamiko were dashing out the door on the other side.

Hand in hand. Laughing excitedly.

What was that all about? Frowning, Giovanna went over to the receptionist, trying to come up with an excuse for her nosiness. "I'd hoped to speak to Tamiko. Did they say where they were going?"

"When I gave them a golf cart key, she said something about a secret mission. A fun one, from the way they were smiling."

"Thanks. I'll catch her later."

Fuming, she headed back to her cabana. Tamiko was Zane's girlfriend. Where on earth were she and James going, and why were they so damned happy? Wasn't one handsome older man enough for the lovely young model?

Halfway to her cabana, Giovanna realized she'd again forgotten to get a book. *Dio mio*, she was so distracted, it was almost as if she was jealous.

That certainly wasn't the case. She just hated to see James make a fool of himself over a younger woman. She hated to think that Tamiko might be a cheat.

Did Zane know what his young lover was up to?

Of course, it might be something entirely innocent. But would they have been so excited—holding hands—if they were going to the grocery store?

How ridiculous to obsess over this. She'd head to the bar and find some company. Have a little sex on the beach. What a pity the liquid kind would be all she'd be getting on this trip.

In the Toucan Bar, a couple of Danny and Bella's male friends vied for Giovanna's attention, and she enjoyed flirting with them. Sweet boys, but definitely boys. All the same, they gave her ego a boost.

After a couple drinks, the second one virgin, she returned to her cabana to bathe. Then, clad in a short silk robe, she pondered what to wear.

She selected a dress Fabiana had created for her. Though Giovanna often wore vivid colors, this one was a subtle golden shade that brought out the highlights in her hair. It also came close to matching her skin color and, on first glance, a person might think she was naked.

After adding dangly gold earrings and bracelets, she was ready.

The young model might be a photographer's darling, but most men preferred a real woman with curves. Not that she was competing, of course.

Certainly *not* for her ex-husband's attention.

Carrying strappy high-heeled sandals, she walked through the sand to the lobby, paused to put on her shoes, then stepped through the door to make her entrance.

Across the room, she saw Ric gazing at her appreciatively. She blew him a kiss.

Dramatically, he caught it out of the air, then pressed his hand over his heart.

She smiled at the gesture, then glanced around the room in time to see a man enter.

James? *Dio mio*, he looked amazing.

Finally, he'd gotten an excellent haircut. It took ten years off his age, made him look modern and stylish. As did the clothes, the deceptively simple kind only a designer could create. Well-tailored linen pants, great sandals, a slim-cut short-sleeved blue shirt worn open-necked and untucked. The right shade of blue to complement his eyes and light tan.

He looked seriously hot.

He'd done all this to impress Tamiko?

When he'd never once responded to Giovanna's pleas that he spruce up his style?

The model had arrived and was talking with Zane and Ric. Giovanna glared at her. What a little slut!

She glanced back at James, who now had three young women hanging on his every word. Why did it hurt so much to see other women swarming around him?

Giovanna tossed her head, then realized Tamiko was heading toward her.

The model gave a shy smile. "Hello, Giovanna."

Her anger spilled over. "What are you *doing*?"

"Doing?"

"You already have Zane. Isn't one handsome man enough for you?"

Tamiko paled and glanced around, as if checking to see whether anyone could overhear. "What do you mean?" she whispered urgently. "Of course I'm with Zane. There's no other man. Honestly. Zane's my guy, and I'm crazy about him."

"Pah! You're protesting too much."

"No, honestly, there's nothing between me and—" She broke off, eyes narrowing. "Wait a minute. What are you talking about?"

"James! You sneaking off with James. I bet Zane doesn't know about that, does he?"

The tension eased from Tamiko's face, and her lips curved. "Actually, I told him all about it. He approves completely."

"He what? He doesn't mind if his lover—?"

Tamiko interrupted. "Does a makeover?"

"A what?"

"A makeover. I love helping people change their look and feel better about themselves."

"You wanted to make him over? That's *all* you wanted from him?" Like Giovanna was going to believe that for a single moment.

The model's eyes gleamed. "James is such an attractive man, don't you think? But that kind of got lost, with his haircut and choice of clothes. So I sounded him out, and he went for it."

"I saw the two of you leave together."

She nodded vigorously, excitedly. "We went into San Pedro, to this shop Zane and I discovered. Great men's clothes. The shirt Zane's wearing came from there, too."

She rushed on. "I gave James advice on what suited him, and he bought a bunch of things. Then we went to a hairstylist the salesclerk recommended, and she and I put our heads together on a style. I think she did a wonderful job. Don't you?"

Tamiko's face was as bright as a kid's at Christmas. Either she was as good an actor as she was a model, or all she'd done with James was revamp his image.

Giovanna felt relieved, which was absurd. And embarrassed, which was more than warranted. "Yes, I like his hair," she muttered. "And the clothes. They're flattering."

Then she thrust back her shoulders. "I owe you an apology, Tamiko. I'm sorry for jumping to conclusions and for that . . . rant."

"Don't worry about it. Honestly."

"How did you convince him?"

She crinkled her nose. "It wasn't very hard. I told him he was a handsome man, but his good looks got hidden because of the not-so-great haircut and wardrobe."

"*Si pigliano più mosche in una gocciola di miele che in un barile d'aceto,*" she muttered.

"What?"

"My grandmother used to say you can catch more flies with a drop of honey than in a barrel of vinegar." Giovanna had nagged rather than told James he was handsome. But surely he'd known she found him attractive. After all, she'd fallen in love with him and married him.

Tamiko glanced over at James and grinned. "I told him I'd have him turning heads in no time, and it certainly worked."

Giovanna snorted. "So he wants to turn young female heads, does he?"

"Uh . . . Well, I mean, not in any serious way."

"Hmph. Not serious, just a holiday fling?"

"That's not what I meant. I don't think he's the fling type." Tamiko shook her head, looking embarrassed. "Sorry, that sounded presumptuous. You know him much better than I do."

"I doubt that." Not now, and not back then. She'd been so intimidated by his transformation from fun-loving tourist to career-driven academic, she'd wondered if she'd ever truly known him.

He should have married another professor rather than a waitress, but Giovanna had gotten pregnant, and he'd done the right thing. Then he'd constantly criticized her. And she hadn't known how to cope, except to yell at him. In her family, people yelled, cleared the air, then they kissed and made up. But James never yelled back, just got disdainful and criticized her.

She had felt second-class; she was always disappointing him. It was like he wanted to subdue her, to banish the vibrancy he'd seemed so attracted to in Italy. No, she'd never understood him.

Tamiko darted a glance through long eyelashes. "I asked if there was anyone special back home who'd be upset if we changed his image."

"Oh?" Giovanna pretended disinterest.

"He said no, he'd never done well at relationships. Which surprises me, because he's so nice, as well as handsome."

Relieved, and annoyed at herself for feeling relieved, she said, "His first love is history. Maybe he's never met a woman who could compare. And no woman enjoys coming second to a stack of fusty old books."

Tamiko gave her a sharp glance.

"Sorry, that was bitchy. Obviously, my ex and I have issues."

"Yes, but—" She broke off, ducking her head.

"What?"

"You also still have feelings."

Giovanna sniffed. "That would be foolish."

The other woman sighed. "Sometimes you care for someone even though it's silly to." Her gaze drifted past Giovanna's shoulder.

Giovanna turned to look. And saw Zane, who was still chatting with Ric.

The model was falling for her celebrity lover. "I'm sorry. I know he has the reputation of being a ladies' man." Giovanna touched Tamiko's arm sympathetically.

"He does?" Her eyes widened in what looked like shock, then

she recovered and gave an artificial smile. "Oh yes, Zane likes the ladies. But I knew what I was getting into. And I'll be so busy with Sakura, I won't have time to worry about a bruised heart."

How strange. For a moment, Giovanna had the impression Tamiko had been thinking about someone other than Zane.

# Chapter 4

DINNER tonight was at an Italian restaurant in San Pedro. Sarah's seating plan put Giovanna with Danny's father and some other relatives of Danny's. James was at Bella and Danny's table.

Studying the menu, Giovanna saw it was traditional, as were the red-checked tablecloths and Chianti-bottle candles. Entrées like spaghetti bolognese, lasagna, and fettuccine Alfredo took her back to her childhood when she was a simple girl living in a small town.

Before she became James's wife, and eventually Giovanna of Venezia Cosmetics.

She ordered a tossed salad and fettuccine Alfredo.

Al smiled. "It's nice to see a pretty woman with a healthy appetite."

"Life is full of pleasures to be enjoyed." Her body would always be curvy, and whether or not that was fashionable, she was entirely happy with how she looked.

When the fettuccine came, it was excellent, rich and creamy and sprinkled with lots of freshly grated Parmesan cheese and ground black pepper. "Your chef is Italian?" she asked the waitress.

"Yes, from Milan. Milano, as he calls it."

Milano. Where she and James had once had wild sex in a restaurant bathroom. "Please give him my compliments. From a Piemontese girl to a Milano chef."

A few minutes later, a short, dark-haired man in a chef's white jacket and a beret scurried from the kitchen. He greeted her excitedly in Italian, and they spoke in that language for a few minutes, reminiscing about Italy and talking about the upcoming wedding. It was all very Italian and very satisfying.

When he excused himself, he kissed her hand.

Danny's brother laughed. "You have an admirer, Giovanna."

"I suspect she finds those wherever she goes," Al said, a gentle twinkle in his eye. He was a dear man, one whose heart belonged to his deceased wife.

As she glanced around the table, filled mostly with Danny's relatives, she thought it sad that only she and James—who could hardly bear to speak to each other—were here to represent Bella's family.

James was an only child, and his parents, a scholarly couple who'd had him late in life, lived in England and didn't travel. Nor did Giovanna's own much larger Italian family, who insisted they were simple country folk.

When dessert and coffee had been served, the waitstaff appeared bearing trays with shooters, which they ignited.

Giovanna laughed in recognition. "*Sambuca con mosca.*"

"What is it?" Danny's sister-in-law asked.

"Sambuca, an anise-flavored Italian liqueur, with coffee beans." She didn't tell them that *mosca*, translated literally, meant flies.

The chef had appeared to claim a glass, which he raised high. "My compliments to the lovely daughter of the beautiful Giovanna, and to the lucky man who is marrying her. The three coffee beans are for happiness, health, and prosperity. *Salute!*" He lifted his glass.

Everyone else did the same, and drank the toast.

After, Giovanna told him, "*Grazie mille.*"

"For you, anything." Again he kissed her hand, then returned to the kitchen.

A few minutes later, Giovanna went to the ladies' room to touch up her hair and lipstick. When she emerged, James was walking toward the men's room.

They both stopped dead, then he gave a tentative smile. "That was nice, Giovanna. Arranging the toast."

Caught off guard—he looked so hot, so young and vital, and was he actually being nice to her?—she smiled back. "I wish I'd thought of it, but it was the chef's idea."

His eyes gleamed with humor. "He seemed quite taken with you."

Who was this man? The old James would have accused her of flirting.

She shrugged casually, trying to ignore the impact of those beautiful eyes, not to mention his sensual lips. Those lips had kissed every inch of her body, a body that was currently very aware of his presence. "He was pleased to meet another Italian. He doesn't see many in Belize."

A crazy instinct urged her to take another step forward, to caress the lightly tanned skin at his throat. A nearly irresistible instinct.

She fought it. Feeling awkward, nervous, almost like a girl on a blind date with a very sexy guy, she said, "You look very nice. Tamiko knows what she's doing."

"Thanks." He gestured toward her, almost as if he, too, wanted to reach out and touch. "You look really good, too."

Her eyebrows went up. This was certainly new. Her dress had a scooped neckline and hugged her body like the outfits he'd always complained about. "Uh, thank you." A woman shouldn't look a gift horse in the mouth, but she had to ask. "You don't think it's *inappropriate*?"

He gave a rueful grin. "I think I'm a man who doesn't know much about women's clothing and isn't always objective."

What on earth did that mean?

But he was going on. "And I think that's a beautiful dress on a beautiful woman."

Her freshly painted lips opened in a stunned, "Oh."

His indigo gaze fixed on her lips.

*Dio mio.* A spark jumped between them. Or maybe it was a magnetic field, because her body felt irresistibly drawn toward him. Her nipples tightened, her blood almost sizzled, and her sex throbbed with raw need.

She had to touch him. Had to have him.

This was how she'd felt when she'd first met James.

The air was thick. She couldn't breathe, couldn't think.

His hand rose in slow motion. As it moved toward her, she took a half step closer.

He touched her cheek softly, so softly, wonderingly. The caress made her feel nineteen again, little more than a girl, meeting a man who made her feel things she'd only imagined before.

She turned her head slowly into his palm. Feeling the strength of his hand, the softness of his skin. Breathing in his male scent. Opening her mouth and letting the damp inside of her bottom lip drag across his skin.

Footsteps clicked their way, fast, accompanied by breathy female laughter. "Did he really?" someone asked.

She and James jerked apart. Giovanna's breath stuttered, and her chest heaved as she sucked in air.

His gaze locked with hers: dark, stunned, passionate.

Two of the young female guests came down the hallway toward them. "Sorry," one murmured as they passed, then they both ducked into the ladies' room. "So, what did you—?" Giovanna heard before the door closed.

She pressed a hand against her breast, trying to steady her racing heart. "What were we thinking?"

"Remember Milano? The bathroom in that little restaurant?"

"Of course I do. But . . . that was then."

He sighed. "I know. A nice memory, all the same."

She closed her eyes against an unanticipated and utterly ridiculous surge of tears. Things had seemed so simple then, so wonderful, falling in love and dreaming wild and crazy dreams.

She raised her chin, opened her eyes, and flicked back her hair.

For once, she couldn't think of a single thing to say. Besides, she wouldn't have trusted her voice. So she simply turned and walked away.

James stared after Giovanna, watching that curvy ass sway. Through the blood roaring in his head—and filling his cock—all he could think about was getting his hands on her.

They'd had sex in a restroom before, and it had been amazing.

"Damn!" He shuddered as he fought the primitive urge to rush after her and grab her. Instead, he went into the men's room, slammed the door, and rested his forehead against it.

Lust. It was lust, pure and simple.

Shared lust, from the fire in her eyes as she'd stared back at him, from the way she'd turned her lips into his palm.

How embarrassing it would have been if one of the wedding guests—or, God forbid, Bella—had come along and found them twined in a passionate embrace like horny teens.

He moved away from the door and stood at the sink. He needed a cold shower, but he'd have to settle for splashing water on his face.

Except, when he stared at his palm, he saw the red smear of her lipstick.

JAMES rose Thursday morning after a restless night filled with torrid dreams of Giovanna. Day by day, she was pissing him off less and turning him on more.

And that was dangerous. They both knew how hopelessly incompatible they were.

Except . . . he'd judged her unfairly. It wasn't just his clothing sense that had been stuck in a rut, but his opinion of Giovanna, too. Jennie and Tamiko had made him realize there'd never been anything wrong with her clothing or her manner. It had taken Belize and two nice young women to clear the prejudice from his brain and make him realize that Giovanna's style reflected her confident, sensual personality.

And also to realize that, as a husband, he'd been a jerk. Looking back, he could even understand how it had happened. He'd been so damned insecure, so jealous of every man she spoke to. The Baby Brit had been afraid his gorgeous, vibrant wife—the woman who'd been forced by pregnancy into an early marriage with a boring professor—would find a more handsome, exciting man.

But she hadn't in the years they'd been together.

Well, he couldn't remake the past—and he and Giovanna were still polar opposites—but perhaps he should find an opportunity to apologize.

Mainly, he needed to get through the next few days without doing anything embarrassing, and see his daughter happily married. Then he could retreat to his ivory tower, where life was so much less complicated.

As he dressed, he chose clothing Tamiko had picked: tan shorts and a dark blue polo shirt. He owned shirts like that back home, but this one had cost four times as much. She'd also made him buy a size smaller than usual, saying he had nice muscles and should show them off.

He studied his reflection, an activity he rarely engaged in, and had to admit he liked what he saw.

Would Giovanna?

Damn, why couldn't he stop thinking of her?

He left his room to go for breakfast. He was in a three-story block off the lobby, along with most of the other guests. As he walked down the hallway, another door opened, and Al Trent, Danny's father, emerged.

The man Giovanna had been spending so much time with.

James had wondered if they were romantically involved and felt absurd twinges of jealousy.

"Morning." He tried to sound friendly. If this man was attracted to Giovanna, and vice versa, it was none of his business.

"Hi, James. Going for breakfast? Why don't we sit together? Seems like it's time for the two dads to get to know each other."

"Sounds good," he said. "Er, you weren't planning to sit with Giovanna, were you?"

"No." Al's gray eyes met his in a level gaze. "I know the two of you have issues. I'm sorry. My wife and I were lucky. We loved each other from the moment we met in high school, and that love grew until the day she died."

James had fallen for Giovanna from the first moment, too. "I'm so sorry you lost her."

Al sighed. "She went too young, but I often feel she's still with me."

In the restaurant, Bella came over to hug them both and invite them to join her and Danny and some friends. James exchanged glances with Al, then said, "Thanks, sweetheart, but Al and I want to chat."

The men took a table for two, and James said, "Tell me more about your wife."

Al smiled. "Have you got all day?"

As the other man spoke, James found himself both envying and feeling sorry for him. Al had found the love of his life, and they'd shared wonderful years, but then he'd lost her. It was clear he was still in love with the woman.

Giovanna, who had a knack for getting people to open up, would have discovered the same thing. She got along with Al because she liked him, not because she was looking for romance.

That shouldn't be a relief.

He and Al were still talking when Giovanna entered the restaurant. She paused near the entrance, checking out the room, vibrant in a figure-hugging red top and a full skirt in a red and white pattern.

Arousal heated his blood, fueled by the memory of their encounter last night. He curved his fingers into his palm, protecting the memory of her lips against his skin. The near kiss he'd so hated to wash off.

He saw the quick rise and fall of her breasts when she caught sight of him and Al. She gave a brief smile, then joined some other wedding guests.

"She's dressed for dancing," Al said.

"Dancing? Oh yes, Sarah's scheduled lessons this morning." Salsa, which he knew and enjoyed, and some Belizean dance he'd never heard of.

"My wife and I did a mean foxtrot and loved to jive." Al gave a nostalgic smile. "I haven't done much of the Latin stuff. How about you?"

"Actually, a fair bit. There's a woman in my department—a happily married one—who loves to dance. Her husband doesn't, but he likes her to go out and have fun. She talked me into taking lessons, and I enjoyed it. Now we go dancing every month or so."

Guiltily, he thought of the times when Giovanna had wanted to go dancing or out for a drink or movie. She'd been bored, tired, restless. Only twenty years old, she had a baby to look after, and her only social life was hanging out with much older professors and their spouses.

Somehow, with him and Giovanna, everything had turned into a fight. If he'd been as open and flexible with her as he was with his colleague Helen—

"Think I'll give the lessons a pass," Al said. "I've lost the only partner I want to dance with."

The man should let the past go. And yet, here was James, spending most of his time thinking about his ex.

The two men continued their conversation until it was time for the lessons, then James headed over to the lobby. If the Belizean dance was fun, he could teach it to Helen.

A dramatic dark-skinned couple, obviously the instructors, were talking to Bella and Danny, and Giovanna was by the reception desk with Ric and Sarah.

Sarah's eyes widened when she saw him, and she scooted over. "James? You're not here for dance lessons?"

"Yes. Is that a problem?"

"Bella said you didn't dance."

He must never have told her about Helen. "All the more need for lessons." Wryly he added, "I'm sure Giovanna and I can behave ourselves." At least as long as they stayed on opposite sides of the dance floor. Otherwise, sparks might fly and it was fifty-fifty whether they'd be ones of anger or of passion.

"Thanks." She touched his arm. "Have fun. And by the way, you look great. You're easily the best-looking man here."

Even as she spoke the compliment, her gaze darted across the room toward Free Lafontaine. Hmm. That was interesting.

But he forgot that thought—and any other one—when the instructors taught them the Belizean punta, and he saw Giovanna's hips sway in time to the catchy beat. She was made for this kind of sexy dance.

Unlike the young woman he partnered with, who laughed a lot and kept snapping her gum.

The instructors asked people to change partners each time the music changed, and themselves took turns with the guests. When he got a dance with the female teacher, she winked. "Nice to be with a man who knows what he's doing."

James moved on to a middle-aged woman who had two left feet but at least didn't chew gum.

The male teacher was dancing with Giovanna. The instructors had said the dance could be as sexy and suggestive as the partners wanted to make it, and those two were getting into it.

He wanted to dance that way with her. Like making wild, hot love standing up. Something they'd done more than once when they first met.

God, his lust was flaring out of control. He had to stay away from her.

He managed to do it during the short break between dances, then the instructors began the salsa lesson.

It was a dance James knew well, and he guided his partner through the basic steps. She caught on quickly, swaying her hips, hamming it up, smiling vividly. They were having fun, and he'd even stopped watching Giovanna.

Then his ex stalked up. To him, she said, "Let me show you how it's done." Then, to his partner, "You'll excuse us, won't you?"

James's jaw dropped.

A moment later, Ric stepped up, saying to James's partner, "Want to dance?"

"You bet, Ric."

Which left James with Giovanna.

So she intended to show him how it was done, did she? Well, he was the man, and the man damned well led.

He took her hands firmly, gazed into her eyes, and they began to dance.

Her eyes flared with surprise as he gave her strong leads and she followed. Oh yes, she knew this dance, too. He moved beyond the steps the instructors had demonstrated, and she followed without hesitation, their movements as harmonious as if they'd been dancing together for years.

Or making love together, because that's almost how it felt. The dance steps were sexy, passionate, and James's and Giovanna's were perfectly attuned.

Her eyes blazed, her breasts bounced softly, and her hips swayed seductively. He spun her out, skirt swirling around shapely legs, and she came back. They joined both hands, twisted and twined this way and that. Now his hand was on the bare skin of her shoulder, now on her supple waist under the thin top.

They moved apart, together, sideways and back. Whatever they did, it was as if an invisible thread—a thread that vibrated with sexual tension—joined them.

She stared at him the way she had that first summer, as if he was the sexiest man she'd ever laid eyes on, except now she did it with an adult's fiery passion.

He knew he was staring back with the same passion, his expression naked, telling her she was the most desirable woman he'd ever met. There was no way he could prevent it.

She held him in her spell.

Her posture was confident; she never lost her balance for a moment. Each move was fiery and sensual, matching his.

She worked the dance for all it was worth, her entire body in motion: feet constantly moving, hips gyrating, torso swaying to the music, arms gracefully expressing the beat.

He wanted to kiss those glossy red lips, imbed himself between those full hips, feel those red-tipped nails bite into his back, and make her cry out first with need, then with release.

Her leg lifted, twined seductively around him, and then was gone.

He spun her out again and this time brought her back so she was facing away from him, her back to his front. His arms were across her chest, brushing those full breasts. Her curvy ass swiveled an inch from his groin

Thank God they were moving quickly, doing intricate steps—each step a quick tease rather than a lingering seduction—otherwise he'd have had an erection.

The music ended, and he dipped her, bending low himself.

They held the position, both breathing hard, eyes locked together.

Then he raised her.

Their bodies stopped moving but still touched, and their gazes still held.

"I want you," he mouthed, unable to stop himself, not wanting to stop himself.

She gave a soft gasp, then whispered, "My cabana, Wild Ginger. Don't let anyone see you."

A moment later she was gone. He didn't watch her leave; he stalked away in the opposite direction.

# Chapter 5

INSIDE her cabana, Giovanna pulled her hair back from her flushed face with trembling hands.

James.

*Dio mio*, the man was sexier than he'd ever been. Like wine—and Giovanna herself—he'd improved with age.

She wanted to taste him. All over. Her entire body ached for him.

But this was insane.

When he opened the door and stepped inside, she planted her hands on her hips, tossed her hair back, and glared at him. "We don't even like each other."

He locked the door and gave a ragged chuckle. "No, but we sure as hell—" Then he pulled her into his arms and bent his head, his intent utterly clear in the indigo blaze of his eyes.

She groaned with relief, lust, God knows what, flung her arms around his waist, and clung as his lips brushed hers.

That first touch was sweet yet potent, like those tropical cocktails she'd been drinking. Deceptively innocent, just a brush of lips against lips, and yet behind it passion surged with an intensity she'd never felt before.

"Damn you, James," she said against his lips as she pressed closer, feeling his lean hardness, a body that was new yet achingly familiar.

"Damn you, too," he returned, then thrust his tongue into her mouth and claimed her.

Their teeth clicked, their lips ground together, their tongues thrust and parried as their mouths made love and war at the same time.

His mouth was a wild, wet world where she could lose herself.

He grabbed her butt and squeezed, pulling her belly against his rigid shaft.

Everything inside her turned to molten heat and raw yearning. She squirmed against him, rubbing against his cock as shamelessly as a cat in heat.

She pulled up the hem of his shirt and ran her hands up his bare back, hard and hasty. Not taking the time to learn this new landscape, just enjoying how wonderful he felt.

But it wasn't enough. She tore her mouth from his. "Take it off."

"You, too."

Gazes locked, gasping for breath, they each fumbled to yank off their clothing.

She tossed her top and skirt aside and stood in front of him proudly in her red lace bra and bikini panties.

His gaze left her face and roamed her body, his lips curving with satisfaction. "God, Giovanna, you're lovely."

He had pulled off his navy shirt, revealing a torso that was stronger and more sculpted than when they'd split up. Now he slid his shorts down to reveal crisp white boxers, the slim-fitting type, stretched tight over his impressive erection.

She grasped him through cotton, felt him jerk at her touch. Her sex craved him, and she felt hot dampness between her legs.

"I want you, damn it," he said.

"This is insane." She shoved the boxers down his hips and had to stifle a moan at the pleasure of seeing that gorgeous cock. He had the most beautiful one she'd ever seen, and she'd missed it.

Missed his penis. Not the man himself, of course.

Her hand closed around his shaft.

He didn't bother to stifle his moan. "I don't want to want you, but I do."

She pumped up and down, enjoying the smooth, warm glide of her fingers on his flesh. Imagining that hard organ inside her, thrusting fast and deep. "We'll fuck once." Deliberately, she used the harsh word. "Get it out of our systems."

"Yeah." He unfastened the front clasp of her bra and peeled it away. Then he cupped her breasts as she thrust them forward, seeking his touch.

"You have the most beautiful breasts," he muttered, sounding more annoyed than pleased.

Her nipples were hard, and when he ran his thumbs over them, his touch was rough, needy. She whimpered, felt fresh moisture between her thighs. The pulsing ache in her sex said, *Do me, do me, do me NOW!*

She hooked her thumbs into her panties and pulled them off.

He gazed down, touched between her legs where she was swollen and juicy.

She pressed hard against his hand as he stroked her, then pulled away. One more touch, and she'd explode, but his fingers weren't what she wanted. "Scrap the foreplay," she commanded.

He stared at her, expression intense, unreadable. Then he grabbed her and hoisted her into his arms. He carried her across the room to the couch and dumped her, almost roughly.

But she didn't care. She didn't want gentleness, finesse, anything that smacked of romance. She wanted James inside her, hard and fast.

He went over to his shorts and pulled a package from his wallet. Ripping it open, he strode back to her, cock thrusting rigidly up his belly.

She wanted to whimper with need but forced herself to be quiet.

As he put the condom on, she stretched out on a towel on the couch—a piece of furniture that hadn't been designed with sex in mind.

But comfort wasn't the point. Hard and fast was. Getting the orgasm her body so desperately craved, and getting the man out of her system once and for all. She spread her legs.

Silently, James sprawled across her, his tall body too long for the couch.

She reached urgently for his cock. Her body was simmering, at the flashpoint. She needed this—him—now.

The head of his penis probed her soaking-wet folds, the sensation so delicious she moaned, "*Dio mio.*"

His lips captured her moan, and he plundered her mouth. But she gave as good as she got, meeting his tongue with hers in a dance that was—like their salsa—as much a duel.

His hips jerked, and he plunged deep inside her in one strong thrust.

She gasped with shock and sheer pleasure. Then her body exploded in a wrenching, shuddering, spasming climax that gripped him and milked him, that made her scream out and rake her nails down his back in passion, anger, maybe even love.

"Giovanna!" Her name grated out of his mouth as his own orgasm ripped through him in convulsive strokes that drove all the way to her womb.

He collapsed on top of her, and they lay for a long moment, bodies plastered together with sweat, chests heaving.

That had felt amazing, but what the hell had they been thinking?

James pulled out of her, rose, and headed to the bathroom.

Despite the tremors that still rippled through her body, she forced herself to sit up.

He returned a few minutes later, hair damp around the edges, and stood, staring down at her. He scrubbed his hands across his face and through his hair. "Sorry," he said gruffly. "If we were only going to do it once, it should have been better than that."

She shook her head. "We both got carried away." But yes, despite the screaming orgasm, she felt as if her appetite had been whetted, not satisfied.

Would one more round hurt?

His naked body was so tantalizing, and arousal still heated her blood. "You're in better shape than when I last saw you," she said a little grudgingly.

"Basketball."

Basketball? "And dancing." He'd looked so sexy doing the punta. And their bodies had moved so naturally, so erotically, in the salsa. Casually she crossed her legs to stop herself from squirming against the need between her thighs. "Where did you learn to dance like that?"

"A friend."

"Pah! A lover, you mean."

"No. Just a friend who wanted to take dance lessons and needed a partner."

She tossed her hair back and lifted her chin. "You never had time to go dancing with me."

Something flashed in his eyes. Regret? "Maybe that was a mistake."

"Oh, it was," she said, slowly and silkily.

His lips twitched. "You always have to win, don't you?"

"But I never won." The words burst out. James had always been so much smarter, and when they'd fought, he'd gone cold. She might yell and throw things, but he turned icy and froze her out. Of course, she'd been fighting with all the pain of a wounded heart, whereas he only cared about his precious career.

He studied her for a long moment. "Seems to me, neither of us won. All we did was hurt each other."

Had she hurt him? She'd certainly meant to. What a pair they'd been. She nodded. "Yes, that did seem to be our fate. Olive oil and tonic make a nasty combination."

His eyes gleamed. "We didn't do so badly a few minutes ago. Even if it was too quick."

Need quivered through her. Her fingers trembled with the desire to touch him.

And his cock—that lovely cock—was swelling again.

She raked his body with a blatantly sultry gaze. "It looks like once wasn't enough for you."

"We barely got started." He held out his hand. "What do you say? Want to go upstairs where it's more comfortable?"

"I'm not sure *comfort* is what I have in mind," she purred, taking his hand and coming to her feet.

His arms went around her shoulders, hers circled his waist, and they stood, naked, holding each other loosely. Their bodies touched lightly here and there, and she breathed in his scent with hungry nostalgia.

The urgency was gone, and the anger. But the desire remained. Slower, lazier, like thick, warm honey running through her veins. "Yes, let's go up to the loft."

She let him lead the way, not wanting him to notice that her curvy bottom, while still firm, was an inch or so lower than it had once been.

His own butt seemed to be doing just fine, taut and sexy, the muscles flexing as he took the stairs.

When he stepped into the loft, she couldn't resist. She swatted his backside playfully. "Basketball suits you."

"Thanks. And whatever you've been doing suits you. You barely look a day older."

Yoga, walking, lots of water, healthy eating, minerals and vitamins, spa treatments, the skin potions her company developed. Yes, she devoted time and money to her appearance, but in her industry, health was important, and image mattered.

And yes, her vanity enjoyed it when men turned their heads admiringly.

Though none of those appreciative glances had warmed her the way James's expression did.

He was staring at her the way he used to. As if he was worshipping a sex goddess. And his cock was erect again.

She raised her arms, stretching her breasts high, and ran her hands through her tousled hair, preening for him and enjoying the heated caress of his gaze.

The shutters were open, letting in sunshine and soft ocean air, making her feel earthy and uninhibited. She threw back the covers, lay down, and stretched like a cat.

James smiled as he watched Giovanna. Sensuality came naturally for her. She couldn't be any other way if she tried—and it had been wrong of him to ask her to, foolish of him to want her to.

He sat on the edge of the bed and gazed appreciatively at her naked body. She was curvy and firm in the right places, and slender where she should be. Her measurements probably hadn't changed much, yet there was something different about her: a maturity, a lushness. It was very womanly, very appealing.

On the upper curve of her right breast, just low enough to be hidden under most bras, was a small, chocolate-brown beauty mark. "I remember this." He bent to kiss it. "I remember the first time I found it."

"We were in my apartment in Rome, and it was . . . what? About two hours after we met?"

He nodded. "At the bar, you'd asked me what kind of coffee I wanted, and I made you describe them all, just to keep you there, so I could hear you talk, look at you."

"You chose cappuccino, which I'm sure is what you'd intended all along."

"It was." He shaped his palm to her breast, which filled it perfectly with soft fullness.

"Then you made me tell you about the pastries, and you chose a *cornetto*."

"And when you brought the coffee and *cornetto*, you asked where I was from and why I was visiting Rome." He molded her breast, squeezing gently.

"A good waitress is always polite." Her eyes twinkled. "Then, when I had to go serve someone else, you asked me for sugar for your coffee." Under his fingers, her areola was tightening, her nipple perking to attention.

"Even though I didn't take sugar." He took that bud between his thumb and forefinger and rolled it gently, remembering how sensitive her breasts were. "I just wanted you to come back."

She gave a husky chuckle and stroked his thigh. "I brought you a glass of water, then another cappuccino, and another *cornetto*, and—"

"I tore off a piece of pastry and offered it to you, and you ate it from my fingers. The way your lips brushed my skin was the most erotic thing I'd ever experienced."

"You led such a sheltered life in England," she teased, fingers drifting high on his inner thigh, grazing his balls.

He sucked in a breath. "I asked if you'd go out with me that night, and you said—"

"Why wait until then?"

"I was so relieved. I'd have gone mad waiting for evening to come."

"I was such a bad girl." Another quick brush of her fingers across his sac, then higher, featherlight, across his swollen shaft. "I told my boss I was sick and had to leave early. I'm sure he guessed the truth." Her hand explored higher, caressing his pecs.

His skin quivered under her touch. "Your boss probably would have fired you." He slipped his hand over to her other breast and began to fondle it.

"If I hadn't quit the next day."

"It was a crazy thing to do. Quitting your job and taking off with a stranger to travel around Italy."

She shrugged, eyes gleaming. "You were pretty hopeless, you spoke so little Italian. You needed a guide, so I took pity on you."

"Ah, is that what it was? And here I thought it was lust." He tweaked her nipple gently. Traveling with her had been incredible. He'd been the tourist who'd won the Italian goddess—the one who turned heads, talked easily to everyone they met, found interesting places to explore. And to make love.

Her lips pressed tightly against a smile. "Lust? Perhaps there was a bit of that, too."

Their gazes met, soft and affectionate, yet tinged with wryness at how things had worked out in the end.

"If you'd known then how things would turn out," he asked, "would you still have gone with me that first day?"

"Yes. I've asked myself that same question many times. When I was particularly mad at you, I'd say no, never. But honestly, yes. Because of that summer, that wonderful summer, and mostly because of Bella. She was an accident, yet such an amazing gift to two young people who didn't deserve her."

"Very true."

"And you? Would you have stopped ordering *cornetti* and walked away without having the best sex of your life?"

An arrogant assumption, but a correct one. "I've thought about it, too." About what his life would have been like if he hadn't given his heart to Giovanna.

But for her, he might have loved a fellow prof or a graduate student, married and had kids, maybe coauthored a book with his spouse. It was the life he'd wanted and planned when he left England for that summer in Italy. He'd traded all that for one grand passion, one incredible summer followed by months, years, of pain.

Yes, he might have made a different choice if it hadn't been for Bella.

"As I said a couple days ago, Bella's the best thing in my life. It's inconceivable to think of her not existing."

He leaned over and kissed the soft tummy that had once housed their daughter. Giovanna's sexy, musky scent made his head spin and his groin tighten. He kept on kissing, heading lower through springy dark curls of hair.

She gave a sigh of pleasure, shifted, parted her legs wider in invitation.

Giovanna had never been shy about her body or about letting him know what pleased her. He remembered how firmly to press his tongue against her slick, swollen folds, giving her long, sure strokes, pausing to dip his tongue inside her to taste the juicy essence that rewarded his efforts. She was still so responsive.

She hummed approval when he eased in a finger, then a second one. As he stroked in and out, her walls tightened around him in rhythmic contractions, and his needy cock throbbed, wanting that same touch.

He took her clit between his lips, tonguing and sucking it.

"Oh yes, James, just like that." Her hips writhed, and she pressed against his mouth. When they'd had sex on the couch, it had been greedy, desperate, and this was so much better. This was about giving and sharing pleasure.

With the tip of one finger, he found her G-spot and caressed it lightly, making tiny circles.

She gasped, and her body tightened, tensed, held still.

He gave her a bit more pressure, and she climaxed with a cry, deep waves pulsing through her and around his fingers.

As they slowed to ripples, she gave an earthy, satisfied groan. "So good."

He eased out of her as she said, "And now it's your turn."

There were so many things he wanted to do. Kiss her breasts and suck on her nipples, see if that spot behind her left knee was still ticklish, nip the supersensitive lobes of her ears.

But he also wanted to feel her lips on him.

So he lay back on the bed, wondering where she'd start.

They'd often done this in the past, taking turns with foreplay. It was something she'd taught him: to focus on one thing at a time, either the giving or taking of pleasure.

He'd just done the giving, which was as much a turn-on for him as for her. Now it was his turn to lie back and let himself be pleasured, to concentrate totally on the sensations.

Giovanna rose to her knees lazily and lifted both hands to scoop her hair back from her face. She studied him like he was a plate of rich, creamy pasta, and she a woman who was savoring the moment before digging in.

Then she said, "Ah, I have so little willpower," and lithely slid down the bed until she was lying between his legs.

# Chapter 6

HE raised up on one elbow. Her hair tumbled across his belly, and he smoothed it aside so he could see her full, rosy mouth poised above his erection.

His cock pulsed, straining for her touch.

She gave a darting lick, and it felt so good he let out a groan.

Delicately she licked all over the crown, under it, then, more vigorously, down his shaft, stimulating every centimeter of skin and making him groan louder.

She carried on, licking his sac then widening her mouth to gently suck in his balls.

He tensed, hoping—

Yes, she began to hum. No particular tune; she'd always told him she made them up as she went along. And damn, it felt good.

Her hands were under his butt, holding him firmly.

Not that he had the slightest intention of moving away.

When he neared the point of no return, she sensed it as she always had.

Moments later he was sheathed and she was straddling him, lowering herself to take him in. Bracing her hands on his chest, she glided up and down on his shaft.

Damn, it felt unbelievably good. And the sight of her riding him was so sexy. The fire in her eyes, the tumble of dark hair, the bounce of her full, rosy-tipped breasts.

The knowing curve of her lips. "You like this, don't you, James?"

No one else had ever made love with him this way, with lack of inhibition, pure sensuality, giving herself totally to the moment. "It's wonderful. You're an amazing lover."

"How true." She grinned. "But it takes one to know one."

He raised both hands to caress her breasts, and when he squeezed her nipples gently she moaned and threw her head back. Her breasts thrust more firmly into his hands, and he admired the lovely stretch of her throat.

In the old days, he'd never understood what such a gorgeous woman was doing with him, and in some ways he still felt that way. But Tamiko's makeover and the attention paid him by Jennie and some of the other women had helped his confidence.

He pumped his hips, thrusting hard to meet Giovanna as she sank down on his shaft, and she made a throaty sound of pleasure.

Then she started to swivel her hips as she rose up and down. Stirring him up, she used to call it, and it truly did. "Giovanna, that's incredible." He felt the provocative sensations all up and down his shaft.

The need to come built inside him, and he pumped upward while she did that swiveling thing.

"Oh yes," she panted, "do that again."

So he did, and he dropped one hand from her breast to tease her plump little clit, slippery with her juices.

"*Ancora*," she demanded, staring down at him, eyes glazed with passion.

Italian for "more," he remembered. And he obeyed, thrusting hard, caressing her clit, feeling his climax gathering in the base of his spine.

"Now, James," she said. "Come now. With me."

He let his body take over, driving to orgasm, driving her along with him until they both cried out as their bodies plunged together to satisfaction. He thrust into her again and again, feeling her body shudder and spasm around him, until he had nothing more to give.

Gradually their bodies stilled.

"It appears we haven't lost the knack," she said, giving him a smug smile.

"You can say that again."

She peeled herself off him and came to lie curled up beside him. He put his arm around her shoulders and drew her close, enjoying clasping her lush, warm body. She rested her head on his shoulder, hair tumbling across his chest.

When he'd come to her cabana, he'd thought a quickie would get the craving out of his system.

But the woman was addictive, especially when the sounds that came out of her mouth were sighs of pleasure, not barbed criticisms.

He gathered his courage. "Giovanna, this has been wonderful. Want to meet up again while we're on the Caye?"

She gave a soft laugh. "You just mounted a rather persuasive argument."

"It's strange, us connecting like this. After years when we made every effort to not see each other."

"Mmm. Bella told Sarah she had to keep us apart."

"I know. Sarah's efficient; she tried her best."

"Blame it on the salsa." Giovanna pushed herself up to a sitting position and gazed down at him, eyes sparkling with humor.

He stacked his hands behind his head and looked up at her. God, she was beautiful. "You shouldn't have danced with me. I was doing okay until then."

"No, you weren't. But nor was I. Every time we looked at each other, the air sizzled."

"Yes. You're right."

"Besides, are you saying you're sorry this happened?" Her tone was teasing. She knew the answer.

"I'm delighted it happened. But what do we do now?"

"You suggested a repeat performance."

"Yes, but when? How? Do we let people know we're, er . . . ?"

"Lovers?" She shook her hair back. "How embarrassing, when everyone thinks we're mortal enemies."

He chuckled. "Perhaps not mortal, but yes, I agree. Besides, this is just some . . . aberration, isn't it?" Amazing sex and a temporary truce.

"An aberration? Not the prettiest compliment I've ever received."

When he started to explain, she waved a hand to silence him. "No, no, you're right. It's lust, it's sex—fantastic sex—and that's all. If people found out . . . Imagine if Bella discovered that her long-estranged parents were going at it like rabbits. How humiliating for her and for us."

A pang of regret went through him, but she was right. They'd proved years ago they were too incompatible to live together. She'd never loved him, only married him because she was pregnant. There was no point thinking in terms of a relationship.

And yes, it would be mortifying if people knew the two of them were having a purely sexual fling. At their daughter's wedding, no less. "So what do we do? Find a way to meet secretly? And in public we'll avoid each other?"

"I think that's how it must be." Was there a touch of sadness in her voice?

He couldn't see her expression, because she was sliding off the bed and into a robe.

"We've missed lunch," she said. "I wonder if anyone noticed?"

"They'd assume we had a fight on the dance floor and stalked off to sulk."

"What if someone sees you leaving my cabana? Maybe we should stage a fight. We could pretend you came here to, uh . . ."

"Complain about the immodest way you were dancing? Not to mention the plunging neckline on your top."

"That top is perfectly respectable," she responded heatedly. "In fact, it's made by—" She broke off when she saw his grin.

"Hah. Got you," he said. "I like what you were wearing today."

"You do? What's different about today's outfit?"

"Nothing." He climbed out of bed and walked over. "Before, I overreacted to the way you dress. I didn't like the way other men looked at you."

Her chin went up. "You thought I looked slutty."

He winced. "Not exactly slutty, but sexy. Not the way academics and their spouses dress. I shouldn't have said the things I did."

"No, you shouldn't." She waited, a puzzled expression on her face, as if she figured a *but* was coming. When it didn't, she said slowly, "When we were at Tufts, perhaps I should have toned it down a little, tried harder to fit in. But I felt so out of place. I knew I'd never belong in your world."

"I'm sorry." He touched her shoulder. "We really did belong in different worlds, didn't we?" Even if she had loved him, they might not have been able to make their marriage work.

Slowly, she nodded. "Perhaps I shouldn't have called you stuffy, but you were so different than in Italy. You dressed and acted like a much older man."

"Yeah. I was the youngest person on faculty, and I wanted to appear established and dignified."

"I never knew that."

"You never asked. Just yelled at me."

She glared at him. "And you stalked away rather than explaining."

His temper rose automatically, then he gave a quick laugh. "And we've both *grown up* since then, right?"

She snorted. "Mmm. Apparently not as much as we should have." Eyes gleaming wickedly, she said, "I think we should be able to stage a fight, don't you?"

"Just so long as we remember it's only make-believe."

DINNER that night was at a resort called the Crown Jewel. Riding in the Toucan minibus with Bella and some other guests, Giovanna knew she should be looking forward to the evening, but all she could think about was James. The sex had been wonderful, and it had been such a joy to talk rather than fight.

Tonight, after everyone had returned to the resort, he'd sneak over to see her.

Her body felt ripe and lush and utterly, earthily female.

Why had she never found another man—a more compatible one—who made her feel this way?

Deep down, she knew James had been the love of her life. But she also knew they were oil and tonic, and could never mix. So, she would take this interlude for exactly what it was.

They'd have great sex, watch their daughter get married, then go home to their separate lives. With any luck, relations between them might be less strained in the future, which was probably the best wedding gift they could give Bella.

She realized the minibus had arrived, and Bella was climbing out. When Giovanna followed, her daughter was explaining to Sarah that Danny wasn't there because he'd instead chosen to drink beer with his friend Free.

They were all miffed at Danny, so Giovanna linked arms with Bella and said, "Sarah, I'm sure there's a sunny patio somewhere, and drinks for Bella and me."

Sarah guided them through a bar, and Giovanna went on. "Warm sun and a cold drink. What more could a woman want? Except, of course, for an utterly charming and devastatingly handsome man."

They stepped onto a sunny patio, and she stopped dead. "*Che bello!* From my lips to God's ears."

Yes, the man who lounged by himself at a white patio table definitely fit the bill. He was movie star handsome, with wavy black hair, classic features, and a Mediterranean complexion. His lean, toned build was revealed nicely by the white shirt he wore open over khaki shorts.

He raised his drink in their direction. White teeth flashed in a devastating smile and a diamond ring winked in the sun. He rose and came over. "Ladies, this lovely day has grown even brighter."

Giovanna laughed appreciatively. There was nothing like good old-fashioned European charm.

Beside her, Bella whispered to Sarah, "Over the top, but God, he's cute."

Sarah whispered back, "You're engaged."

"Tell that to my missing fiancé." Bella's voice rose.

Enough so the man caught the last word. "Fiancé? No, don't tell me you're engaged. I'm desolate." He glanced at Giovanna. "Tell me you're not engaged or married."

Amused, she said, "Let me guess, you're Italian, yes?"

He gave another dazzling smile. "My father was from Assisi. How did you know?"

"No one but an Italian could be so outrageous and get away with it."

"Shall we leave you two to your flirtation?" her daughter asked dryly.

Giovanna touched her shoulder. "Oh, Bella, don't be silly."

"Bella? Now, there's a perfect name for such a beautiful young woman." The man held out his hand. "I'm Jeff Tomaso."

Her daughter reached out as if to shake it, but Jeff kissed it instead with a Continental flair. "I just arrived, and I'm lonely. Will the three of you do me the honor of letting me buy you a drink?"

"That's the best offer I've had all day," Bella said.

"How kind of you. I'm Giovanna." She gave him her hand.

"Giovanna." He lingered over the name, then kissed her hand.

He turned to Sarah.

"I'm the wedding planner," she said, not sounding pleased and not offering her hand, "and *I* have guests to look after."

Humor glinted in his eyes. "My loss. But I shall console myself with these two lovely women."

After Sarah went into the hotel, Giovanna and Bella ordered mojitos, at Jeff's suggestion.

Giovanna asked him what brought him to Belize all on his own.

"London was so rainy and dismal, I decided on a whim to visit Belize."

"You live in London?" Bella asked.

"I have a flat in London, one in Manhattan, and of course one in Rome." He glanced at Giovanna. "Near the Villa Borghese gardens."

"A lovely area." And an expensive one. "If you don't mind my asking, what line of work are you in?"

"I'm afraid I'm one of the indolent rich. I invented a . . . I won't give you the technical term, let's call it a gizmo, used in diamond mining. It made me an embarrassing amount of money. How about you two?"

"I'm a slave laborer," Bella said with a grin. "Still trying to find a job that suits me." Giovanna had offered her a job with Venezia, and Bella had said she'd decide after her honeymoon.

"And I'm in the cosmetics industry," Giovanna said.

"An interesting choice," he said, "since a woman as lovely as you has scant need of cosmetics."

"Which only goes to show how extraordinarily effective my cosmetics are."

For the next while they chatted happily, and he flirted mildly with both of them, though mostly with Bella, who lapped up the attention.

Giovanna kept wondering when James would arrive. At one point she thought she saw him inside the bar; then he was gone.

A little while later, Danny finally turned up, coming toward them with Free and Sarah.

Bella glanced up coolly. "You decided to show up."

Jeff said, "You must be the fiancé. I congratulate you. You're a very lucky man."

"I know," Danny muttered.

Jeff rose. "I must go and dress for dinner." He bent down to Giovanna, and they kissed cheeks in the European manner. "Giovanna, such a pleasure."

The he took Bella's hand. "A delight, *bellissima* Bella." He kissed it again, the kiss more of a caress this time. "An utter delight."

"Thanks for the drink, Jeff." She was blushing.

"I will hope to see you both later." To Sarah, he said, "And you, the unnamed wedding planner. And of course the groom and his friend."

They all watched him stroll away, confident and graceful.

"Gotta hate guys like that," Free said. "All smarm."

Western men. Honestly! Giovanna shot him a nasty look. "*Charm* and *smarm* are two very different things. A man should let a woman know she's appreciated." Though perhaps Jeff had gone a bit far with that last hand kiss.

Danny reached out to Bella. "Come on, sweets." He winked. "Let's find a private spot, and I'll show you how much I appreciate you."

Giovanna really did need to have a talk with her future son-in-law.

Bella studied him, making him squirm a little, then smiled and rose to hug him. "You're incorrigible."

Sarah gave a relieved smile. "Don't sneak off too far. It's almost time for dinner."

When the three of them had gone, Free and Giovanna studied each other for a long second. There was an odd tension about him that made her uncomfortable. Without a word, he turned and walked away.

Giovanna wandered inside and explored the Crown Jewel resort. Glancing into a book-lined room, she saw James at a desk, head bent over some heavy tome. How predictable. Did the man *always* have his head in a book? If she went in and proposed a little late-afternoon delight, would he even look up?

Ah well, when he came to her cabana, she'd make him forget everything he'd ever learned about history and concentrate entirely on the present. And her.

# Chapter 7

DINNER was delicious, and Giovanna enjoyed the food and conversation while she tried to resist glancing over to the table where James sat. It was a pleasant evening, and the background piano music complemented the mood.

After coffee had been served, Danny came over to their table. “Some of the ladies are into listening to this sentimental music, and us guys want to have a drink in the bar. Who’s gonna join us?” His speech was more than a bit slurred.

The last thing he needed was another drink, but a groom was entitled to get drunk with his friends once before his wedding. At least the hangover would happen tomorrow, not on his wedding day.

“I choose the music,” Giovanna said, turning to see the piano, which she’d been sitting with her back to. “Oh my, that’s Jeff Tomaso.” The rich inventor was also a talented pianist?

“You know him?” one of the women asked.

“I met him before dinner.”

Over the next few minutes, the guests reorganized themselves, most of the men going to the bar and the women moving to empty tables closer to the piano. Al joined the women and, after several moments' deliberation, so did James. He glanced at Giovanna but took a seat well away from her.

A wise decision. Romantic songs aroused her passions.

Many of their group ordered fancy coffees or liqueurs, Giovanna choosing a grappa. She glanced at James's glass and wondered if he still favored Laphroaig whiskey.

To this point, Jeff had only been playing, not singing, but now he began to sing. The song was "It Had to be You." His voice was true, and his gaze lingered on Bella.

Giovanna glanced at her daughter, sitting beside her. She was smiling and mouthing the words. Bella had always loved romantic songs, and she had a pretty voice.

In the middle of the next song, which Giovanna recognized as being from *South Pacific*, a musical she and Bella had seen on Broadway, Jeff broke off. "Bella, you can sing this, yes?"

"I know the whole soundtrack. It's old-fashioned, but . . ."

"Romance is never old-fashioned." He patted the piano bench. "Come, *bellissima* Bella, and sing with me."

She raised her hands to flushed cheeks. "I can't."

But it was clear she wanted to. Her fiancé was having his fun, drinking with his guy pals. Why shouldn't Bella have a special experience of her own? She was in love with Danny; it wasn't like she'd be wooed by Jeff's mild flirtation. Giovanna touched her bare arm. "Oh *tesora*, do it. You have a lovely voice, and when will you ever again have an opportunity like this?"

Bella went to join him, hesitant at first, but after a few minutes of singing together, she'd lost her nervousness. Her voice blended well with Jeff's, and she was clearly having a ball.

She looked lovely, too, in a clean-lined linen dress, its blue complemented by her sparkly sapphire and diamond pendant and earrings.

Giovanna lifted her glass to her daughter, then, beaming proudly, she couldn't resist catching James's eye.

He nodded and smiled back.

However badly the two of them had messed up, they'd managed to raise a wonderful daughter.

When the pair at the piano finished the next song and received their applause, Jeff kissed Bella's cheek. "You are a delight, *carissima*."

"You gonna let him do that?" a loud male voice asked.

Giovanna started, and turned to see Free and Danny standing at the back of the audience.

"They're just singing," Danny said, not sounding happy.

"Get a grip. That rich dude is hustling your girl." Free muttered something else Giovanna didn't catch.

Danny's expression changed to anger. Sounding drunk and obnoxious, he said, "Hell, no!" He headed over to the piano, weaving a little, and grabbed Bella's shoulder. "We're going. Now."

She stared up at him like she didn't know him. Certainly Giovanna had never seen the easygoing Danny behave this way.

"Hey," Jeff said. "Take it easy with the lady."

"Back off. She's *my* fiancée, and she's going with me."

*Madonna mia!* No man treated her daughter that way. Giovanna began to rise, then saw James was already on his feet. She sank back, perching on the edge of her chair.

Bella, scarlet with embarrassment, tried to shake off Danny's hand. "Stop it. You're making a scene."

James stepped up to them. In a calm, authoritative tone, he said, "Danny, you've had too much—"

Danny interrupted, saying to Bella, "And you're acting like a slut, throwing yourself at this rich guy."

"Oh!" She leaped to her feet, dislodging his hand.

James jumped between them, both hands raised, palms toward Danny. "Calm down."

Perhaps he might have, but Jeff got into the act. Rising, he put his arm around Bella. "Yeah. Stop insulting her and go sleep it off."

"Who the fuck do you think—?" Danny went for Jeff, but James, thank God, got between them.

Her James. Taking control. To Danny, he said firmly, "You've had too much to drink and you're overreacting. Bella was just singing."

She loved how he defended their daughter. Yes, she'd been flirting a little, but it was harmless. She'd no more cheat on Danny than Giovanna ever would have on James.

Free came up beside Danny. "Singing love songs like she meant them."

Damn him. Why was he interfering? Between him and Jeff, it was almost as if they were deliberately trying to cause trouble between Danny and Bella. She'd like to slap both their faces.

And she'd do it, too, except it would cause even more of a scene and further embarrass her poor daughter.

Sarah seemed to have no such qualms. She strode over and glared at Free. Voice shrill, she said, "This is your fault. You got him drunk."

"I'm not drunk," Danny said. "I'm mad. Bella, what the fuck are you—?" Danny tried to lunge for her, but again James blocked him, hands firm against his chest.

Sarah said to Bella, "Maybe it's best if you just take Danny home."

Bella crossed her arms and stuck her jaw out. "I have no intention of going home with a drunk. It's Free's fault. He can take him home."

"I'm not going without you," Danny said belligerently.

"Yes, you are." James's voice and Bella's sounded together.

"Let's everyone just—" Sarah started.

"Bella, you don't have to put up with this," Jeff said. "Come, I'll buy you a drink. I bet you could use one."

"I don't think that's a good idea," Sarah said. "Bella, I'll take you back to the resort."

Giovanna, who knew her normally easygoing daughter could only be pushed so far, wasn't surprised when Bella stuck out her jaw again. "No, thanks. I'd rather have a drink with Jeff." She gave him a smile that was dazzling but didn't reach her eyes. "It's so nice to be with a man who knows how to treat a woman."

James shot Giovanna a questioning look, and she shrugged helplessly. She hadn't a clue what they could do to make this better.

As Bella and Jeff walked away, Danny started to follow. This time it was Sarah who got in front of him. "Stop. You'll only make things worse. Go home and cool off, then apologize in the morning."

"Crap, I—"

"Apologize?" Free said belligerently. "What's he got to apologize for? He's the one who got dumped for a richer guy."

Dumped? Talk about overreaction. Surely this was just a foolish lovers' quarrel, brought on by a combination of jitters, alcohol, and Jeff Tomaso's presence.

Sarah was in Free's face, white-faced and spitting mad. "Shut up! You've done enough harm."

Then she collected herself and turned to the guests. "A prewedding spat. Happens to the best of couples. They'll sort everything out in the morning. Time to get back to the Toucan."

To Free and Danny, she said, "Go!"

After they did, and the guests began to follow, James came over to Giovanna. "That was nasty."

"Yes, but it was wonderful how you stepped in."

One corner of his mouth curled up. "Figured if I didn't, you'd probably sock Danny."

"I was tempted, believe me. Not to mention Free and Jeff."

"What do we do now?"

Giovanna was deliberating when Sarah said, "James, Al? Could you get everyone back to the resort? I'm going to stay and talk to Bella."

"As will I," Giovanna said. "You go, James, and try to settle people down. It probably is just a stupid quarrel, and they'll soon kiss and make up."

He nodded, and went to join Al.

Giovanna sipped grappa as everyone left. She resisted the urge to rush melodramatically after Bella, not wanting to give the guests even more to gossip about.

When everyone had gone but the wedding planner, Giovanna rose. "Let's find her, Sarah. Knowing Bella, she's about to crash."

They went to the bar where Bella, sitting with Jeff, gave them a phony smile. "Hey there."

She sat beside her daughter and hugged her. "I see you've inherited my flair for the dramatic."

"Danny's a whole different person tonight. I don't know what got into him." Her smile had gone, and her whole body drooped. Softly she said, "He doesn't trust me."

Giovanna drew in a breath. Was that true? She remembered how it had hurt when James hadn't trusted her. Yes, she'd always enjoyed talking to men, doing a little harmless flirting. That was her nature. She'd never have cheated on James, and he damned well should have known it.

"He was jealous. And drunk," Sarah was saying bitterly. "And Free Lafontaine's an asshole."

"Free's never wanted us to get married," Bella said. "I thought he liked me, so I don't get it."

What? Bella had never told her this.

"He hates marriage in general," Sarah snapped. "He thinks he's saving Danny from a fate worse than death."

"What?" Was Sarah right? How would the wedding planner know? Giovanna turned to her daughter. "You didn't tell me this."

"Mama, I'm an adult. I can handle my own problems."

Hurt, Giovanna wanted to snap that she wasn't doing such an amazing job of it, but she restrained herself.

Sarah glared at Jeff. "Then there's you. You sure didn't help matters."

Giovanna felt guilty for having encouraged him. Still, she really didn't see anything wrong with a little flirting and singing. People could be so uptight.

"Hey, if the lady prefers my company, I'm not going to complain."

"But I don't," Bella said. She flushed. "I'm sorry, that came out wrong. You're great company. I've enjoyed talking to you, and singing together was amazing. But I'd never . . . I mean, I love Danny."

Exactly! Danny should have known that.

"You do?" Jeff took a sip of what looked like brandy. "But does he really love you? He's insecure and possessive, and a bully. Better you find out now, before he's your husband."

"I don't know." Bella's eyes were tearing. "Everything's gone wrong."

"He'll apologize in the morning," Sarah said. "Yes, he acted stupid, but this is all Free's fault. And Jeff's."

Maybe so. But there was merit to what Jeff had said. Giovanna didn't want to see Bella repeat her own mistake. "I hate to say this, but perhaps an apology isn't enough," she said slowly. "I've never seen this side of Danny before. And ultimately, he's responsible for his own behavior."

She gazed into her daughter's troubled face. "Bella, you can't be with a man who doesn't respect and trust you. Believe me, I learned that lesson a long time ago."

"N-no. I can't." Bella was crying now.

Heart aching for her daughter, Giovanna hugged her tight. "Let's go back to the resort."

"I d-don't want to see Danny," she sobbed.

"I know, *tesora*."

WHEN the guests arrived back at the Toucan, James quietly took Danny and Free aside. A primitive instinct made him want to crack their heads together—damn it, they'd hurt his daughter—but he clamped down on it. There'd been enough drama and irrational behavior for the night.

"Danny, I don't know what's going on with you and my daughter, but I'm not impressed. You've had too much to drink, and you're being insulting and obnoxious. Sleep it off before you see her. Stay away from her tonight."

"But I—" Danny started to say, but Free interrupted him.

"Like he wants to be there?" He sounded self-righteous, as if Bella, not he and Danny, was at fault. "Danny'll bunk in with me."

Putting an arm around his friend's shoulders, he led him toward the room block off the lobby. "Come on, buddy."

Al, who'd been saying good night to the guests, came over. "Has Danny gone? I wanted to talk to him."

"Free's putting him to bed." And right now, James was pissed off with Free, too. "Maybe you should go talk to him anyhow."

Al looked uncertain, then shrugged. "They've been best friends for ages. Free has Danny's best interests at heart."

"That's not how it looked."

Al's lips tightened, pressed together. "What the hell is going on? Have the kids lost their minds?"

The kids? Danny was the one who'd been drunk and obnoxious. Sure, Bella'd been having a good time, but Danny'd let jealousy get out of hand.

As James had when he was married to Giovanna. So he was in no position to judge too harshly. "Pre-wedding jitters, I guess, as Sarah said."

"Everything had been going too smoothly. Something was bound to happen. They'll sort it out in the morning."

"I suppose." If he were Al, he'd have tried to talk some sense into his son. But then, Danny wasn't in much of a state to listen at the moment.

"They love each other, and they're great together," Al said firmly. "Gosh, even my wife and I had the occasional spat. Didn't mean we didn't love each other."

He said good night and went off to bed, but James stayed in the lobby.

It was good that Giovanna and Sarah had stayed to look after Bella. If she was mad at Danny, they'd keep her from doing something foolish. If she was hurt, they'd comfort her. Women did this kind of thing so much better than men.

All the same, he couldn't go to bed until his daughter returned.

Eventually a taxi pulled up outside. He walked across the lobby and watched as the three women emerged. Giovanna put her arm around Bella.

His lovely daughter looked small and lost as she clung to her mama, face tear-swollen, damp curls of blonde hair plastered to her cheeks.

"Oh, sweetheart." He hurried out the door toward his little girl.

She looked up, then gave a gulping sob. "Daddy."

She ran into his arms, and he hugged her tight as she buried her face against his shoulder and wept. Stroking her hair, he murmured, "It's okay, Bella. Hush, sweetheart, everything's going to be okay."

And he really wanted to believe it. Bella and Danny loved each other. Surely they'd work this out.

Giovanna came up beside them, with Sarah right after her.

"He's not at the cabana," James told the three women. "He's staying with Free."

"Free." Sarah spat out the name. "This is all his fault."

"He supplied the fuel," Giovanna said, "but it's Danny who screwed up."

James looked from one to the other, realizing they knew more about the situation than he did. But this wasn't the time to ask. "Let's get you to your cabana," he murmured to Bella.

He tucked her under his arm, half supporting her weight as she slumped against him. They made their way slowly through the lobby and across the sand, with Giovanna and Sarah following.

When they reached the Azure cabana, Giovanna told Sarah, "We'll look after her."

"Are you sure?" In the soft porch light, the wedding planner's face looked almost haggard. "I mean, you and James . . ."

"We'll be fine," Giovanna said.

Sarah looked doubtful but exhausted, almost ill.

"Get a good night's sleep," James told her. "Hopefully things will look better in the morning."

Her lips pressed tight, then she forced a smile. "Of course."

As he, Bella, and Giovanna entered the cabana, he had the incongruous thought that this was the first time the three of them had been alone together since he and his ex had broken up. Would that the circumstances were different.

Bella dropped onto the couch, face buried in her hands.

Feeling helpless, he said, "What can I do for you, sweetheart? Mix you a drink? Get you some water?"

She shook her head. "There's nothing anyone can do." Her voice came out muffled from behind her hands. "It's over. It's all over," she wailed, and began to cry again.

Giovanna hugged her shoulders. "I'm going to get you a sleeping pill, *tesora*. You get ready for bed, and I'll be back in a minute."

When she passed James on her way to the door, expression worried and sad, he for the first time noticed the fine lines around her eyes and mouth. He touched her arm, and she paused, caught her breath, and he saw the sheen of tears in her dark eyes.

Then she went out the door.

Bella dragged herself off the couch and headed for the bathroom, and James paced the sitting room, hoping she was okay.

She was just coming out when Giovanna came back and gave her a pill to take.

James hugged his daughter but didn't know what to say. Things will look better in the morning? Surely they would. And yet Giovanna's expression wasn't hopeful.

"Daddy? Will you stay? In case I wake up? Or D-Danny comes?"

"Of course, Bella. I'll be right here."

"And so will I," Giovanna said. "Now come to bed, and I'll tuck you in."

He watched them go up the stairs. His brokenhearted daughter, his lovely wife.

No, ex-wife.

# Chapter 8

FROM upstairs came the murmur of female voices. When Bella had been little, he'd missed out on a lot of bedtimes, too busy with work to spend time with his family. It wasn't until he and Giovanna had divorced and Bella had come to him on weekends that he'd discovered the joy of toothbrushing, baths, bedtime stories.

While he'd been working so hard to get tenure, he'd been flunking fatherhood. Ironic that it had taken divorce to turn him into a decent parent.

And he had become one. The older Bella had gotten, the more time she'd spent with him until, in her teens, she'd chosen to divide her time evenly between him and Giovanna. That had meant so much more to him than his damned tenure.

The voices upstairs had stopped, and finally Giovanna made her way down the stairs.

She collapsed onto the couch. "She's asleep," she said softly. "And I need a drink."

"Let's see what they've got." He checked and reported, "Water, beer, passion fruit juice, and a bottle of rum. I could mix up rum and passion fruit. Or go see if the bar's open."

"Rum and passion fruit sounds fine. Heavy on the rum." She leaned back, ran her hands through her hair, and sighed. "What a night."

He made the drinks and came to sit beside her. "Is it more than just nerves?"

"Maybe." She took a healthy slug of her drink. "For some reason Free's anti-marriage. Bella says he's been on Danny's case."

"He's what?"

"Yes. I had no idea. Bella wanted to handle it herself. She thought it was petty stuff, and Danny was immune."

She told him about Danny and Free drinking, Bella and Giovanna meeting Jeff. Bella, miffed at Danny, enjoying Jeff's attention. "But she made it entirely clear she was engaged."

"Look, I'm not criticizing Bella, but I can see why Danny might have felt jealous. She and that guy were having a lot of fun and really connecting."

Giovanna studied him. "You said you go dancing with a woman friend. If someone saw you, would they think you were having fun and connecting?"

Ruefully, he said, "Yeah."

"Dancing passionate dances? Mightn't they assume you were lovers, or about to become lovers?"

He sighed. "Perhaps. For the record, she's happily married, and we're not turned on by each other. And yes, you've made your point."

Her lips twitched. "Thank you."

"But maybe Danny's as Neanderthal as I am."

"He should have trusted her. She loves him."

James tried to put himself in Danny's shoes. If Giovanna had loved him and he'd seen her flirting with his colleagues, what would he have felt? Perhaps he wouldn't have been insecure and jealous but proud she'd chosen him. "You're right, he should have trusted her. And he shouldn't have had so much to drink. But he's human."

"Drink can bring out a person's true nature."

"So, maybe Danny's insecure. Is that so awful?"

"Insecure?" She tilted her head. "He's never seemed that way to me. He always strikes me as a confident, outgoing young man."

"He does. I've always liked him. He's rich, but it hasn't spoiled him."

She sipped her drink, nodding. "He works in the family business, he knows how to have fun, and he's always treated Bella wonderfully well. Until now."

"Then likely it's a one-off thing. There must be some reason for it. Last-minute nerves, Free being a jerk, jealousy of a man who can play the piano and sing love songs."

"A man who lets her know he appreciates her. And who's even wealthier than Danny," she added.

"He is?"

"So I gather."

He sipped his own drink. "Well, I hope Danny apologizes, and they make up."

She bit her lip. "Until tonight, I thought they were perfect for each other. But if he really doesn't respect and trust her, then no, it'll only bring pain."

He sighed. "When she marries, I want it to be forever."

"Yes. Happily ever after. She shouldn't repeat our mistake."

But what else should he and Giovanna have done? Not had the baby, or given her up for adoption? No, impossible. Should Giovanna have remained in Italy and raised Bella, with James sending money? Then he'd have missed out on his wonderful daughter. "I think we did the best we were capable of at the time."

"Maybe so. I only hope they're capable of more."

He nodded. Seeing her drink glass was empty, he asked, "Want another?"

She shook her head. "This is nice. That we can talk like this without fighting."

"It is. I wonder if it's having sex that did it, or mutual concern about Bella?"

"Maybe some of both." She sighed tiredly. "Or maybe we're middle-aged and just don't have the energy to fight."

He smiled at that, then put his arm around her and drew her close. "Want to go to your cabana and get some sleep? I'll stay here."

"No. I want to be here if she needs me."

"How did I know you'd say that?"

As she relaxed against him, he became very aware of her soft, yielding curves. Until now, concern over Bella had overwhelmed everything else, but now Giovanna filled his senses.

The smooth skin of her bare arm, the delicious pressure of her breast against his chest, the silkiness of her hair, the soft brush of her breath as she sighed. And her scent, that spicy, sensual one she now wore.

"You've changed perfume. What's the new one?"

"Giovanna."

He chuckled. "Oh yes, there's a lot of you, but there's perfume as well."

"No, I mean it's called Giovanna. It's my signature scent."

He'd heard of places where women could get makeup or scent designed specifically for them and knew Giovanna worked for a cosmetics company. "It's perfect for you."

"Thanks. I'm pleased. It's done very well for us, too."

They were both exhausted. That must be why her last words didn't make sense. "Well for who?"

"For Venezia. My company." She pulled away to look at him. "Oh, I guess you don't know. We've had that zipped-mouth policy about not talking about each other with Bella."

He nodded. "To avoid sniping about each other in front of her." Besides, it had been easier to avoid thinking about his ex.

Her mouth quirked. "I did overhear her on the phone a time or two. Congratulations on being appointed department chair. I remember when your biggest dream was getting tenure."

"I worked so hard for that."

"It was more important to you than I was."

When he started to protest, she waved her hand. "Old history. Let it go."

"Well, I'm sorry if that's how it came across. Anyhow, yes, I'm chair, and I've authored a text that's done well."

"And you go dancing and play basketball. Why basketball?"

"One of my students got me into it. It's with disadvantaged teens. Kids who have family issues, problems with school. The ones who could tip in either direction and need some healthy activity and influence in their lives."

"My gosh." Her tired face had brightened. "That's wonderful, James."

"I needed to do something more than just be a professor. And yes, you can say 'I told you so.' Now, how about you? I heard you work in the cosmetics business? For this company called Venezia?"

A mischievous sparkle lit her eyes. "When we divorced, I looked for a job that suited me and did well doing makeup and selling cosmetics. I took some courses, got into a business program."

"You studied business?" He'd never thought she had any inclination toward business or schoolwork.

Her eyes gleamed dangerously. "I'm not as brainless as you thought. I graduated with honors and worked up to a very good job with Estée Lauder. I saw a niche the cosmetics companies weren't targeting, so I put together a team and a business plan, got financing, and started my own company. It's called Venezia."

"You have your own company?" He was stunned. When he met her, she'd been a waitress, barely out of high school. "OK, I'm flabbergasted. I admit it. And very impressed."

"It turned out I have a flair for this."

He'd thought she was clever and charming but an intellectual lightweight. Now he cringed at what an idiot, and how hurtful, he'd been. He took her hands. "Giovanna, I'm coming to think you'd have a flair for anything you turned your mind to."

"That's very sweet of you." She squeezed his hands. "Maybe this is the time to tell you: I've asked Bella if she'd like to come work for me."

"Really? I know she's been drifting since she graduated from college. I've been hoping she'd find a job that suited her or go back to school. So what did she say?"

"She'd like to do it, but not if it would be awkward. Given our"—she waved her hand—"situation. And she doesn't want to disappoint you."

"Disappoint me? Why would I be disappointed?"

"The cosmetics industry?" She arched a brow.

"Okay, I confess, I'd have loved it if Bella'd become a history prof. But what's important is that she finds something she enjoys. As for cosmetics—well, I'm learning there's nothing wrong with people wanting to look their best." He smiled at her. "Like you always do."

"What a lovely compliment." Her smile was radiant.

His heart turned to mush. He might have disliked Giovanna, tried to forget her, had serious relationships with other women, but no one had ever taken her place.

His heart was hers to claim.

Except she hadn't wanted it back then. Was there any reason to think she might now? Any reason to think they'd do any better a second time around?

She nestled close again, and he put his arm around her. Gently she kissed his cheek. "This is nice, James."

"It is." That lush mouth, so close to his, was too much temptation to resist. He turned to meet it in a soft, whispering kiss.

"And this is nice, too." She licked his top lip, his bottom one, in damp, darting touches, then dipped inside.

Each touch ignited sparks of arousal. His tongue met hers, danced with it, and his cock hardened.

She raised a graceful hand and ran her fingers through his hair, cupped the back of his head, and held him exactly where she wanted him. Her mouth slanted across his, harder and more demanding, turning the slow dance into a fierier, more passionate one.

Breathing hard, he pulled her closer, cupped her breast, then ran his thumb over the hard nipple.

"Mmm," she murmured. "So nice. We should—" She broke away. "James, Bella's upstairs."

"Damn." His gaze flew to the loft. Beyond the half wall that set it off, the room was dark. "I forgot. How potent was that sleeping pill?"

"There's no guarantee she won't wake up. Besides . . ."

"I know. Having sex in a gondola is one thing. Having sex with your adult daughter sleeping in the next room is different."

"You remember that gondola in Venezia?"

"I remember all the places we made love."

"Why, James, I'd almost think you were a romantic." Her tone was light and teasing, saying she didn't believe it for a moment.

And he supposed he wasn't. Only a man who would never forget the days when he'd believed a beautiful Italian girl was falling in love with him.

He sighed. "This isn't the way any of us had hoped tonight would go." Rising, he held out a hand to pull her up. "The couch converts into a bed. Now that we've agreed we'll behave ourselves, let's get some rest."

If such a thing was possible, lying beside Giovanna.

GIOVANNA woke to a mix of sensations: an earring digging into her cheek, a male arm wrapped around her.

Her daughter's voice, screeching, "Oh my God, you *slept* together?"

She and James jerked away from each other, both denying it loudly.

Bella, clad in a robe, stood halfway down the staircase, looking stunned.

Quickly Giovanna slid out of bed. "Fully dressed. Even to my earrings." She smoothed her hair, her dress, knowing she must look dreadful. "*Tesora*, we wanted to be here in case you needed us."

James—rumpled and sexy—was sitting up in bed. "How are you feeling, sweetheart?"

"Like crap. My life is over." Her face crumpled, and she stumbled to the bathroom and slammed the door.

"Poor kid," James said, tossing the sheet aside and rising.

Giovanna saw why he hadn't before. He had an erection. From sleeping with her, she hoped.

He walked to the window and tipped the shutters to see out. "We slept late. It's breakfast time, and people are wandering around."

"No sign of Danny?"

He shook his head. "Why don't I go grab a shower and change clothes, and I'll bring back fruit and muffins."

They shared a quick kiss before he left, then Giovanna folded the bed back into a couch, found her purse, and ran a comb through her hair.

When Bella emerged from the bathroom, face red and tear-swollen again, Giovanna hugged her. "My poor baby."

"Where's Daddy?"

"He went to shower and change and get some snacks for us."

Bella pulled back in the circle of her arms so she could see her mother's face. "The two of you really spent the night here because you were worried about me? Without killing each other?"

"We did."

She sniffed, then hauled a tissue from the pocket of her robe and blew her red nose. "Sorry I said that thing about you sleeping together."

"It's all right."

Bella drifted over to stare out the window and gave a heartfelt sigh. "Danny will come, won't he?"

"Once he wakes up and gets over the worst of the hangover. He's going to feel awful in all sorts of ways this morning."

"I hope so." She turned from the window, rubbing her forehead. "I feel like crap. Headachy, groggy. I'm going to try to go back to sleep. Wake me up when he comes, Mama."

"I will." Giovanna tucked her daughter into bed, then went into the bathroom and cleaned up as best she could, given the meager contents of her purse. She was contemplating borrowing Bella's makeup when a light tap sounded on the door of the cabana.

She hurried to open it, expecting a penitent Danny.

But it was Sarah. "How's Bella? And have you seen—?"

Giovanna stepped outside. "Bella's trying to sleep. Let's talk out here. And no, we haven't seen Danny."

She glanced past Sarah and saw Free Lafontaine approaching. "You! *Faccia di merda!* Stay away from my daughter."

He glanced at Sarah. "I wasn't going to—"

Furious, Giovanna said, "Get lost. If you make Bella cry again, you'll have James and me to answer to."

She turned to go in. Behind her, she heard Sarah say to Free, with equal vehemence, "You heard her. Stay away from Bella."

Inside, Giovanna took deep breaths, trying to calm down. Where was Danny? He should be here, crawling on his knees to beg forgiveness. Last night—the trust issue—had been one huge strike against him, and this was another.

Shortly after, James returned, looking exceedingly good, which made her all the more conscious of her own appearance. "I think Bella's asleep," she whispered. "No Danny yet, but Sarah came. Then Free, who I told to get lost."

"Good. That asshole."

"I need a shower and fresh clothes. Will you stay? She asked to be woken if Danny comes."

"Of course." He gave her a quick, gentle hug and handed her a pineapple muffin.

When she'd gone, James ate a banana and a muffin and did a lot of pacing. Where the hell was Danny? Once Giovanna got back, he'd go see that young bastard and give him a piece of his mind.

"Daddy?"

He gazed up to see Bella looking over the loft's railing. "Hi sweetheart."

"Danny hasn't come?" she asked plaintively.

He shook his head.

Tears streaked her cheeks. "It's true," she sobbed. "He really doesn't love me. If he did, he'd come."

He took the stairs, catching her in a hug. "I don't know what to say. Maybe he's sick or feeling too guilty. Yes, he should apologize and explain, but things aren't always straightforward."

"I thought he loved me," she wailed.

"I thought so, too."

Damn, he wished Giovanna would hurry. Danny's time was up. He was going to get a visit from a pissed-off father.

A knock sounded on the door.

"That's him!" Bella said, breaking the hug. "I look a total mess. Give me a minute to at least comb my hair." She rushed to the bedside table and grabbed a comb.

James hurried down the steps and flung the door open.

To Free Lafontaine, damn it. "Haven't you made enough trouble?"

The other man ducked his head, then raised it again. "Yeah. I've come to fix things."

*To fix things?* "Are you sure?"

"Positive."

James peered into his face, looking for the truth. What he saw was a swollen nose and the beginnings of a black eye. "What happened to you?"

"Danny."

"Ah." He smiled. This was a very good sign, and the man thoroughly deserved it. "Bella," he called, "Free's here to see you. I'm going to send him up."

"No!" she screeched.

He winced but gestured to the stairs. "Give it your best shot. And if you hurt her again, you'll be feeling my fist, too."

Free took the stairs, and James heard Bella say, "Asshole!"

Free replied in a lower voice, and Bella responded.

James began to pace again. Should he have sent Free up there?

Danny had punched out his friend. What did that mean? Was Free really being honest when he said he wanted to fix things?

He couldn't hear the conversation, but occasional words stood out. Money, freedom. Ruined. Trust. Jealous. A name, Kimberly. Jeff.

A feminine "Ooh!" and something that sounded like a pillow flying. And connecting, because Free let out an "Oof."

James froze. But Bella didn't call him, and the voices resumed. He paced some more.

A hard knock on the door made him jump, then he heard Danny. "Bella, I'm such a jerk. I don't deserve you. Let me in."

James waited a minute or two until Bella called, "Daddy, let him in."

Free came down the stairs as James opened the door. Danny, face as swollen and blotchy as Bella's, surged through, then stopped and stared at Free. "Well?"

"I explained everything. I think she understands. She may hate me forever, but she's prepared to give you—"

Danny rushed up the stairs, and James saw Bella standing at the top.

"I am such a total idiot," Danny said.

James's lips curved. Accurate, and not a bad start to an apology.

"You are," Bella announced firmly, but her own mouth was softening into a smile.

She glanced past Danny and said, "Thanks, Daddy. You can go now. Tell Mama and Sarah, will you? We'll be okay."

And he had the sense that they really would be. He and Free left the cabana not speaking.

James walked first to Sarah's cabana to give her the news, then to Giovanna's. He knocked on the door. "It's James."

Inside, putting on earrings, Giovanna heard him. "Come in!" She hurried to meet him. "Is Bella all right? Did Danny show up?"

His smile, tired but relieved, reassured her. "Free came—bearing the marks of Danny punching him in the nose."

"Good for Danny."

"Free said he wanted to fix things and talked to Bella upstairs. Then Danny showed up, looking as haggard as Bella, and I think they're going to work things out."

She let out a long, grateful sigh. Then, "I wonder what Free said?"

"I imagine we'll find out eventually." He moved toward her purposefully, a gleam in his eye. "We missed out on our rendezvous last night."

Refreshed from her shower, skin lotioned, clad in a purple top and wraparound skirt, Giovanna felt like a new woman. The appreciation in his eyes confirmed that she was an attractive one. "Rendezvous?" she teased. "Is that your word for it?"

"I don't care what we call it." He touched her bare shoulder, caressed gently down her arm. "It was torture sharing a bed with you last night and not being able to make love."

Last night had been good, though. Being parents together. But if she said that, he'd think she was complaining about all the times during their marriage when he hadn't been around for her and Bella.

Her skin quivered under his touch, arousal quickly flaming to life. "Are you suggesting we make up for it now? I want to, but someone—Bella—might come looking for us."

# Chapter 9

"WE'LL lock the door." James looked so determined, so intense, and an erection was rising to tent the front of his shorts. "And make it a quickie."

Heat pulsed through her veins. Desire. Need. She walked over and clicked the lock on the door. "Upstairs."

She led the way, provocatively swaying her hips.

Above the bed, a wooden ceiling fan stirred a lazy breeze.

The breeze might have been lazy, but James wasted no time unbuttoning her sleeveless top. Then he tackled the bow that secured her wrap skirt, and she twirled herself free of it, until she was down to a pink lace demi-bra and panties.

"My turn." She stripped off his shirt and shorts. "Tamiko does have excellent taste." When he was clad only in form-fitting blue cotton boxers, she asked, suppressing a twinge of jealousy, "Did she choose the underwear, too?"

He shook his head. "The male salesclerk politely suggested that the boxers I was wearing belonged either on an old man or one of those kids with pants halfway down his butt."

"You're definitely neither of those." She slid her hands over the fabric that covered his lean hips. "I like these."

She ran a hand across the front, clasping his erection. "And I like this." It throbbed in her hand, and her pussy pulsed in response.

Then she hooked her fingers in the waistband. "But this is even better." Deftly she peeled them down until gravity took over and they fell.

Then she stood back to admire. Such a sexy man. He looked like a basketball player, a dancer. Definitely not a stuffy professor. Why hadn't he been like this when they were married?

Shoving away regret, she reached back to unfasten her bra, skimmed off her panties, then lay on the bed and held out her arms. "Come here. A quickie, remember?"

"I wish we had more time." He donned protection then lowered himself, hips brushing the insides of her thighs, erection hard against her belly. "Tonight we'll do this slowly."

Then he kissed her hungrily, and she answered, raising her legs to twine them around him. Opening herself to him. When his cock brushed her moist folds, she shuddered with pleasure. "Come inside me. Now, James."

"Are you . . .?" He reached down, between them.

When he caressed her, she squirmed needily against his hand. "Ready? I've been ready since last night."

"So have I." In one quick surge, he filled her.

Oh, how good he felt! Her legs locked around him, and her hands grabbed his firm butt as their bodies rocked together.

His hands framed her face, and his mouth claimed hers. They kissed hungrily, a little sloppily, panting for breath as they did it. Even after all these years, their bodies were perfectly attuned as they raced toward orgasm.

Arousal coiled tight in her. "Faster," she commanded, tilting her hips. "*Ancora.*"

He obliged, finding exactly the angle that rubbed both her clit and her G-spot.

"Oh, yes," she gasped as pleasure peaked unbearably high. Then she came apart—"James!"—and he pumped into her with a groan, finding his own release.

They clung together, breathing hard. "So good, Giovanna," he gasped.

Good enough that . . . "I feel guilty. I forgot all about Bella's problems."

He dropped a kiss on her nose and eased off her. "Hopefully they've been doing the same thing we have."

"Yes. But I hope she didn't take him back too easily. If he doesn't trust her . . ."

"Should we go to her cabana?"

She bit her lip. "She wouldn't want us interrupting."

He rolled off the bed. "Let's get cleaned up and go for lunch. They'll turn up."

"I guess we should go separately." She watched as he pulled on his boxers. "This is still our secret, right?"

"Bella sounded pretty upset this morning when she thought we were sleeping together."

"It would be embarrassing for all of us. Her parents acting like sex-crazed teens at her wedding." Giovanna clasped a pillow across her chest. "Besides, last night was quite enough drama for the week."

He glanced up from fastening his shorts. "Thought you were the one who liked drama," he teased.

"Very funny. Not that kind. Or the kind that involves looking foolish." After all, it wasn't like they were getting back together. This was only a holiday fling.

A fling with the only man she'd ever loved, a man who was sexier and more considerate than ever before.

Damn. Sex was supposed to get him *out* of her system, not deeper into her heart.

He was nodding. "Okay, back to being barely civil." Dressed now, he came over and touched her cheek. "But I want to see you tonight."

Not wise, yet she couldn't resist. "I think that can be arranged." Nor could she resist turning her head to kiss his palm.

After he'd gone, she started to worry again about Bella. Had she and Danny made up? Had they really dealt with the trust issue?

Quickly she freshened up and hurried over to the restaurant. No Bella or Danny.

James sat with Al. She probably shouldn't join them and would rather not sit with the wedding guests, either. They'd ask about the kids, and she didn't know what to say.

The elderly English couple, who she'd heard were celebrating an anniversary, were at their usual table. They so clearly belonged together.

Why couldn't she and James have ended up like this?

Impulsively, she went over. "Please tell me if I'm intruding, but I wondered if I might sit with you?" If anything could calm her nerves right now, their company might be it.

"We'd be delighted, dear," the woman said in a charming English accent. "We're Ellie and Bill Everleigh."

"Giovanna Moncrieff."

"The mother of the bride," Bill said. "Or, er . . . not that we listen to gossip, but we couldn't help overhearing. There's been a problem?"

"I think they've sorted it out. I hope they have." She held up crossed fingers.

"Do they really love each other?" Ellie asked.

"I thought so. But behavior speaks louder than words."

"You need both," she said. "Behavior can be misinterpreted."

Bill chuckled. "Like the time you saw me buying a diamond necklace with Penelope Wright, and thought I was having an affair with her."

Ellie winked at Giovanna. "He put it around her neck, then gave her a big hug. I saw them through the shop window."

"Let me guess. He was buying it for you and asking a friend's advice."

"There, you see?" Bill said. "*She* understood right away, love."

"What I lost track of," Ellie said, "was that I knew Bill loved me. He'd been busy at work, often didn't make it home for dinner, hadn't told me he loved me in months."

"I was bidding on my first landscaping contract," he explained, "and didn't tell Ellie in case I didn't get it. When I did, I wanted to buy her something special to tell her how much I loved her. I wasn't very good with words back then. The typical reserved Englishman."

"The pendant was beautiful, but the words mean more to me." Ellie gave Giovanna a mischievous grin. "I whipped him into shape, and now he tells me every day that he loves me."

"And you know he means it." James hadn't been much for speaking words of affection, and when he had, he'd sounded stiff. Because, she knew, he hadn't loved her.

He had said the words a few times, and at first she'd believed him. But then, at Tufts, she'd realized the truth. She was the opposite of what he wanted in a wife. Summer lust had resulted in pregnancy, and he'd married her out of duty, not love.

For her, though, it had been love, all the way.

And yet she'd criticized him and fought with him.

She'd told him she loved him, but her behavior hadn't backed it up. Had he believed her?

She was pondering that thought when raised voices made her turn her head. Bella and Danny were coming up the steps to the restaurant, arms wrapped tightly around each other.

They stood in the entrance, beaming so brightly their red-rimmed eyes were barely noticeable. "It's official," Danny said loudly. "I'm a jerk, and Bella's a generous, wonderful woman. The wedding's still on."

Cheers, whistles, and applause exploded.

Giovanna smiled, yet she needed reassurance that the pair had really dealt with their issues. "Would you excuse me?" she asked the Everleighs.

"Of course," Ellie said. "And, whatever the differences between you and your husband, you've raised a lovely daughter."

"Thanks." It was only after she'd moved away that Giovanna realized Ellie had forgotten the "ex."

She went over to her daughter and Danny, who were getting

hugs from their friends. "I want to talk to you two." James and Al came to join them.

The other young people moved away, leaving only Bella, Danny, their parents, and Sarah hovering nearby.

"I'm concerned, Bella," Giovanna said. "I want to know you've really resolved things. I'm sure both your father and Danny's father do, too."

James spoke up. "We love you, sweetheart. We saw how upset you were, and we need to be sure you know what you're doing."

Bella squeezed Danny's arm. "You're right. Let's find some privacy and talk. And Sarah, too. She's put so much into this wedding." She hugged the wedding planner.

Their group assembled around a table in a quiet corner of the bar, and Danny and Bella explained what had happened.

"So," Danny concluded, "Free deliberately pushed my hot button, Kimberly."

Giovanna noticed Sarah frowning, as if something didn't make sense to her. Probably, she wondered why Free had confessed about his meddling. It was a real about-face from his behavior last night.

"I knew in my heart Bella was nothing like Kimberly," Danny said, "and I was an idiot to let Free get to me."

"You were," Bella agreed, leaning over to kiss him.

Giovanna gave a sigh of relief and exchanged a surreptitious smile with James. Yes, Danny truly did respect and trust their daughter. He hadn't simply won her back with a quick apology and protestations of undying love.

"People can do unfortunate things when they're emotional," she said, thinking of the times that, feeling unloved and inadequate, she'd yelled at James.

"You won't treat Bella that way again," James said to Danny. It was a statement, not a question.

"No, sir," he said firmly. "I won't."

* * *

THE next afternoon, James dressed for the wedding in the beige pants and white shirt Tamiko had selected. They were the same kind of clothes he'd worn at Tufts, but the styling and fabrics—and price tag—made them very different. She'd told him not to cuff the shirt but roll the sleeves up and leave a couple buttons undone at the neck.

Was he going to remember her instructions when he got back to Medford?

Would he give a damn how he looked?

To be honest, wasn't he dressing for Giovanna, to enjoy the way her eyes lit when she saw him?

What a day this would be. His little girl would become another man's wife. And he and his ex-wife—his lover—would share one last night before they both headed back to their own lives.

It had been an amazing week. In many ways, it would be a relief to get back to his normal life. And yet . . .

He'd miss Giovanna desperately.

Maybe this was why he'd avoided her—avoided even thinking of her—all these years. Because he still loved her and had sensed seeing her would mean falling for her all over again.

A knock sounded on the door of his room. Was it her?

But no, it was Sarah, pretty in a peach-colored dress, carrying the ubiquitous clipboard, a nervous expression on her face. "James, I know this is last minute, but Bella has a request."

"And it's her day, and we're supposed to humor her. What does she want?"

"Uh, well, it's about walking her down the aisle and giving her away."

"She doesn't like the way we did it yesterday in the rehearsal?"

"No, um, well . . . She wondered if you and Giovanna could do it together. Because, you know, you're, uh, getting along better?"

The idea struck him as perfectly fitting. Should he protest, as Sarah clearly expected him to? Stage a mock squabble with Giovanna?

No, he didn't want to, and it wasn't necessary. Bella would be shocked if she knew about her parents' fling, but she seemed happy that he and Giovanna were, as Sarah said, getting along better.

"I think that's a great idea."

"You do?" She frowned. "Really? I mean, you think the two of you can do it without . . ."

"We'll behave ourselves. Shall we go find Giovanna?"

As they headed off, he said, "You look wonderful, by the way. That dress looks great with your hair." Yes, he was learning to appreciate such things and to give compliments.

"You look great, too. I'd barely recognize you as the pale, buttoned-up guy who got off the plane last Sunday."

Another reminder that tomorrow he'd be getting back on that plane and going home.

Barefoot, they crossed the sand to the Wild Ginger cabana. The door was open.

Sarah knocked. "Giovanna?"

"Sarah?" A moment later Giovanna came down from the loft, hair swept up in a casual style that left tendrils dangling, voluptuous body clad in a lovely cinnamon-colored dress.

She took his breath away.

Sarah said, "Oh my God, you look fantastic. I *love* that dress."

"Thank you." Giovanna's gaze focused on James. "Well?"

"Yes. What she said." He couldn't find the words to tell her how wonderful she looked.

Fortunately, her smile told him she got the message. "You look pretty good, too"—sparks of mischief glittered in her eyes—"for a stodgy professor."

Sarah tensed, but James laughed. "We've come to ask you something. Bella would like us both to walk her down the aisle and give her away. I said I thought it was a good idea, and that we could do it without arguing. What do you think?"

Giovanna's eyes moistened. "Yes." She blinked rapidly. "No arguing. But I can't promise there won't be tears."

"Good," Sarah said briskly, making a note on her spreadsheet. "Now, I'll fill you in on what's involved."

"I can do that," James said. "I'm sure you have other details to attend to."

"Only a million." She gave a quick smile. "Thanks. To both of you. Bella will be so happy."

When she'd gone, James turned to Giovanna. "Here it is, our baby's wedding day."

She wiped a finger under her eyes. "When she was born and we knew she was a girl, I imagined this. I imagined all the days: her christening, first day of school, first date, high school prom, and her wedding."

"Did you?" He'd been too stunned by holding new life—their baby—in his arms to be anything except thrilled and scared shitless.

Giovanna sniffled. "Back then, I hoped we'd be beside each other for all of them. And we didn't even make it to her christening." Her mouth tightened. "You were too *busy* giving some stupid lecture."

That was unfair. "I'd have been there if you'd bothered to check my schedule before you booked the date. But you never gave a damn about my work commitments."

"Ooh!" She planted her hands on her hips, eyes flashing as she glared at him. "You—"

"Wait, stop. I'm sorry. We're emotional and on edge. I shouldn't have said that." He took a breath. "But what you said about the christening hurt. I really wanted to be there, but I'd committed to that lecture."

She nodded slowly. "I'm sorry, too. I was jealous of your work, and I think subconsciously I wanted you to choose me for once. Or at least Bella. I put you in an impossible situation."

"And I wasn't a very good father."

"We were young and we both made mistakes. And James, I know you turned into a good father. I was jealous when Bella said she wanted to spend half her time with you, yet I was happy, too. For her. And for you."

"Thank you." He took her hand and interlaced their fingers. "What a pity we couldn't have talked this way back then." If they had, if he'd understood her better and been more considerate, might she have fallen in love with him?

"Yes." Her brow wrinkled. "You reminded me of something the Everleighs—that elderly English couple?—said to me. I'll tell you tonight when we have more time."

She gave him a tremulous smile. "Right now, I have to help our daughter into her wedding gown."

A little while later, the guests had all assembled by the beach where the wedding would take place. The layout was simple: rows of folding chairs, a sandy aisle scattered with flower petals, and a trellised arch. Everything had been decorated with a profusion of tropical flowers, and the air smelled of orange blossoms.

Danny stood side by side with his brother, the best man, beaming his head off. James noted that both men were dressed very much as he was. Free, the photographer, was in long pants for the first time this week, and Tamiko, arm in arm with Zane, was lovely as usual in a lime green dress.

A couple of local musicians were playing guitars, and the officiary had arrived.

Sarah came over to James, blue eyes sparkling with excitement. She held up her clipboard. "One last item: collect the beautiful bride. Over to you, James."

"Thanks for everything you've done."

"It's been my absolute pleasure. Now, let's give Bella and Danny a perfect wedding."

He headed over to the Azure cabana and knocked lightly. "Ready to go?"

Giovanna opened the door, smiling proudly. "Wait until you see her."

"Daddy?" His daughter stepped into view.

Damned if tears didn't fill his eyes. He remembered the tiny red bundle that had been thrust into his arms at the hospital. Now, here she was, without question the most beautiful bride who had ever existed. He cleared his throat. "Danny Trent is one hell of a lucky man."

Then he went over and embraced her gently, careful not to mess the softly tousled blonde hair strewn with fragrant white blossoms or the incredible dress, delicate and floaty and utterly perfect for her. He kissed her forehead. "You're so beautiful. I'm so proud of you, sweetheart."

He hugged Giovanna, too. "And you. For creating her and raising her."

She smiled back. "You had some small part in it yourself."

Then, all of them barefoot, arms linked together with Bella in the middle, they walked across the sand toward her wedding.

"Sweetheart," James said, "even though you're going to be Danny's wife, you're still our daughter. Your mama and I will always be here for you."

"I know, Daddy." She squeezed his arm, and Giovanna gave him a warm smile.

Then they were there, starting down the aisle.

And now, all too soon, he and Giovanna delivered Bella to her fiancé and sat down.

Side by side, his shoulder touching his ex-wife's, his lover's, James listened to the ceremony, watching the way Bella's and Danny's faces glowed. Sarah was indeed giving them a wonderful start to their married life.

He and Giovanna had married in a registry office in Medford. No parents. They didn't even have friends in the new city. Their witnesses had been strangers.

Not the best way to start a marriage. Nor was the baby Giovanna had been carrying. Nor the fact that she'd left behind the life she'd wanted—the carefree life of a beautiful nineteen-year-old girl—for a strange country, a man she barely knew, an unplanned baby.

They'd been young and made so many mistakes.

Now they were older, and this week they had gained some wisdom.

Was there any hope that this time she might really fall in love with him?

Medford wasn't far from New York. They could see each other, and he could woo her properly. With great sex, yes, but also with compliments, consideration, and understanding. They'd go dancing, do fun, sexy, spontaneous things like they had in Italy.

Had his daughter's wedding given him a second chance at love?

# Chapter 10

AFTER the wedding dinner, Giovanna walked back to her cabana, hoping everyone would retire early so James could sneak over.

Tomorrow, they'd be boarding separate planes and flying home.

And after that, would they keep seeing each other? If they did, might the new Giovanna be more successful than the old one in winning his love?

If she wasn't, could she bear to keep seeing him?

God, she was an emotional mess. This week had been almost more than she could handle.

When she opened the door and stepped inside, her bare foot brushed a piece of paper that must have been slipped under the door. She turned on a light and saw James's handwriting.

> Lovely Giovanna, will you rendezvous on the beach with me at midnight? Meet me past the point of land to the north of the resort.

She laughed with delight. How about that? In Italy, they'd done romantic, spontaneous, sexy things. But once they were married, that side of James had disappeared.

Excited and curious, she changed her Fabiana creation for a sarong dress—a large rectangle of Belizean fabric wrapped around her and tied at the neck. Taking only one small item with her, she slipped outside and hurried down the beach.

When she rounded the point, a figure materialized out of the strip of bushes and trees that lined the beach. "Giovanna."

"James." She went toward him. "Should we be meeting here? Someone might go for a late-night walk."

"I found a private spot." He glanced past her to make sure the beach was deserted, then gave her a quick, intense kiss. "Here, come through the trees."

She followed him. "Oh, my!"

He'd spread out a large beach towel, and there was a bottle of Prosecco—Giovanna's favorite—and flute glasses.

He handed her a red hibiscus blossom, a huge, perfect double one. "For you, my lady."

"How wonderful. I'm"—she gazed around in wonder—"stunned. It's the kind of thing we did that first summer." She tucked the flower in her hair, and they both sank down on the towel.

He gave her a lingering kiss. "I was an ass after we got married."

"I didn't understand a thing about your work, yet you were totally absorbed in it."

"I know. The Baby Brit, who had to prove himself."

"The what?"

"That's what they called me. I didn't tell you because it was humiliating. But it wasn't just about proving myself, Giovanna. I wanted to get tenure—financial security—because I had a wife and child to provide for."

So it hadn't only been career ambition but the pressure of having a family. "Not what you'd expected to come back with when you went to Italy after graduation."

"No. But then I saw you, and my life changed in an instant." He sighed. "And so did yours. You went from being young and carefree to being a mom, a wife. Not just any wife, but a stuffy professor's wife."

"The Baby Brit's wife." She laughed delightedly. "Oh, I wish I'd known about that. It would've helped when I felt so intimidated by you."

"You felt intimidated? But you always seemed so confident. And, er, critical."

"It was an act. I did have some pride, you know."

"Damn, Giovanna, I shouldn't have made you feel intimidated."

"No. And I should have been more supportive of your career." She shook her hair back. "Let's stop rehashing the past. We're supposed to be having a sexy night on the beach. How about opening the Prosecco?"

"After I kiss you again."

Which he did, in a lingeringly erotic way that made her almost inclined to say they should skip the wine and get straight to the sex. But James being romantic was too rare an experience to miss.

He opened and poured the wine, and they lifted their glasses.

"Here's to Bella," he said. "For arm-twisting us both to be here. Otherwise, we'd likely never have talked and sorted things out."

"Or had great sex. And that would have been a real pity." Now the question was whether they'd ever have more than that.

They clinked glasses and drank.

Then she raised hers again. "To Bella and Danny. May they be happy together and not repeat their parents' mistakes."

He drank the toast. "I think they'll be okay. Looking at their faces when they said their vows, it was obvious how much they love each other."

"Yes." She remembered the Everleighs, who still looked at each other that way. Softly, toying with her glass, she said, "I know we're olive oil and tonic water, but I've often wondered if we could have made a go of it if you'd loved me."

"Giovanna? What do you mean? I did love you."

"Oh, James, it's all right. I know you didn't. Yes, you occasionally said the words, but you always sounded so uncomfortable. You wouldn't have married me if I hadn't got pregnant. Me, a waitress? I didn't fit your life. But you got trapped and did the honorable thing and—" She broke off, because he was gaping at her as if she'd started talking Italian.

"*You* didn't love *me*," he said.

She remembered her conversation with the Everleighs. "I'm so sorry you thought that. I was a bitch, but I did love you, James." She smiled ruefully. "I loved you from the moment I saw you on the restaurant patio, when you stared at me like I was a goddess come to life."

"You were. But . . ." He shook his head. "You couldn't have loved me. You could have had any man in Italy; you'd never have chosen a dull history professor."

"You weren't dull. Not in Italy." She gazed at him, eyes misty. "And you aren't dull now. You're handsome and fit, a great dancer, you help disadvantaged kids. You're a wonderful father. And a very sexy lover."

She wanted to go on. To tell him she still loved him. But courage deserted her.

His bemused expression made her touch his cheek and ask, "What are you thinking?"

"I'm . . . stunned." He placed his hand over hers, holding it against him. "And I'm thinking that you're still a goddess. And a successful businesswoman, a terrific mother, and the sexiest woman I've ever met."

He took a deep breath, then let it out. "Giovanna, I did love you then, even if the words didn't come easily. I'd never said them before."

Her heart raced. Was this true?

"Once we got to Medford," he went on, "I thought we were wrong for each other. I hated the way we fought. But I still loved you."

He lifted her hand and twined his fingers through hers. "I came here tonight hoping to persuade you to keep seeing me. Hoping I could woo you. Because I never stopped loving you, and I want you back."

"James!" She gave a breathless laugh. "*Dio mio*, I feel the same way. I love you, too."

"You do? Really?" He stared at her, looking dumbfounded.

She nodded vigorously. "More than before. We can talk about things, I can trust you now. And you don't intimidate me. I feel like I'm your equal."

"You always were."

She laughed joyfully. Then, because he seemed too stunned to move, she launched herself at him.

He came alive, laughing, too, kissing her, hugging her, rolling until he was on top and kissing her some more.

They might be older and wiser, but, she thought with great satisfaction, they were as passionate as they'd ever been.

"Do you think Bella will kill us when we tell her?" she asked.

"Kill us or be thrilled to bits. Fifty-fifty chance. We'll wait until they get back from their honeymoon."

He stroked her face. "Let's stay in Belize a few days, Giovanna. Have some privacy, some time to ourselves."

"An excellent idea."

"Time to enjoy being together and figure out how we're going to organize our lives."

"Organize?" She chuckled. "You sound like Sarah. Shall we start a spreadsheet?"

"Perhaps that's a little extreme."

"Mmm." Besides, they could leave the spreadsheet to the wedding planner.

Because there was definitely another wedding in the Moncrieff family's future.

Taking him by surprise, she shifted her body weight and rolled them so she was on top. "If you're going to get all organizational," she teased, "you may need this."

With a flourish, she held up the tie she'd stripped off his neck a few days ago. She'd brought it along, folded up and concealed in her hand.

He laughed as it unfurled to hang down between them. "I figured you'd thrown that out."

"I thought it might come in handy." She draped it around his neck then sat back and pretended to consider. "No, too stuffy and straitlaced."

She attacked the fastenings of his shorts and freed his erection. Then she twined the silky fabric around it and fashioned a loose bow.

Studying her handiwork, she gave a satisfied grin. "Now that is a far more *appropriate* way to wear a tie."

# Epilogue

**Ambergris Caye, Belize—Sunday, February 15**

ELLIE Everleigh rose a little creakily from her afternoon nap and went out to the deck of the Bougainvillea cabana, where her husband Bill was swinging in the hammock reading a thriller Zane Slade had autographed for him.

She watched for a moment, thinking he was still the most handsome, kindest, sexiest man on the planet. Then she dropped a kiss on his bald spot and went to sit on the top step. "Sunday. The day of arrivals and departures. I'm glad we're here another week."

"The last week was different than usual," he said, maneuvering out of the hammock and coming to sit beside her. "It was nice of Bella and Danny to invite us to their wedding."

She clasped his hand and sighed happily. "Such a lovely wedding."

"You've said that at least a hundred times," he said fondly.

"You know I adore weddings. Especially when the bride and groom are so much in love and so perfect for each other as Bella and Danny are."

They gave a friendly wave to a middle-aged couple in travel clothes who were walking toward the Azure cabana, the one the bride and groom had occupied.

"I hope our young friends have a wonderful honeymoon in Placencia," Bill said. "They have a lot to learn, but they came a long way this week."

"Everyone has a lot to learn when they get married."

Across the way, the bright red door to Wild Ginger opened, and a couple stepped out. Healthy, vital, glowing with happiness. The woman, wearing a vivid blue halter top and a flowered sarong, tossed back a mass of wavy dark brown hair that gleamed in the sun and held out her hand to the man. He, in khaki shorts and a short-sleeved blue shirt open down the front to reveal a nicely muscled chest, caught her hand.

Together they went down the steps, then suddenly he swooped her into his arms. She gave a startled laugh as he ran across the sand toward the ocean.

"Well, would you look at that," Bill said.

Ellie smiled approvingly. "It takes some people longer to learn their lessons than others. Isn't it marvelous Giovanna and James got a second chance?"

He patted her leg. "Ah well, I suspect the lady listened to a few words of advice from a far wiser woman."

"And what I told her was so simple. If you love someone, tell them, with your words and your actions."

He chuckled. "Have I told you lately that I love you, Ellie?"

"Yes, but feel free to tell me again."

"I will, if you come and have a drink with me."

"A double incentive."

They rose, knees popping, and made their way across the sand toward the Toucan Bar.

"Don't let me forget I need to buy more sunscreen," she said.

"Best do it now. You know how alcohol addles your brain," he joked.

"Oh, you!" She elbowed him in the ribs.

All the same, her memory wasn't what it had once been, so she tugged Bill toward the lobby to make her purchase.

When they stepped out of the gift shop, a lovely young woman and an adorable girl were crossing the lobby. Both in flowered sundresses, with long dark hair, they looked like mother and daughter. The child's hands tightly grasped a plate full of miniature chocolate cupcakes, and the woman's head was bent, keeping an eye on her.

"Tamiko," Ellie said.

Her head came up. "Ellie! You're still here."

"You, too. And you've been baking?"

"Have a cupcake," the little girl said importantly. "We made them for Daddy, but you can have some, too."

"Thank you, dear." Both Ellie and her husband took a cupcake, and she noticed they were a little lopsided.

The child hurried toward the resort's administration offices, and Tamiko said, "Yes, I've been learning how to make cupcakes, and discovering the joys of licking the bowl."

Then, tilting her head toward the direction in which the girl had disappeared, she said, "That's Mara, she's—"

"Ric's daughter." Ellie beamed. "That young man so deserves happiness. As do you, my dear."

"You told me to follow my heart, and I did." Her smile was luminous. Then she glanced past them, and it turned to a wide grin. "And I told Zane."

She hurried past them, calling, "Graham!"

They turned to see her fling herself into the open arms of a man who'd just entered the lobby. He was slim and attractive, his hair a nice blend of blond and silver.

When the two stopped hugging, the newcomer put his hands on Tamiko's shoulders and gazed into her eyes. "Thank you, sweetheart."

Zane Slade stepped up behind him and took his hand. Gruffly he said, "I'm supposed to be a macho thriller writer, and she's converting me into a romantic."

"There's nothing like a happy ending," Tamiko said, smiling across the lobby at the Everleighs.

Ellie beamed and squeezed her husband's hand.

He kissed the top of her head. "Indeed there isn't. Now, let's go get that drink."

As they strolled toward the bar, he said, "I admit, I didn't see that one coming. Who'd have guessed Zane Slade was gay?"

"I knew there was something strange in the way he and Tamiko interacted, though it was obvious they cared for each other."

"I wonder if those folks know Giovanna and James are here, and vice versa."

"Ric will know about everyone, but he's the soul of discretion, so he may not have let on." She gave a girlish giggle. "I can't wait to see what happens when they all meet up."

"Who knows, maybe next year we won't be the only ones here celebrating our anniversary."

Laughing together, they walked into the Toucan Bar. Alone at a table by the water was Sarah, the wedding planner. She was dressed more casually than usual in a bikini top and sarong skirt, and for once didn't have her clipboard.

"Bill and Ellie!" she said, "I thought you'd gone home."

"No, we're here for three weeks," Bill said. "But we didn't realize you were staying."

Sarah, a redhead with a delicate complexion, flushed. "I decided to stay for a bit of—" She went an even deeper pink as a man stepped up to the table and put down two martini glasses filled with colorful liquid and decorated with hibiscus blossoms.

It was Free Lafontaine, the handsome photographer. He winked at Ellie and Bill. "A bit of . . . now, how did it go? Communication, patience, and compromise? And let's not forget the most important element. Sex—"

"Free!" Sarah broke in.

He grinned and pointed to the glasses. "On the beach."

"Or anywhere else the mood strikes," Ellie said mischievously, thinking that she and Bill could teach all these young folk a thing or two.

And they had!

# ABOUT THE AUTHOR

**Susan Lyons** writes sexy contemporary romance that's intense, passionate, heartwarming, and fun. Her books have won Booksellers Best, Aspen Gold, Golden Quill, and More than Magic awards, and have been nominated for the Romantic Times Reviewers' Choice award. She lives in Vancouver, British Columbia. She has law and psychology degrees, and has also studied anthropology, sociology, and counseling. Her careers have been varied, including perennial student, grad-school dropout, job creation project administrator, computer consultant, and legal editor. Fiction writer is by far her favorite career. Writing gives her a perfect outlet to demonstrate her belief in the power of love, friendship, and a sense of humor.

Visit Susan's website at www.susanlyons.ca for excerpts, discussion questions, writing-process notes, articles, and giveaways. Susan can be contacted at susan@susanlyons.ca.